Strange & Mysterious Tales

Don Reilly

Mystic Publishers
Henderson Nevada

Strange & Mysterious Tales
All Rights Reserved © 2006
by
Don Reilly

ISBN : 978-934051-08-5

This book of short stories is a work of fiction purely from the mind of the author. No part of this book may be reproduced or transmitted in any form or by any means, electronic or mechanical, including photocopying, recording, or by an information storage or retrieval system, without permission in writing from the author.

For information about the contents of this book, or permission to reproduce portions of this book, please contact the author through the publisher at mysticpublishers.com

Published in the United States of America
in cooperation with:

Mystic Publishers
Henderson, Nevada
www.mysticpublishers.com

Acknowledgements

I would like to thank my publisher, Jo Wilkins, for all the encouragement she has given over the years. Charleen Micheles, my editor, for a perfect job of editing and making me more 'aware'. My wife, Shirley, for the constant reminders of, "You can't quit", and, "Get get that thing done, will you." I would also like to thank Andrea Hoarne for the artwork on the cover. Without you folks I couldn't have made it.

Contents

Dumpster
Page 1

Doors
Page 35

Holiday Flight 909
Page 51

Prison Break
Page 55

For Old Times Sake
Page 59

Long Term Care
Page 73

Maniac
Page 99

Giant
Page 121

Homemade Terrorist
Page 157

Prodigy
Page 201

Shadow Child
Page 227

Protected
Page 251

Groeler
Page 319

Strange & Mysterious Tales

*D*umpster

Pleasantville is a small town in central California close to its Eastern border. There are no malls or shopping centers and Wal-Mart hasn't moved in yet. Being a small town, less than ten thousand, there is no one on food stamps, Pleasantville takes care of its own, but this town has it's secrets like any other town. Sometimes people try to sweep too much under the carpet and the lump becomes too big to hide. There are times men have to pay for their sins and full payment for Pleasantville it is about to come due. The issues there are all hush, hush. No one tells; everything is glossed over.

    Sheryl Wheatly is the secretary in the Mayor's office. She is a very mature person in her late thirties. Sheryl is chunky with big brown eyes and an out going personality. By her standards she and her husband are successful people. The have a nice two story house, three new cars, and a boat. Sheryl's husband Dick who is a Deputy cop for the Sheriff's department, has a serious, yet likeable personality. One thing about Dick is he always has his hand out for any extra he can fleece from the public. For a nominal fee he can forget tickets or get them fixed. He's a big guy, six one and very trim with large brown eyes and dark brown hair. They also have a blond seventeen year old daughter that will soon be graduating from high school. Penny is a very happy girl, because her parents give her everything she wants. What she can't get at home she gets from the boys.

It is the last week of June and Pleasantville is getting ready for their Forth of July and County Fair celebrations. The town decided to combine the fair with their July celebration to bring in more money for the town. The fair starts at the end of June and winds up with the fireworks on the evening of the Forth. In the year just passed everyone raved how great the fair was and especially the fireworks finale. Sheryl belongs to the Rotary Club and this year they are taking care of the food stands and disposal of trash. We find Sheryl at the fair grounds organizing the set up of stands and ordering dumpsters to keep the grounds clean. It's the 28th of June and Sheryl is nervous because this is the first time she's handled anything like this and she wants to be as efficient as she is in the Mayor's office. It's not the prettiest job, but she wants to do her best for the community. Some of the other women in the Rotary look down on Sheryl, but she knows things they don't want made public so they remain silent and whisper among themselves.

She is in the parking lot at the entry to the fair grounds, on her cell phone trying to reach the company they rent dumpsters from. When she finally gets through the girl in the office tells her they don't have any available because of a celebration in Brasher Ville, (sixty miles away.) They have decided to make their celebration like Pleasantville's, except the fair will be called something else. Sheryl doesn't like the sound of that because it will cost them attendees. The woman tells her she's sorry but there is nothing she can do at this late date.

Sheryl walks over to the food stand closest to the main gate and orders a coke and sits down in despair. *Where am I going to get ten, twenty-eight yard dumpsters? This thing starts in two days.*

Cathy one of the women with a cotton candy stand on the main thoroughfare walks up. "Hey kid you look like you lost your last friend, what happened?"

"The company that provides our dumpsters every year has

run out because of the celebration over in Brasher Ville. I don't know where else to get them."

"Well I think I may know just the right person. Last month a new company came into my office for a license. And it just so happens they handle dumpsters too. Just a minute I'll get you the number." Cathy calls someone in her office and explains the situation. In a couple of seconds she is reciting the number while Sheryl dials. The message machine tells her they are out on a very important job, but leave a number and someone will call back soon. She leaves her number and punches the end button with a sigh of disgust.

"Just my luck a small company, probably has only three people and they are all out on their first call."

"Don't give up kid." Cathy retorts, "keep calling you'll get somebody." Sheryl makes the rounds and checks to make sure there are enough trash cans by each stand. When she gets back to the main gate she calls again.

Fortunately this time a man answers, "Starlight disposal. How kin I hep yew?" in a voice with a long Southern drawl.

Oh no, not one of these. Lord help me make this celebration work.

"Ah yes, I'm from the Mayor's office in Pleasantville. We are having our annual fair and Forth celebration, and we need twenty-eight yard dumpsters desperately. At least ten of them. Our fair starts day after tomorrow."

"Well never fear sweet lady, we have everything yew need and we can be thar right on time. But rat now the girl is out of the office heping on a job."

Sheryl closed her eyes and groaned.

"Hold on ma'am it's one o'clock. I promise she will call you back in an hour. May I have your number please?"

Sheryl gave him her cell number and waited nervously walking back and forth wringing her hands. She couldn't leave until those dumpsters were on the site. At two-thirty her phone rang and she almost jumped out of her skin trying to dig it out of her purse.

"Hello! Hello!"

"Hi there," a cheery female voice answered, "This is Carol from Starlight Dumpster and Disposal. Are you the lady from Pleasantville?"

"Yes, thank Goodness. It's so good to hear your voice. I'm Sheryl by the way."

" I'm pleased to meet you sorry about the delay. We are just starting out and our team isn't as big as it needs to be, but I'm sure we can provide all you need. Clarence was saying you need several large dumpsters?"

"Yes we need at least ten, twenty-eight yard containers."

"Let me check our stock."

Sheryl fidgeted while she waited. She was sweating from the heat. She dug out a handkerchief and mopped her brow.

"Sorry to hold you up I was checking to see if we could deliver today and we can, but you realize it's quite a ways so you might have to be patient until four or five this afternoon. But please don't worry we will be there, I promise."

"Okay tell the driver I'll be waiting at the front gate of the fair grounds. And thank you very much for your promptness."

For something to do Sheryl drove back to the Mayor's office to let them know the state of affairs. While she was there she took care of some other matters while watching the clock. By three thirty she was back at the fair grounds pacing back and forth. The trucks didn't show up at four and that made her more anxious than ever.

Finally at five-fifteen a big blue truck with a blue dumpster on the back drove into the lot. Sheryl could tell the truck was new because the wheels were chrome and everything shined. Sheryl let out a sigh of relief and walked over to meet it. She shaded her eyes looking up at the drivers window which was tinted so dark it looked black from the outside. Finally after what seemed like a full minute, the drivers window slowly descended and she found herself looking up at a hollow eyed, pencil neck from the hollows of the deep South. He had a funny grin on his unshaven face that showed that several front teeth were missing.

"Howdy ma'am, sorry we're so late. Where can I put this fer ya?"

Sheryl looked anxiously for another truck or group of trucks. Her heart was in her throat.

"Are there more coming?"

"Let me set this on the ground and I'll explain." the man said.

"Put it over there beside the entry." she said stepping back. The man's Adam's apple worked up and down as he put the truck in gear and looked in the mirror. He swung wide and put it in reverse slowly rolling back to the fence. He stopped about fifteen feet from it and shifted into transfer gear. The bed began to rise and slowly the new blue dumpster descended to the ground. A man on the passenger side got out and walked back to remove the hook on the end of the cable. He didn't look much better. Sheryl thought the dumpster's height was just five feet, it definitely would not hold twenty-eight yards. Meanwhile the skinny driver got out to talk to Sheryl. As he approached he eyed her up and down with a lascivious eye. It made her feel uncomfortable. And the grin on his face made it worse. It looked like he hadn't shaved in a couple of days which made him look like a prickly pear. He was dirty and his clothes were sweat soaked. When he got closer he smelled sour and rancid. She tried to hold her breath.

"That girl in the office didn't tell yew what the arrangement was?"

"Uh, no she just said you would deliver ten containers by five o'clock."

"Boy that woman, she always leaves the explanations to me. If I had a wife like that I'd have to slap her around before breakfast just to git her brain a workin. Okay this is what's happenin. We have new technology at starlight that eliminates all that pickup and dumpin. This here's the latest thing a goin. Now if yew will step around here I'll show you how it works ma'am." He went to the truck and took a small plastic bag out of the cab. He approached the end of the dumpster.

"Now you see here; there is a small switch that starts the unit. If you will step up on the edge you will see inside there is a belt." Sheryl grasped the edge and stepped up and looked. The inside looked almost sterile. There was a wide rubber belt down the middle.

"Now that is the secret of our technology it disposes of everything right on the sight. Watch this." He turned on the switch and threw the bag on the belt. The belt started to move slowly when it came to the end it slipped into a slot at the front. The belt stopped.

That's all there is to it?" Sheryl asked.

"Yep all clean and clear."

"Sir you don't know how much trash we are going to have to accommodate. We're talking five days of several thousand people's trash. Ten big Dumpsters almost don't hold it. How do you expect this to do it? It will be full in less than four hours." He held up his hands in defense.

"Okay, okay, don't panic. If it fills up you can call and we'll come out and empty it, but it's not going to fill up. We will put you on alert and can have an emergency unit here in less than an hour. And if there is any mess we will clean it up. How about that?" Sheryl was still skeptical.

"If that doesn't work you people are going to be in big trouble. The City of Pleasantville will sue you to your eyeballs." Sheryl walked around in a circle. Oh Lord, how am I going to explain this to the committee?"

"Trust me ma'am there ain't goin to be no problems. Now if you just sign this contract here on the bottom…"

Sheryl took the contract and looked it over briefly and signed on the bottom line. What other choice did she have?

"Say if you ever have time you might want to stop in to the Buster bar I'd like to buy you a drink and get acquainted." he said with his partially toothless grin. Sheryl didn't answer she just stood and glared at the two guys. The driver and his helper got in and slowly rolled up the windows. Sheryl was sure she saw the guy's eyes begin to glow as his grin became wickedly evil. The window closed and they drove away. Sheryl shuddered with fear. Somehow she felt this was not the end of her problems. She turned and called the clean up boy,

"Tim can you bring one of those trash cans over here please?" The boy brought one of the cans with a quizzical look on his face.

"Dump it in the trash container." The can was about half full. When he tipped it into the dumpster there was trash, ice cream and drinks half finished. The fluid ran down the inside leaving a sticky film. When the trash landed on the belt it started moving slowly. Sheryl and the boy stood on the side and watched the trash slide into the slot on the end. When it was gone so was the soda and ice dream on the sides. It was completely clean again.

"This thing is amazing." Tim said.

"Yeah your right and I hope it keeps people amazed for the next five days."

Sheryl's phone rang in her purse.

"Hi sweetheart, yeah it's mom, I'll will be home in just a little while as soon as I get things wrapped up here at the fair grounds. Is Dad home yet? Okay tell him I'll be there as soon as I can. Maybe we can go to the restaurant tonight. Oh you are! Whatcha fixin? Scalloped potatoes and ham! Hey great. I love you too, bye." *Sometimes having a daughter does pay off.* she thought. She looked at the blue dumpster and shuddered. She couldn't help feeling edgy about this thing.

In the early twilight the next morning the birds were beginning to chirp and fly from limb to limb. Below on the ground a man was behind a tree with a pair of binoculars watching a house across a patch of woods fifty yards away. His watch involved the house of a certain Councilman. The Councilman himself who was away at a convention in New Jersey; wasn't expected back for another three days. Meanwhile his wife, Barbra Witt was in their upstairs bedroom with another Councilman.

Willard Jenks was watching the goings on in the absence of the husband. Any minute now he expected the man to exit the back door and sneak through the brush to his car parked some distance away. The patio door slid open and Willard raised his thirty-five millimeter camera and snapped a picture of the man coming out. He took another shot when the adulterous wife kissed him goodbye. Higher up in the tree he was behind, was a long distance listening device which recorded the sweet nothings and future plans they spoke as they parted.

At this very moment the councilman in New Jersey was in bed with a very gorgeous red head keeping rhythm with the motions of the woman. Of course there was no one there to take pictures, but Willard wished he could have been. He figured something was going on, on both ends. He was right. So the Councilman was in no hurry to get home and his wife was glad.
Willard began to wrap up his equipment as the errant councilman sneaked toward his car some distance away. The wife looked nervously around just before she stepped back inside and closed the patio door. *If she only knew. She was in for a very unpleasant surprise one of these days when the time was right.* Of course the husband was too. Willard had pictures of him with a buxom blond in a motel in Charlesburg fifty miles away.
While in a devil may care encounter, Willard was taking pictures outside a window. They had neglected to close the blinds. His recorder picked up the conversation as well; very damaging evidence.
Willard slipped back to his Jeep hidden further away in the brush. He drove to the local drugstore and knocked at the back door. When a young man answered Willard handed him the roll of film from the camera. They had a deal to keep the goings on secret so the kid processed the film himself and forgot what he saw for a fee, which was more than the price of developing pictures. Willard headed home to prepare for the day which would be light because of the preparations for the

fair. Willard, about six feet tall, with a mess of dirty light brown hair, literally.

He always looked unkempt if his clothes weren't wrinkled, they were dirty. He got the maintenance job because one of his relatives worked in the City Hall complex and pulled strings for him. Now don't get me wrong Willard did a good job, but he was more useful for other things. When he was in Viet Nam he operated as a spy, and a pretty good one I might add. He had no trouble slipping up on the enemy and gathered information. In some situations he made a lot of money keeping track of the off duty actions of his fellow soldiers. These abilities came in handy when he went to work for the city. In some cases he just happened to be outside a door or around a corner when conversations were going on that weren't public information. Soon after Willard went to work he acquired a very expensive camera from a pawn shop in another town. He also collected listening devices and spy ware gathered from a spy convention in Las Vegas. He always kept his equipment ready hidden under a seat in his Jeep. The only one that knew anything about his tactics was a secretary from City Hall he was secretly seeing.

Everyone has their faults. The fun is trying not to get caught. Willard was amused by the actions of the employees of the city. He watched from a small park across the street from the building under the guise of trimming trees and bushes. As people came back from lunch just a little late; giving long backward glances as they entered the front door. Knowing they would breathe a long sigh of relief when they sat down at their desk once more.

When Willard arrived at city hall this morning he was in a mop closet getting ready to sweep the halls when an aide tells him he is wanted in the Mayors office. Willard smiles. He knows the Mayor wants to know how the fair ground set up is going without having to go out there. The Mayor is too busy to be running errands. Willard nods to the secretary as he enters the Mayor's office. He stands just inside the door smiling.

"Good morning Willard." The Mayor says with a grin. "Close the door will you?" Willard closes the door and steps closer to the huge glass topped desk. There is a small cannon with a soldier standing behind it with a tamp rod setting on the desk. The Mayor is a Civil War buff. There are pictures of various battles on the walls, cannon fire and smoke, and some soldiers charging up a hill with bayonets ready. There is also a picture of the Merrimac, a submarine used during the Civil War.

The Mayor now standing leans forward a little and in a low voice says, "What's going on out at the fair grounds? Are they about ready?"

"Yes sir just about. Everything seems to be in tact except for that secretary from the Rotary club. She seems to be having trouble with the trash disposal containers. I saw only one out there yesterday."

"Well you might have to give her a hand. We have to be ready tomorrow when the fair opens."

"Yes sir. I'll check things out and get back to you." Willard turns and leaves. At noon he will go out to the grounds and see how things are going.

Margo Hanley a little old spinster of eighty years is Pleasantville's most adroit gossip. For any contest of conversation she would hold first place bar none. Presently while she is on the phone hashing some juicy morsel probably for the forth or fifth time to hungry ears, her doorbell rings.

"Oh fudge, I'll have to call you back Muriel there's someone at the door." Margo puts the phone back in its holder and creeps toward the front door. Her house is a small cottage, everything is in pristine shape, all is dusted and polished. She makes her way through the array of antiques toward the front of the house. She recognizes the figure at the front door through the glass. It's Gomer Mendez from the garage wanting to collect his money for working on her old Chrysler Vintage 1969. Margo has a habit of putting people off hoping they will forget to collect. She has irritated the grocery clerk a few times that way; telling him she has forgotten her check book, and doesn't have enough cash to cover the charge.

Once at a local restaurant she ate a free meal because the owner was too embarrassed to attempt to collect. Now they make sure she has enough to cover what she orders beforehand. She slowly opens the door.

"Oh good morning Gomer." she says in her high pitched voice.

"Good morning Margo."

"Uh what was it you needed?"

"I came to get the check for the charges you were supposed to bring down to the garage."

"Oh yes! Come on in. I'll get my check book. How much was that now?"

"Eighty-nine thirty seven including parts." Gomer steps inside the door and waits, but not with patience. He looks around the living room at the antique furniture and thinks *This old bitty has piles hid somewhere. I hope I'm around when she cashes in.* It seems like she takes forever to get the check written. But finally she reluctantly hands it to him.

"Thank you Miss Hanley." Without any further conversation he turns and walks out.

"Uh, thanks for coming by Gomer." her voice falls on empty space, Gomer is gone.

Gomer Mendez is a slick tongued mechanic that has a habit of overcharging for everything. At the present he is the only game going in Pleasantville. He is the town's only garage and tow truck owner. He charges to the point that the local Judge hauled him into court and recommended he drop his profits a little. So for the time being he has backed off, but only temporarily.

Gomer and Willard are old drinking buddies. They drink from the same square bottle, literally. When Gomer gets back to the garage he finds Willard waiting for him.

"Hey what's up partner?" Willard says.

"Uh just tryin to collect from Margo Hanley that old gossip."

"How about a drink? I was able to pilfer a new bottle from that family that just moved into the money district." (A small tract of new expensive houses at the edge of town. Willard does maintenance work on the side for a little extra cash.)

Maybe a little later, I can't git started too soon in the mornin or I'll be drunk all day. Heh, heh."

"I'm headed out to the fair grounds to check out the trash facilities. It seems a certain lady with the Rotary has had trouble getting dumpsters. The delivery truck showed up yesterday with only one and gave her a smooth story about new technology. Now she's stuck with *it* and a promise. I'm personally going to stand on the out skirts and watch the fun, eh."

"Hmm, I may have to go out there this evenin and check that out. Maybe you could meet me out there for that drink after dark."

"Okay partner, I'll see you later."

As Willard drives up to the fair grounds he sees Sheryl standing in the parking lot looking at the blue box. Her husband is looking too.

"Howdy Deputy, Ma'am. You all have more coming I hope. Last year ten almost wasn't enough."

"Don't remind me Willard." She answers.

"You know Willard, we might need a back up plan you got any ideas?" Dick asks him.

"Well now that you mention it we have a seven yard dump truck and a front loader at the motor pool. We could use those in a pinch until the trash company shows up."

"Well that makes me feel a little better." Sheryl says.

"Say how does this thing work anyway?" Willard asks.

"Supposedly you just drop the stuff on the belt and it comes on automatically." Dick explains.

"Where does it all go?" Willard asks. They peek over the edge.

"It goes in that slot in the end. Here I'll show you what happens."

Dick walks over to a trash can near the gate and brings it back and dumps it over the edge. The belt starts to move and the trash slides into the slot. When it's all gone the belt stops.

"Well I'll be hanged." Willard walks around the unit looking it over.

"What's really going to impress me is when it's full to the brim and still coming. You know those kids empting those trash cans never stop. By the time they make a round it's time to start over. And from what I hear the crowd is supposed to be bigger this year even though there is another fair over in Brasherville."

"Well we're stuck with it for now. Sheryl signed a contract." Dick says.

"And tomorrow is opening day." Sheryl says with a moan.

That night after Willard and Gomer have looked things over and had a few swigs out of the square bottle, they depart for home. All is quiet in the parking lot and suddenly a stirring begins in the blue box. A twelve inch stainless steel tube descends to the ground from the front of the unit. There are small teeth around its leading edge. It slowly begins to turn and work its way into the ground until it has burrowed down three feet. It stops and all is silent once more.

Opening Day

Early on the day the fair was to open lots of people were already on the grounds feeding live stock, setting up stands, storing salable items in portable cabinets and making things neat in general. Sheryl was there also walking and worrying. Wondering if this one lone dumpster was going to be enough. Over and above that she was fighting a bad feeling that she could almost taste. There was something that gnawed at the back of her mind. It wasn't that there was just one trash collector, but she felt something ominous coming, and couldn't put her finger on it.

It was just after six a.m. Dick had come out here with her in his patrol car to make sure she wouldn't be alone, but finding others he knew from town setting up, he went about his job. Locals were already bringing wrappings and containers they would no longer need after the opening. As they tossed the trash into the blue box Sheryl still wondered if it would hold everything that strange guy said it would. She shuddered afresh as she remembered the eerie glow in his eyes as he drove away. Something bad was coming she just knew it. Seemingly everyone in Pleasantville was awake in anticipation of opening day. Margo was already on the phone, the Mayor was at the kitchen table having his first cup of coffee and Gomer and Wilber were sitting in Gomer's wrecker on the sidelines sipping spiked coffee from the all night convenience store. Ticket takers, mostly teens from the high school, would arrive shortly before nine and a crowd would be building up at the front gate. The Mayor would be there with the high school band for the opening festivities along with the politicians that would be vying for office the following spring. First day would bring the largest crowd of any of the days following, except the fourth which would be the biggest day of all.

The weather was to be perfect, clear and hot, but who cared it was county fair time. There were so many entries the town had to rent some of a farmers property at the back of the fair grounds. They had also brought in a carnival with all the rides and Carney stands with games of chance. It was going to be a big affair this year.

Buford Anson the town's only millionaire, sat in his Cadillac on the road outside the grounds watching and waiting. He had made his money in life outguessing other men. That's the way he made his millions; he was there when it was good and when it wasn't he was gone. He had a sixth sense about situations and just knew when and where to put his attention. As he watched the bustling and hurrying from the road he thought, *I wouldn't put a dime on this one boys. It smells bad from the beginning.* After he had been there at least an hour he started his car and drove away. He didn't know why but for some strange reason he packed a suitcase to take a trip South to the big city.

When the nine o'clock hour finally arrived everyone was ready. The gates swung open and the crowd filed in and waited at the announcement area. The high school Band was playing patriotic songs. The Mayor made an opening speech and reminded the crowd that there were tickets on sale for prizes that would be given away late that afternoon and every day following. A new pickup would be given away on the Fourth. The crowd clapped and cheered; it was time to put their evil deeds behind them and enjoy the celebration.

For a small town this was one of the most corrupt places on the face of the earth. They cheated, lied to one another, stole from each other, embezzled and slept with the another's wife or husband, and they knew what they were doing but they didn't care. They could get away with it, or so they thought, but payday comes some day and for Pleasantville that day had arrived. They were caught up in the pleasures of life and didn't expect it.

By ten thirty the first trash pick up started and the kids on golf carts with small trailers began their rounds. They were all skeptical at first and even the Rotary club President asked Sheryl once more to be sure if everything was going to be all right. It could be very embarrassing if something went wrong. Especially with the dumpster in the front of the fair grounds. Sheryl had had a difficult time convincing her it would handle everything. Sheryl and the club president made their way to the front gate to see how the first drop would go. As the kids dumped can after can over the side the worry mounted. As different ones looked over the edge they saw that the belt was moving and the refuse was going into the slot at the end. They shrugged their shoulders and said,

"Oh well!" But by the time the second round came due it looked like the dumpster was going to handle it. At one thirty when the kids made their third round the worry lessened and they began to forget about it. All day long they dumped everything one could think of and the dumpster took it all and kept running. The trash rose above the halfway point at times, but never any higher. This was truly a modern miracle. People even asked where they could get one of these when they remodeled their homes. One of these would really be handy.

Even with pick up every hour and a half there was a lot of trash at the end of the day and clean up lasted way past dark. Everyone pitched in and helped and soon they were ready for the second day...

Late that night, about midnight, Lolita Alvarez was waiting at her front door for her lover to come. A few moments later Willard pulled up in his Jeep. He hurried to Lolita's door and grabbed her and kissed her. Lolita is a sexy Mexican girl of twenty-eight, she has deep brown eyes that are pools of desire. She and Willard have been lovers for several months now. He can't help himself, he is in love with this woman and he is sure she loves him. While they are inside satisfying each other there is another man out in the shadows. His name is Chico Alvarez he is Lolita's ex husband. He and Lolita have decided to get back together and take Willard for all he has, and go back to Mexico.

Down the street on the same side as Lolita's house there is another man also watching, but he is watching Chico. Gomer from the garage is setting in his wrecker waiting for Willard to come out to go home. Chico is all absorbed waiting for Willard to leave, he sneaks around back of Lolita's house to wait. Gomer picks up his tire iron from under the seat and gets out quietly. He sneaks up behind Chico and slugs him knocking him unconscious. He drags the body to the wrecker and hefts it on the back next to his tool box. He lights a cigarette waiting for Willard. About thirty minutes later Willard comes out the front door and finds Gomer in the front yard.

"Come here a minute man I got something to show you." He takes Willard to the back of the wrecker and shows him the body.

"So who is this?" Willard asks.

"This is her ex and he's been following your act after you leave."

"Why the dirty…" After several expletives Gomer says, "Wait a minute man I got a better idea."

"Something better than killing him?" Willard asks.

With a smile on his face he says, "The dumpster man, the dumpster. It will take anything remember?"

"With a broad smile Willard agrees.

"Yeah man, the dumpster." They drive old Chico to the fairgrounds and wait in the shadows for there are others that have things they need to get rid of. One guy has a knife. Another has some old letters with incriminating evidence. Someone else puts in some rotten meat that has spoiled. An old woman sadly drops her dead dog in and finally they are all gone. Now it's Willard and Gomer's turn. They drive along side the box and roll Chico's body over the edge. The belt starts and Chico moves slowly toward the slot. When his head hit's the end there is a crunching sound and his head now crushed goes in and the rest follows. A few minutes later the body is gone, blood and all.

"You know I should go back there and get Lolita and put her in there with him." "Naw man, it ain't worth it. When she finds out you know about him she'll leave town. You just need to get her bank account before she leaves that's all. So Willard, what happens to all this stuff. You know there ain't room for it in this box."

"Yeah what about that? We need to look this thing over." They walk around the box with a flashlight. When they get back to the front they see the shiny tube in the ground.

"Wait a minute that wasn't there yesterday." Willard says.

"We could lift it up with the wrecker and see where it goes." Says Gomer.

"Okay man lets hook it up."

Gomer turns the truck around and backs it close to the box. He gets out and puts the hook in the steel loop in front.

Slowly he raises the boom. When the tube clears the ground there is a black hole, black as soot. Willard bends down to look inside and a smell hits him in the face so strong it knocks him over gagging and puking. Gomer jumps back and is spared the experience. He grabs Willard's arm and drags him away from the dumpster.

"Oh God, help me man. I'm so sick. Take me to the clinic I'm going to die."

Gomer lifts him into the cab and drives to the small clinic that is open all night with just a nurse and doctor on duty. No one can understand why Willard is so sick and can't quit vomiting. He can't tell them because he doesn't want anyone to know where he got sick. It would mess up the rest of the fair for sure. By four-thirty they finally have him calmed down and in control again. The doctor gave him something to settle his stomach and sends him home. On the way back to his Jeep at Lolita's, Gomer tells him to check with Lolita and let her know that he knows about Chico and see what her reaction is. After talking to her she denies everything. They drive down the street and wait. They see her putting things in her Chevy and she drives away.

"I'll catch her coming out of the bank tomorrow and get my money." Willard says.

Day Two

When the gates open at eight that morning the crowd is as large as the day before. The fair this year is going to be the biggest event in the county. There will be judging's today of the cattle and hogs. Ribbons will be passed out for the best roses, flowers and the biggest vegetables. There will be a chili cook off and lots of indigestion remedies passed out.

When Sheryl arrives she looks in the blue box. There is no evidence of the goings on from the night before. The inside is clean and shinning, but the nagging in her mind is still there. It quietly calls to everyone, *Come with your secrets and the things that bother you and leave them here.* Some of the people who put stuff in the dumpster the night before are at the fair now and they are relieved since some of the things that were bothering them are now gone.

Gomer is at the garage, he hasn't gone home to sleep. He can't sleep he knows he killed a man last night, so he drinks from the square bottle. Willard sits in his Jeep outside the fair grounds listening to his radio waiting for calls. He hopes Lolita hasn't gone to the police to report Chico missing. The women from the Rotary Club are sitting outside one of the sandwich stands drinking coffee and eating danish rolls. They are chattering like chipmunks and giggling at one another. They all feel something lurking in the shadows of their minds but they put it aside for the show must go on.

For the rest of the day the innocent teens load can after can of all kinds of trash, ice cream the kids have dropped, popcorn, cotton candy, cones, hot dogs, bread, and soda. All of it goes into the slot at the end of the wonderful blue box in the parking lot. "Truly a modern wonder," they say.

A black limousine drives quietly by on the road that passes the fairgrounds. The windows are dark and it passes slowly. Inside the man from the disposal company says to the driver,

"Everything is going just like we planned not a single scrap of paper has been lost." He grins his evil grin and his eyes glow behind the darkened car windows.

"We have their money and there is no going back for them." The limo glides away as silently as it arrived.

At noon the food stands are very busy. The attendants can hardly keep up. By the end of the day operators will be going to buy more of everything. Business is great. Profits are nearly what they made last year and this is only the second day.

As the last of twilight leaves the sky, a few of the straggling patrons left leave the fair grounds for home and a feeling of having had a great time. The blue box sits silent at the front gate like a sentry, watching.

Watkins, a Real Estate agent in Pleasantville sits in his

office at home smiling. In his mind he has pulled off the deal of his life. Today he sold a property for a handsome price. A property that sat empty for several years, since the old lady that previously owned it died. The relatives living in another city called and said; "Get rid of it." no matter what it takes. Yeah he had to make a few repairs, but the relatives said he could take the cost out of the final sale. A young couple wanting to move to Pleasantville came in today and looked it over. Their names were Jones. Matthew and Esther Jones. Howard didn't say much he just let them look and assume every thing would be alright.

Of course they had questions, Did the roof leak?, Why no, when in fact it did. Was the water and sewer Okay? Oh yes, never worked better. Termites? Not a single one.

The most critical problem was that the foundation was crumbling at one corner and the whole property was in a low spot. If ever there came a hard rain…? Howard just threw a few shovels of dirt next to the house and let it go. Of course he was going to charge the full ten percent. He had that much coming.

The new couple stayed for the fair and they just loved it. They thought Pleasantville would be a great place to raise kids. In fact in five months the young mother would deliver her first child. What Pleasantville didn't know was, she was a powerful practicing Witch and he was studying to be a Warlock. They needed the age of this house to help them in their practice. They hoped there were spirits in the house that they could summon, but at the present the spirits they were looking for were in the dumpster at the fair.

Day Three

By seven o'clock the next morning all the food stand operators were restocking and getting ready for another great day. Game booths were open and handlers were bring in prizes. The carnies were checking their equipment so they could give the folks the ride of their lives. Charge cards would be moving so fast it would seem like shuffling for poker. It seemed as if the customers had pulled out all the stops and were going for broke and by the end of this celebration that's what they would be. As expected, the day was warm and beautiful and the crowd remained as large as it had been for the past two days. Sales were up for the third day and it seemed everyone was having a wonderful time. The Mayor made the rounds campaigning for votes for the following spring. The carnival was making so much they offered free rides to the kids as prizes. As the old saying goes, 'The Money Rolled In.'

Gomer called Willard and told him he didn't feel so good about Chico.

"Aw forget about it man you were just doing a friend a favor. I would have killed him myself even if you weren't there. I'll go get us a bottle and we'll get drunk and forget our troubles. Willard got a bottle and then Gomer got one and they both passed out. It's a good thing no one called Willard to help with anything at the fairgrounds because they couldn't have reached him.

As the day wore on some of the teens got very inquisitive about the trash box and decided to come back that night to see what made it tick. About nine o'clock a couple of boys sneaked back to the fair grounds with flashlights and looked over the edge. The dumpster was clean and shiny.

"I can't figure out how it takes all that garbage Billy." They walked around it and checked everything. Then Tommy noticed the pipe going down into the ground.

"I'll betcha that's where it all goes man in that pipe."

"Yeah, man your probably right. Lets put a board across the bottom and look in the slot. I'll bet there are some monster teeth that chew up the trash."

Arnie said, "Somebody threw a dead cat in here and it just chewed it up. They could hear a sucking sound as it went in too, but it is always clean inside when it stops. I'll never figure that one out."

The boys found a board long enough to lay across the sloping sides without touching the belt about half way back from the slot. When they had it in solid Billie climbed over the side and put his foot on the board, it held. He knelt down and crawled out to the middle and took the flashlight from Tommy.

When Billie shined the light into the slot he saw a horrible sight.

"Oh God Tommy it *has* got teeth in there!" he screamed. He jumped up intending to climb out, but lost his balance and fell backward on the belt. it started moving slow like it usually did. Tommy leaned over the side trying to reach Billie's hand and missed, twice. Billie was screaming, "HELP ME! HELP ME! Don't let it eat me!"

Just then a man jumped up on the side and reached over and grabbed Billie's shirt just before his foot slid into the slot. Billie was screaming and slobbering all over himself. The big strong arm hauled Billie up the side and over the edge and dropped him on the ground. Billie looked up and saw Willard standing over him.

"Ain't you got enough sense not to git in a thing like that. Now I'm going to haul you over to your dad. And I hope he wears your hide out. And you Tommy, you git yourself home and stay away from this thing unless your parents are with you, you hear me?"

"Yuh, yuh, yes sir." Tommy took off in a dead run for home. Billie took off after him not waiting for Willard to take him home.

"I'm still gonna tell your dad." he yelled after him. When the boys were out of sight Willard reached over the edge and took the board out and tossed it aside. When he glanced back it looked like the slot had spread into a huge grin. Now it was time for him to get out of there he was seeing things. As he drove home he thought, *Wow, it was a good thing I woke up when I did. Wonder what made me wake up. It was like someone was calling me and I had to answer.* Then he remembered the voice, it was his father calling him to pull his brother out of the well. He had fallen and caught hold of a part of the wood that covered the well and was dangling over an eighty foot hole. Willard woke up in a cold sweat, and rushed out of Gomer's house in a dead run to his Jeep. When he was fully awake, somehow he knew right where to go and raced for the fair grounds. Now as he drove home his head began to hurt from the whiskey.

At his small house the first thing he found was the aspirin bottle then he lay down in bed thinking about what had happened to the boys and what had happened to Chico. About all that trash...

Day Four

The next day it seemed like everyone had a hang over. Not a soul showed up until almost eight o'clock. Then there was this sudden rush to get the stands and eating places stocked. Runners were driving around buying supplies and picking up food. Fortunately the crowd was light this morning. Farmers were feeding the live stock and getting ready for the show. But everyone seemed in a stupor, kind of like falling back to rest for it had been a hectic three days. The spirit of the fair didn't come back until almost noon when people sat down to eat. Things began to liven up. Sheryl was sitting at a drink stand having a coke with one of her friends. She was staring at the ground and it was like a wave that came across the fair grounds with a voice whispering, *Wake up!* It was as if people weren't in charge here any more, but a strange force they couldn't see.

After one o'clock the crowd grew surprisingly fast and they had a full house once again. Willard and Gomer showed up late; checked out a few things, and just sat in Willard's Jeep most of the day.

"Willard, something is wrong here I can feel it in my bones." Gomer grumbled.

"When this is over I'm going to close up and go down

South to LA for a while."

"Yeah I hear you man. Somthin strange is going on here but it's hard to put a handle on it." Willard said.

The boys that had been there the night before passed and gave Willard a feeble wave. He waved back not wanting to think about what could have happened.

The trash seemed unusually heavy when the kids made the pick up at two o'clock and the dumpster was almost full when they finished, but it took all they put in. Some of the teen aged girls looked at it and wondered where all that trash was going. Sheryl walked over to her daughter who was among them.

"Pretty amazing the technology they have today huh kid."

"Yeah I guess, but can't you feel the strange aura around this thing Mom. I mean it's like death." Her mom's eyes opened wide. Her mouth, while open, didn't have any words. Her daughter was saying what she felt all this time. For a long moment they just stood and looked at one another.

Then one of Penny's friends said, "Weird huh girl."

"Yeah let's get out of here." She felt relieved as they walked away.

Sheryl stood there stunned. The full impact of this steel box had finally hit her. She knew something terrible was going to happen and there wasn't anything she could do about it. There was too much riding on this fair and fourth celebration to start a panic. Her subconscious mind told her, *I'm going home and get things packed we are going to have to leave here or die.*

She spent the rest of the afternoon packing clothes and things they would need for a trip and set the bags in the back of the closet. If nothing happened she could say that they needed a get away for a few days. When she finished she went to the store and bought a case of bottled water not really knowing why. The had a water treatment system par excellence in their home. She put the bottles to one side in the trunk of the car. Once at home again she made up a first aid kit out of compulsion. Sheryl didn't know why, but she knew they would need it. The image of that man's glowing eyes stayed in her mind. She shuddered. She picked up her cell phone to call her husband, but thought better of it; he wouldn't believe her, he always seemed to shrug off her feelings. Law enforcement always had the answer. With things as ready as she could make them now Sheryl paced the floor.

When Dick came in he asked, "Do you want to go by the fair grounds?"

"No I've seen all of the fair I want to see until tomorrow night when we will want to see the fire works. Look Dick, Penny stopped to look at that trash collector and she said she sensed death in it. I'm afraid something bad is going to happen baby."

"All right, all right, if it will make you feel any better pack a couple of bags in case something does happen so we can get out of here."

"Oh Dick I'm so glad to hear you talking common sense." She threw her arms around him with relief.

"I've already packed, the bags are in the upstairs closet." she said. Dick grinned as he held her.

Willard went back to City hall; they had a couple of things to fix and some cleaning up to do. He was glad to know this would be over day after tomorrow.

The Jones's arrived in Pleasantville in their small RV. They decided to transfer their bed pads from the RV to the bedroom of the house. It would be so cozy sleeping in a bedroom. Of course they didn't have any power but they hooked up a circuit to their bed room from their small generator. They could eat snacks and watch their nine inch T.V. When Matthew turned it on all the channels were blank. All they could get was a white screen. They took it back out to the RV, but it was the same. Suddenly the screen went black. None of the channels would come in. Esther went into a trance and started talking in strange gibberish. Matthew stared at her waiting for a message to come forth. Finally she fell over in a dead faint. He had a difficult time reviving her. When she was alert again the TV screen started showing explosions. When Matthew tried changing channels, they were all the same. He shut it off and grabbed Esther by the shoulders and shook her to bring her around. When she came to he jumped in the drivers seat and turned the RV around and drove up the road toward the highway into town. The second he drove onto the state road the trances and feelings left them.

"Esther I think for our own safety we should spend the night on the side of this road and maybe we will go back tomorrow if everything seems all right."

"Yes maybe we should. I felt so funny down there. Do you think we should stay here Matthew?"

"Oh Esther there is so much power in that house we would be missing the chance of a life time. Let's just wait until morning and see how it goes. Okay?"

"All right if you think so Matthew." Now Esther felt very weak and tired so she lay down on one of the padded seats and was soon asleep.

Fourth of July

Everyone in Pleasantville woke up excited this morning. Especially the children. This is our nations birth date. On this day everyone is patriotic. The flag goes out on the front porch and the people mix their favorite drinks and celebrate. Most fathers and sons had spirited off to some distant secret place and gotten the fireworks that no one sold in Pleasantville. They bought cherry bombs, big Roman candles, M-80's, and strings of small firecrackers and naturally they are all there waiting with the famous Coca-Cola bottle that holds the bottle rockets. As usual the fire department is on hand to give a show at the fair grounds and what a show it will be.

Even Matthew and Esther wake up in a better mood and when they go back into their little house every thing is all right.

When he fires up the generator the TV is working just like it should. Some of the neighbors from the neighborhood up the hill from them bring them gifts and welcome them. There is joy all over Pleasantville. All over town errant fireworks can be heard being exploded by the kids. Occasionally a tin can, can be seen rising into the air fired from an M-80.

Wilbur wakes up in a fog from last night. He takes a few minutes to get straightened out and get his head working. It's nine thirty, he realizes he is late and should be at the fair grounds, but he doesn't care. He hears a knock at the front door. He pulls on his shirt and goes to answer. Its Gomer in a sweat; the City Hall wants Willard out at the fair grounds and couldn't reach him so they called Gomer to come and get him.

"Hey man they need you at the fair grounds. I guess like me you slept late huh?"

"Yeah and when I get there I'm going to look for somebody selling tomato juice." Gomer smiles he feels a little that way himself. On the way to the fair grounds Willard stops at the local liquor store and buys a miniature vodka for his tomato juice.

At the fair he stops by the City's information stand. One of the other stands needs help part of the walls collapsed and a delivery truck is stuck on the midway. Gomer pulls in to help move the truck with his wrecker and Willard goes to fix the stand. When they get things straightened out Willard walks over to one of the food stands.

One of the girls from City Hall that is helping out shouts, "Hi Willard. What can we get you this fine day? Coffee and a danish?"

"No coffee today Winnie. Tomato Juice is what I need."

"Well now let's see do we have tomato juice? I see orange and pineapple."

"It's under the counter on the end", and sure enough under the counter in a pan of ice is an open can. Willard hands her his glass.

"Wow, need a double portion this morning huh?"

"Yeah Winnie, Please I'll pay double for it." She sets the full glass on the counter and Willard uncaps the vodka and dumps it in looking around to see if anyone else is looking. Winnie gives him a long plastic spoon to stir it. While she stands smiling Willard pours half of it down before he comes up for air. He drops two dollars on the counter and sits down at one of the tables. He looks around to see what's going on. The crowd is pretty good for ten in the morning. Vendors are walking around passing out miniature flags in hopes some of the patrons will buy the larger one for their homes. The mood is light and airy and everyone seems to be enjoying themselves. Willard waves at people he knows and some of the seniors stop to talk.

Around noon the teens emptying trash notice the dumpster is filling up to the brim. They set the trash cans down and wait for the level to go down. But now it seems to take longer to empty. One of the girls finds Sheryl.

"Hi Sheryl. The trash collector is getting ready to run over."

"Oh no. Tell them I'll be right there." she takes out her cell phone and calls Willard's phone.

"Yeah this is Willard."

"Yeah this is Sheryl Wheatly and I may have to get you to take a look at the dumpster. The kids say it's getting ready to run over."

"Okay I'll meet you over there." Willard says as he gets up to leave. He calls back over his shoulder,

"Thanks Winnie, just what I needed."

When Willard and Sheryl reach the parking lot the trash level has started to recede. Sheryl sighs a breath and says,

"Thank God it was only a false alarm." Willard turns to her and in a soft tone he asks, "Does this thing give you a funny feeling?"

"Yeah it does, but I've not wanted to say anything to cause problems. The town needs the money and I've saved them a bundle on this thing alone. Rental fees are horrendous for the other kind. I've got a feeling in my gut that tells me to be careful. You too?"

"Yeah, me too," he nods his head and looks off into the distance.

The rest of the day goes without incident and sales are good. As the sun sinks on the horizon people are getting anxious for dark and the fireworks. About eight-thirty the crowd starts finding seats at the baseball field and waiting for the festivities to begin.

At long last just after nine several concussion bombs go off and scares everybody to death.

Then a voice comes on the PA system, "Welcome to Billings field Ladies and gentlemen and welcome to the Pleasantville Fourth of July celebration. We will start with a ground display this year and we think it will be one you will enjoy." Another concussion bomb goes off and someone lights a massive display on a rack that becomes the U. S. flag. Everyone stands up and cheers and the band starts the National Anthem. More concussion bombs and then the ground display is started. When the time comes for the aerial display the crowd is really oohing and ahhing over the display, huge circles of color lighting up the night sky. Some bursts overlap others and make it more majestic. When the display is over at ten there is a roar of appreciation.

The cheering goes on and on. Dick shouts in Sheryl's ear, "See I told you it was going to be great."

Sheryl smiles and nods. Meanwhile Penny and her friends are jumping for joy.

By eleven-thirty nearly everyone has gone. It's over for one more year and everyone is tired. The cleanup will start tomorrow. They put away what has to be stored and go home. Gomer and Willard sit in the Jeep on the sidelines watching things wind down. By the time everyone has left the dumpster has emptied itself and it once again is clean and shiny.

Up the road from the fair grounds a couple of miles the blue truck from Starlight Dumpster and Disposal is setting along side the road waiting. When the last of the patrons from the fair leave they will go into action. They don't know that Willard and Gomer are watching from outside the parking lot in a patch of trees.

Just past midnight everyone is gone and Clarence starts the truck and drives into the parking lot of the fair grounds. He backs up to the blue dumpster, and sets the brake. He and his helper get out and walk back to the unit. Clarence takes a key out of his pocket and inserts it into a hidden switch. When he turns the key the twelve inch tube retracts from the ground. He shuts off the power switch and the quiet motor winds down. His partner holds his breath and puts an insert into the black hole and lays a plastic cover over it.

Then he takes a shovel and puts a mound of dirt over it and pats it down. He is chuckling all the time he works. Meanwhile Clarence puts the cable hook through the steel loop, he goes to the front and engages the wench. The truck bed tilts and the cable tightens slowly as the dumpster rolls up the bed. The bed settles down to level again and stops. Clarence begins to laugh, then his partner joins him as they crawl back into the truck. The windows are down and Willard and Gomer can hear their cackling on the night air.

The truck pulls out and as it leaves the parking lot Clarence's voice can be heard, "GOOD BYE NOT SO PLEASANTVILLE!" They continue down the road and their laughter can be heard until they are out of sight.

Willard has goose bumps on his arms, he looks over at Gomer and his hair is standing up on the back of his neck. They wait until the truck has had time to get to the highway and they drive home.

Pleasantville's Last Day

The sun is just coming up over the horizon, the birds are already chirping. A squirrel runs down a tree trunk looking for breakfast. It's a beautiful July fifth. No one is going to want to get up early this morning because they have to face the cleanup from the day before.

Bliss and sweet rest is all they want now. In the Wheatly house they are also sleeping peacefully. But the buzzing feeling of a nagging fly begins to bother Penny then she smells something funny and awakes with a start. She sniffs the air and notices the bathroom door is open slightly. Did she forget to flush last night? She slides off the bed slowly expecting nothing more than a smelly toilet bowl. She creeps to the door and a horrible smell hits her in the face. She chokes and dives for the hall. Opening the hall door she staggers out and screams at her parents. They both come alive in an instant and run into the hall. Penny grabs Sheryl and screams, "ITS HAPPENING MOM, ITS STARTED!" They don't know what to do it hasn't registered yet what is happening.

"In my bath." Penny cries. They bolt for the bath. When Dick opens the door and turns on the light he is greeted by a black goo in the sink. It is bubbling up from the drain. Then he hears a noise from the tub. It is also bubbling black goo. And the smell gags them and they run for their bedroom.

Sheryl shouts, "Penny get dressed and run for the car."

Sheryl hurriedly puts on her clothes and Dick is doing the same. Sheryl runs into the closet and grabs the suitcases and breaks for the hall. Dick picks up the rest of the things and runs after her. Penny is running after them down the stairs. Sheryl sprints into the kitchen trying not to smell the stench. Sure enough the kitchen sink is full, and nearly running over. She looks in the downstairs bath, it's already running over the edges of the sink and shower and advancing toward the door. Sheryl bolts for the front door. In the driveway she shouts, "It's all over the house. I think we should wake the neighbors. There is more to this than we think." Penny bolts across the street and starts banging on the neighbors door. Dick and Sheryl go to the adjoining houses on either side of them. The neighbors come staggering out wondering what's going on. By the time the smell hits them they know. The Wheatly family don't waste any more time, it's time to get out of there. They pile into the car and drive for the highway out of town. Somehow they know they have lost everything, but they are alive which is more than some will have in the coming hours in Pleasantville.

Margo Hanley is already up and making her morning tea she puts water in the teapot and turns on the gas flame to set the pot on. There is a giant explosion and her little cottage and antiques are obliterated in a huge ball of flame. What no one is thinking of is the methane gas this black soup is generating. Now explosions start all over town in the houses that have gas water heaters. The fiery debris flies onto the neighboring homes which are just ten feet away from each other, most with wooden fences. In a few minutes whole neighborhoods will be on fire from the black death coming out of every drain in Pleasantville. An explosion rocks Willard's house and he is on his feet in an instant. He smells a familiar odor and breaks for the front door. He jumps in his Jeep and heads for Gomer's. He meets him a few blocks down the street coming his way.

Without stopping he shouts, "Head for the highway!"

Gomer turns around in the middle of the street and follows.

Muriel hears an explosion and jumps up in bed. When she steps out she puts her foot in something black and sticky. She looks down and begins to scream. The goo is burning her foot. She has an older gas stove in her house; it has a pilot light. When the methane reaches the kitchen its all over.

The Mayor lives in the better district of town. He has a new two story, three bedroom house. A funny smell wakes his wife. She slides out of bed and puts her robe on and goes to the bathroom door as she opens it and something spills out, all over her feet. She starts to scream, her husband wakes and sees the mess. He's nobody's fool, he runs for the hall to go downstairs; a terrible smell gags him when he tries to descend, then he sees a black liquid all over the floor of the living room. He thinks of his fishing boots and remembers his wife screaming in the bedroom. Could he get to the closet? It was worth a try. When he gets to the bedroom door he sees spots that haven't been covered yet. He jumps across them and into the walkin closet, he grabs his pants and puts on his boots. He ignores his wife's screams, he's getting out of there. She has fallen down and is rolling in the goop. Meanwhile down the hall in his oldest daughter's room her bathroom door is also closed. She is into far Eastern religions and has candles burning. She smells the odor and gets up to see what it is. When she opens the bathroom door… BOOM!

Mrs. Witt and her Councilman lover are in the bedroom sleeping it off. The black ooze runs under the door and the smell wakes them with a gag. Out in her kitchen it's all over the floor and running into the living room and has come under the door from the hall bath. The flame clicks on in the gas water heater and the methane seeps into the vent.

When Mr. Witt gets home from New Jersey he will discover he has nothing to come home to.

The explosions continue and fires run rampant through the town. The burning debris falls onto the adjoining structures. People who do get out of their houses are killed by the explosions because they don't get far enough away from the house. Businesses on main street are also lost because of the fires from the electric water heaters in the bathrooms. When the explosions started they just went from one building to the next. In just over an hour all of Pleasantville was in flames.

The last house to be affected was the Jones house. They lived down hill and the black mess was headed there at a quick pace. The sewer pipe was six inches in diameter that passed their house. They had gotten up wondering what was going on; when they heard the explosions they went into the house and closed the door. When they went into the kitchen with their TV the dead bolt locked the door on its own. When the goo hit the T in the pipe it came with full force spraying out of the kitchen drain and the shower drain until it hit the ceiling.

Esther screamed and then a serious look came over her and she said in a quivering voice, "I command you to stop and go back, we are the children of the master and we have his protection."

The force of the spray slowed slightly, but kept running onto the floor.

"Stop! I command you." she shouted. The ooze slowed further, but still kept coming over the edge of the shower stall.

The stench was overpowering as Matthew tried to open the front door. By now he was gagging and throwing up and couldn't get hold of the lock.

The smell overcame Esther and she passed out falling into the puddle covering the floor. Then the burner in their old gas water heater came on and the methane gas drifted out of the vent; there was a tremendous explosion. What was left burned. Now you can't tell which Witch is which.

Other towns miles away seeing the column of smoke that used to be Pleasantville and soon start sending fire trucks, but by the time the trucks arrive it's too late; nearly the whole town is gone and the black substance has evaporated in the flames. Everything else is burned black.

There is an old proverb that says;
Be sure your sins will find you out.

*D*oors

The old house sat back at least two hundred yards from the road. Yet it was big and ominous enough to be recognized at that distance. When one got closer its features seemed to soften a little. It had an air of peace and solitude. The house was empty, but there were lots of windows and they sparkled in the morning sun as if they had just been washed. The inactivity around it would make a person wonder where the family was that owned this beautiful place. As everything around it was so neat and clean. This tranquil atmosphere seemed to draw people and they would want to sit on the front patio and lush green grass and appreciate the comfortable furniture that was spread around a glass topped table. I always imagined a pitcher of cold lemonade setting on the table and ladies with large brimmed white hats sitting around it. Their conversation would be light and they would be laughing as they enjoyed a perfect morning. The house itself was two story built of all solid hardwood. The many windows were tall, had partitions and brightly colored drapes that were drawn back to reveal part of the rooms within. There were large pots on each side of the entry with lush plants that hung over the sides. Purple blossoms graced each of the plants and made the atmosphere homier. It would make a person want to linger and drink in the freshness of the day. The front door was a massive four foot opening with deep set panels. There was a large brass knocking device that had very ornate features and it shined as if some butler or housekeeper had just polished it. This door was solid oak, two inches thick and supported by four large brass hinges. When opened it swung back silently. The jambs on the frame were thick timbers mounted solidly. The knob was an ornate brass lever handle, but the lock was a larger version of today's dead bolt separate from the handle. Set in the upper part of the door were letters carved deeply into the shining wood.

Welcome

Around the North side of the house was a separate four car garage built of the same hardwood as the rest of the structure. The doors of each individual bay were also of oak and had a slot of windows across them at eye level. The concrete floors were free of oil and grease as if they had just been finished. There were cabinets inside but nothing in them. No tools or garden implements hung on the walls.

There were gables on the second story of the house with wide windows in them. The roof was covered with large slabs of black slate, but it lent a certain grace to the structure. Upstairs there were five bedrooms, two sitting rooms, and three full baths. One of the baths adjoined the master bedroom, which was nearly twenty feet square. The entire house was furnished with early Victorian furniture. Inside this house it seemed to glow. All around it for a hundred acres were trees of all origins. From the air it looked like a lush green patch of forest with a house in the center. The house was located in the extreme Northeastern sector of New York State in the middle of the forest with a gravel road leading to it.

In the late eighteen hundreds a rich railroad man, J. Barnaby Walden, built the house as a summer dwelling for his family. He and his wife and three children enjoyed many peaceful days there in the summer. When the children were in their teens Mrs. Walden contracted a cancer for which there was no cure and after several months of suffering passed away. The family was thrown into depression and had a very difficult time of recovery.

Needless to say things were never the same with the rest of the family and the house seemed to take on a melancholy atmosphere. Mr. Walden finally closed up the place and stopped coming because he couldn't stand the memories.

Inside the deserted house the atmosphere changed from joy to sorrow. One night late the wind was blowing and there was no moon when a spirit materialized outside the house. After it stayed in one place for a while, perhaps considering the house, it moved through the front door. The spirit breathed a mist on the door as it came through and then went on to do the same to every door in the house. Then it moved outside and drifted away.

This spirit was the spirit of a man that had worked for the Walden railroad company. His name was David Marne. He was hired to correct some mistakes that had been made when a car was assembled. When he attempted to right the wrong, he did it incorrectly. The brakeman on the train discovered the mistake and approached the repairman and an argument ensued. The brakeman threw the repairman off the train and his head hit a rock when he hit the ground, he died a few hours later. The brakeman left the body beside the tracks and never reported the incident.

Mr. Walden hired people to maintain the house and grounds, but after many years incidents started occurring for which there was no explanation. Once a month a group of workers would go to care for the grounds and dust the interior of the house. It was on one of these days something occurred. It was late in the summer and the day was sunny and cool. There were two women and three men that made their way up the gravel road that day. The birds were chirping loudly, as the ladies went inside as they always did and prepared to do the light cleaning and make sure everything was secure. When they went in they found all the interior doors open all the way to the wall behind them. One woman made a comment to the other about thinking they had closed all the doors to the rooms when they left the last time. Then they went about their duties forgetting about the doors.

    Agnes started in the kitchen and Marie went up to the second floor. Marie was using a dust mop to sweep the hardwood floors where there was no carpet. As she swept the dust mop back and forth a dust bunny rolled into one of the bedroom doorways. When she bent down to pick it up there was a swish and a thud. The door swung shut and the knob hit her at the top of her forehead at the hairline. She didn't have time to scream and was thrown across the hall into the wall. When she fell to the floor she was already dead. The knob on the swinging door had cracked her skull and left a hole the size of the knob. Blood oozed out of the hole and down on the freshly polished floor.

    Agnes, the woman down stairs, heard the noise and wondered what had happened. She went to the bottom of the staircase and called up to the woman above.

    "Marie are you all right? No answer. Curiosity over came her and she climbed the stairs. As her eyes came even with the floor she saw Marie lying in the hall. She bolted to the woman's side. Approaching the body she saw the large gaping hole in her forehead with blood and gray matter leaking out. She screamed, and screamed, and screamed, unable to move.

    One of the men out side, a large burly fellow named Jason heard the screams and ran to the front door. When he grabbed the knob it was locked. In panic he wrenched and pushed but the door wouldn't budge. He called out to one of the other men to go around to the back and see what was wrong with Agnes. The other man took off running to the back of the house.

    Upstairs Agnes was still screaming horrified by what she had found. She became faint and staggered across the hall and laid her hand on the doorjamb to steady herself. As she sobbed for her friend she hung her head and put her other hand on her forehead. There was another swish as the door swung shut again with a slam. In horror Agnes looked at her bleeding hand. The door had severed four of her fingers. She screamed afresh now as she dealt with her own increasing pain.

She held her bleeding hand and hugged it to her as she ran for the stairs. How could this possibly happen? There was no one in the house but the two women.

Outside the man at the front door heard more screams and picked up a stone and began smashing the panels of the nearest window. When he crawled in the opening the shutter swung shut hitting him in the face. Angered he grabbed the shutter and tore it off the hinges. He then dashed to meet Agnes at the stairs. He was shocked to see her holding her bleeding hand.

The man at the back had broken the glass in the door and was climbing in when the door swung in fast and he hit the wall behind the door. He fell back and grabbed the frame to keep from falling. The door swung shut with such force it took off his fingers. He fell onto the patio holding his bleeding hand yelling. Jason grabbed Agnes and headed for the front door, as they approached the front door swung open and began swinging back and forth at mind boggling speed. The wind from the swing door blew their hair and clothing. They dare not get in the path of the door at that speed it could easily break a bone. For a few seconds they stood there hypnotized by the motion. The door swung so fast it was little more than a blur.

The third man ran around the back to help the one who had lost his fingers. He led him around the house toward a vehicle as fast as he could.

In the front room the big man picked up a Victorian side chair and threw it in the path of the wildly swinging door. It managed to get between the door and the jamb. The chair became splinters in an instant.

Things turned from peaceful serenity to total chaos in a matter of minutes. Then just as quickly in another minute it all stopped. The big front door slowed and closed and the latch locked itself and the house became quiet again as it was when they arrived. Then there was a thundering sound as every door in the house closed at once. It was a cold final sound that left chills running up their backs as if the house had turned away to attend to other matters.

    The burly man Jason, realizing quickly what had happened, stepped to the side of the door and tried the latch. It opened. He quickly grabbed Agnes and hurried her through to safety outside. The third man Willard wrapped a T shirt around Jakes fingers to slow the bleeding. He and Jason then ran back inside to retrieve Marie's body. Once in the vehicle they drove as fast as they could to the nearest hospital, which was a long way from them.

A few days later the Estate of J. Barnaby Walden was notified of the catastrophe. The closest living relative was his great granddaughter who had inherited Mr. Walden's empire and attended to its affairs. Demmie Walden was a pretty blond lawyer who was educated in Estate law and handled her great grandfather's estate. She was thirty years old and stood at five foot ten with a very trim frame; and was very hard to beat at tennis. She gave many a corporate lawyer a real run for their money. Demmie was a smart woman. When the tennis match was over she wouldn't compete in a match for her heart. Consequently she was still single and very rich. When her secretary brought the message of the injuries to the employees she immediately arranged for all the medical bills to be paid for and a very lavish funeral for Marie. She met with the families personally and gave her heartfelt condolences to the family of the departed.

    A couple of nights later when she lay down to rest she thought of the house and what a beautiful structure it was. All of the pains her grandfather had gone through to make his family comfortable in that house blocked her sense of understanding. She had no idea how any of these things could have happened. What force would make the doors move of their own accord? Why would the hired help suffer the pains of torture and death? She decided to visit the estate in the next couple of days to see what was going on. Demmie was not one to worry incessantly so she slept soundly that night.

Two days later she drove her new Lexus Sedan North to the property. The gravel road that allowed approach to the house seemed longer as she hadn't been there for a few years. She loved the house almost as much as her grandmother had. Going to Walden house was such a peaceful get away. It was quiet and one could think things over without interruption. She remembered that in the library there were all kinds of books and classics shelved and she remembered the fine leather recliners that gave her such comfort while she read. The lighting was perfect. The kitchen was spacious with an island for preparing meals. She enjoyed fixing some of her grandmother's recipes at other times when she had been there. What would she find now?

When she stopped in front of the house all seemed as peaceful and serene as it had been in the past. Demmie thought, *I can't let myself be lulled into that kind of thinking. There has been mayhem committed here. I've got to get to the bottom of this.* She got out of the car and took her overnight bag from the back seat. For a moment she stood there in the drive looking at the place.

"Well no time to chicken out now. Whatever's happening is happening inside so look out, here I come." She said in a low tone.

Walking toward the door she saw the blood spots on the concrete. When she looked up she noticed the broken window on the left side. She walked up to it and peered inside. The broken shards were still on the floor and the splinters from the broken chair were strewn across the tile. Demmie kicked a piece of the chair aside and walked up to the door. She put her hand on the lever handle pushing it down, the latch released and the door slowly swung open. After she looked around inside she stepped in and away from the arch of its travel. While she was looking around the door slammed shut and locked. Demmie turned around and took a step back and in a loud voice said,

"I am the owner of this house and I will not tolerate the actions that have been going on. You will stop this right now and return the door to the position where I left it."

The silence that followed was deafening. Then the latch released and the door opened slowly and swung to the place where it had stood ajar.

Then she said, "I'm going to go through every room in this house including the garage and you will do me no harm."

She turned to go into the kitchen first. As she walked her heels clicked on the bare floor, which was the only sound in this big empty house. Demmie noticed the damage and the blood that had dripped on the tile. If she tried to send someone out to clean up and make repairs they could be hurt or killed too. So she had to get to the bottom of this first. Apparently whatever or whoever was there was listening now since she had made a positive statement. It had let her in, but would it let her out when she wanted to leave?

The glass was broken in the kitchen door. When she opened it she saw that blood and flesh was still on the jamb from Jakes fingers, accompanied by a rotten odor.

Out on the back patio blood stains could be seen splattered everywhere. She remembered the police had made a thorough investigation. Demmie turned and went through the rooms on the ground floor and garage. In the garage Demmie noticed several steel shafts lying on the bench at the back. As she approached the bench she noticed they were all sharpened on both ends and about twelve inches long. For some reason the word impaled came forcefully to her mind. Another thought came into her mind, no a memory, when her grandmother had taken her to church when she was a child. The teacher that Sunday told them the story of a King taking advice from one of the prophets. He said that, *Many shafts tied together are stronger than one.* She might need a couple of these. Her eyes went to the pegboard above the bench. There on the end was a roll of black electrical tape. She took it down and began to wrap three of the shafts together. Her purse was just long enough to hide the rods. She slipped them inside. The rest of the doors on the first floor opened without incident.

She climbed to the second floor and viewed the carnage there. She was amazed that the police, when they examined the house, called all of the injuries accidental. No amount of persuasion by the workers could convince them differently. But she felt there was something here, a presence of some sort. Maybe a displaced spirit had wandered in, but who's spirit. She would have to remember to read up on this sort of thing.

When she reached her grandparent's bedroom she reached for the doorknob, but the door swung open on its own.

"Thank you." She said in a cocky manner, and strode in. The door was three feet wide as she reached its outer most arch of travel she did a quick double step. There was a swish as the door slammed shut narrowly missing her.

"Ha! You missed." She mocked. The door swung back the other way slamming against the wall. The knob knocked a hole in the plaster.

"Stop that!" she shouted. It started swinging back and forth at blinding speed just inches from where she stood. Demmie never moved. She could be just as stubborn as the door.

"I have oil for your hinges and polish for your beautiful surface. It could keep you from getting dried out and make you shine. You are really a beautiful door you know. I realize no one pays any attention to the pretty doors in this house that's why I came." The swinging slowed as if the door was considering what she said. Demmie reached out and let her fingers brush the edge as it passed. It was meant to be a caress. The door stopped. She touched it gently again. The door backed up until the edge was in front of her. She rubbed her hand down the surface of the thick edge careful to keep her hand away from the front or back of the door. She heard a sound like a moan in the distance. In her mind she thought, *I've got to get out of here. There is a treacherous presence here. If one of these doors knocked me into the jamb it wouldn't* stop until I was pulp. And if there were ears to hear they could probably hear laughter of the spirit that's doing this. If I can get through this one the only other door is the front entry. As she stroked the door she felt the presence lift. The door moved freely. She moved it back a little and touched the face. Then she took a step and jumped through the opening. In that half second it took her to land in the hall the door slammed behind her with such force it seemed to shake the house. Just what she expected. Now she could feel anger, no rage, in the presence that was there. She took off her heels and ran for the staircase.

Once downstairs she crossed the large living room as quickly as she could. In her excitement to get out she forgot momentarily what she was facing. When she reached the range of the front door it swung open narrowly missing her face.

"Whoa girl." She whispered. There would be no pacifying this big beast. The door swung back to the wall, waiting. She put her hand on her purse touching the rods inside. The zipper was open now if she could get her hand on the rods, but she needed a diversion. She dropped her heels and lifted her left foot turning in a circle like a karate fighter. She let out a scream, "Whaa!" As she turned Demmie pulled the rods out and continued to turn. The door started to move. As it came even with her she buried the sharp ends in the face of the door. It continued until it slammed into the jamb, burying the points in the wood. The opening was about ten inches wide. Demmie thanked God she wasn't a heavy person. She quickly slipped through. It was a tight fit and the door exerted pressure, trying in vain to close. Finally she squeezed through and ran to her car. As she started the car she could hear the rest of the doors slamming. This was truly a mad house. Relief swept over her as she drove down the gravel road toward the highway.

Finally all of the doors closed and silence took over again.

Strange Visitors

Oscar Bennington III decided to get away from the city. It

was too crowded, too many street people to compete with. So he thought he would try the countryside out in the open. His clothes were tattered; he was dirty and in need of a bath for many days. Once Oscar had been part of a prominent business and an upstanding citizen, but like a lot of poor people in the world he fell on bad times because of alcohol and lost everything he had because of his drinking.

He had wandered along this two lane road for several hours. Now he was hoping he would come to a house where he could beg a meal perhaps. People out in the country would usually feed a fella. He wouldn't ask for money that way they might have pity on him. He would have plenty of time to scrape up enough to get a drink when he got back to town. Awhile later he came to a gravel road and noticed there were fresh tire tracks. Maybe there was a house out there somewhere. So Oscar started up the road walking alongside the gravel so the rocks wouldn't hurt his feet. The soles of his shoes had worn thin and one had a hole in it.

About thirty minutes later he came within sight of the Walden estate.

"You're a long way off the main road old boy." He muttered. The sight of a big house gave him encouragement. A big ham sandwich would be good about now, but it would probably be more like cheese and mustard. As he drew close he noticed the front door was open a little. Wow, this place was big and kept up too. Oscar approached the front door and leaned toward it a little. "Hello, anybody here?" There was no answer. He saw the rods sticking in the wood. "Hello, hope there's nobody hurt." His curiosity continued to grow until he leaned against the door and gave a push. It didn't budge. He lunged against it until the rods gave way on the jamb side of the door. "Hello anybody here?" Oscar peeked inside. He saw Demmie's shoes lying on the floor with her bags. *Maybe someone's hurt.* He thought. Pushing the door open he stepped in. "Anybody here?" he called. He happened to look down and saw the blood spots and said aloud, "My God, someone is hurt."

He wandered around the first floor calling, but there was no answer. He opened a door to one of the rooms and looked in. There he beheld a glorious sight. In the middle of one wall was a bar and behind it was all sorts of liquor. An evil smile came across his face. *Why not. He could have an drink and a bite and get out of there before any one came back.* He tiptoed over to the bar not wanting to arouse anyone's interest now. There wasn't any ice in the bin but all he wanted was the hard stuff anyway. He picked up a glass and a bottle of fine scotch, broke the seal and poured. The aroma hit his nostrils and he took a deep breath. *Ah, his luck had never been so good.* He took a deep drink. The burning felt so good going down.

He thought he better find some food before this booze messed him up so bad he couldn't get out of here. Oscar put the glass down and set out to find the kitchen. Opening the frig he found it bare so he moved on to the cabinets. Then he noticed the pantry. Inside he found all manner of canned goods, chips and nuts in bottles and cans. He put one of the bottles of mixed nuts in his pocket and took a couple of cans of soup. Next to the stove he found an opener and a pan. In a few minutes he was slurping warm soup. After he finished two cans he rushed back to the bar. He finished the scotch and decided to try the bourbon. Excellent. Then he tasted a wine or two right from the bottle. Not too good, he went back to the liquor. By the time an hour had passed he was thoroughly soused. He decided to sleep it off outside under a tree so no one would see him.

As he passed through the open front door the rods bent away from the jamb a little. The door swung shut spearing him between the shoulder blades. When it slammed, the jar threw Oscar out onto the patio with three rods sticking out of his back. Dead. Pretty serious security system.

The smell of blood brought the fox out of the woods and soon a raccoon followed. The fox licked at the blood on Oscar's back and then the scent of food caught his attention. He went through the window to find what was in the kitchen. The coon moved in to try out the nuts that had fallen out of Oscar's pocket when he hit the pavement. The jar had broken when it hit the concrete and the coon was stuffing them in his mouth as fast as he could. Meanwhile the fox was up on the table in the house finishing the soup in the pan that Oscar had left there.

The next morning a couple of wolves found the carnage on the front stoop and tore into Oscar's body, literally. When it was over the flies got the rest. Demmie would not be back for several days. What was left of Oscar's body would probably be decayed by then.

Demmie Walden sat at her desk pondering what she had found at the house. She doubted if it would do any good to go back out there until she found someone that could help her. She knew the police weren't interested. The spiritualists were mostly people who would do or say anything for money. Well, she thought she would have to shelve this for the moment she had an Estate meeting with some Indians who had inherited a lot of acreage from their parents. There were five people involved. Demmie told them she would meet with them in the board room. She looked at her watch. They should be here by now. She picked up the phone and called her secretary. Ann had already seated them and given them coffee and water. When Demmie walked in she noticed that there were six people in the room. The sixth person was a tall handsome Indian man wearing a suit and tie. When she greeted them she asked who the gentleman was. One of the daughters introduced him as the tribal Medicine Man, or Shaman, Running Bear. She also said he would be able to tell if Demmie's spirit was honest.

Demmie turned to him and asked, "Well, will I pass for an honest woman?"

When he spoke his voice was a rich baritone. "If you don't mind I would like to sit and listen for awhile before I speak. Although I do detect a troubling in your spirit. Something weighs heavy on your mind."

Demmie nodded and sat down.

"Alright then shall we get started?"

When the meeting was over everyone seemed satisfied with her decision and they would retain her as their lawyer. Running Bear had not said anything during the meeting.

When they stood to leave she said to him, "Could you stay behind a moment I'd like to talk to you." He smiled and told the others he would follow shortly. When they were alone, she said, "You were right about my spirit being troubled."

"How may I help?" he asked.

"I have a house that my grandfather left me when he died and some strange things have been going on. People have met with death in this house. The police investigated and deemed it accidental. And when I looked the situation over I realized there is more to this than an accident." Running Bear looked at the floor in thought.

"I would have to go to this house and maybe touch the structure to feel what is there. There is a ritual I have to go through to prepare my spirit."

"Could you meet me here Friday we could go together? I would repay any expenses that might be incurred." she pleaded.

"I don't think that would be necessary, a few hours in your company would be payment enough."

"You are very kind sir. Perhaps that and expenses." she said.

"What ever you say. I will do what I can to help."

"Shall we say Friday morning at seven then?"

Very well I'll be here at seven." he said with a pleasant smile.

She went into the restroom and looked in the mirror and smiled saying, "I love the voodoo that you do." She batted her eyes at herself and laughed.

Friday brought a bright sunny morning with a cool breeze. Demmie decided to take her convertible and let her hair blow free in the wind.

When Running Bear arrived he was wearing a buckskin

shirt and trousers with Indian designs on them. His moccasins looked new, but handmade. As he approached Demmie said, "Well now, don't you look like an Indian medicine man."

"Speaking of clothes, were you wearing this outfit when you went to the house last time?"

She was wearing a pink suit with skirt and top. Her sleeves were three quarter length.

"No."

Afterward they drove North to the house in Demmie's car.

When they arrived and they were going up the gravel road Running bear said, "It's a shame I can't get out more, I love being in the woods." he took deep breaths all along the way.

When they drove onto the circular drive way Running Bear shouted, "STOP! He climbed up onto the seat and jumped over the door and ran back toward the gravel road. Demmie quickly got out surveying the horrible sight in front of the house. She looked back to see what had happened to Running Bear. He had stopped where the gravel met the pavement and was pulling a small leather pouch out of his shirt. He took the leather string from around his neck and poured some of the contents into his hand. He began sprinkling, dancing, and chanting as he went. First one foot then the other. Demmie stood there watching Running Bear. She could feel the hair standing up on the back of her neck. She felt she dare not move, at least not yet.

The front door swung open and the knob bumped the wall behind it.

"Hey ya, Hey ya, Yi, Yi, Yi Hey Yi, Yi, Yi." he chanted as he turned in circles lightly sprinkling powder as he went. Demmie stood and waited to see what would happen.

Finally after fifteen minutes Running Bear stopped and beckoned to Demmie. She walked over to him. Just then the front door slammed, opened, and slammed again.

"We have to leave now. The ritual I performed will give us safe passage to the highway. Stay here I will go get the car." he held out his hand for the keys.

"What are you talking about. There is another dead body at the front door. We have to do something."

"We will go to the next town and call the police they will handle this. We dare not go into the house or we will die. You will die and I will die. We must leave now. I will explain when we get to the highway." Finally she handed him the keys. He ran quickly and jumped over the door into the seat. He started the car and sped in reverse to the place where she was standing. She got in and he made a u-turn and sped down the gravel road.

When they came to the highway, he said, "I am sorry there is death and destruction in that house. No one can temper or drive out that spirit it is fierce and powerful, there is no medicine against it."

"What can we do?" Demmie asked.

Burn it down or people will die every time they enter." The next week after she had thought it over carefully she hired a man to bring a flame thrower and diesel fuel. He approached the front, sprayed the door and lit it with the flame thrower. He went around back and did the same to the kitchen door. In a few minutes the whole structure was in flames. In a couple of hours the roof and second floor had caved in onto the bottom floors and soon it was all ashes. Demmie stood and wept.

Surely the spirit had gone with the flames. She wept all the way home. She felt so bad. Once at her house she called Running Bear and told him it was over. He said it was the best thing she could have done.

As she hung up the telephone the front door of her home swung open and the knob knocked a hole in the dry wall behind it. Then it swung the other way and the slam thundered through the whole house. All of the other doors in the house began opening and closing.

Holiday Flight 909

This year at Dulles Airport in Washington, flights were scant to some of the smaller cities. Flight 909 was one of those flights. Scheduled for Oklahoma City, not all the seats were filled in coach and had only one passenger in first class. The airline thought this very unusual and in the days just previous to the holiday offered seats at a reduced rate. Still no one bought tickets, but rather reserved seats on other airlines.

Tonight flight 909 will be taking off at eleven-thirty, the only seat in first class is occupied by a fifteen year old boy. James Desmond has told all he has spoken to that he is going to visit his grandmother in Perry, Oklahoma. He has a pleasant voice and is mild mannered wearing a neatly pressed colored shirt and black slacks and loafers, at five foot ten, and thin with light brown hair he looks considerably older for his age. His baggage includes a small carry on bag and a portable radio, which security has disassembled as much as they can. And they have asked James to remove the batteries and carry them with him in a small bag. He put the batteries in his carry on after they finished checking his shoes, he was allowed to board the aircraft. James' demeanor during all this was calm and polite. When he reached his seat he put his radio and bag in the overhead compartment, which is in the forward area just behind the pilot's cabin.

The stewardesses teased James about his good looks and he smiled in a shy sort of way. Judy, the stewardess for first class, was to take care of James' needs. She asked about his progress in school. He told her he lived in an area outside Washington and the school was an unknown school where he was in the ninth grade and very excited about being in high school this year. He mentioned that he was at the top of his class with a 3.9 grade average. Judy said he must be a very smart boy.

After take off James asked for a coke. Judy brought him a glass of ice and left the coke can on the tray. When she went to help the other stewardesses James quickly drained the coke can and left some in the glass. He then put the can in the magazine pouch under the window with his napkin wrapped around it. When the aircraft reached seven hundred miles an hour, its cruising speed, James asked to use the restroom as Judy was passing. She directed him to the lavatory door and went into coach to help the other stewardesses. James waited for a second and stood up. He then took the coke can and slid it into his pants pocket. The restroom was just three steps away. He made it without attracting any attention and locked the door. Inside he unbuttoned his shirt and raised his T shirt and began to peel off clay that was taped to his midsection. He tore it into strips the height of the coke can. James took a small can opener from behind his belt buckle and cut the lid off the can, rolled up the clay and put it in the can. He had enough strips to fill the can. He then pulled a thin strand of copper wire from the collar of his shirt, hooked it to a tiny delay powered by two hearing aid batteries and plugged the ends into the clay. The toilet flush valve empties into a tank where the hole was big enough to let the coke can pass. He dropped it and straightened his clothes. The delay would hold for fifteen minutes. James returned to his seat, but before sitting down he reached into the overhead baggage compartment and pushed a small button on his radio. Two small hearing aid batteries activated a signal and a timer for thirteen minutes. He slid a small black bag out of his carry on and put it down on the floor in front of the seat. James learned of another passenger from the area where he lived and asked the stewardess if he could go back and speak to her.

In the rear, seat ninety-nine-A there was a woman from the same town James was from. James had checked the passenger list and found she would be on the plane.

He made his way down the aisle to her seat. He introduced himself and told her one of the stewardesses told him someone from his hometown was on the plane. They talked for eleven minutes. He then told her he thought the man in seventy-nine C was acting strangely and might be a terrorist.

The man, a Greek, not an Arab, was olive skinned and had black hair and a shadow from a fast growing beard. He was an American business man traveling to Oklahoma City on business. That didn't matter the word was out now and as James excused himself he moved back toward the front of the plane. He took a second to look at the business man in seventy-nine C as he passed. The woman in the rear noticed and being a woman she was panicked and not wanting to die at the age of forty-five, she signaled for the stewardess. The atmosphere on the plane became tense. The stewardesses moved into the rear portion of the plane. This included Judy the stewardess from first class.

James Picked up the flat bag and slipped his arms into some straps on the backside and snapped them together. He turned and ran into the coach class cabin screaming he had seen a device in the overhead baggage compartment and it might be explosive. Because he had been so calm up to now they believed him and called the Capitan. James was still moving toward the rear of the plane. The lady in ninety-nine A was on her feet calling for the stewardesses to arrest the man in seventy-nine C. An on board Federal Marshal jumped to his feet and tried to calm the passengers as fear took over. When James arrived at the last escape window he stepped in next to the window and took hold of the release.

At that moment there was an explosion behind the pilot's cabin and a few seconds later one in the restroom. The plane depressurized and the explosions caused the front of the plane to fold back on the body.

James Desmond pulled the window release and the window blew out and he was sucked out with it. The plane now nose down was falling at a faster rate of speed and left James in the air, who had pulled a cord on his back pack which was a small parachute. As he glided toward the earth he watched the plane hit the ground nose first and explode in a residential area.

His next flight would be from Atlanta To San Francisco.

Prison Break

Out in the desert of Southern Nevada there is a maximum security prison. It houses murderers, pedophiles, drug dealers, rapists, and kidnappers. Most of their crimes involve death. Also the men in this prison are in here for life. There are those however, that think of nothing but escape. Joe Morris is one of those guys. Joe is a big fella and his light brown hair is cut short. He is six one and weighs one-eighty. Joe is in superior shape from working out in the weight room and keeping his meals down to a minimum. He is in prison for a double murder and narrowly escaped the death penalty.

When he was given life without parole he muttered under his breath, "I'll make my own parole."

Joe has finished his first year in prison and he is making plans to get out of this hell hole. It's Friday night, the guards are anxious to get their shift in and start their weekend. A small oversight puts Mr. Morris in the duct work and headed toward the vent in the laundry room. He has to spring the lock on the door to the outside yard. After forty-five minutes of crawling he finally comes to a vent and releases the cover from the inside.

Once out in the room he replaces the cover and listens. All is silent. He goes to work on the lock on the side door where the laundry truck parks. While he was on the outside he learned to make lock picks. Finally, he gets the door open and slips out into the yard and waits for a friend inside to create a glitch in the yard lighting. The flood lights in a section across from him falter for sixty seconds. In that short space of time he is able to sprint to and open up a hole under the wall. On the outside of the wall is rock that covers the hole. Joe moves it with his hand and wiggles out. As he puts the rock back he grins and takes a deep breath. Freedom!

He doesn't hear any shouts or alarms so he knows he made it without being noticed. Someone told those dumb guards to have the lights checked when they flickered before and they ignored it. Just what Joe needed. If he can make it to the highway two miles from here he should have a ride waiting. He sees the lights flicker once again that's the signal for him to break for a creosote bush fifty yards away. From there he will be outside the lights and will move for a ravine that goes toward the highway two miles away.

He is beyond the lights crawling down the ravine when he hears something behind him. He stops and stares into the darkness. He sees someone crawling up behind him. Now he wishes he had taken that knife Lou offered him. It was only a butter knife, but it had been ground to a point and sharpened. Joe gets ready for a fight he is not going back now.

When the body gets two feet behind him a woman's voice in a whisper says, "Hey, they sent me to show you where your ride is."

"I know where my ride is lady. What are you doing out here?"

"No honest he had to move further up the road. The highway patrol made him move. He said to stay off the road going that way. If you will follow me I'll show you. It's out this way." she runs across the sand keeping low.

For a moment Joe thinks about it. He has planned this for months and now things change? The guy that was supposed to pick him up was off the road far enough not to be seen by the highway patrol. Something was messed up here. Where did she come from anyway? How did she know about his pickup? When she notices Joe is not following she turns back. She lays down in the sand a few feet from him.

"I'm not lying to you Joe. The guy is further down the road and I can show you where and we can get out of here." *She knows my name maybe he did send her.* He raises up slightly, but he can't see the car it's too far away. He looks back, all is quiet at the prison.

"Look woman, Jerry never mentioned any woman to me. If you are putting me on I'll break your neck."
"You know Jerry he never lets anyone down. He brought me along in case anything changed and it did."
"Why didn't he come out here?"
"Joe we ain't got time to discuss this. Let's get out of here and I'll explain it when we get down the road." Her voice is velvety and smooth. She sounds believable; but something feels wrong. Joe can sense it in is gut. He doesn't want to go on, but if he does miss Jerry, a mile can be along way moving through the sagebrush. There's worry because he can't see her face in the dark. Joe likes to know who he is dealing with.

"Come on Joe, we don't have all night. Let's get out of here."

She gets up and moves away. Joe gets up and runs after her. They run a half mile through the desert and she drops down into another ravine. This one is deeper. Joe slides in beside her and she turns and lands on his chest snarling. Her teeth clamp onto his neck over his jugular vein. He fights, but her claws dig into the flesh on his arms.

Wow, This broad is strong was Joes last thought. When she is finished she leaves Joe in the ravine and starts toward the road.

Now to get that guy in the car.

Back inside the warden is talking to the head of the guard detail, "Hey Bentley did Joe Morris get out all right?"

"Yeah he was gone about twenty minutes ago. She's got him by now. You know she doesn't miss warden. We'll pick up the body when the sun comes up. Who do we have on the list for next month?

For Old Times Sake

The old soldier sat outside his ancient trailer in the afternoon heat remembering times from many years before. The trailer was one of the old Air Streams about twenty feet long. He stared off toward the sandy expanse of the Nevada desert. It was dry and hot with nothing growing but sagebrush and creosote bushes. His little plot of land was many miles from any of the cities that advertised gambling and the other vices of life. It was peaceful out here, but he yearned for the days he had spent in the army during the second World War where his duties were those of a sniper.

He thought of the enemy officers he had lined up in his sights as he lay behind a rock or a mound of dirt. How they fell before they knew what had happened. Everyone around them startled by the shot that made a man's head explode and his lifeless body drop to the ground. And he would be gone before they had a chance to send soldiers after him. Shooting from six hundred yards or more they didn't have a chance of hitting or catching him.

He also thought of the M-1 he kept wrapped in a sheet and covered with a blanket. It was grooved for a scope and he had the best one money could buy. As far as he was concerned it was the best rifle they had ever made. Occasionally he would take it out and clean it though it didn't need it. The old man was hopeful for a chance to use it one more time.

As he sat staring out in the desert he heard a vehicle approaching on the gravel road that ran past his place. He rose up from the battered lawn chair and turned to see who was coming. Incased by a dust cloud was a semi truck towing half of a doublewide mobile home. A hundred yards behind that was the other half also raising dust. Where did they come from? He hadn't noticed anyone surveying land out here. The semis passed his place and continued down the road about a hundred yards before they pulled off the path. The second truck slid in beside it and in seconds the drivers were out and preparing to set the tongues on large blocks. In a few minutes the trucks were going back the way they came. The two halves, now less than a foot apart, sat abandoned in the sand.

The old man watched the road for a long time expecting someone to follow, but no one came. Now he would have neighbors just a hundred yards away. Well it was lonely, maybe he would have someone to talk to.

Next morning the old soldier was up just before the sun rose. He paced back and forth watching for someone to come up the road anxious to know who was going to be his neighbor. He waited as the morning sky began to lighten in the East. Finally he tired of watching the road he went inside to make a pot of coffee and even then he found himself peeking out the rear window toward the gravel road.

Later that morning he decided to drive his ancient car, a 1950 Dodge, down to the nearest neighbor's, which was nearly a mile away. When he arrived the man was out in his yard trimming a tree.

"Hey Jeb, what brings you out so early?" The neighbor asked.

Getting right to the point the soldier asked,
"Did you see that trailer go by here yesterday?"
"Yeah I did. It was a beauty wasn't it?"
"Yeah it was. They done parked it about a hundred yards down the road from me."

"Well it's hard to believe; Jeb's going to have neighbors."

"Yeah, I hope they're good Southern folk. I don't care for them Yankees too much."

He heard his neighbor laugh as he made a u-turn in the sand and drove back toward his trailer.

The next morning about ten o'clock Jeb had moved his lawn chair to the end of his trailer and with coffee cup in hand he watched the road. Finally a cloud of dust appeared in the distance. Someone was coming. When the vehicle got close enough to recognize he could see it was a flat bed pickup with a lot of equipment tied on it. As they went by, the guy on the passenger side waved to Jeb. Jeb waved back and watched as they went on to the trailer up the road. The truck stopped beyond the mobile home and the men started unloading some of the equipment. It wasn't long before they were digging holes and mixing bags of ready-mix for the foundation. By the end of the day they had twenty holes, two foot square, filled with concrete. Jeb was fixing dinner when they left.

By the time the sun was up the next morning another truck with more men was on the site. Some unloaded lumber while others began to dig a foundation trench. Ten o'clock brought a semi with a special hitch and a concrete truck behind it. As the sun got to the late side of the afternoon one of the men came down to Jeb's.

"Howdy old timer. Say we would like to leave one of our trucks out here. You don't think anyone would bother it do you?"

"Naw, there ain't no body here but me and I shoot folks that come out here and mess with things at night." The man smiled and said.

"Okay thanks partner. We'll see you in the morning then."

Jeb nodded and waved. He sat and rubbed his chin and he wondered who his new neighbors would be.

By the middle of the next week they had finished the groundwork, had the trailers on piers and laid the blocks for the foundation. Kinda funny though no one else had been out here looking to see how things were going. Jeb just couldn't see a family movin out here in the sand and sagebrush with no one else around but him. It just didn't fit in his mind. He would wait and see how this came together.

That evening as Jeb watched the news on his nine inch TV the anchor warned of possible terrorist attacks at sites on the west coast.

"Sure would be nice to get a shot at some of those rag heads." He thought.

The mobile home sat for the better part of the next week then late one evening just before the sun went down a new car worked its way down the road slowly trying to keep the dust off its shiny surface. Jeb slipped inside his trailer and dropped the blind on the front window. He stood back in the shadows watching as the car went past. It was a new silver Chrysler and everything about it sparkled. As Jeb watched the car stopped by the mobile and a darkened window slid down. Jeb put his binoculars to his eyes and sighted in on the car. Soon a hand came out the window and a bony finger pointed toward something. Jeb could see the skin was dark on the hand. The hand retreated and the window slid up. The car sat there for a few minutes and the driver made a u-turn and glided back toward civilization.

That dark hand had piqued Jeb's interest.

In the days that followed nothing happened, but that didn't keep Jeb from his vigil. He even woke up in the middle of the night and looked things over. At the end of the second week on a Saturday afternoon Jeb heard another car coming down the road. He hustled to the back bedroom and peered out the window. The car was moving at an average speed and dust was billowing out from under it as it moved along. It looked like one of those midsized Fords. As it passed he could see the windows weren't tinted and there was a man at the wheel, and from the looks of it he was alone.

He pulled up next to the house and got out. He had on

khaki pants and a white shirt with the sleeves rolled up. His hair was black and his skin was a dark olive color. Hmm! Jeb could see through his binoculars that his shoes were new and shiny. The man walked to the steps and climbed to the door. He took out a key and opened the door and went inside. Jeb then focused on the window on the end of the house, but there was a mini blind covering it.

After about a half hour the man came out and got back into the car and drove away.

The car didn't turn around but continued on the gravel road until it became a dusty trail in the distance. That trail went into the mountains on the far side of the valley. The mountains were probably twenty miles away. Jeb knew because he had been up there, but he had never crossed over. He figured it went to a paved road somewhere on the other side. The thing that got Jeb's attention was that the man seemed to know where he was going. The man didn't look like he was wondering where things went. He just drove off like he was headed for home. Tomorrow morning Jeb would be going for a ride. He had to know where that road went.

With the rising of the sun the old Dodge crept up a dirt road that went into the mountains. As the rocks began to rise on either side of the car the path took twists and turns. Jeb knew there was a fork in the road a little ways ahead. When he came to it he took the left side for he knew he could see part of the right fork below as he drove through. After gliding along about a thousand yards Jeb stopped and got out of the car. He went over to a split in the rocks and looked down. He could see the other part of the road below. He continued on until the road came to a paved two lane. He turned left and drove toward town. Now he knew where he was and tomorrow he would take the right fork to be sure where it went.

Jeb picked up some groceries in town and it was late afternoon by the time he got back. When he was a long ways off he could see a car at the house. He stopped and turned around heading back toward town. He didn't want his neighbor to see him just yet. When it was dark he returned and the car was gone. He parked and went inside and lay down to rest. About one in the morning he awoke and made his way to the front window. No one was at the house up the road. He ate some cereal and went back to sleep.

The next morning the sound of tires on gravel woke Jeb with a start.

"Dagnabit I slept too long." The brass alarm clock on the little stand registered just past eight. Jeb hustled to the other end of the trailer in time to see the young man going inside. Shortly before ten a box van rolled up to the house. The young man came out to meet it. As the men got out of the truck Jeb noticed one of the men was wearing a turban. The young man grabbed him and pulled him around the front of the truck where no one could see. When they continued into the house; the turban was gone.

A few minutes later the driver backed the truck up to the door and the three began to carry boxes into the house.

"Don't look like furniture to me." Jeb said to himself. Finally they unloaded some office chairs and a couple of desks. Lastly they took in some long lumber and folding chairs. Jeb watched with great interest. Where's he gonna sleep and eat? Jeb wondered aloud. He hadn't seen a bed or a dining table being carried in.

Later that afternoon the box truck showed up again. This time they hauled out a bed and more furniture. Jeb set up his lawn chair back a ways from the window to keep his night vigil. About ten the house was dark and he decided the young fellow had turned in for the night and decided to go to bed.

About two in the morning a noise echoed through the desert silence and brought Jeb hustling toward the kitchen window. He could see a dark form outside the house probably a pickup. A man got in and had slammed the door. He started the truck and drove off in the direction of the mountains. The driver waited until he was about a hundred yards down the road before

Strange & Mysterious Tales

♦

he turned on the headlights. The house was still dark.

The next morning Jeb was still sitting in the lawn chair watching.

"They're bringing in something and I don't think its vittles." Jeb mumbled to himself.

Jeb opened the front window and the morning breeze brought the odor of food, but it was not bacon and eggs. This fellow was cooking some of that Middle Eastern food and it smelled a little of curry and other strange flavors. There was probably a pot of rice setting next to whatever he was boiling. Jeb decided it was time to go visit his new neighbor. He stepped outside and started up the road toward the house. By the time he got even with the door, it opened and the man stepped outside and closed it behind him. Jeb's suspicions were confirmed he was from the Middle East.

"Mornin, I'm yer neighbor. Thought I'd stop by and welcome you to the neighborhood."

"Good morning sir so nice to meet you." He stood there silent. Starring.

" I noticed you were moving in and if you need any help I'd be glad to oblige."

"Thank you if I need any help I will call."

"Okay my names Jeb." The man nodded and smiled. Just then a longhaired German Shepard slipped out of a space in the foundation. Faintly Jeb heard the man snap his fingers. The dog sat down.

"Well just thought I'd stop by and welcome you in."

"Thank you sir." Again the silent stare. Jeb turned and started back down the road.

"Friendly fellow. I don't think I'll have to worry bout him bothering me." Jeb thought.

As Jeb started into his trailer he noticed out of the corner of his eye the blinds were open on this end of the man's house. Jeb went in and retreated to the back of his trailer. There was something funny going on and Jeb could feel it in his bones. If he could keep is mind sharp there would be an opportunity and he didn't want to miss it. He sat down on the bed and stare down the hall toward the kitchen thinking. He picked up his binoculars and looked down the hall. As he focused on the window up the road he saw the Arab standing at the window with binoculars up to his eyes.

Jeb didn't think the man could see him this far back.

"Okay the war is on. Now we see who comes out on top." Jeb mumbled. He picked up the army blanket that covered his rifle and began to unwrap the weapon. He laid the blanket aside and lay the rifle across the foot of the bed. He took a new clip of ammunition out of a box and loaded the gun. He lay another clip next to it.

In the house up the road the Arab went to the other end into what would have been the master bedroom. In this room there was a long bench across the room with equipment spread beneath it. There were boxes all long the length of the bench. He sat down in one of the chairs in front of the bench and began soldiering connections on a piece of equipment. In his shirt pocket a cell phone rang. When he answered he spoke in Arabic. He finished speaking and hung up. As he did so he went to a drawer and took out a .45 caliber pistol and put it in his belt. If the old man got nosey he might have to get rid of him. The dog would let him know if he got too close. He might have the leaders send in a woman to make things look more natural. The rest of the team would be in late tonight he needed to get his part done. They would have to come across the desert so they wouldn't be heard.

Just after midnight a truck rolled silently across the sand up to the back of the house. Three men got out each one carrying a small box. They stopped close to the back of the house and one tapped on the door. The door opened and they slipped inside.

"Allah be praised my brother we have found the perfect place to prepare for mayhem." One of the men whispered.

Jeb sat in the dark watching. They had this timed right he thought. No moon out tonight total darkness. Good time to bring in explosives. In the morning he needed go to town to get some equipment.

As the Eastern sky began to glow with the coming of the sun Jeb was already making his way to the small community of East Las Vegas. Beside the highway there was a small gun shop. The owner was inside having a cup of coffee preparing for the day ahead. As Jeb entered a small bell sounded marking his entry.

"Mornin old-timer, how you doin today."

"It's a good day to go huntin Marvin, I come to get some ammo. A box of those special 30-06 rounds you mentioned to me last month." The owner reached under the counter and laid a box on the glass top.

"And I noticed you had a blow gun the last time I was in. I'd like to have one of those."

Marvin took down a long narrow box and laid it next to the shells.

"I have darts for this thing if you need them." The owner said.

"Naw, I make my own out of paper and a nail, but I could use some of that treatment you mentioned." The owner reached into a drawer and took out a small vial and placed it with the rest.

"That night scope you was telling me about; do you have one of those?"

"Well it just so happens I have a new model that came in last week. Better image, longer range."

"Good, give me one of those."

The owner stepped up to a small ladder and placed it along the shelves behind the counter. Climbing to the top he took down a box and set it on the counter. Jeb wandered the small isles and looked at this and that seemingly uninterested in what was on the counter.

"These babies could take out a deer at four hundred yards

if a fella could see him." The owner said of the shells; kidding Jeb about his age.

"Don't you worry I can still see him at four hundred yards and even further if I have to." The old man said.

"You must have spotted a big one up in those mountains."

"Yeah he's a prize. I may save the head and bring it in." The old man smiled slyly. Marvin was never sure what the old man was talking about. He hoped he was still referring to deer.

"Some dark skinned folk moved in up the road from me. If they show up here you might want to call the FBI. They might be puttin together some serious stuff out there." The owner knew what Jeb was referring to for they had talked about this kind of thing before.

"Okay, I'll keep my eyes open. What am I looking for?"

"Young fella, probably thirty, five foot eight, a hundred and fifty pounds. Look out the window he might have a dog with him. Shepard, black and brown, long hair." The owner made a note on a pad lying on the end of the counter.

"All right sir, what do I owe you for this?" The owner tapped a few numbers into a calculator and said, "That'll be about $407.50." Jeb pulled out a worn wallet and fished out four hundreds. The rest he took out of his front pocket. As Marvin made up his receipt, Jeb picked up his goods.

He tucked the paper into Jeb's shirt pocket and said, "Good huntin, partner.."

"Yeah, it will be." Jeb answered with a grin.

When Jeb returned the Ford was sitting outside the Arab's house. He carried the equipment in and took it back to the bedroom. First he replaced the shells in the clips he had on the bed. Then he set the night scope on a small table in the middle of the isle and covered it with a towel. The blowgun he removed from the box and mounted the mouthpiece on one end of the tube. He then started rolling small paper cones and gluing them. After he made several he dropped small finish nails, that he had sharpened, into the cones and taped them in and fitted them to the tube. He marked the cones with a pencil where the cones met the tube. He cut them off at the pencil line. A perfect fit. Jeb dropped one into the tube and pointed it toward the other end of the trailer. He drew a lung full of air and blew. In a half second the dart lodged in the trim just below the window. Jeb smiled and set the tube aside. He took the small vial of poison and put it in his pants pocket. He raised the mattress and put the M-1 under it with the extra clip. Now he would wait to see what happened next. He raised the binoculars to his eyes and saw that the blinds were open up the road.

He would have to take care of the dog first so he would wait until the moon was up and then he could see his adversary. Just then he heard a vehicle pass his trailer rolling slow. It was a pickup with two men in it. When they got to the house they started hauling small boxes inside.

"I better git with it or they will have enough stuff made to blow up the rest of New York." The men came out and drove back past Jeb's place going toward town.

That night there was a half moon in the sky. There would be enough light to see the dog when he came at Jeb. He put on his fatigues, boots, and pulled his camouflage hat over his scarce hair. He crept straight out from his trailer into the desert about a half mile. In his right hand he carried the blowgun; a couple of darts stuck through his shirt pocket. The vial of poison was in his pocket and his hunting knife was on his side. When he'd gone about two hundred yards he crossed over to his neighbor's property and started back toward the house making enough noise for the dog to hear him. When he was within seventy yards of the house the dog came around the backside. Jeb waited. The dog stood his ground. Jeb picked up a rock and threw it at him. It fell way short, but that didn't matter it was an aggressive act to the dog and he bolted toward Jeb. Jeb waited for him to get close enough to shoot. Now the dog was growling and dodging through the brush. When the dog was ten yards away Jeb raised the blowgun to his lips and blew hard. The dart hit the dog in the throat. The dog landed on Jeb hard, and his teeth grabbed Jeb's arm, but it was too late the poison was already working. In a few seconds the dog released his grip and fell over panting hard. In another minute he was dead and Jeb grabbed his collar and began to drag the body out into the desert. A mile away he covered the dog with rocks and sneaked back to his trailer. He lay back on his bed waiting for morning.

The Arab didn't come out to feed the dog until after nine. When there was no response he was down on his hands and knees calling under the house. Jeb was watching from the hallway of his trailer. After awhile the man started looking toward Jeb's trailer. Another man came out of the house and joined the Arab looking confused. They walked down the road to the property line but never crossed it. After looking around they went back to the house. Jeb knew they wouldn't mention anything to him because it would arouse suspicion. From then on the blinds towards end of the house up the road, stayed open. The next day there was a lot of hubbub going on. Three more men came to the house and went inside. Jeb knew he would have to act fast because there would be a lot of bomb material leaving there soon.

Straight across the gravel road out about three hundred yards there was a rise in the land and would be a good spot to shoot from. Jeb would check it out in the wee hours of the night, but now what he needed was a chance to check out the inside of the Arab's house. He got his chance after dark that night. He was watching through his night scope when three men came out of the house and got into the Arab's car and drove down the road toward town. Jeb took a small pry bar and sneaked down the road behind the house. He took his hunting knife with him in case they left someone behind. When he reached the back door he stood close to the trailer and tapped on the door and waited to see if anyone was going to answer. He couldn't hear any noise inside so he put the pry bar in the frame of the aluminum door. It didn't take much force to pop the door open. He was up the steps and in the back room in seconds. All was dark inside. He took out a small flashlight and shined it around the room. Sure enough they were making bombs and there was plenty of explosives to do the job.

"Nice of these boys to leave me enough stuff to make a bomb of my own." He chuckled as he surveyed the equipment on the bench. On the floor beneath the bench he found a case of dynamite. Jeb sat down in one of the chairs and plugged in one of the small soldering irons and began to put together something of his own. He ran a wire and a detonator to the front door and then hooked it up to the dynamite.

"This should take care of their little operation," He muttered to himself. Now he would go to the desert to wait until they came back and watch the fire works. Jeb went back to his trailer and got his car and drove out into the desert across from the house. About three hundred and fifty yards away he parked the car behind some bushes. He walked back to the top of the rise and lay down to wait for the Arabs to return. When the fire works went off there would be enough light to get anyone that was left. About two hours later the car returned with a pickup following. There were three men in the pickup and one man in the car. The truck backed up to the front door just like Jeb thought they would. The three men rushed in and before they realized anything was different the whole house erupted into a ball of flames. The pickup landed on top of the car and the man inside was struggling to get out. As he crawled out and stood up a bullet from Jeb's M-1 hit him in the forehead.

"When they don't hear from these fellas someone else will be out to see what happened." Jeb said to himself. So he settled in to wait for anyone else that might show up. Since his location was so far out in the desert there wasn't anyone to put out the fire so it would have to burn itself out. Jeb waited about an hour and a half before the car showed up. It was the Chrysler he had seen before. There were two men in it. They both jumped out to survey the damage. Jeb hit one in the back of the head and the other one in the temple, they both went down like a ton of brick. Jeb went down and loaded the three bodies into the Chrysler and drove off toward the mountains. It would be a long hike back but this wasn't the first time he had to walk a long way.

Besides he would have to wait until the investigation was over before he could come home.

"Yes sir the land of the free and the home of the brave," he said as he saluted.

Long Term Care

Park Dale care unit was located on the outskirts of a small town called Clarksburg. It was built by a private party for the Seniors of Clarksburg so they wouldn't have to go away to a big city and their families could visit them everyday without a long drive. Park Dale wasn't like some of the places in larger cities, run down and always short of personnel and money to operate. The millionaire that built Park dale set up a fund to keep it running. They hired the best nurses and paid good wages to care for the elderly of Clarksburg and surrounding towns. They had room for forty patients and the unit was always full. You probably know about all that though so we will get right to the point. This narrative is about a patient at Park Dale. His name is Riley Clemmons and he has been here for four years. Riley is seventy-four, tall, thin, white hair, and has a perpetual smile on his lips. No matter how harried the situation gets around him, he is always smiling. You know, sometimes poor old patients mess the bed and everybody gets excited, because no one wants to clean it up. Riley keeps his smile.

When asked why he always smiles he says, 'That way nobody knows what you're up too."

His room is at the back of the unit, at the end of the hall. His room mate is Alvin Amery. Alvin is eighty-one and not able to get around as well Mr. Clemmons, but Riley looks out for

Mr. Amery as much as he can. When it gets too involved he calls the nurse for him. Incidentally every nurse knows they have to answer Riley's call for he has spoken to the Medicare folks once already. They don't want that to happen again. Having a patient blurt out conditions in the hall while they are having a semiannual inspection is not good for business. Something about matching funds. So now they prepare a pill for Mr. Clemmons when the Medicare folks are supposed to show up and he sleeps very peacefully.

Earlier in Riley Clemmons life he lived in the old family home on the other side of town that had been left to him and his brother Johnson Clemmons. Johnson is ten years younger than Riley so that makes him sixty-four at this time. They and Riley's wife Sarah lived in the old house for many years after the parents passed away. When Riley was seventy his wife was taken by a heart attack and of course he was devastated by his loss. Johnson was afraid Riley was never going to get over it. So he sat down with Riley one day and recommended Park dale. Riley told him he would think about it.

That night about midnight Riley felt someone shaking him out of his sleep by the arm. He awoke to see a shadowy figure bending over his bed. When the visitor was certain Riley was awake, he said in a gruff voice, "Riley Clemmons you must go to Park Dale they need you out there."

To which he replied, "I'm an old man, I can't help them people."

"Yes you can, and you will you hear me." Whoever the guy was he sounded threatening. "I have something special for you to do and you will enjoy life out there very much. So when you get up just tell Johnson you've decided to go and pack your things, today."

With that the shadowy figure let go of his arm and melted into the wall. This scared Riley very badly he thought maybe he might just get up and pack. After Riley had gotten a few things together he sat down in his recliner and dozed until about 7:00.

When Johnson came into the kitchen Riley had the coffee made and was working on breakfast. Johnson was surprised apparently Riley's mourning was ending.

"Johnson I've thought about it and maybe you're right, maybe I should go out there."

"Well you know I love you brother and I will never leave you out there alone. I'll come everyday if you want me to."

Riley knowing the nature of people said, "Well let's not get feisty too soon here. You got a life too you know so we'll take that up later. Maybe you could call and keep tabs on me though, but really I think things will be all right." Riley was thinking about what the dark figure had said earlier. He might need time to get lined out.

Just before lunch the two men drove out to Park Dale and sat down with the Administrator. After they talked about Riley's condition awhile they filled out the paperwork to admit Riley and introduced him to Wilma the head nurse. She was a very pleasant person and didn't seem rushed about anything.

Finally she said, "Well Mr. Clemmons if you have decided to live here we have a room right here next to the nurses station if you like."

To which Riley replied, "Well no, I think I would like to have a spot in that room at the end of the hall back there." He pointed in that direction. Something strange came over him as he said this. How did he know there was an opening in the last room?

The nurse looked surprised and said, "I don't know if we have an opening back there sir, but I'll check." And sure enough there was an opening in the last room, a patient had passed away the night before.

Wilma just couldn't figure how Mr. Clemmons knew, but in the future she would learn that there were more strange things about Riley Clemmons. So Riley packed his things and moved in the next day.

About six weeks into Mr. Clemmons stay, things as promised were going well. He knew all the nurses and most of the patients by name. He stopped to speak to everyone at breakfast and to enquire of their welfare. All the ladies thought Riley was 'charming'.

Park Dale hosted a bingo party every week and Riley was right there in the middle of everything waiting to win a prize. He called Johnson nearly every day and Johnson came to visit about twice a week. On his last visit Riley told his brother that he wished he could help Alma one of the older patients. It seemed that her doctor had made some demands about her bill that she couldn't meet. And her family was hard pressed to come up with the money for the treatment she needed. Riley thought the woman might not live too long if she didn't get it. So he asked Johnson if he could help out, but Johnson reminded Riley that Social Security was paying for his stay and the house he was living in was the rest of their inheritance.

"Well don't worry about it brother, I may be able to come up with it."

"What are you doing playing the numbers on the side?" Johnson joked.

"Naw, I just have a feeling something good is going to happen. It will work out don't worry."

That night Riley felt someone shaking his arm again.

At first he thought the night nurse had come to take his vitals. When his eyes were open he was struck with fear once more for that dark figure was standing beside his bed. The thing that made this guy so terrifying was you couldn't see his face. All of him was dark as if he had no features, a shadow that had taken on solid form.

"Riley get up, I have something for you." In the glow of the night light Riley noticed that the man held a glass.

"Here I want you to take this pill and drink all that is in this glass." Riley took the pill and drank the fluid, which tasted a little salty.

"Enjoy yourself." The man said and faded into the wall beside the window. Riley sat and wondered what was going to take place, but soon he was drowsy again and lay back and slept till breakfast time.

"Mr. Clemmons wake up. It's time for breakfast. You're almost late." When Riley looked at his alarm clock it read 7:45. The young aide gave him an endearing smile. Maybe he reminded her of her grandpa or her father. When he got up he felt different for sure something had happened to him. *What's next?* He wondered as he wandered toward the bath.

When he entered the dining room he was passing a table and a patient knocked a glass off the edge. Riley Clemmons caught it and set it back on the table never breaking stride, his cheerful smile never faltered. An aide looked at him with amazement as he passed. He sat down at his usual place and said good morning to everyone. His room mate and two ladies occupied the table with him.

"Alma you're looking good this morning and things are going to get better." He leaned across the table and squeezed her hand as she stared off into space as if she were alone. Then she jumped slightly and looked his way and smiled.

"Why hi Riley, you're looking good too. Did you sleep well?"

"Yes Alma as a matter of fact I did."

"You know Riley when we have our dance party this week I'd like to dance with you if I may."

"Why Alma I'd love to. I'm so glad you asked."

Alma looked across the table at he friends and said, "Good morning Nina what are you having for breakfast?" Nina just sat smiling. She was so surprised to hear Alma talking so clearly.

"Oh yes, breakfast. I think I'll have eggs and some cereal." she said.

Riley rose from his chair and walked around to Alvin his roommate and whispered in his ear, "Your appetite is better this morning. You are hungry and you will be able to eat without dropping it all over you."

Alvin's eyes cleared up and he smiled for the first time in months. He mumbled, "Thanks Riley."

At the end of the dining hall a pair of eyes were on Riley as he talked to his friends and they noticed the changes that came over the two he had spoken to. The mind behind those eyes thought, *Something very interesting is going on here, I'm going to have to find out how he does these things. Lip reading for the deaf comes in handy at the strangest times.*

After breakfast Riley stopped at the nurse's desk and asked the nurse on duty if he could sit in the therapy tub for a few minutes.

"I'm sorry sweetheart, I don't have time this morning. Someone needs to be in there with you so you don't fall. Maybe in the morning, Okay?" Candace casually approached the desk and said, "I can go in with him I have a few minutes."

"Oh, okay Candace you can go in with Riley." He continued to smile, but he felt something suspicious going on. Her eyes sent a message, one he wasn't sure of yet...

In the tub room Riley took his clothes off but left his shorts on. Candace held the door open to the vertical tub while he stepped in. Candace was a big woman, but there was no fat on her. She had dark auburn hair and heavy dark eyebrows with serious brown eyes. Almost menacing. She had started at Park Dale just three weeks before. She stared at Riley as she put her hand on the knob to turn on the water.

In a low voice she said,"Riley Clemmons I want to know what's going on here. People have started changing since I came here." She gave the knob a twist and the water started flowing.

"I think you got something strange going on with you." She stood and stared at him for a minute and her eyes seemed to Riley to get bigger and more threatening. He didn't answer her, he just sat and stared back. Finally she turned and left.

Later in his room he thought about what Candace had said and then he thought about what the stranger told him. He knew he felt different since he took that pill in the dark last night. He didn't think he would have to worry about her for too long. So he would just go on helping the aged and enjoying himself in the process.

After midnight Riley woke with a feeling of strength in his body. He couldn't describe it, but it was there. Something had changed in him although he didn't know what it was. He got out of bed and checked on Alvin his roommate. Alvin was snoring softly enjoying blessed rest. Riley moved quietly over to the door and peeked out into the hallway. There was no one in the hall and he could hear the nurses and aides talking at the desk. He looked across the hall. The first room was a restroom and the next was the tub room. In this building the nurse's desk, medical supplies, tub room and restroom were built down the middle of the building giving them a hall down both sides. The tub room was Riley's destination. He loved those whirlpool baths. As quietly as he could he shuffled across the hall. He reached for the door lever to see if it was locked. He was overcome with shock as his hand went through the knob. He slowly pulled it back and stared at his hand for a moment. He heard one of the women at the desk laugh. He looked down the hall. No one was coming. He then shoved his hand all the way through the door, and then his body followed. Inside the tub room it was pitch dark. Riley stood with a big smile on his face. Then he flipped the light switch and started for the tub. Riley dropped his pajamas on the floor and stepped inside the vertical tub and sat down. After he popped the door shut to the tub he turned on the water, which took a few minutes to fill the tub. The controls to the whirlpool were along the armrest next to the water knob. He punched his choice and sat back in pure pleasure. Riley knew he couldn't stay too long so when the whirling action timer went off he emptied the tub and got out. He took a towel from the linen cabinet, dried and put on his pajamas. Now he had to deal with the door. He stepped into his slippers and went right through once again. He looked down the hall grinning. Back in his room he lay down and slept until the aide called him for breakfast. Earlier, out in the hall, in a doorway further down, Candace had taken in all that had happened. A smile came across her face.

This morning there would be a difference that Riley had

never felt in his life. He had ability now that he had never had before. He also knew why it had been given to him. He could now help all his friends at the care unit. After he had greeted everyone and sat down at the table to wait for his plate he thought about the events of the night before. He realized that he had the ability to take care of things that needed to be attended to, only it would have to be at night while everyone else slept.

It might not be a bad idea to learn something about those computers. It might help me get things done quicker. He thought.

"Riley your breakfast is getting cold." Riley glanced up to see Alma looking at him across the table.

"Oh yes, breakfast. Sorry, I was woolgathering." The aide had set his plate down and moved on to serve others. Riley was so engrossed in his thinking he hadn't noticed. He'd have to be careful about that. The sense of the abilities he possessed had begun to grip him.

At the end of the week a woman came from the Clarksburg Library with magazines and books for the patients to read. Riley stood in line waiting his turn. Patients could also order books on loan and the librarian would bring them the following week when she came. When Riley reached the table he sat down and asked the woman to find him a book to help him learn computer operation. She searched through her laptop and came up with a couple that she thought would be pretty simple. The center had a computer for patients to practice on. In a few weeks Riley Clemmons would be a computer operator... and more.

Candace Moon sat at the table in their kitchen while her husband ate supper.

"What's the matter hon, not hungry?" he asked.

"Yes sweetheart, but not hungry for food right now. I have a story that you'll love. There is a patient at the care center that has an ability to do things you wouldn't believe.

"Jack," she said, "if it's the way I think it is we will be able to retire early and travel all we like. The problem is I've got to catch him outside the unit at night and I don't think it will be long before he has to make a trip to a bank or a loan office after hours. When he does, I'll be waiting for him." Jack sat with his mouth open in shock.

"How do you know that?"

"Jack, get ready for the shock of your life. Hold on to your chair. You ready?"

Jack nodded with a mouth full of food.

"This old guy can change the disabilities of the old and heal minds lost to Alzheimer's. I saw an old woman come to herself after this guy talked in her ear for a minute. And she has been cognizant ever since. His roommate doesn't suffer from arthritis like he used to before the old man moved in. Now, get ready for the good part. I went back to the unit last night and told the night nurse I forgot my stethoscope. I stood in the doorway of one of the rooms down the hall from the old guy's. I saw him come out into the hall and cross to the tub room. He likes to sit in the whirlpool tub, but they don't want him doing it too much." Jack," she grasped his arm, "he walked right through the door into the room. He didn't open it and walk through he went through the door. About twenty minutes later he comes through the door again and crosses to his room." Jack starred into space for a moment then it came to him and he began to smile.

"Candace we could be rich." he declared excitedly.

She put her hand across his mouth and said, "Shh."

The next morning…

Candace was in the employee's locker room just it was before time to start work.

The door opened silently and someone came in. When she turned to see who it was she jumped, Riley Clemmons was standing right next to her grinning. He said, "You know Candace, watching people goes both ways." He turned and left. She stood there staring at the door. She thought *He doesn't know I know what he can do. I'll still know when he tries to extract funds from a financial institution.* As the days went by she started sleeping for a couple of hours at odd times just after dark and at dawn. She spent her nights in different places along the road outside Park Dale. She waited six weeks and was about to give up when Riley made his move.

One night about 10:00 he came through the side wall of the building and waited for a taxi. When the cab drove away Candace started her car and followed. The cab went to another town not far away and dropped Riley on the town square. Candace pulled up on a side street with her lights out, shut off the engine and waited. She saw him cross the grass on the square and the street on the other side and head toward the payday loan office. Riley knew the man that owned the office and his interest rates were off the chart. So Riley took an interest in him. Candace got out and crept to the corner and watched as he melted through the glass front door. No alarm sounded because the door hadn't been breeched. Candace moved around to a car parked along the curb not far from the loan office. She squatted behind it and slid her feet under the car and leaned over where she could see around the back tire.

Inside Riley went to the cash drawer and slid his hands inside. He removed all the bills from the cash tray probably five hundred dollars. He looked up to see if anyone was roaming the town. There was no police car and no one walking the street. He turned to the back room and found a safe in a closet. The door was wired so he melted through the wall next to it. Putting his hands through the side of the safe he removed about a hundred thousand dollars. The owner thought, *This is a small town, no thieves, so I'll keep it in here and not worry about transporting it to the bank every day.* His attitude would change about 7:30 the next morning. Riley found a paper sack on a table in the back room. He put the money in it and folded the top neatly. He raised his head and looked at the wall on the end of the room.

Something in his head said, "Come this way."

He walked through the walls of all the stores to the end of the block. When he came out he went back to the house where his brother Johnson was sleeping. He went into the bedroom where he used to sleep and put the package on the shelf of the closet at the end. He went back to the square and called the taxi from the gas station. It picked him up and dropped him at Park Dale. By 11:30 Riley Clemmons was back in bed sleeping peacefully.

Finally Candace got tired of waiting in the street as she tried to slide out from under the car she put her hand in something wet. A sprinkler had come on not far away and water was running down the gutter. Something was wrong here Riley had not come out the way he went in. She went over to the window; the place was deserted. She let out a sigh and went back to her car. She realized Riley had left another way, but like the compulsive gambler she would keep trying. She went back to her watching mode.

At 7:30 the next morning, the owner came into the loan office, the first thing he did was go to the safe. When he opened it his gun was there, but the money wasn't. He ran to the cash drawer in front. It too was empty. His first thought was the police, but he didn't know how the thief got in or how he opened the drawer and the safe. He stood behind the counter stupefied. Now he needed a loan.

At Park dale Johnson Clemmons was talking to his brother on the phone.

Riley said, "I need to see you as soon as you have time to get here."

When Johnson arrived they went into the family room where patients visited with relatives in private. Riley sat in a chair facing the door that had a glass panel on each side. He could see the nurse's station from where he sat. Johnson sat in a chair across from him. Riley said, "Sit over here." He pointed to a chair next to him.

"Is this a secret matter?" Johnson asked. "If so we can go

out to the car."

"Just hold on Brother." Riley raised his hands and placed them together in front of his mouth in thought.

"I wanted to let you know my numbers came in. Now don't look surprised. Remember how we used to keep secrets from mom and dad? We discussed them right in front of their eyes." Johnson smiled at the memory and turned his face toward the door.

Riley said, "There is a package in the closet in my bedroom on the shelf on the left side against the wall. I want you to take it to the bank in Carbondale and deposit in the account of the person's name I give you. I'll get you the account number and info you need to make the deposit. Now don't ask any questions yet. I'll tell you what's going on as soon as I can. Somebody needs help and I have the chance to give it to them. I'll call you when I get the info." They both sat and stared at the door for a few minutes. Then Johnson got up and left.

The person watching the security camera walked away from the monitor.

Riley went back to his room waiting for the aide to walk Alma by the door on her exercise regimen. When he saw her he would go out and walk with her and convince the aide he would stay with Alma and she could go do other things that needed to be attended to. Mary, the aide, trusted Riley so he was confident she would leave them alone and he could explain the situation to Alma; get the necessary information and Johnson could make a deposit into her account.

During the bingo session that week Riley sat at the table next to an old gent named Willard Carson. Riley had talked to one of the nurses about Willard and she told him about Willard's condition and that she felt sorry for him. Willard was still very sharp in his thinking even though he was seventy-eight. He feigned to be helping the old fella with his card while between games he gathered information about him. He had rheumatoid arthritis and his hands were starting to cripple. He needed treatment from a specialist, but there wasn't any money for the bills. Riley wrote a note on a slip of paper and laid it on the table in front of Jenks. Willard read it and looked at Riley with surprise.

It read: **I have some money that I can give you for treatment, but you have to let me know how I can get it in your bank account. Don't say anything now.**
After Carson read it Riley took the note and tore it up and put it in the pocket of his robe.

They went on with the bingo games, neither one said anything. Candace was standing at the door, watching what was going on. In her mind she knew there would be another extraction from a financial institution soon.

When Riley convinced Willard he wasn't trying to fleece him he got an account number and went to work looking for a place to provide funds for treatment. At one point there was a slight glitch in the plan because Alvin his roommate woke late that night to discover Riley was gone and he wasn't in the bathroom. When Alvin approached him about it the next morning he told him he had a special meeting with someone about private business. This seemed to satisfy Alvin. Riley went on with business as usual. He went into the dining room which was empty after they cleaned up from breakfast. Looking around he lifted the handle off the wall phone and dialed nine followed by his brother's number. He had made sure he knew where Candace was before he dialed.

"Hi Johnson, here's the info." his took a slip of paper out of his shirt pocket and read the name and number and the bank. "Don't talk to anyone, you hear?" He hung up and went back to his room.

He knew he couldn't get too many people involved because someone would wind up going to jail if they got caught. He'd heard there was a gaming casino across the border in a neighboring state. Some of the patients went over there with their relatives on weekends. He couldn't take a cab, something would look fishy if he came back from a Casino with a big piece of luggage or even worse, a big sack. While Alvin was at the exercise room Riley went outside of the building and sat down on the patio to think this through. After a few minutes he felt someone watching him. The window to his room was behind him so he couldn't see who it was. When he turned the window was empty.

He put his hand in front of his mouth and said, "That woman is getting to be a pain. I may have to tell the shadow to get rid of her." Surprisingly a strong thought came to him; *Give her a bag of money. There's plenty for everyone.*

Then Riley smiled and said to himself in a low voice, "Sure, you're supposed to be helping people, help them too." Just then he saw the rear door open. He got up and went around the end of the building and slid through the wall into his room. He sat down in the chair next to his bed. He watched through his window as Candace looked around wondering where he was.

Five days later Beatrice Olney passed away. A fine old institution in the care unit. Even though her health was bad she had a wonderful sense of humor and made everyone around her laugh. Riley was hit hard at her passing and tired to comfort the family when they came to claim her. Some of these people were a sense of history and had great experiences to tell. He wished some of the younger folks could hear the stories in the lives of the aged. He thought, *It would be a wonderful and eye opening experience for the high school kids to hear some of the stories of lives of fifty years ago.*

This event made Riley more determined to help the aged at Park Dale. He would get his plan in gear and provide for his friends. That night just after midnight he went over to see Johnson at the house.

"I'm sorry to wake you so late, Johnson you need to help me so I can help others."

"Riley where did you get all that money. There was close to a hundred thousand in that bag."

"Did you put it in her account?"

"Every dime. Now where did you get it?"

"Johnson, this money comes from people that steal from other people right under their noses. I'm just putting it to good use that's all."

"You're not answering my question brother. Where did you get it?"

"Johnson, I'm not going to answer your question because then we both would spend the rest of our lives up North looking through a twelve foot chain link fence. Now will you help me get an old car so I can get around?"

Johnson sat in silence for a moment. "Why does it have to be an old car?"

"Johnson, you ask too many questions. You gonna help me or not?"

"Well it might take me a day or two to find something."

"No it won't. Just go down to Parson's car lot. He's got more junk than the wrecking yard over in Coleman. If I can get something to get around in I'm going be able to get funds to help people that need it."

"How much do you think I ought to pay for a car?"

"I don't know six, seven, eight hundred dollars might be all right. Just something that runs, you know. You might have to front me for a couple of days until I can get across the state line."

"Now you know the folks never wanted us to go gambling Riley."

"If I go there I won't be going to gamble. I got to get out of here. Call me when you find something." Riley got up and went back to the care unit. He entered through the end of the building into the hall. As he went into his room he found Alvin sitting on the side of the bed.

"Where you been Riley?" he said in a low tone. Riley sat down beside him and said,

"I can't tell you where I've been Alvin. Just you be satisfied knowing that I'm helping people live a little longer. And quit asking so many questions, you're worse than my brother. Now let's get some shuteye."

When the sun shined in the window at 7:00 the next morning Riley blinked and sat up. The day nurse was just coming on duty and was making her rounds.

"Good morning fellas. Anybody hurting, I got pain pills."

"Give us time to get our eyes open and come out of the fog." Riley said.

"All right Alvin sweetheart can you sit up? I need to take your blood pressure. That's a good boy."

Riley slipped off the bed and sat down in his chair. Waiting his turn.

"Well you're up a little this morning sweetie. You stayin off the salt like the doc told you?"

"Yeah, they even took the salt shaker off our table." Alvin answered.

"Okay Riley your turn." She began wrapping the cuff around his arm. She put a thermometer in his mouth as the cuff pressurized.

"Hey partner you're looking pretty good 110 over 70. Cool as a cucumber my man Riley is." Riley sat and smiled.

When she finished she said as she went out the door, "All right guys get cleaned up breakfast is at eight." The dining room was all abuzz everyone seemed to be talking at one time telling of their pains and their prejudices.

At the next table Riley could hear Homer Skoggins saying, "You dang tootin I'm gonna vote. If I can get somebody to cart my bones to the booth I'll put my two cents in like I always have. That guy they got up in the state assembly ain't doin nothin but sittin with his feet up and drinkin coffee and sometimes worse than that. Vat number nine you know what I mean." Riley smiled. Yeah he knew what he meant. He was anxious for his brother to call he wanted to get the show on the road.

When breakfast was over Riley sat drumming his finger on the arm of his chair when the phone rang on his side of the room.

"Hello? Yeah, that's great. No don't need anything better

than that. Yeah just something to get around in. You think you'll have any trouble getting it registered. Okay, I'll drop by later and take a look at it."

He hung up and sat smiling. It was Johnson and he had found a car down at Parsons that wasn't in too bad a shape. It was a 1990 Nissan and whoever had it took pretty good care of it. Johnson had whittled him down to six hundred and he didn't think it would take too much to fix it up. He would spend the day checking it out. That was good for him. It would give him something to do beside sit on the porch and gossip. Now Riley was more anxious than before to get started. In a few minutes they would have the dining area set up for game time. Riley thought he would wander down and see what kind of mischief he could get into and give Candace something to worry about.

When he went in the door he spotted Grace Hutchins working on a jigsaw puzzle. It was a big one too about 1500 pieces. She had the border finished and was filling in the middle.

Riley sat down beside her and said, "Your doin pretty good you just started this yesterday didn't you?"

"Day before. Help me find this green one they're all starting to look the same."

"If I find it will you help me?" he said his eye searching the pieces.

"Now what?"

"I need to know who has to have help the most." Grace looked up glaring into his eyes.

"My God Riley we all need help in this place. That's including the staff. One less Medicare check and we could all windup alongside the road." Riley chuckled at her humor. He picked up a piece and put it in the hole. And then followed it with another.

"What's that guys name in the wheelchair, the one that just started using it? He was walking just last week."

"Yeah that's Joe Belgrade he's got muscular problems in his legs. He needs therapy, but probably no money for it."

"We don't have any therapists here?"

"Not the kind he needs. He needs specialists. They would have to take him to a special unit out of town. Probably everyday to start, then the sessions taper off as a patient begins to walk more and they send him back here when they release him."

The reason Grace knew about all the serious cases was because she hung around Wilma's office talking to her a lot. There were times when even Wilma needed someone to confide in.

"I wish I could get the money these people need. I'd give it to them." Grace looked up at him.

"Where you gonna get thirty thousand for therapy?" He didn't answer he just shook his head.

"Well I gotta get out of here I think my brother is coming tonight to take me over to the house for a while."

"You tell Johnson he can take me to his house anytime he wants." Grace said with a smile. Riley chuckled and got up. At the other end of the hall he worked his way into a checker game. Even Alvin was playing checkers again. Riley gave a big sigh. He was glad to be able to help these people. As soon as he could move around he would get more help.

About 7:00 that evening Johnson came in looking for Riley. "Come on Brother I got something to show you."

"Okay, I'm comin right away."

They walked outside after Riley signed out and told the night nurse he would be back in about an hour. Outside they got into Johnson's car and went to the house. The Nissan was dark green, almost black.

The only time one could see the green was when it was in the sun.

"Not bad looking for a 1990." Riley said.

"It's in pretty good shape. The radiator needs to be cleaned out and it might need an alternator. The head lights look a little weak. Here let me turn them on and see what you think." Johnson slid in and started it and turned on the lights. When he revved the motor the lights got brighter.

"Yeah go ahead and put a new one on and get the radiator fixed and have it winterized," he said over the noise of the engine.

You want to drive it?" Johnson asked. Riley nodded and Johnson got out and went around to the passenger side. They drove around the block a couple of times then they came back and Riley parked it along the curb.

Half a block away on a side street Candace watched the two men evaluate the car then followed when Johnson took Riley back to the unit.

A couple of evenings later Johnson called Riley in his room.

"Okay Brother you owe me eight hundred eighty-four dollars. That includes registration, insurance and plates."

"All right I'll get it to you tonight or tomorrow night. Leave it on that side street about a half a block from here. I'll find a place to hide it later. No one is supposed to know I got a driver's license so I don't want anyone to see me driving it. Thanks Johnson, you've been a big help."

Candace hadn't expected the car, but she expected something to happen soon so she kept a close eye on Riley and sat outside the care unit all night waiting to see if he would leave.

Outside the rear of the unit was a patio and a grassy area about twenty feet wide. Beyond that was lined with trees planted fairly close together. Candace stood in the trees in line with the corner of the building so she could see which side of the building Riley came out of. About 11:00 Riley got up and dressed to leave. Something felt out of place. He knew somehow he couldn't go out on his side of the building. So he walked across the hall to the end room on the front side of the building. The drive was circular with lights all along it. There were big floods at the front door, which was locked after 8:00 o'clock. The nurse's desk was back from the main entrance so if Riley walked straight out and made it to the road from his end of the building neither the nurses or the watcher in the back could see him. Once across the road he would be in the dark. He could travel back up the street to the car from there.

Candace also had a funny feeling and moved out of the trees and in her peripheral vision she saw something move out on the road, but in a half second it was out of sight. She ran on her tiptoes across the lawn hoping to get to the road in time to see if it was Riley leaving. Her foot caught a small tree limb that a gardener had forgotten to pick up and she fell hard. Fortunately for her she was on the grass and didn't get hurt, but it knocked the wind out of her. She jumped up and hurried to the street as quick as she could, gasping for air. When she got to the street it was empty. Down the street and around the corner Riley was sitting in the car, back from the intersection…smiling.

Candace went back to the building and went around to the window of Riley's room. She looked in the window to see if Riley was still there. At that same time Alvin got up in the dark to go to the restroom. He saw someone outside the window and started hollering for the nurse.

"Hey! Hey! There is someone looking in our window." He pulled the emergency cord for the nurse's signal at the desk. Everyone came running. Candace bolted away from the building running toward her car. By the time Alvin got the message straight and they got out the rear door Candace was gone, but where was Riley? They began searching.

Out in the car the dark figure slid in beside Riley and said, "Go back inside they know you are missing."

Riley went back the way he came out and at a moment when everyone was looking the other way he rushed into his room taking his clothes off at the same time. When they found him he had his PJ bottoms on and was working on the top.

"Riley, where have you been?"

"Jane, I was in the tub room. Sorry to give everybody a scare."

This explained his having his shirt off. He had thrown his clothes inside the wardrobe door. Now if only they didn't open it. No one did. Once they got calmed down they had a male nurse search the grounds with a big flashlight. He didn't find anyone.

Riley considered this night a total loss and went to sleep. He woke up about 7:00 and lay there making plans in his mind for the next night. It occurred to him that there would be more money in the Casino on the week ends. They might possibly count the cash and put it in holding and have Brinks pick it up on Monday. If he could find the room where they sent the cash until the count team came in he could take what he needed and they would never miss it. He could take pillow cases to carry it in and go back and pick up more. When he was through he would just put them in the dirty laundry. Then he remembered his computer training. If he got good enough he could transfer funds and never leave his room, but he had to do something with Alvin. He could take care of that when the time came.

It was about 8:00 a. m. when the phone rang. Riley picked it up and said hello and listened. The voice on the other end said, "Riley listen and don't say anything in case there is someone else in the room. There is a tax free trust set up in your name for large deposits. Money can be deposited either by electronic transfer or by cash. All you have to do is write a check for the bills you want to pay. There will be a trust stamp on the signature line so you will not have to sign them. Everything will be operated through the trust. Now get a pen and take down this phone number and account number. Don't write anything else on the paper." Riley sat up and pulled his nightstand over to his bed and took a pen and a tablet out of the drawer. He wrote down the numbers and folded the paper and put it in his wallet and hung up. Well he didn't have to worry about large amounts of cash after all.

The next Friday night Riley visited the Casino about 1:00 a. m.. He sat around playing nickels watching what went on. He hit a hundred dollar jackpot, which he didn't expect to do, but now he had money to keep playing until something happened. They paid him twenty-five in nickels and seventy-five in bills. He also got a free meal.

About 2:30 the pick up began to roll. The cash carts stopped at the live tables first and then they started on the slots. When a cart were full they took it to the soft count room and locked it in and left. All together there were about twelve carts jammed full of bills. The counters would be busy later this morning. Riley took notice where the soft count room was in relation to the rest of the building. He waited until the collection was finished and cashed in his nickels. He casually wandered outside and around to the end of the building, watching for security. Standing in the center of the structure he estimated where the room should be. He moved over to the wall and melded part way through. He discovered the wall was twelve inches thick. He slowly moved further in until his eyes could see what was in the room. Straight ahead the collection carts were in the middle of the room and the counting machines were positioned around the outside of the room. He waited and listened.

After Riley thought it was safe, he moved into the room and walked around the carts noticing that there were tags on each one with instructions for the counters. He looked at what might have been the last one pushed in and as he thought, it wasn't full. He slipped a pillow case out of his shirt. (There were four wrapped around his waist.) The stacks were banded with wide rubber bands and they were all different thicknesses. His eye searched for the hundreds, there weren't as many as the ones and twenties, but still a goodly amount. He cleaned them out and replaced them with a stack of ones from the bottom. When he had two sacks full he started on the twenties. When he had all four bags filled he went through the wall and set them down in the dark outside next to the building and waited for security to pass. After the golf cart passed he went after his car. Five minutes later Riley parked along the curb, opened the back door and watched the valet until he drove away in a Lincoln, to park it. He ran back after the bags, loaded them quickly and drove out of there. His clothes were wet with perspiration. He wiped his forehead with his trembling arm. He was sure he had over a million dollars back there on the floor.

When he arrived at the house he pushed the button on the garage door opener and stopped in the driveway. The door rolled up noiselessly. He hauled the bags into the garage and set them behind a sheet of plywood Johnson stood next to the wall. Once outside he closed the door and backed out never making enough noise to wake Johnson. After he parked the car in a spot in the trees he walked around behind the care center. He stopped behind one with a big trunk. Carefully he peeked around it and there not five feet from him stood Candace, watching the rear of the building muttering curses under her breath. Slowly he bent down and searched the ground for a rock. He found one about three inches in diameter. Then threw it behind her. When it landed it bounced a couple of times. Her head snapped around in that direction. Riley moved around to the opposite side of the tree. Candace ran. She was probably thinking the male nurse was searching the grounds. Riley smiled. He would remember how easily she was spooked. He moved quietly into his room, changed into his PJ's and slipped into bed. The clock said 4:30. Not a bad nights work.

The next week Riley was going to make use of his computer training. The simple things he picked up quickly typing with two fingers, operating the mouse, scrolling, finding files and booting up and shutting down. The nurses were sort of excited for Riley they loved to see any of the older folks trying out new technology, so they helped him all they could. When one of them would come by they would stop and show him things and correct his mistakes. In the next two weeks he got pretty good. On Monday of the third week Johnson came in with a new IBM, the latest model that had all the bells and whistles. He had unwrapped the unit and monitor at home. He also brought a small table to set it on. Johnson sat down and Riley noticed he was trembling.

"What's the matter buddy. "

"Riley, do you have any idea how much was in those packages?" (He didn't want to say pillow cases.)

"No." Alvin wasn't in the room and Riley went to the door to check the hall. He came back and sat down.

"A million-eight hundred thousand. What are we going to do with all that?"

"Go buy enough suit cases to hold all of it and leave it in the garage and I will come and pick them up and deposit the money. Don't worry we got it covered. I just need to get to the bank." Johnson left shaking his head.

The room had been wired with a data plug and Riley was online in a couple of hours. AOL was the most popular provider so he went with them, the money didn't matter. He accessed the bank so he could transfer funds in the future. The next thing he did was establish a link to a chat room so he could get messages. The 'shadow' might want to talk to him.

Now it was time to talk to Candace and he knew she wouldn't be far away. She took the time to stop in everyday while she was working; ask a few unrelated questions, stare at him a minute and then leave.

It was 2:00 o'clock when she came into Riley's room.

"Well how we doing today partner?" She accented the word 'partner'. Riley was sitting at his table working, accessing web sites. He stood up smiling and stepped toward her, she felt his mood and backed up.

"Could I speak to you out in the hall for a moment?" She stepped out in the hall and turned around with a worried look on her face. Riley was right behind her.

"If you could find it in your heart to take me to lunch Sunday I might have a very nice surprise for you and your husband." Candace felt a chill go up her back.

"We would be thrilled to. Would you like to go to the steakhouse?" she said in a friendly tone.

"No, I would like to go to the chicken shack out on highway 342." It was a mom and pop restaurant that did very well on weekends. Though an old frame building it had been added on to several times to accommodate the abundance of customers. The extra wings could be closed during the week when it wasn't so busy. Candace smiled and said,

"We will pick you up after Chapel service." The service ended usually about 11:30 or so.

Candace and Jack laughed and giggled nervously from Wednesday until Sunday, in anticipation of Riley's intentions. When they arrived to pick Riley up they saw Johnson was with him. They looked at one another. The Clemmons brothers walked over and opened the back door and got in.

"We really appreciate you coming to get us. I really enjoy that chicken out at the shack." Jack Moon reached over the seat and shook Riley and Johnson's hand.

"I'm Jack Moon and it is indeed a pleasure to meet you gentlemen." When they arrived at the chicken shack. The first thing Riley noticed was an aide and one of the night nurses headed inside with their husbands. Riley suggested, "Let's wait until they get seated and we can sit somewhere away from them." They sat in the car until the others were seated.

"Okay I think we can go in now." Candace said. Once inside they asked for a different wing from the other employees. The waitress seated them at the end of one of the long tables. They ordered meals and the waitress left. Candace and Jack were grinning like a possum eating briars.

Riley said, "Now to the point. We have an envelope here with a gift we think you will be happy with."

Riley withdrew the envelope from his sport coat pocket. It was a business envelope with little flowers pasted on it with Jack and Candace's name on it.

"Please don't open it until you get home. Now something else we wanted to do is deposit an amount in your account as a retirement fund. You may want to retire right away or you may want to continue to work for a while. It's up to you. After the deposit is completed there will be a block put on it so that no one can gain access to our account. We started our endeavor to help the aged in the care unit. The serious cases will get the treatment they need and no one will know where it came from. We are swearing the two of you to secrecy from this point on. Now if I was in your position I would invest some of this, money goes quick these days." Jack and Candace both nodded.

"Johnson and I will not benefit from this except to accomplish our mission."

"But Riley one thing mystifies me. How did you get this power?" Riley's smile faded. He just shook his head not saying a word. Candace nodded.

When Candace and Jack arrived home they sat down at the kitchen table hearts beating fast. Candace opened the envelope. Inside was a cashier's check for $500,000. The deposit made the next day was for a million dollars. A couple of days later Candace resigned her position at the care center in favor of caring for sick relatives. (In the Bahamas.)

When Johnson was sure she was gone he asked Riley, "How much did you give them?"

"Well I think it was about a million and a half." He rubbed his hand across his mouth and looked away saying, "You see brother that's the difference between us, I don't care about the amount as long as we get the job done. 'The shadow' wants me to help these people whatever it costs. No limits. And I'm sure he will make sure we have a retirement fund in our own bank account. So don't worry we ain't gonna run out. So if you need a new car to accomplish your part in this, go buy one. But if I were you I would keep it low key. Somebody might start asking questions if you show up in a new Cadillac or a Lincoln. It might be hard for your social security check to meet the payments.

"Oh by the way since I'm on the internet I won't be using that Nissan so you can sell it."

Well Riley and Johnson Clemmons went on paying for treatments, operations, therapy and the like and no one seems to know where the money comes from. The patients are happy and the doctors are happy and the donors, well lets just say, ignorance is bliss in a situation like this.

Maniac

George Crafton and his ten year old daughter Karen lived on twenty acres near the small town of Hugo Oklahoma not far from the Red River, deep in the Southern part of the state. A few years earlier they suffered the loss of Lilly, beloved wife to George and mother to Karen, from Cancer. But they'd had time to recover and try to go on with their lives. They both missed her very much for she was the center of their lives. It is a terrible disease this cancer that takes loved ones out of peoples lives so quickly; leaving despair in the minds of the patients and doctors alike.

George and Karen did the best they could with the crops they had planted and this year a bumper crop had come up so they were trying to make provisions to do all the canning they could to save their vegetables. Maya Little Fawn, an Indian woman, that lived a short distance from them had committed to help them can the food when they harvested. Karen stayed at her house after school everyday until her dad got home from his job in town.

On the Crafton property there was a corrugated metal shed with a water tank inside that held about seventeen thousand gallons of water. Karens dad had built a walk way around the top because the tank was eight feet high. There was a two inch pipe that ran from it to a manifold. They used the water to flood the rows between their garden and water the one horse they had and the few scant chickens. Karen liked to go out to the shed in the summer and sit inside the door. Sometimes when she was working with her dad she would go there and climb up to the walkway to wash her hot face in the cool water and sit down to rest. She was especially resilient this ten year old and her father was proud of her. She tried hard to notice what had to be done next so she could make her dad's job a little easier. If he needed the hoe she would be standing there with it in her hand waiting to give it to him.

"You're as handy as a pocket on a shirt Karen." he would tell her. She would laugh. She was an inquisitive child and she learned the farm chores quickly. Always asking questions that would help her understand farm work.

"What can I do now Daddy?" Sometimes he would grab her and hug her and tell her to sit and rest a minute until he got ready for something else.

She was also doing very well in the fourth grade in the country school. The teacher told Karen she would be a smart girl when she grew up. When she got home from school she would make sure she had any homework done so she could do the dishes after supper. When her dad fell asleep while trying to read the paper, she would take his boots off and cover him with a blanket.

There was an inner strength in this little girl that even she wasn't aware of yet.

George's temperament was mild and easy going. George tried to get along with everybody.

Just before Karen's eleventh birthday her dad called her in one day from her chores and told her they were going to town.

"But Dad, I got to feed and water Butch." Butch was their horse.

"Don't worry he'll keep until we get back. Go put a dress on and let's get out of here. We need a little time off. To much work is not good for anybody."

It was almost noon by the time they got to town so they had lunch at the Chinese restaurant and went to the Matinee movie. Karen was in heaven. Disney's Cinderella was playing and George bought her a coke and popcorn. After the movie he took her to the ladies store and bought her some clothes. Karen was ecstatic; she hung on to the bag like it was full of gold. Then he took her to the shoe store and bought her some dress shoes. There wasn't a happier girl in the State of Oklahoma.

Far Away in a Kansas State Mental health facility there was a patient that was uncontrollable if he wasn't on medication, Thorizane and stronger drugs like it. When he was a boy of twelve Michael Denton had been subjected to torture from a stepfather that was also deemed crazy. Poor Michael's mind snapped and resulted in his becoming a wild man. He ran away from home and was able to elude the authorities for several years until one day he tried to steal food from a convenience store and killed the guy that tried to stop him. The police found him easily; for he had no control and ran around screaming constantly. He was running down the street of a residential neighborhood screaming and someone called the police. With great difficulty they caught and cuffed him and put him in the back seat of a police car, but the officers couldn't get him to stop screaming. So they called the paramedics. When they arrived they called for authorization to give him a sedative. They took him to a hospital emergency room and when Michael woke up he went wild and they almost couldn't restrain him. When he was finally subdued the State mental institution was his next stop. In a medicated state he wouldn't talk or answer questions. They didn't know what to do with him. By some miracle his mother found out where Michael was and came to the hospital. That's how they found out his name and how old he was and what had happened to him. Armed with that information the doctors formulated a method of treatment for him, but he still didn't cooperate much and he was always restless. He acted as if he was in a constant stupor and walked in circles around the enclosure.

All it takes is one inexperienced employee to make one mistake and terrible things can happen. The male aide that brought his food didn't notice a fork left on Michael's tray, when he picked up the tray after Michael finished he didn't notice the fork was missing. Michael was only allowed to eat with a spoon. He had taken the fork and put it between his legs under his hospital pants. No one saw what happened. The aide realized what had happened and he knew he'd made a mistake. Not wanting to lose his job he didn't tell anyone, but went back to Michael's room to see if he could retrieve the fork.

The timing was right. The nurse that administered Michael's medication's was on her way to his room and was distracted with a call about another patient. He came to and his eyes grew wide. The minutes passed and he crept over to the door and backed up to the wall beside it. The innocent aide came through the locked door and saw Michael standing next to the door, but before he could react the fork was sticking out of his throat. Michael threw him across the hall into the wall and took off down the hall toward an exit door. Again the timing was perfect. A nurse who had been outside smoking came in as Michael was going out. Fortunately for the nurse all he did was knock her down. Then he began to scream again running for the twelve foot chain link fence. He climbed like a cat and went over the barbed wire like it wasn't even there. He vaulted off the top strand of wire and landed on his feet and ran. By the time the hospital employees got to the fence Michael was gone with a trail of blood following him.

They called the Kansas Highway Patrol and the local police who started a search statewide.

A bulletin was put out and announced on radio and television, but no one had seen Michael Denton. The maniac traveled South staying in the wooded areas. He would go to gas stations and convenience stores at night and take what he wanted. The clerks were terrified and waited until he took food and when he ran out they called the police. Fortunately for many months no one was hurt; but they couldn't catch Michael either. Sometimes he could be heard screaming near farm houses late in the night. When the authorities were called there was no sign of him. Michael was now almost twenty years old and his condition hadn't gotten any better; only he didn't scream as much. His dark beard grew and his hair was long, hanging down his back. He truly looked like a wild man. When he screamed it wasn't a man's scream or a woman's for that matter. It sounded like some wild animal in pain.

Michael went into campgrounds and took peoples clothes and shoes. In one instance he found a hunting knife and took that too. Now he was really armed and dangerous. The blade was broad and came to a sharp point. The owner was one of those sharp fanatics. The stone he used had to be an Arkansas hard so that the finished edge would cut deep without any undue pressure. Somehow Michael continually traveled South. After a couple of hours he came to a state road. There was no traffic, but across the road was a single light on a pole that lit a small parking space. Below it was a bait store with a light in the window. Michael sat in the bushes staring and drooling. The saliva dripped off his chin and down onto his shirt, but he was unaware of it. He heard a car approaching and looked up the road just as a pair of headlights came into view. When the car came to the store it turned in and parked next to the door. An old man got out and hunted through his keys. His white hair looked like he had been in a wind storm. Finding one, he opened the front door and went inside. Michael began to breathe faster. For a few moments he sat and stared at the shiny blade turning it over and over. His eyes grew wide.

"Uhhh, Uhhh, Uhhh." He grunted and a sardonic smile appeared on his lips. He slid out of the bushes and crossed the road. When he came into the store the little bell tinkled at the top of the door.

A voice from the back called out, "Be there in a minute."

Michael wandered through the small isles picking up things

he wanted to eat. Especially sweet things like miniature pecan pies, chocolate cup cakes and candy bars. When all that got into his system he would be on a screaming binge for sure. He carried the sweets to the small counter and dumped them on the rubber place mat. He stood panting and grinning, waiting for the old man. The old man came out of the back room hurrying along behind the counter.

"Morning what can…"

The instant the old guy saw Michael he lost his voice. He realized this was the wild man they had announced on the radio and on the TV. He dropped the stryrofoam worm tubs and ran toward the back of the store. Michael was after him in a flash. He loved things that ran from him. When the old man slammed the door it was too late Michael's hand was inside. Anyone else would have screamed in pain, but for him it was pure pleasure because probably all that was on his twisted mind was getting his hands on the old man.

On the other side of the door the old guy was pushing on the door as hard as he could muttering, "Oh God please help me."

Next to the door was a 2x4 with a fork cut in the end. He grabbed it and jammed it under the knob and kicked the bottom wedging it tight hoping he could make it to the back door. There were two dead bolts and a large bar across the middle. Country security. The old man hobbled down between two rows of shelves digging for his keys again. He was shaking uncontrollably he parted through the keys twice before he found one that opened one of the locks. He pushed it into the bottom lock. No good. He pulled it out and put it in the top and turned the latch. He pulled it out and fished out the one next to it and put it in. No good. He tried the other side.

Michael pulled his hand out of the opening in the door splintering the edge of the door and the jamb. That left the door a little loose. He slammed into the door with all his crazy might shearing the knob off on the back side and taking out the two three and a half inch hinges. The door fell in against a shelf. Michael threw the door aside roaring as he ran toward the back. He started down the isle between the shelf and the wall as the old man clicked the second lock. He was pulling the bar out when Michael grabbed him. The bar was too heavy and too long to use as a weapon. He tried to hold it between them and Michael knocked it out of his hands. The old man gasped and clutched the top of his bib overalls. He was having a heart attack. His head fell back against the door as he grimaced in pain. Michael was standing over him grinning.

"Aaahh!" The old man cried. In response Michael gave a scream that shook the rafters. He raised the knife and plunged it into the old man's chest. Then he pulled it out and began to hack, and hack until there was nothing left but a pile of flesh and bones. He stood there bloody panting and grinning at his success when he heard a noise in the front. It was someone coming in.

Then he heard a voice, "Hey you old fart get out here I need some bait. Grubs, worms, marshmallows and a can of corn. Them catfish are bitin today."

Silence.

"Hey old man what you doin back there?"

No answer.

He started towards the back. As he reached the end of the counter he saw a dark head of hair raising from behind it. When those eyes cleared the top he knew immediately something was wrong. When he could see the guys mouth with the spittle dripping he turned and ran for the door. Michael was after him, but the fat guy was just far enough ahead of him to get out the door and into his truck. By the time Michael had a hold of the door handle the truck was moving. He drew back his hand to break the glass as the guy backed up dragging him with him. After being drug out to the road Michael finally let go. Inside the truck the guy shifted into drive while trying to dial 911 on his cell phone. Remembering his booty Michael ran back inside the store to pick up the candy and cakes and fill his pockets. He blasted through the door and lopped across the highway like a big ape who had escaped from the zoo.

Twenty minutes later two deputy's the Sheriff's department arrived with guns drawn. When the second car arrived they went in together searching the isles. When they reached the back room they found what was left of the old man lying on the floor at the back door. One of the officers went outside and threw up. The other one checked the rest of the store and called in the incident asking for more men as backup. They were way too late though Michael was deep in the woods running South.

Late that afternoon he lay under a tree exhausted. He had been running for hours. He lay down and passed out. When he woke up it was almost dark. He dug into his pockets taking out the cakes and candy. He devoured all of it in no time and could have eaten more. He fell back again and began to snore.

When he woke up it was almost light. The Eastern sky was turning a prism of blue. A squirrel was at his feet cleaning up the scraps. When it saw Michael waking up it scampered away.

"Ooohhh, Ooohhh, Aaahh." he moaned his head was hurting from all the excitement. He got up and wandered around among the trees for a while and came to a small stream. He dropped to his knees and dipped his hands and face in the cold water and wet his hair. He sat on his knees for a long time staring at the water. After a while he stood up and staggered around laughing and giggling. Finally he stumbled Southward again. The Sheriff's posse hadn't reached the place where he had slept yet and probably wouldn't for another couple of hours. By that time Michael would be far away. He was now approaching the extreme Southern part of Kansas and soon would cross the Oklahoma line.

Three days later

In a truck stop North of Tulsa, a trucker had delivered his load and stopped to fill up before picking up his next load going

South. He had left the latch open on his roll up door. Out in the tall weeds and grass beyond the station Michael Denton watched as the driver walked back toward the cab of his rig. Michael jumped up and hopped over the barrier and slipped up to the back of the truck. He lifted the door and crawled inside. The trucker drove away.

The Kansas State Police notified the State of Oklahoma that possibly this man was traveling South and would enter the state soon. The Oklahoma Highway Patrol posted cars on every major and minor road in the Northeastern part of the state. Especially near gas stations and convenience stores. In Tulsa the trucker stopped and picked up the load that was to go to Hugo Oklahoma and then stopped at a truck stop for fuel. During the stops Michael crawled under a truckers blanket in the front of the truck. Since it was going to be a full load the driver left the delivery close to the back door. He simply didn't notice anything funny; so he didn't check the blanket.

When the driver climbed down and rolled the door down Michael lay listening, but the drivers footfall moved away from the truck. He crawled over the boxes and slowly raised the door enough to crawl out. He looked around and saw people filling coolers with food and pop. The families with kids bought more. Finally he zoned in on one family with a cooler that had a single handle. Michael edged his way around to the row just the other side of the station wagon. He ducked down and watched the man put the food in the cooler. When he closed it he walked to the front of the car and raised the hood. Michael eased around the rear of the car and ran stooped over. He snatched the cooler and kept going. Hopping over the steel roadside barrier was no challenge, or the one on the other side of the road. Michael was out in the brush in seconds. When the man came back to put the cooler in the wagon he saw it was gone and began looking around hoping to spot whoever had taken it. Meanwhile Michael was having lunch barbaric style. Tearing wrappers and chewing noisily. He waited until the man and his family went around the other side of the store to start over with another cooler and the contents. Michael ran back to the truck and slid up the door and got in. A few minutes later he felt the truck start and move out of the parking lot. He sat up behind the boxes and began to eat more of the contents of the cooler.

    Late that afternoon the truck began to sputter and the engine started coughing. The driver found a place to pull over. He got out and released the front of the hood of the truck and leaned the whole hood and front fenders forward to check the engine. The driver discovered the problem was more than he could fix, so he crawled back into the cab and picked up his cell phone and called the number of a mechanic in Hugo. He had made deliveries there before and was carrying one now. Unaware that he might not be alone he walked up the road away from the truck. At the same time Michael climbed down with the cooler and ran off the road, up into the trees. He stood peeking around the trunk of a pine, watching the driver walking around talking to someone. Somehow he understood this would be the end of his ride. He turned and moved up to the top of the hill and looked around. He could see several farm houses in the distance from where he stood. This was the calmest he had been since he killed the old man.

    Highway 271 was too busy a road to follow. There were lots of trucks, RV's and cars. He stayed a good distance from the road so he wouldn't be spotted by the Highway Patrol. An hour later he came to a small country road running out into the farmland. He turned right and followed the road.

Earlier that day...

On the small plot of acreage outside Hugo, Oklahoma the morning was bright and sunny. It was spring and everyone was happy. Karen had fed the chickens and watered and fed the horse. She was in her bedroom getting ready for school.

    "You ready Karen, the school bus will be here shortly." her father called.

"Okay daddy I'll be there in a minute."

George walked Karen to the road and they waited for the bus. After Karen left he drove toward town.

That evening George drove up to Maya Little Fawn's house at 5:00 o'clock, she and Karen were outside waiting. The first thing George noticed was a hunting knife on Maya's hip.

"Hi daddy." Karen said.

"Hi sweetheart."

As Karen ran around the front of the truck he said to Maya, "What's the matter Maya? Going hunting?"

"If he comes here I'll gut him like a carp." she said in a soft tone, but George could tell she was talking through gritted teeth. "You haven't seen the news have you?"

"No what's going on?"

George you need to turn your TV on once in a while. The news is on at four, five and six o'clock on at least three channels." She turned and hurried toward the house. George heard the door close and the dead bolt snap into place. He sat and stared for a moment, watching as Maya put sticks diagonally across the top of her slide up windows

"Karen did you see what happened?"

She threw her arms around his neck and gave him a kiss. "Yeah daddy, a crazy man broke out in Kansas and he's headed this way. It's been on the news all day. The highway patrol has road blocks on the State Line up North and on all the roads coming into Oklahoma. The man on the TV said to go in the house and lock the door and don't open it for anybody."

"Boy this guy must be bad."

"Yeah he must really be bad." she said. George drove to the house and together they fixed supper. Afterward Karen carried a small TV out of the bedroom and set it on the kitchen table; she plugged it in and found a news program. They told about the old man in the bait shop, but they couldn't show any pictures. There was an old lady crying in the parking lot. The anchor told about the break out and the male nurse being stabbed with the fork. Just then the phone rang. George got up and answered it.

"Hello. Yeah Sheriff this is George."

"George before you go to bed tonight you better make sure your windows a locked and you might want to set your shotgun out. Loaded."

"God Sheriff this guy is wacko huh?"

"Yeah they say he's the craziest one they have ever seen. Running around screaming like a Banshee tearing up everything he comes in contact with. I hate to think of you and the little girl out there all by yourselves. If anything funny happens don't hesitate to give us a call huh?"

"Okay Sheriff I sure will, thanks for callin us. Karen go make sure the back door is locked and put the stick under the knob." They also had a 2x4 with a strip of wood nailed to the floor at the right distance so the stick would wedge tight. George got up and locked the front door. It would be dark soon and he didn't want to forget.

"Dad the water is still running out of the tank into the garden. You want me to go shut it off?"

"No baby that's not something we worry about tonight. It's not on full anyway."

George went to the hall closet and took out his shotgun; it was an old single shot that his dad had given him. He had a new automatic twelve gage in the bedroom closet but he didn't think he would need it. He checked to see if it was loaded and it was, but the shell was #7½ bird shot he used for dove. He thought for a moment then went into the bedroom and took out a box of duck loads which were #4's. That would take a man apart at ten feet or less. He stuck one in and put a couple in his pocket and put the box back.

Karen had moved the TV back into the living room and was watching a game show.

"Did you do your homework hon.?"

"We didn't have any tonight so I thought I would read a book."

"That's a good girl. Mom would have wanted you to be a

good reader."

After the game show was over Karen went into her room and selected a book off her bookshelf. Dad had kept her in books that she liked. She sat down on the bed and leaned against the headboard.

"Karen, he called from the living room, Why don't you come out here until it's time for bed. You can read under the lamp in my chair."

"Okay daddy." When she was in the chair she looked at George and said,

" It's really scary huh Dad?"

"Well sweetheart it would be foolish not to be careful. If Mom was here she would probably make us go to town and get a room, but I think the Lord will keep us."

So they sat and read in the peaceful atmosphere of their home. Occasionally George would raise his head and listen to the night sounds. Nothing seemed out of place.

"Well Karen honey we better get some shut-eye it's nine o'clock and we got one more day ahead of us."

She crawled up in his lap and grinned lovingly, "Daddy can we go to McAlister this weekend?"

"Got an appointment at the toy store maybe?" he said. She grinned and hid her face in his shirt.

"Maybe you've got an appointment at the ice cream shop too."

He laughed and stood up taking her with him. He went into his bedroom and put her down on the bed.

"I gotta sleep in here?"

"Sorry kiddo just for tonight okay, so Dad don't worry so much."

"You gonna get the gun? Bring my pajamas please?"

"Oh I guess I might." he went into the living room and retrieved the shotgun and went to his daughter's dresser and pulled out a pair of pajamas. Outside he heard a noise in the corral. Butch was acting up and he didn't usually do that at night.

"Lord don't let nothing be wrong." he prayed in the hall. Then it got quiet again and he went on.

In the bedroom George asked Karen, "Would you pray with me honey before we go to sleep?"

"Yes daddy." They knelt beside the bed and prayed together for the Lord to protect them through the night and keep evil away. They got into bed and turned out the light. In a few minutes they were asleep.

Outside...

His eyes seemed to almost glow in the darkness. Earlier he had seen the man and the girl go in the house. They were in there now with the lights out and they would soon be sleeping. Not much longer now. His breathing began to quicken as he readied himself to go after them. He longed to hear the man scream in terror. And the little girl, oh the little girl. He almost laughed out loud. He had to put his hand over his mouth to keep it in. He grinned in the darkness and the drool ran down the corner of his mouth. Slowly and silently he moved toward the house. He tried the front door. Then he grinned and turned and went around to the back of the house. There were three windows slowly he went to each one listening. At the third one he put his ear to the pane and heard the man snoring. He turned around and walked back three or four paces and ran at the window. He jumped just before he hit the glass.

The window exploded in and Michael landed on the floor on top of the glass and the stick.

George came awake immediately and rolled toward Karen and grabbed her pajamas and threw her over him onto the floor screaming, "Run, Karen run!" That was all he had time to say.

In another second the maniac was on him screaming.

"Yaaaaa, Yaaaaa!" He grabbed George and jerked him off the bed. The first blow hit George in the face and almost knocked him out. The second was just as quick. George tried to block the next one and hold onto his arm. The maniac threw him into the wall next to the window. When his head hit the wall he lost consciousness. While they were struggling Karen ran out the front door and into the yard. Once outside she ran to the water shed. Inside she quickly slipped around to the back. She hunkered down behind the tank listening. She trembled in fear. What could she do? Oh how she hoped her daddy stopped the crazy man. She could still hear him screaming in the house. She crawled around the tank and peeked out. The man came out of the house dragging her father. He drug him across the yard and up to the barn. Then he started doing something, but she couldn't make out what it was. She slipped around to the side of the barn and in the light from the house she saw the maniac wrapping something around her father. Then it came to her. It was the roll of baling wire that her dad kept in the barn. He didn't stop at tying his hands and feet he kept wrapping it around his whole body. He continued wrapping until he'd used the entire roll. Her dad was wire from his ankles to his shoulders. With a scream of victory the maniac lifted George Crafton and carried him toward the watershed laughing wildly. Karen followed at a distance going around behind the shed.

Inside he slammed George against the tank and started to climb. After he had stepped up two steps he reached down and grabbed the wire at George's back and hefted him up on the catwalk that surrounded the top of the tank. He climbed onto the catwalk and stood George up and plunged him into the tank. Then he turned around and jumped off the catwalk screaming and laughing. Now in his twisted and demented mind he thought of the girl. He ran out into the yard and headed for the house.

When George hit the cold water he came to. He wasn't at the bottom, because the last four strands of wire wrapped around his shoulders had snagged a bolt below the waterline. All that was above the water was his nose. He tried to hold his breath until the water quit making ripples. Slowly he began to breathe.

With the tips of his fingers he felt the wire and realized what the maniac had done. The only things that moved were his toes and his head. He tried to lay his head back to get his mouth above the water.

"Daddy, I'm here." She whispered.

"Karen! Go get the wire cutters out of the tool box in the truck." he bubbled through the ripples in the water. In an instant she was gone. Outside she crept across the yard while the maniac screamed and threw things through the windows. Karen hid behind the bumper of the truck for a few seconds. Then she climbed up into the truck. She crept forward and pulled the latch to the lid of the tool box. Slowly she raised the lid and laid it against the cab. The darkness frustrated her she couldn't see anything as she reached inside and began to feel around. She knew what the cutters looked like but she couldn't see anything. She felt around pulling out handles. First pliers nope. Then snips nope. Finally she pulled out the side cutters. She hugged them to her and crawled out of the truck. When she got down she listened; the noise in the house had stopped. Crouching close to the ground she peeked around the back tire. He was standing out in the yard listening. He ran toward the shed again and went inside. She slid under the truck next to the tire on the other side. It seemed like an eternity before he came back out. Then he went to the barn and she could hear him throwing things. She crawled out and ran for the shed trying not to make any noise. Inside she scampered up the ladder and slipped into the water next to her dad.

"Karen listen," he whispered, "Don't start at the top. If those wires break I'll drown. You'll have to go down and start at my feet. Don't try to hold your breath too long. Come up for air as often as you need to." Her head went below the surface.

Click, click, click, click she cut the wire one or two strands at a time. Slowly her head came above the water. She breathed as quietly as she could. She took a deep breath and slid below the surface again. Click, click, click, click Karen came up with her head back. She moved over beside her dad listening. She could hear him raging. She went down again. Click, click, click, click this time she was down longer.

George began to worry. "Karen don't drown on me I need you." Finally she came up.

"I'm up to your knees Dad."

"Take it easy honey get your breath." Her head disappeared again. Click, click, click, click she was down longer this time or it seemed like it. When she got to his waist she started on the wires around his arms cutting close to his right arm. As the wire came loose he began to bend his arm. Pulling at the wire around his legs. Finally she came up and gave a long gasp. She took deep breaths for a half a minute and sank again. When she reached his shoulders the wire gave way and he sunk to the bottom. For a few seconds he wrestled with the wire then broke for the surface. Karen was hanging onto the side. He grabbed her and kissed her and hugged her.

"Listen baby do you think you can get to the corral?" She nodded.

"Put the bridle on Butch and ride for Maya's as fast as you can go. I can take care of this guy now. Tell Maya to call the Sheriff." he helped her out of the water. She went down the ladder without a sound. She peeped out the opening. She could see flames in the kitchen. He was burning the house down. Karen saw him pass a window. She ran for the corral. Karen came in on the back side and slid under the bottom bar. Butch's ears jerked up and he grunted.

"Shh be quiet butch. Come here boy, come here butch." he dropped his head and started toward her. She went into the shed and pulled his bridle down as he approached. When she tried to put the bit in his mouth he bobbed his head and she couldn't reach his mouth.

"Come on Butch. Put your head down boy." he lowered his head and she slipped the bit between his teeth. Now to get the strap over his ears.

"Get your head down boy I got to get this over your ears."

She stretched and finally he put his head down far enough for her to slip the strap over his ears. She scrambled on as quick as she could. Leaning forward she whispered, "We got to get the gate open."

Butch moved over to the gate as if he understood. Karen pulled the latch and Butch broke out in a run. It was then she saw the maniac running across the yard. Butch was moving so quick she almost lost her balance. Michael was running as fast as he could, but the horse was just ahead of him. He dove for the horses tail and missed. Karen was gone in a flash.

George was working the last of the wire off his shoulders when Michael landed on his face out in the yard. George ran out of the shed and headed for the trees behind the barn. He stopped at the corner of the building and turned.

"Hey Crazy, over here." Then he turned and ran. Crazy followed with the hunting knife in his hand, screaming all the way. George hurried into the trees and found two small pines close together, he wrapped a piece of wire he had been carrying around one tree and then the other. He stood between them and yelled.

"Come on nut, hurry up!" Michael was furious that this guy wasn't afraid of him. He wanted to cut him in pieces. When he was almost to the trees George darted away into the shadows. Michael went between the trees and caught his foot on the wire and went down hard. It knocked the breath out of him. Before he could recover George was on him. He slammed Michael's hand on the ground and the knife flew out. George grabbed the handle and with both hands he drove the blade into Michael's back, all the way to the handle. Michael struggled for a few seconds then his face dropped into the dirt. George waited for a second or two before he released the handle. The maniac was dead.

George could hear the siren coming up the road. Then the flashing lights came into view. The whole house was in flames by this time. It would be a total loss.

The Sheriff and his deputies jumped out of the car with

guns drawn. They split up looking everywhere.

George waited a few seconds and then called, "Over here Sheriff, over here in the trees."

Three or four lights shined that way. They came rushing to him. They grabbed him with a sigh of relief.

"Where's he at?" they said in excited voices.

"Back there between those two small trees. They ran that way, and when George followed there were four lights shining on the maniac's body.

"Well that's the end of him." the Sheriff said. Several more cars were in the yard. More deputies and several farmers that were listening to scanners in the night were waiting to see what had happened.

"All right everybody let's go back out in the yard." The Sheriff held his hand up and they stopped a little ways from the group.

"Listen up everybody we need some help, but the first thing I need to tell you all is no one says anything about what you see here tonight. This mess stops here. We are going to take care of it and forget it. Now here's what I want. Carl you take Bill and park his truck across the gate and don't let anyone in. Pete you got any of that heavy black plastic?"

Pete nodded.

"Go get it. And hurry back. George, you and the deputies come with me." The Sheriff started back toward the trees. When they got to the body he said, "When Pete gets back we are going to wrap this thing up and take it to the grave yard and bury it. No marker, no cross, nothing. You all understand." They nodded in silence.

"Don't tell anyone what happened here. This has been bad enough I don't want no stories goin around. And we don't need any National press in Hugo."

A few minutes later Pete was back with a roll of black plastic. They wound the body and tied it with the wire that he had used on George.

"George can we use your truck?" the Sheriff asked.

"You betcha." he backed the truck to the edge of the barn and dropped the tail gate. The men slid the body in and the deputies rode in the back.

"Stop in town at the hardware store. We need some shovels and a pick." After they had picked up the tools they drove to the cemetery. The Sheriff directed them to the back corner of the land. When they got out he showed them where to dig. They took turns digging three at a time.

"I want it deeper than six foot." the Sheriff said. So if any one ever checks they still won't find him."

When they got down deep enough the sheriff measured the depth; seven and a half feet.

"That should do it boys." They dropped the body in and it made a plopping sound as it hit the bottom. They wasted no time filling it in. When they had it filled the Sheriff told them to drop rocks on top until it was covered.

While the burial was going on Maya was comforting Karen.

"Daddy will be back soon. Don't worry everything will be all right." She said as she hugged her tight.

"Maya, could we move into your house?" she asked innocently while staring off into the distance.

"Yeah, maybe that's not such a bad idea after all." She said with a grin.

It was getting daylight when George drove up to Maya's house. Karen ran out to meet him. Hugging him fiercely.

"I love you Daddy." Maya came up to him and put her arms around him laying her head on his chest.

"Thanks Maya, I don't know how I could ever repay you for all you have done for us.'

She pushed him back a little and grabbed the front of his shirt, and jerked him close to her.

"Well I know how you can repay me." she said in a husky voice.

"Marry me and take me as your dependant and you can move into my house since you don't have one anymore."

George was staggered. He looked at Maya with a sheepish

grin. "Well I didn't know you felt that way Maya."

"Yeah I know, men are such dunces. She reached up and kissed him. "Come on I'll fix you two some breakfast."

They all three went into the house together.

Giant

Patricia Woods is on her way home from work. She comes out of the office building into the parking garage. Her car is just a few spaces down the wall on the left from the elevator. Her office is on the twelfth floor and the car is on the third level. Being careful she already has her keys out and has her purse open so she can reach the can of mace spray. She knows of a girl who was attacked in the recent past and she doesn't want to be the next victim. As she walks toward her new Saturn she looks between the cars making sure no one is squatting down between them. Patricia hurries to her car, pushes the door opener and it chirps. As she reaches for the door handle... Thump! She goes down unconscious and a man picks her up and puts her in another car. This one is a Lincoln Town car. The car drives away.

    Three days later Patricia Woods comes to behind the wheel of her Saturn in the parking garage. The headache she is enduring is a jack hammer headache. She is confused and doesn't know what happened. She remembers reaching for the door handle, but doesn't remember getting in the car. What she doesn't realize yet is that it's three days later.

    She looks toward the opening between the floors and it doesn't seem like five minutes after five in the afternoon. The day is bright telling her it's morning. She looks at her watch and the date window says it's three days later. Patricia shakes her head.

"What happened?" Her hand goes to the top of her head and there is a bump there and it's very sore. Patricia decides to see if she can still get in the building. The door is open so she tries the elevator. When she reaches the twelfth floor she steps out into a bustling office crew. She sees her office manager Marge looking at her wide eyed. Marge runs over to her and wants to know where she has been.

"Patricia where have you been for the last three days? The police have been looking for you. We thought you had been kidnapped. Your family has been looking for you. Someone saw your car in the garage and felt something was wrong so we called the police. Are you all right?"

Patricia stares open mouthed. Then closes her eyes and faints. When she comes to she is laying on one of the couches in the break room with people all around her. The company nurse is attending to her; wiping her forehead with a damp cloth.

Her vision swims a little and her head still hurts. She puts her hand to her head and says, "My head hurts, someone hit me with a club or something." The nurse gently checks her head and sure enough there is a bump there. She picks up the phone and calls an ambulance.

"You could have a concussion we better have you checked out." the nurse says.

The CEO comes over and takes Patricia's hand,

"Don't worry we'll take care of everything. And from now on there will be security on every level of the garage."

A few minutes later two paramedics arrive and put Patricia on a gurney and take her down to a waiting ambulance. One of the girls that works with Patricia goes with her to explain the situation to the doctor. For some reason Patricia fades in and out on the way to the hospital. Patricia is a slight young woman with long brown hair and big brown eyes. She is only five foot two and weighs a hundred and twenty pounds. She has her Mother and Father and a Sister for family. The four of them are very close.

Marge the office manager is on the phone with Patricia's mother. "Yes she walked in a few minutes ago looking starry eyed and fainted when I spoke to her. The company nurse looked her over and we discovered she had a nasty bump on her head like someone had hit her pretty hard. So we sent her to St. Mary's hospital. She's probably still in the emergency room right now. Okay please let us know how she is. Thanks. Bye" The rest of the Woods family rush to get to the hospital. When they arrive they are told Patricia is in radiology getting a cat scan. And blood tests will be taken then evaluated. Her family walks the floor of the waiting room full of anxiety. After the testing is complete the doctor determines that there is no concussion but Patricia needs rest and pain medication. He sends her home with her family. A week later Patricia is allowed to return to work. Everything seems normal. Her fellow employees are happy to have her back.

Six weeks later

Patricia wakes one morning sick to her stomach. She vomits several times, but the sickness hangs on. She calls in to work and tells them she will have to take the day off. Finally about noon she begins to feel better. She thinks it's her period starting, but there is no period. Now she begins to worry, so she goes to the doctor. She really wants to know what happened during those three days she was out of contact with reality.

"Well Patricia, after taking these tests, you and your husband will be happy you are going to be a mother. You are pregnant. That is the reason for the sickness; it's called morning sickness. Otherwise you are very healthy." Patricia sits staring at the doctor with her mouth open.

"Doctor I'm not married, I've never been with a man."

"Well I don't know what to say but you definitely have conceived a child. Maybe someone did something to you during the three days you were missing." When Patricia gets back to her apartment she calls her mother.

"Mom we have to talk I'm in trouble and I think it's from those three days I was gone. Are you going to be at home today? Okay I'll be there in a few minutes." When she arrives at her parents house her mother is in a tizzy. She hugs her daughter and cries. Her sister tries to console her. Patricia waits until the family settles down and she and her mother can talk alone. Later in the day they sit in her mothers bedroom and she explains what the doctor told her and the confusion from the experience.

"Mom I don't know what they did to me. What can I tell the police? One minute I'm at the door of my car and the next I wake up sitting at the wheel and it's three days later with no evidence of what happened. My clothes weren't even wrinkled. How can I go to work blown up like a balloon and not even have a boyfriend. To say nothing of my reputation."

At that moment her father comes into the bedroom and closes the door. He sits down beside his daughter. "Pattie honey, I realize this is awful and it's a terrible blow to your mother and I. I'm not a violent man, but if I could find out who did this… Now sweetheart there are ways to take care of this and I've thought about it and this isn't your fault. You are being used by some vicious Frankenstein for some twisted purpose and I think we should stop this as soon as we can."

Patricia agrees and they start calling clinics and finally get an appointment to go see the doctor in one of them. The doctor has a quiet personality and speaks very kindly and gently with understanding.

"Miss woods I understand your situation and I whole heartedly agree with your decision. This procedure will be painless. After the procedure we will send samples to a lab and try to find out what happened. We can give the results to the authorities and maybe they can catch these criminals. We

can do the procedure this Friday if you feel up to it."
Patricia agrees and makes an appointment to come in Friday morning. She and her mother go home and continue to worry. Her father and her sister try to console her.

That night a dark figure approaches the back door of the clinic and inserts a lock pick into the lock and forces the tumblers. He goes inside and finds a closet and closes the door and sits down in the dark and goes to sleep. The next morning at nine the nurse comes in and prepares for the day. It will be busy for they have several cases to handle. Foolish young girls, most of them, who really don't know yet what life is all about. Of course the people in this business are in it for the money and they are making a lot of it.

While she is getting things ready for the day the stranger in the closet slips across the hall to the operating room and waits. At ten the doctor shows up and the first patient comes in. He and the nurse discuss the events for the day. The nurse goes into the operating room to prepare for the first procedure as she steps in a mechanical hand grabs her by the throat and jerks her in and quietly closes the door. She can't scream because the mechanical fingers are squeezing her throat so tight blood is leaking around the fingers. He lifts her off the floor and lays her body on the operating table and still using only one hand tears out her throat and throws the handful of flesh on the floor. Unfortunately her heart is still beating. The man plunges the mechanical hand into her chest cavity and pulls out her heart and drops it on the floor next to the remnants of her throat. He then steps over to the door to wait for the doctor. When the doctor steps in almost the same thing happens. Except the man grabs the doctor by the back of the neck and takes him over to the table and pushes his face into the nurses chest cavity and then pulls him out. The doctor is sputtering blood when the guy plunges the metal hand into his chest and throws his heart down next to the nurse's. Then he lays the doctors body face down on top of the dead nurse. He takes time to wash the blood off his hand at the small sink. He then slips out the back door the way he came.

Two hours later there are Police and crime scene people all over the place. The next ones to show up are the press.

The next morning when Patricia's dad picks up the newspaper there is death all over the front page. He goes inside to tell his wife about the horrible catastrophe and when she sees the front page she faints. He carries her into the bedroom and tries to revive her. When she comes to she says in a hushed voice.

"Jack, that is the same clinic that we went to for an appointment for Patricia!" Jack stared off into space with his mouth hanging open.

Patricia came into the bedroom pale as a ghost. "That is the same clinic we went to Mom!"

Her sister is right behind her crying. "Oh Dad they are going to kill Patricia!"

"Oh no their not. I'll kill every one of them who tries to get in here."

"Dad they have taken my life away from me. I won't even be able to go outside." Patricia says with tears streaming down her face. Her mother picks up the phone and dials the police. She tells the woman that answers the call she thinks the crime committed the day before, is related to her daughters appointment made a few days earlier. Two hours later the same two detectives arrive.

"What makes you think these incidents are related Ma'am?"

Patricia and her mother tell them about the report of her disappearance months before and the discovery of her pregnancy.

"Someone must want my daughter to give birth to this child awfully bad to kill a doctor and a nurse because of it."

"Well now we don't know that for sure ma'am. But we will keep that in mind because I remember the incident when you folks reported it. It is possible and we will check that avenue to make sure."

"Patricia we can still do something about this because we don't know for sure if your are even involved. That doctor may have been involved in some crime we don't even know about." Her mother says after the detectives have gone.

"Maybe if we went out of the country and had it done…" Jack says.

After worrying for a couple of days Patricia calls the company where she works and takes an extended leave of absence. She then tells her father maybe this will be the best way. So Jack decides they will sneak out just before dark. The whole family gets into the station wagon and they drive South late that afternoon. When they get across the state line into California they stop for gas and a pit stop. The restrooms are around the side of the building. Pattie's sister is inside the store picking out junk food to eat along the way. Her mother goes to the ladies room alone and is inside for a long time and Patricia starts to worry. Finally mom comes out and Reba emerges from the store and goes to the restroom. When she steps inside the light is out; she closes the door and flips up the switch. When she turns around, she opens her mouth to scream and a hand with a cloth in it covers her face. A few moments later a man comes out carrying Reba. He goes to the back of the building and puts her in the Lincoln, gets in and they drive away.

Jack begins to wonder what has happened to his youngest daughter and goes around to the restroom door and knocks. A strange woman comes out.

"Oh I'm sorry ma'am I was looking for my daughter."

"There was no one in there when I went in." she says. Jack begins to search the area behind the station. He finds Reba's shoe laying in the open lot behind the building. He grabs it and runs around to the car.

"Mom is this Reba's shoe?" She puts her hand up to her mouth and screams. Jack runs inside to call the Highway Patrol. After many hours of questions and filing out a report the patrolman sends them on their way.

Several hours later they arrive home tired and distraught. They stumble inside and fall on the couch and in the easy chair. Finally Patricia goes toward the back of the house to the bathroom and as she passes Reba's bedroom door she sees, in the faint glow of the night light, her sister laying on the bed asleep.

"Mom! Dad! She's in here!" They come running. Confused. They turn on the light and sure enough there is Reba asleep. Mom and Patricia pile on her hugging and weeping for joy.

A couple of hours later Reba starts to come around waking gradually.

"Oh baby what happened?" Mom asks.

"Well I remember going into the restroom and turning on the light and a man pushed a rag in my face and I must have passed out."

"Do you remember what he looked like?"

"No he had a black mask over his face and all I could see were his eyes. It happened so fast."

"Well that takes care of going out of state. They, whoever they are, are watching us and pretty closely too." Dad remarks.

"We need to call the police in the morning and tell them what happened." Pattie says.

Jack goes to the closet an takes out his twelve gauge shotgun and says, "I'll stay up and watch, you girls get some sleep."

No one argues; they are dead tired. Dad sits in a straight chair in the hall with the shotgun across his lap. It is loaded with double 00 buckshot. A couple of hours later about four in the morning he nods and dozes for a moment or two. He is jolted into reality by a scream in the bedroom. He jumps and runs in. When he turns on the light there are only two women in the bed. Patricia is missing again. The bedroom window is open. In total rage he climbs out and looks around but there's no one or evidence of anyone having been there. The next thing he does is call the police. The same two detectives answer the call and Mr. Woods explains what happened on the trip to California. One of the officers calls the CHP and explains the situation and that the missing daughter has been found and they can cancel the search for her, but now they have to start looking for Patricia again.

When the officers get outside one says to the other. "I've got a sneaking hunch that no one is going to hurt this woman. This I think is related to the medical world and they are checking her progress. I'll bet my next weeks salary she'll show up in a day or two, so let's sit on this a while and see, but we won't tell the family. This woman means a lot to someone out there. I can't help wonder what's going on."

The next morning one of the detectives is sitting in the bushes across the street on a neighbor's property. About seven he doesn't think anything is going to happen so he goes to the rear of the property and drives away in his car. The rest of the Woods family rises about ten dejected and tired of all the worry. They are sitting in the dining room eating donuts and drinking strong coffee. Trying to come out of the fog from the night before. They hear a thump at the front door. Jack jumps up and runs. The women follow. When he opens the door the top half of Patricia's body falls in. He bends down and picks her up and carries her to her bedroom. Reba is pulling her hair back and Mom is washing her face with a wet cloth. She looks like she has been drugged.

A strange voice says, "You people don't catch on very quick."

They all jump with fear and rightly so, for the guy is holding Jack's shotgun. He is dressed in black. He's about six feet tall and looks to weigh in at about two thirty. Jack decides that he will listen calmly to what this guy has to say.

"Now let me tell you the game plan and don't miss a word or it could cost you your daughter's life. She is going to have this child and there is nothing you can do to stop it so just sit back and relax. There will be a lot less trouble if you do. When the baby is ready to be delivered we will come and pick her up and when it's born and stable we will bring her and the baby home. So clam down and quit calling the cops." he walks out the door with Jack's shotgun. The last thing they hear is the front door closing.

Jack rushes into the living room and sees his gun propped against the wall next to the door.

In the bedroom Reba notices the windows open. She figures that's how the guy got in.

Jack comes back with his gun and says, "Well at least he didn't take my gun. So I guess we know now that they don't mean to harm her. So we can relax a little."

During her forth month Patricia came up missing for a day. The next day she was back asleep on Reba's bed. The bad side of this was the baby was growing at a phenomenal rate. Patricia was already the size of a woman ready to give birth. And she had five months to go.

At the end of eight months and six days Patricia had grown to a state where she could not walk and the family had to rent a large wheel chair to move her around. That day someone knocked on the front door. When Jack opened it there were two men in ski masks looking at him.

"We came for the girl. The doctor says the baby will have to be taken C-section or she won't make it."

"What have you people done to my daughter?" Jack says in an angry voice. A big ten millimeter automatic comes out of both their coats.

"Go get her and bring her here." One of the men says in an equally angry tone. Jack goes out on the patio where the women are sitting having breakfast.

"They have come for you Patricia and they have guns." Mom starts crying and Reba has an frightened look on her face. Dad steps around and takes hold of he chair handles. When he turns the men with the ten millimeters are in the door watching. He pushes his daughter toward the front of the house. Outside they take over, putting a black hood over her head and then put her in a black van. The family watches as the van drives away.

Patricia is gone this time for a week. The family is walking the floor worrying. The following weekend they return her to her parents home. When she comes into the house she almost can't carry the child it is so big.

"My Lord Patricia, what happened."

"They took very good care of me and the C-section went well, but this kid is the hungriest boy I've ever seen. When he was born he weighed fourteen pounds and was twenty-three inches long. He has already started to grow at an amazing rate. He weighed twenty-one pounds this morning and had three bottles of formula, which they will deliver each week until he starts eating solid food." The rest of the family stood and looked at the child laying on the bed. Yes, he was huge for a newborn. His appearance was normal except for his size. His hair was light brown, his eyes were blue and a little small for his size.

"What are you going to name him?" Jack asked.

"They already took care of that. You see it's about him not me. They said I would call him Anak. I have no choice they have already submitted the paper work to the office of records."

Grandma was already playing with him touching him on his cheeks and he smiled as she cooed at him.

Later when Anak was hungry he started to cry and he could be heard all over the house and everybody came running. His cry was husky and very loud.

"Wow this kid has got a good set of lungs." Dad said. Patricia came into the bedroom with three bottles of formula.

"He takes that much.?" her dad asked.

"Yeah this much and as he grows it will be much more before we are giving him mashed cereal." The doctor at the laboratory said he should start on solids sooner than normal children. I'm going to try to be ready with his bottles tonight or he'll wake the whole neighborhood."

In six weeks Anak was taking solid food and clamoring for

more. His growth was amazing. By the time he was a year old he was twice the size of a normal one year old. A few days after his first birthday, he came walking into the living room on his own. Everyone sat with their mouths open in shock. He wasn't stumbling like most kids do when they first start walking. It was one foot in front of the other. When Grandpa held out his hand Anak grabbed two of his fingers with strength.

"Hey! Big guy let up on your old grandpa. Man he's got a grip." Patricia tried to set him down to play with some of his toys, but he kept backing up and wiggling away from her giggling all the time.

"I've never seen a kid with such balance. When he doesn't want to sit down he won't sit down." Reba said watching him.

"Do you like your Aunt Reba?" Patricia asked him. He put his hands together in front of his face and made a noise pointing to his Mother.

"Gaa."

"What does that mean?" Reba asked.

"Gaa," he repeated with a serious look pointing to his Mother again.

Patricia took hold of his hands and said, "Ma ma." pointing to herself. His beautiful blue eyes focused on her face.

Forming his first question he repeated, "Ma…Ma?" Patricia was so happy she could have almost cried. She nodded and said, "Mama." She knelt down grabbed him and hugged him and kissed his cheek. When she let go there was a scream of joy from Anak she hadn't expected.

"Eeeeeeiii!" He slapped his hands together and fell back on his rump. The screech almost deafened Patricia's ears.

Everyone else in the room stared in shock.

She held her finger to her lips. "Shh say it quietly." She said in a whisper.

He put his finger up and gave her a slushy shhhh, grinning as he did. Then he said it again.

"Ma ma?" Then he lunged forward and grabbed her around the neck.

"WOW, Son I've got to teach you how to hug too." She held him tight and rocked him back and forth. Then she remembered how he had come into her life and felt a pang of sadness. Deep inside she felt that one day they would want to take him away from her, but this was still her child and she loved him in spite of what he was or would be.

The next week the family took Anak to a photo shop and had pictures taken with the whole family. She wouldn't let the photographer take pictures of Anak alone for some reason. She didn't know why, but it just didn't seem right. They ordered lots of 5x7's and one 8x10 of the whole family. Then they went to a framing shop and bought a fancy frame for the 8x10. When Patricia picked up the pictures she was so happy she was almost giddy. She picked up the large frame at the same time and went by Wal-Mart and bought several 5x7 frames. On the way home she felt like hiding one of the 5x7's of Anak and her so she did. When Patricia came in everybody was excited over the pictures and they all participated in putting them in the frames. Times like this seemed to draw them together. Everyone was happy even Anak. He seemed mesmerized by the big picture of he and his mother. He held it for a long time and stared at it as the rest watched to see what he would do. Finally he held it up and tried to kiss the photo leaving a smear on the glass.

Patricia took the picture and Anak looked up and said, "Ma ma."

"And Anak too." She said. He squealed and rolled backward and grabbed his toes.

Patricia took hold of his arms and said, "Anak, Can you say Aunt Reba?"

In a quiet voice he said, "Ank beba."

They all laughed.

That night while Patricia listened to Anak breathing in his crib (which would soon be too small) she breathed a prayer of thanks for this child. She felt he was truly hers. The men from the lab hadn't bothered them in several months now and she began to wonder when they would intrude into their lives again. She was sure they would consequently there was always a feeling of apprehension. Slowly she closed her eyes and dozed off.

The next morning the whole family went grocery shopping. It seemed they all wanted to be together. The closeness gave them a feeling of safety. They were all feeling the same thing and asking the same question in their minds. When? While they pushed the cart they took turns playing with Anak and he loved every minute of it. Finally he got tired and fell asleep. When they were getting in the car Jack had to lift Anak into the car seat because he had gotten so big.

"Boy you are a bundle." his Grandpa said.

Patricia covered him with a blanket and he slept all the way home.

When they arrived at the house Jack pulled over to the curb across the street and stopped. For a second he sat looking at the house.

"What's the matter Jack?" Thelma asked. The two girls sat in rapt silence.

"They've been here while we were gone. I feel it."

The two girls were holding their breath afraid to breathe. Fearful that if the silence was broken they would know something terrible had happened. Slowly Jack put the car in gear and pulled into the drive way. Carefully they all got out and moved toward the front door.

Once inside they began looking around for evidence that someone had been there. It took a while before it registered, then Thelma burst into tears.

"What Mama, what!" Reba cried.

Jack saw it after Thelma. And said, "Oh no." Patricia noticed and ran for the bedroom. The sight in there was even worse. She cried out in anguish. Everyone rushed in behind her with their mouths open. Someone had come in and taken all the pictures of Anak and all of his toys and his swing. They had even removed his baby bed and in it's place was a short version of a twin bed. In the middle of it was a pile of clothes that were made to fit him. They were all plain colors blue, green, yellow and red. They had robbed the Woods family of their memories, and left a drab future in it's place.

"Why would they do this. These things couldn't do any harm." Thelma cried. Patricia repeated the line she had spoken before.

"It's not about us; it's about him." She thought of the picture she had hidden.

Five years went by and they had almost forgotten about the incident. When Anak was six they were trying to decide what to do about kindergarten. Anak was so much bigger than the rest of the children he would be going to school with. The answer came with a knock at the front door. When Jack opened it there was short man with a stern look on his face standing there.

"Yes may I help you?"

"We will be sending a car by next week on Wednesday to pick up the boy for school." With that he turned and walked away. Jack stood there dumbstruck. When he turned around the women were staring at him.

"Mom, Dad, Reba come in here a moment I have something to tell you."

They went into the living room and sat down.

"Listen everyone, they have, and will continue to take everything we have of Anak and there is only one thing left that they can't take and that's our love. If we will show him and tell him we love him he will not forget. I don't think there is anything else we can give because they will take it away."

"You talk like they are going to take him for good Patricia." Reba said.

"Yes I think this is the beginning, first school and then less and less time with us. Eventually Anak will belong totally to them and won't be able to come back here at all. That's the reason we must let him know what love is and maybe they won't alter his mind and he won't forget us. If so he will find a way back."

The next few weeks they all talked to Anak and explained the best they could how much they loved him and no matter what happened they would never forget him and hoped he would never forget them.

"I can't forget you Mommie. Why do you think I would? I love you very much." he said as he hugged her.

"The reason we are telling you these things is because we know things about these people that you don't know and we want you to remember us."

Eventually things happened just the way Patricia had said. By the time Anak was twelve the school wouldn't let him go back to his family. They gave him a private room and locked him in at night. His tutors were bland and uncaring answering him mostly in one word answers. They offered very few explanations for the type of life he was made to live.

Anak was an intelligent boy and did well in his schooling understanding whatever he was taught. When he was thirteen he had grown to an enormous eight feet in height and weighed three hundred and twenty pounds. The size of his quarters were increased and he was given a ten foot bed. His clothes were specially made and he was dressed very neatly. The only time he was allowed to leave the facility was on Sunday. At times the chauffer would just take him for a drive and then at other times he would take him to a gym and let him play basketball. After a few days Anak had no trouble hitting the goal every time from the half court line. During the rest of his time he was in class or was being examined and given tests at the clinic. When he asked what they were doing he was always told it was of no concern of his. A few months later he was given a shot that increased his growth rate and by the time he was fifteen he was over nine feet tall and weighed another hundred pounds. Because of the growth hormone they were giving him; there was a lot of pain in his joints.

By this time he realized he was nothing more to them than an experiment. The next week when they wanted him to lift certain weights he refused. After he had gone to sleep someone slipped in during the night and put a steel collar around his neck and chained him to the wall above his bed. Then they put iron bars across the wall where the door had been. They told him he would not be permitted to leave the cell if he didn't do what they told him. Anak's food portions were cut down and he was hungry most of the time now. After several days he grew weak and couldn't stand. The headmaster told him they would let him die, that he meant nothing to them. He had one last chance to take orders, it was up to him. Finally he said he would do whatever they told him. They brought him plenty of food and sports drink. His strength began to return. They gave him another shot and the pain in his joints returned for a couple of days. They took him to an exercise room and told him to lift a bar. The trainers asked what it felt like. Anak told them it was nothing. When they added a hundred pounds he hefted it and shrugged his shoulders. They added another hundred and Anak lifted it with ease telling them it was still easy. They added another hundred and he said it was heavy. When another hundred was added he told them he couldn't do it, he would need practice. But what was really happening Anak was forming a plan in his mind. His strength was far greater than they knew, but he didn't want them to know that. The trainers suspected Anak could lift more, but they didn't know how much more.

By the time Anak was eighteen he was ten feet tall and weighed another hundred pounds. Which brought him to a little over five hundred pounds, but he was still agile and fast.

The trainers still chained Anak to the wall at night, of course they had increased the link size of the chain to half inch, and he chuckled to himself. As he lay there in the dark a thought came to him. He remembered the love his mother had shown him when he was little. How his Aunt Reba, used to play with him. Oh and Grandma and Grandpa. How he missed them. It had been so long since he had thought about them and it would be so good to see them again.

He whispered in the darkness, "I love you Mom. I love

you Aunt Reba. I love you Grandma and Grandpa. Suddenly a pang of desire came over him so strong he couldn't contain himself and he wept. As he lay there in the darkness weeping his muscles began to ripple. If he wanted he could go and see them and the robots with no hearts in this place couldn't stop him. Anak reached up and took hold of the chain. When he pulled the chain his muscles rippled again and the concrete in the wall cracked. He smiled and went to sleep.

The next morning when the male nurse came to take Anak to the clinic, he didn't notice the crack in the wall. After testing all morning they let him go to the dining room and have lunch. Of course his lunch consisted of a lot more than most people could eat. Today he had six sandwiches and two large pieces of cake. Then he finished off a gallon of milk. They never gave him soda pop or candy only water, milk or sports drinks. After lunch Anak went back to his room. He sat on the side of his bed and looked at the window. He studied the frame. The pane was made of half inch bullet proof glass, but Anak thought he could punch out the whole window. They hadn't made the frame as strong as the glass. The screws around the frame were too small to be of any use. He stood and pushed on the frame in the bottom corner. Two of the screws sheared off. He pulled the frame back into place.

The male nurse came to get him.

"Anak it is time to go the gym for exercise."

Anak turned and followed the nurse.

Günter Radic sat in his office studying the test results they had left from Anak's testing that morning. In his mind he thought if he could get this boy to cooperate, Anak would be the strongest man in the world. So far he wasn't giving them his best and Radic knew it, but there were ways to get things out of him. If events went the way he wanted them to he could produce an army of these men from the DNA he had stored in a freezer in the lab under the ground where Anak had been produced. First though he must be sure that things didn't go awry just when the project was about to be completed. A couple of years and no one could stop this boy. There were certain things that could be done to the kid and the authorities couldn't even find him under their noses. Gunter leaned back and smiled as he thought of his staff, how faithful they had been on this project and the excitement they had for its completion. Even they didn't know what Gunter had in mind and the serum he had developed in private. If things went well it would make Anak invisible when he really wanted to be, but Gunter would save this matter for the very last.

In the old country Gunter's father had been a German scientist before they were called geneticists. Gunter had been born with a brilliant mind and he learned things very quickly and was soon learning in his father's laboratory as a prodigy. The old German family they came from was rich beyond belief and he and his father were able to continue their experiments unnoticed. When his father died Gunter came to the United States and started setting up a laboratory as soon as he was established as a citizen. He met a German girl (Marsha Leipzig) and they were married a few weeks after he met her. She became his faithful assistant and they prospered and gained government projects that they performed in secret, but even the American government didn't know about Anak.

As he stood at the half court line he finally grew tired of throwing swishers. There was no one his size to play with or present any opposition. He was too big and too strong. After the last basket he let the ball drop to the floor and started toward the weight room. There weren't enough weights to present a challenge, but he continued to lift them not wanting to reveal his full strength. When he concentrated his muscles would ripple and he felt like he could lift a house.

Once when they were taking him out for a ride the driver forgot something and went back inside for a moment. Anak went over to one of the pickup trucks parked in the drive and lifted the rear end above his head and set it down again. The whole truck weighed forty-three hundred pounds and he was lifting at least half. He stood smiling while he waited for the driver. He thought he could throw the driver at least a hundred feet. Hmm!

What the driver went back after was the mechanical hand that he put over his and connected to a small hydraulic unit under his coat. With this he could control Anak if he got rough. With the talons on the hand he had torn out the hearts of two people already.

While Anak lifted the weights he thought it was such a waste of time when he could lift three times that much, but while he was in the weight room he made it look like he was straining while he did a free press or a bench press. The company bought him a BOWFLEX machine and the first time he used it he set it on the highest setting and broke it. They took it back to the Sporting Goods store and got their money back telling the clerk that there was a fault in the machine.

Perhaps he would break out tonight and go to see his family. He had brute strength, but he could be very cunning and sneaking out would be no challenge for Anak. In the early hours of the morning Anak sheared off the rest of the screws in the window frame except one on each side at the top, which made a sort of hinge and let the window swing open while Anak crawled out. He quickly crept to the gate of the property and climbed over. He bent two of the arrow points down and crawled over and then bent them back into place. Once out on the road he looked around and discovered he was not where he thought he was. This research laboratory was made to look like the one he had been in the town his mother lived in. But he soon realized he was nowhere close to his family.

He started to run in a Easterly direction hoping he would find a town not far away. When he had run for five miles he finally came to a small town. The first house he came to he knocked on the door and when the woman opened it she ran back away from the door calling her husband. He came to the door and looked up at Anak in surprise.

"I'm lost sir. he said, could you tell me what town this is

and what state I'm in.

"Billings Missouri son." he then realized he was eighteen hundred miles from home in Nevada.

"Is it possible that I could use your phone sir?"

"Well I don't think you would fit in our house. Wait just a minute." He went back into the house and returned with a cell phone. The man dialed Anak's grandfather's number and held the small phone to his ear. Anak hoped his family still lived in the same house.

The number began to ring. Finally someone said, "Hello, this is the Woods residence."

"Hi Aunt Reba, It's Anak."

He heard a squeal on the other end.

Anak! Where are you we'll come and get you."

"No Aunt Reba that isn't possible. Could I speak to Mom a moment?" he heard her calling Patricia to come to the phone quick.

"Hello?"

All he had to say was, "Hi Mom."

She screamed and burst into tears.

"Anak my baby. Where are you honey?"

"I'm in a small town in Missouri. Billings I think it is. Look Mom, I'm going to come home to visit. Don't tell anyone. The research center might still have people watching your house. I'm about eighteen hundred miles from you so it might take me a couple of days to get there, but I'll be there. I gotta go now I love you all. Bye." he moved away from the phone and took out a couple of twenties and handed to the man.

"Here sir I hope this will cover your bill for this month. Thank you very much."

"Yeah well anytime son anytime." As Anak walked away the couple stood in the door way gawking still not able to believe their eyes.

As Anak approached the road he turned back and called to them, "Which way to the next town with an airport?"

"That would be St. Louis, twenty miles North of here."

"Thanks again." He waved as he walked toward the main street of Billings.

When he reached the main street he pulled out another twenty and went into a restaurant. He had to duck low to get into the door and then keep his head down to keep from rubbing the ceiling. He went to a table and sat down. A hush had fallen over the people in the place and they were all staring at him. Finally the waitress got enough nerve to approach him.

"Good m-m-morning." she said in a shaky voice.

"What's the matter you never saw a giant before?" he smiled sweetly.

She shook her head and finally found her voice again. "Can I getcha somthin?"

"Yeah, how many orders of ham and eggs with twenty dollars buy?"

She turned her pad over and began to calculate. Finally she said, "Five sir."

"Okay bring me five orders and five large glasses of milk." the waitress wrote the order and went to the cook's window and hung the paper on the order rack. The people were still staring when the waitress walked away.

Anak looked around and said, "Hi everybody beautiful morning ain't it?"

They all jumped at one time and looked away in embarrassment. Anak shrugged his massive shoulders and picked up the menu to read. When his breakfast came the cook had put three orders on a large oval plate and two on another. The waitress had to bring the milk on a second trip. Anak dove in and devoured everything. The reason he had money was in the test laboratory some of the staff had hid three hundred in twenties for lunches. Anak found it and took two hundred, not nearly enough for this trip. But if he could find a plane he could ride he could use a credit card he had taken from one of the staff women.

When the waitress came back to give him the check she asked, "Will there be anything else sir?"

"Yes, do you have any pie?"

"Yes sir the cook made some berry pies fresh this morning. Would you like a piece?"

"Could you bring me a whole pie, a plate and two more glasses of milk please."

Her eyes grew wide as she looked at Anak.

"Sorry I'm pretty big on breakfast."

"Oh yeah how silly of me."

When he was finished he paid and walked to the door and could feel their eyes on him. When he reached the door he turned and said in his best southern voice, "Ya'll have an nice day now ya hear."

Once outside he roamed the main street of town until he came to a Greyhound loading passengers. He said to the driver, "Is there a bus that goes through here going to St Louis?"

"Yeah I'm going to St Louis, you got twenty dollars I'll take you with me."

Anak pulled out another twenty and gave it to the driver who punched a ticket and handed it to him.

"You'll probably have to sit in that seat across the back, you're too big for the others."

Anak nodded and the passengers watched him all the way to the back. From now on Anak would have to watch for the press. The minute one of those guys saw him it would be all over the country and the research lab would know right where he was.

"I've seen some big boys in my time, but that one is the biggest," the driver said.

In St. Louis Anak found a shuttle that would take him to the airport. He found a private company that would carry him to Las Vegas. He wouldn't fit in the seats on a commercial flight. And if they had to take out a seat divider he would have to buy two tickets. The plane arrived just before midnight that night. He left the airport with everyone watching him.

When the private plane was just leaving the ground in St. Louis two black sedans drove onto the tarmac and several men jumped out, but they had arrived two minutes too late, Anak was already in the air.

An hour later the men reported back to the lab and the doctor said, "All right we know where he is going so you men take one more man and go to Henderson where he grew up. If you can get him before he makes contact with those people put him to sleep and bring him back here. If you take the Leer Jet you may even get there before he does."

When the men arrived in Las Vegas they were ahead of the small plane that Anak was on by several hours and they weren't sure of the name of the company he rented the plane from. As it worked out the men were tired and their watch grew a little lax. One man went to the men's room and another stopped by the snack bar and the third guy just plain missed him. Once Anak got onto the road outside the airport he went out into the desert and cut across country. He hadn't run into anyone from the press but in the daytime he knew he wouldn't be so lucky. He arrived at the Woods home after three in the morning. He climbed over the wall in the rear of their property and tapped on the patio door. When Patricia and Reba heard the noise they were at the door in a second. He was kneeling down when Patricia leaped into his arms kissing his face. While Reba and Grandma and Grandpa hugged him from all sides.

"Oh Anak it is good to have you home again, but you are so much bigger now. What are we going to do?" At five hundred pounds he could no longer sit in regular chairs so he sat on the concrete patio. Grandma put down pillows and a blanket so he would have some padding to sit on.

"It will not be long before they come here looking for me so it would be wise to turn off the patio light. I guess you know I can't stay here. They will come in and hurt you if they find me here. So I will come at strange times or meet you in empty places where they won't think I will be. Can you bring me the phone?"

Patricia handed it to him.

"They will find me soon enough then I will have to give

them trouble to stay free. If they take me back to the laboratory that will be the end. They will take my mind and I will have no will of my own. This man Gunter Radic is an animal. He created me from a DNA that he spliced and enhanced and he has more in a place underground in Missouri to create an army of giants. One of his servants told me some of his plans and we must do everything we can to stop him or he could cause havoc around the world. As I understand from books I've read the information highway is the best way to stop him. If we expose him he will not be able to proceed and by then maybe I can get in and destroy the rest of the experimental cells."

The rest of the family sat in silence finding it hard to believe that it had grown to this stage.

"Okay I've got to get out of here they will be coming soon. You don't have to deny that I was here. Just tell them you don't know where I went and point out there into the desert. It would do no good to lie to them, that might cause you harm. If they try to take anyone hostage it will do them no good because I know their ways now and I can stop them. Grandpa get some long nylon ties, some small nylon rope and duct tape I will need it when I come next time. Put it over there close to the fence."

He moved out into the yard and hugged everyone and was gone over the fence in a couple seconds.

The Woods all went into the house like nothing happened. Though they didn't know it, Anak remained on the other side of the block wall at the end, sitting in the dark waiting for his enemy. He wanted to give them a taste of what they had put others through.

The Woods turned out the lights like they had gone to bed. They knew it would not be long before they had company. At five-thirty just before it got light outside the front door burst in and two men walked in and turned on a light in the living room. As a third man started in the door, something grabbed him and covered his mouth and silently jerked him back. He didn't have a chance to yell and the first two were concentrating on finding the Woods. They started toward the bedrooms.

Outside Anak covered the man's mouth and twisted one arm behind his back. He whispered in his ear, "If you resist I will break your arm and if you make a sound I will break your neck. You know I can do it."

He lifted him and carried him to the car. "Open the trunk." Inside just like he thought there was rope and tape, he put tape over the guy's mouth and tied his hands and dropped him in and closed the lid. He went back to the door and stood outside waiting. Finally they came out looking for the third man. He grabbed both of them and lifted them high, one in each hand. He spread his massive arms and slammed them together knocking them unconscious. He tied them up and taped their mouths. They were dealing with a different Anak now. Now they were dealing with a giant. He tied them up and put them in the car, took the keys and walked away.

Patricia told them that Anak had gone over the fence, and that was when they missed the third man. They went back to the front door to see what happened and Anak stepped in and grabbed them.

Anak was running in the early light at an easy pace not even breathing hard. His conditioning was an asset to him now. The sun was coming up and he noticed that there were a lot of concrete buildings at the edges of town. When finished these concrete walls would become office buildings, but until they were inhabited it might make a good place to store bodies. When found, the work crews might call the authorities. These guys could be embarrassed into holding back and convinced to leave the Woods family alone. He hoped his mother remembered to find a way to stay in contact with him.

Anak ran until he got to Black Mountain and began to climb up into the higher rocks. In the morning sunlight he could see the area where the Woods house was. He sat on an outcropping studying the lay of the land. He was going to have to get some warmer clothes. Even though it was spring it might be chilly out here at night.

Back at the Woods house Dad was fixing the front door

and the girls were making sandwiches, lots of them. They prepared a couple of back packs with water bottles and crackers and peanut butter snacks. They would put the sandwiches in when Anak came back.

Anak spent most of the day on the mountain watching and thinking. He watched the freeway and how the traffic moved and when it was most crowded. At the Woods house they had called the police and told them about the car outside. When the police arrived, they released the men but because of the conditions that made them suspect and they couldn't say anything about their mission so the police took them into custody until they would talk.

At the research center in Missouri, Gunter tried to get in contact with his men, but no one answered their phones. He had no idea what was happening. His wife suggested they take a trip to Nevada where they could handle matters themselves.

"We need to know what has happened first. I will wait for a call. If they are not dead they will call. Then we will take action." he told her in German.

Later that morning one of the men in black was allowed a call to the lab and notified Gunter that the three of them were in custody for possession of weapons without a permit to carry them. They could be bailed out, but the authorities would confiscate the guns. Radic told them he would take care of the bail and they should check in to a hotel and sit tight until someone else arrived. He would be sending a professional that would put the giant on ice and take care of shipping his body East. They were to assist this man and do whatever needed to be done to finish the job. Radic hung up and made another call.

"Hello Boris, this is Radic. I have a very important job that needs to be done. All right I don't care about money, there is someone that needs to be returned to the lab as soon as possible. This man is an experiment and he is highly dangerous to me while he is running loose. He must be found at any cost and returned to the lab. I want him alive if at all possible. Please!

Don't worry me with fees and extras this man must be found and returned here. He is in the state of Nevada in the town of Henderson somewhere. He is with a family by the name of Woods at this address..." He relayed the rest of the information and hung up. The man, Boris Clinkoff a Russian hit man had done jobs for Radic in the past. He was very good. In and out clean and quiet. Clinkoff was just across the Canadian border North of New York. An hour from then he would be on a plane headed for Las Vegas.

Radic turned to his wife, "Marsha, listen to me I want you to do exactly what I tell you. Right now is not a time for thinking for yourself. I want you to go upstairs and pack a couple of bags and prepare to travel. I will tell you what we are doing later. Do you understand?"

"Yes Mien Heir." she said as she smiled and glided away.

Gunter huffed in disgust at his wife's attempt at humor. He made another call to the lab and spoke to the head scientist.

"Carl, Prepare to shut things down and leave the country. I think the cat is out of the bag on the big boy. He's on the loose out West and I'm not sure we can get him back before he causes immeasurable damage to our experiment and I do not want any of our staff to fall into the hands of the FBI or the CIA. I want all of you people on planes traveling East do you understand? Very good."

Gunter went to a wall safe and removed a hypodermic needle and a vile of serum that was intended to be the final injection to complete the condition in Anak's life. He put them in his suit coat pocket. If he was able to give the injection it wouldn't matter then wherever Anak hid Gunter be able to find him because of the changes this injection would make.

In a matter of a few hours the scientists from Radic's lab would all be on a jet somewhere flying toward Europe. Hungary, Austria, Germany or somewhere in the Eastern bloc. The equipment in the lab below ground would be sealed off perhaps for use on some future date. Right now the important thing was to get out of the country before they were exposed.

Deep in the earth another place on the property had been reserved for the experiments that had gone amiss. It had a secret entrance, where creatures, that was the only thing they could be called, were locked away, some to be disposed of, some to be studied and some to be dissected for use in other experiments. In this huge tomb there were cries that rang all throughout the night. There were horrible grunts and groans of suffering. For these things there could be nothing normal, they were just genetic experiments and had to be disposed of now with the utmost haste.

A scientist's assistant ran out the back door of the lab to the entrance of the tomb. He went in and hurried down the stairs to a depth of thirty feet to a steel door with a thick glass set in the upper part. To the right of the door there was a red handle to a valve that held natural gas. The assistant looked inside once more and observed the cages then pulled the handle down and gas began to fill the sealed room. He stood a moment watching as they began to writhe and twist at the smell of the gas. Soon they all would be dead. He turned to go back to the lab and a look of horror came across his face. Someone above had already pushed the button that would fill the cavity. Dirt was pouring into the stairwell and sliding down. He ran to meet the earthen onslaught, but he had been too slow. The rushing earth drove him back to the door as wet cement mixed with the dirt. He screamed, but there was no one to hear him. And in a few hours the staircase would be a solid rock.

On Black Mountain the sun had just set and night was coming on, and it was time for Anak to get back to his home hoping there would be something to eat. He hadn't eaten all day and he was ravenous. He climbed down among the rocks hurrying as fast as he could. When he was at the bottom he turned and looked up at the face of the mountain thinking. Tomorrow, if tomorrow came, he would search the mountain for a cave if there were any. It would be good to have a place to hide out of the weather and the sight of other men. He continued on toward home where his family waited anxiously for him. After he had circled the street and observed the surroundings he went to the back wall and climbed over. The rest of the family came rushing out to meet him. They hurried him inside and put him on a low stool at the table and set food before him and told him of the back pack they had prepared. He tried, between ravenous bites, to put it on his shoulders. It was too small. Dad cut the straps and added rope to supplement the length. Patricia hugged him and told him how glad they were that he was home again. Inside Anak had a wonderful feeling of peace here, but he knew it would be short lived. They were coming and he could feel it. Once Gunter's employees were bailed out of jail they would probably be back too. He must be ready. He ate hurriedly and stood up bent over trying not to hit his head on the ceiling. He went out the front door this time and straight across the street to a neighbors yard and climbed up into a large pine tree in the front. Two thirds of the way up he straddled a limb and sat watching. The limb sagged with his weight, but fortunately there were limbs below him he could rest his feet on.

 Hours later when the small foreign car stopped in front of the house he leaped out of the tree just in time to catch the thin man getting out of the car. The man didn't quite have time to reach his balance point when Anak slammed the door against him knocking the wind out of him. The last thing he expected was this huge man picking him up by the front of his jacket. He began struggling to get a commando knife out of his pocket. When a button was pushed the blade came out the end of the knife. When his hand found the knife he wasn't sure if the blade was pointing in the right direction. That half second hesitation saved Anak's life. Anak grabbed his arm and bent it back and the bone snapped. The man screamed in pain struggling now to stay alive; he knew this huge thing meant to kill him. For all the years he had trained to overtake his opponent this one mistake would cost him his life. Anak grabbed him by the throat and twisted his head breaking his neck cleanly. He dropped the body in the street. When he looked up the whole family was at the door watching.

"Go back inside." he said in an angry tone. They fled. He stuffed the man's body back into the car, started it and wedged his foot on the gas pedal and jerked it into gear. The car flew off down the street speeding ever faster as it went. When it reached the intersection the car veered off to the right and jumped the curb slamming into a wall. The way the accident looked the man could have easily broken his neck without a scat belt. So much for the assassin. Now Anak would go to the back of the property to wait for the others. What he didn't know was they were trying to get a flight out of Vegas. By the time the sun rose the next morning he knew they weren't coming.

When Gunter tried to contact his man in Henderson there was no answer. He knew something had gone wrong. He called the other three men and they were on a plane headed East. What a miserable failure. How could something as simple as this operation go so wrong? He sat down in a chair at his desk and tried to think. *The best thing to do is get out of the country. I could come back and straighten this up sometime in the future. I must think of mine and my wife's safety first.* He picked up the phone and made reservations on the first flight out of the country going to Germany. The flight would leave three hours from now.

He called up stairs to his wife, "Marsha hurry we're leaving we have to get to the airport.

When she heard Gunter call she grabbed the bags and ran for the stairs. The staircase at the top had six stairs that veered to the left as a finish. She took the first six stairs with ease, but as she turned one of the bags bumped her leg and when she started to take her next step the toe of her right foot caught on her left heel causing her to trip. She tumbled down the staircase head over heels. When she hit the bottom; she was dead, she had also broken her neck.

Radic heard the commotion and ran out into the hall and gave a cry of despair as he saw Marsha's body lying at the bottom of the stairs twisted. He tried to lift her head, but it lolled in death. He didn't have time to waste he would have someone else take care of her later he had to get out of here. He ran to the garage got into his car and drove to the airport. Anak went back into the house, he wanted to talk to his Grandpa. He opened the patio door and called to Jack. Jack stepped outside and sat down at the table.

"What is it son?"

"Grandpa I need help. There must be a way I can hide in society somewhere, but I can't think of anything at the moment. I have a feeling I'm never going to be able to be free, but for a while I must have somewhere to go where they can't find me."

"Anak I think I have come up with the perfect idea. The women won't think so because they are frightened. They don't think you should be out in plain sight, but sometimes the most obvious place to hide is in the open. Here is my idea and see what you think. If you were to join a circus you would fit in better because of all the strange things that are associated with the circus. Not as a giant, but as a big clown; the make up would hide your identity and the clothes would hide your size. They travel all over the country so you would not be in one place very long. When the circus came to this area, which would be at least once a year, you could come to see us."

Grandpa looked at Anak as he stared of into the distance thinking.

Finally he said, "Grandpa, that would be perfect. At the same time I could look for Radic. He would never suspect me of being in a circus. I would be in an element that would accept me and circus people are secretive. Something must have gone wrong at the research center or they would have been here hours ago. Nevertheless I must go there and try to stop Radic. The women would never understand my feelings, but I'm struggling for my life here. As long as he is in control I will never be safe and life is going to be hard enough for a giant without that shadow over my life."

"This spring a circus will come to town for about three days that would be your best chance. And I know they would take you," He said with a big smile.

The family spent the next few weeks in harmony and peace waiting for the circus to arrive. Barnum and Bailey's show moved into the Thomas and Mack center for three days as Grandpa had predicted. The family slipped Anak in before the night show and the circus manager was delighted and took Anak in right away. There was some disagreement at first about his being billed as a clown, but when they explained the situation, he signed Anak up immediately as a clown. The family came back to see him the last day before the circus left. Patricia took him to one side and told him she loved him and that was the reason he had been saved because of the love between them.

"I know you will be all right now Son you have a cover. Please be careful when you go back to the lab we don't know what's going on."

"I love you Mom. Don't worry I will prevail now. When I find him I will break his neck for all the trouble he has caused all of us."

When the circus left Anak was with them in a 'special' trailer. He learned as he went and became a great help to the circus and made a good living as a clown and no one was the wiser. The circus gave him a different name and he went into obscurity for a time.

Radic couldn't forget his experiment and a year later he came back to the Research lab. He sent out a couple of men he hired to find Anak. They came to Henderson and kept the Woods family under surveillance. When Anak didn't try to contact them, they had the phone tapped for a while, but decided it was useless and gave up.

Not long after Gunter moved back into the center he opened up the lab and began to experiment with the giant DNA once more. He kept an eye out for Anak and continued his work quietly. Not attracting any attention. There had been quite a stir over his wife's death but finally he was able to cover it up and go on. His plan was to create a second giant and work in another area of the country perhaps right there in the South. At that time he was perusing the internet for a subject to give birth to the child. He thought he had someone he could use when he met a young girl in a chat room. With so many young women being kidnapped the police wouldn't be surprised at one more. Then mysteriously she would come home and things would calm down until the baby was ready to be taken. If this child came to be; it's personality would be very different. Radic had changed things in his mix of genes. The CIA might be interested in this new child as a warrior. The giant could be dropped in an enemy area to wreak havoc before the sun came up the next day. Then a helicopter could pick him up and fly him out. Radic would be a millionaire many times over. He already had people in Congress working on passage of a Bill permitting gene splicing and cloning. Things were working out better than he thought. Now if he could only find Anak his problems would be solved.

Radic never expected Anak to show up at the lab. His mind was on his work when he came into his office that morning. He never even noticed Anak standing behind the door. As Gunter swung the door shut a deep voice whispered,

"Good morning Papa." When Gunter turned his mouth dropped open in shock. He didn't have time to activate an alarm as a big hand grabbed the front of his shirt and snatched him up off the floor. Anak held him close to his face and glared into his eyes.

"Now it is time for you to die Papa. You have made your last experiment and your last dollar."

"No! No! Please I will give you your freedom and never bother you again. I promise. I will give you whatever you want. Don't hurt me, we have so much at stake now. I am working in another area now. I can make you very rich. Please, please." The expression never changed on Anak's face as he reached up and grasped Radic's head with his massive hand.

"I will tell you ahead of time Papa I'm going to break your neck and bury your body outside where no one will ever find you. An then I will burn this place down." Gunter thought of the hypodermic needle, but it was in vain he had taken it out of his pocket long ago. Slowly Anak began to twist Radic's head. He tried to scream, "Nu! Nu! Aaaaggg!"

Snap!

His spinal cord broke and left him hanging there in Anak's grasp, lifeless. Anak went into the lab where a couple of men were working that Radic had brought back to the country with him. When Anak stepped in he hung Radic's body on a hook on the back of the door. He turned to face the scientists. They were in mortal fear and knew what was coming. One of the men tried to punch in 911 on his cell but Anak saw it and was on him in a flash. He grabbed him and raised his body and broke his back over his knee. The other man ran out the door and Anak followed. He caught him outside in the driveway. He grabbed him and smashed a giant fist into his back splintering his spine and several ribs. Then he twisted his head completely off. He took the body back inside and set the building on fire, then took Radic's body out to the rear of the property and dug a deep grave and covered him up. Anak walked away a free man now without a shadow hanging over his life.

He went back to the circus, but not before calling his mother to tell her he loved her very much.

Homemade Terrorist

Wilma Mason lived in the town of North Las Vegas in a small house at the end of a side street. She hadn't always lived in this broken down house. She once lived in a big fine house on cocktail party row. She was married to a Scientist that worked at the Nevada Test Site and was a very popular lecturer in the scientific community. They had everything, home, summer cabin, cars, boat; they traveled and essentially enjoyed the best of everything in life. That all ended one day when Wilma came to Thurston and happily announced that she was going to have a child. The few years they had been married she never realized that Thurston Mason did not want any children. His efforts to prevent having children never registered with her because she was so busy attending to his needs and traveling on the lecture circuit. Wilma truly loved Thurston and she thought he loved her, but apparently that wasn't entirely the case. Now baby would make three and that wasn't what he wanted. He liked having his woman on his arm and Wilma made the perfect scientist's wife. She had a lovely smile, she spoke eloquently, and she made good martini's, which was all Thurston wanted. When she told him of the coming event, he just stood there with a blank expression on his face.

"Thurston are you all right?" she asked. He turned and went upstairs without a word. A while later he came down with his briefcase and a small suitcase.

"I will have to be gone for a day or two, I have some legal matters to attend to." He announced and walked out. He just left her standing there with her mouth hanging open. The divorce papers came in the mail the next week. Wilma was in shock and didn't know what to do. How could he just cut off this portion of his life without a word? Wilma had just met the real Thurston Mason for the first time in her life. Inside he was a cold cruel animal who would never return to her. In addition, he proved it in court when Wilma discovered she wouldn't receive any alimony and he took their joint account with the use of a very sharp lawyer. She was out in the cold, so to speak. After the legal proceedings the lawyer announced she would be given time to get her belongings out of the house before it was sold and a sale was pending.

Wilma sat down and thought about her condition. She was thirty-five and good looking. She was not a defeatist so she decided she'd get through this calamity somehow. If he was that type of person she didn't need him anyway and she certainly wasn't going to go begging for any of his money. Wilma had a separate account she hadn't told Thurston about with several hundred dollars in it. She rented the small house in North Las Vegas to hide from Thurston and because it was all she could afford. After she settled in, she applied for a position at the North Las Vegas City Hall and got it. Meanwhile she found a doctor for her prenatal care. The doctor was a very kind Middle Eastern woman that helped in many more ways than just medicine. She helped Wilma get through the red tape of bureaucracy housing, food, and temporary financial help.

By the time the baby was to be born, she had already gotten a raise at city hall. She would do the very best she could for this child. When he was born she decided his name would be Tom, not Thomas, just Tom. After his birth, she got back on her feet as soon as she could. Wilma had become friends with a Mexican woman on her street that had several children. She was a plump little woman that wanted to help everyone in the neighborhood. So Wilma asked Maria if she would keep Tom while she worked. Of course Maria Lopez was thrilled to keep little Tom while Wilma worked. Maria was a single mother with four children of her own, three girls and a boy. Her husband had passed away from a heart attack. three years earlier.

Twelve Years Later...

Tom was sitting in the living room playing with a Nintendo game he found in a second hand store, while they were on their weekly forage for clothes. When he picked it out of the discarded bin, his mother said,
"Tom it's broke and there is no way we can make it work."
"I can fix it Mom, and I have a dollar left from last week."
When they got to the counter to pay for everything the woman gave Tom a couple of games to go with the Nintendo. When they reached the house, Tom helped his mom carry things in and took his game to the bedroom. Later Wilma went to Tom's room to tell him lunch was ready. Tom was sitting in the floor amidst a pile of wires and parts.
"Oh Tom, I'm afraid you've wasted your money sweetheart."
"No Mom, I've just about got this thing figured out. You know these games are really simple."
"How do you know that son? You've never studied electronics."
"Well, he said with an impish grin, I've been doing some reading at the library."
Tom was a voracious reader and a brilliant student. His grades were the highest in his class. Of course that was the way it would be all his life, way ahead of the others. Tom didn't mix well with other students though. He chose his friends very carefully. Because he had been practically raised in the Lopez household, he and Maria's son Lupe were inseparable. He even picked up a little of the Spanish they constantly spoke.

Now twelve years old he began to ask questions about his dad which his mother tried to answer as honestly as she could. Tom was unsettled with the answers he got and didn't understand his fathers' actions. His mother's answer was, "I don't understand him either Tom." A silent anger and determination began to burn in his heart against the way he and his mother had been treated by Thurston. When his mother asked if he would like to see his father he asked where he lectured in town.

She told him about the college and that he would be speaking at Ham Hall the following Saturday.

Tom decided to go and see what his father was like. He took the bus to the college and went to the hall where his dad lectured. The lecture had already started when he arrived. Tom slipped in and found a seat in the bleachers. As he sat and listened to Thurston Mason, he recognized the arrogance and pride his mother mentioned. He really was all wrapped up in himself. When Thurston finally finished people in the stands rushed to shake his hand and tell him how good his subject was. Tom slipped out the door and waited outside. When his father came out Tom stepped back into the shadows and watched as he and a very beautiful blond strolled to a waiting black Mercedes. Tom memorized the license tag; something he would keep in his mind for many years. He hated his father even more now that he knew what he was like. He decided Mr. Mason would pay for what he had done to them.

As he came in the front door, he saw his mother was waiting up for him.

"Well Son what did you think of his lecture?"

"You were right Mom, he was just like you said, he was trash in a tuxedo." Tom went to his room without saying any more.

By the time, Tom was in his first year of high school his teachers began to recognize the genius in him and his counselor called his mother in to talk to her about Tom.

"Scholastically Wilma your son is so far ahead of the

students around him it's hard to measure his abilities. Tom doesn't have many friends and of course, this is a concern with us here at the school. I've talked with some of his teachers and Tom doesn't show any attraction toward any of the girls or boys for that matter. It appears that Lupe Lopez is the only boy that he hangs around with. Sometimes geniuses get bored with life because other people have trouble understanding them. I think we should find out what Tom likes and cater to those interests to keep him stimulated."

"I've talked with a psychologist and Tom doesn't show any of the tendencies that usually follow the gifted. He's just overly determined to achieve. He loves electronics, maybe we could get him in touch with someone that works in that field." Wilma said.

"All right Mrs. Mason I will see what I can do to get him started in that direction. I really appreciate your coming in today and I won't say anything to Tom about it."

In the following days Tom was introduced to an electronics engineer that was to teach at the high school and was scheduled to have a class with him.

In their first session Bill Walton was amazed by what Tom had already learned in the library. Tom was the only student in Bills class to begin with then finally a few of the other boys came to join them. Mr. Walton brought in projects for the boys to do. Tom always had the circuitry figured out in his mind. When tests were given Tom sailed through them waiting for the others to finish.

On Saturdays when he finished helping his Mom he would ride his bike out in the desert and study the insects and animals he came across out there. As he rode over a hill one morning he spotted a group of boys and a man in the distance. He wondered what they were doing. He rode a little closer and saw they were going to send up a toy rocket. He watched with interest as the rocket streaked into the sky. It went up a couple hundred feet and burned out and as it fell back to earth a parachute unfolded to protect its landing. They gathered around the spent rocket and Tom rode over to ask about how it worked. Of course the man was delighted to explain and tell Tom where to get one of his own. He also told Tom the safety measures he needed to take to keep from getting burned. Tom thanked him and rode for home. When he got there Lupe was waiting for him.

"Where you been Bro?" he asked with his congenial smile on his face. Lupe understood Tom and knew just how to handle him when he was moody. They were an odd pair Tom blond standing at almost six feet and Lupe dark haired and five foot five.

"Ah out in the desert watching some kids fire a rocket. The guy with them said I could get one that went up five hundred feet."

"Wow that's getting up there man." Lupe said with a look of awe. You gonna get one?"

"I think I'm gonna make my own that will go up a mile." Tom said with a grin and held his fingers to his lips, which meant don't tell Mom.

"What you gonna make it out of?" Lupe asked.

"The one I saw today was cardboard with a wooden nose."

"Yeah but to go that high you need a lot of fuel man."

"C'mon in the house I'll show you what I thought." Tom said.

They took a soda from the frig and went into Tom's bedroom.

"You see Lupe I can get the mix for the fuel off the Internet. We can make the body from a piece of cardboard tube like they roll carpet on."

"Yeah man, cool." So when Tom came home with a carpet tube and some wood his mom wanted to know what he was doing. He told her it was a project for the science fair at school. He got a kid in wood shop to make the nose cone and he cut the fins out of the wood he brought home. After a few days work it began to look like the real thing, but what no one knew was that it was really going to work. Secretly Tom found the materials for a battery operated guidance system which was a joystick pad and had it working in no time. Lupe ran back and forth from place to place getting materials and helping to assemble the rocket. In the library, Tom found pictures and articles on rockets and how they were made. He adapted his accordingly. By now Lupe realized the name of this thing was going to be different. The name of this was 'Missile.'

One day he asked, "This ain't gonna be a rocket is it Tom?"

"No my friend it isn't, but don't say the word."

"We could get in trouble doing this man. I mean FAA stuff you know?"

"If you want out it would be best to go home now and stay gone until I get done. Cause I'm gonna finish this project and test it out in the desert."

"I don't want you to go to jail man." Lupe said with a serious tone.

"I'm sly man they won't catch me. You don't have to stay if you're scared."

"I'm not scared for me man I'm scared for you. What about your mom man who's gonna take care of her?"

"Quit worrying man I'm not gonna get caught. Your not going to fink out on me are you?"

"No Bro I'd never do that, never." Lupe was serious now.

"If you don't want to stay it's okay I won't feel bad at you. Something in me says I've got to finish this."

Lupe thought for a minute then he said, "Okay bro. I'm in. We're like blood and we grew up together so you know I'd do anything for you."

They embraced. Something Maria had made them do when they were little and they had been fussing over something, but now it was something more, much more.

"We can try this out in the desert, a long way from the roads where we can get away before anyone can get to us." Tom said.

When the project was finished they rode their bikes out

into the desert several miles. Tom carried the tube and Lupe carried the controls. As they set up in the sand the sun was just coming up, Tom checked the sky for aircraft or helicopters. They backed away at least a hundred yards. Tom pushed the fire button. He had adapted a joystick from a game pad. Fire exploded from under the missile and for a second they thought it wasn't going to go up, but then it streaked toward the sky so quickly Tom almost didn't catch the control soon enough. It was up almost a thousand feet when he turned it and flew it in a circle until it ran out of fuel. It fell to earth and landed in a creosote bush. Seemingly it was like the rest of the world was involved in something else; because no one saw the launch. The tube was broken, but they took home all the pieces. They were grinning and throwing high fives the rest of the day. The boys had to stay away from the house for a long while for fear their excitement would show.

The next week, Tom asked his mother if he could use the tool shed for a workshop. She agreed, for mothers of genius's think they're children do no wrong.

So secretly Tom developed a better control and made more fuel for a new larger fuel cell. He also worked out some of the glitches that were in the first missile. He made the body out of a cardboard carpet tube eight feet long. Now he would befriend one of the boys in metal shop. He needed a metal nose cone for the next one.

Three Years Later...

The year Tom and Lupe graduated from high school Tom wanted to develop a solar car and Lupe wanted to start a car repair shop. They didn't go their separate ways, but it put enough space between them to give them an independence they needed to be businessmen. Lupe got an older Datsun body for Tom to use for his solar project. Tom took out the motor and transmission and mounted a large electric motor in its place. Lupe rebuilt the motor and transmission and sold them to finance

Tom's solar project. Then Tom adapted solar cells and mounted them on the roof. Another little item he invented was called a solar intensifier, which looked like a small glass insulator. He made four and mounted one on each fender and wired them to the solar cells. When the sun shined on them the cells developed four times as much juice. He hooked up a forward and reverse switch with a shift stick. In theory the further forward he pushed the stick the faster the car would go. When the stick was pulled back from the stop position it would go in reverse. Everyday Wilma would check on Tom's progress for she began to think Tom's car might work. To be able to drive a car without gas or oil would be a dream.

"It's going to work Mom, but I don't want anyone in Detroit to find out. I've heard that other inventions like this have disappeared over the years. So let's keep this a secret for the time being." When Lupe came over he swore him to secrecy too. When Tom explained the project to him he got very excited.

"You can make a million dollars bro."

"Not yet bro. For the time being I just want cheap transportation." When the project was ready to be tested, Tom called his Mom and Lupe and put them in the car. He pushed the lever forward almost all the way before it began to roll. Slow and easy it rolled away from the curb and began to pick up speed. The speedometer read 10, then 15, then 20, and it leveled out at 25. Wilma and Lupe began to cheer and slap Tom on the back. At the end of the block, Tom pulled back on the stick and made a u-turn at 10 miles an hour. He pushed the stick forward to 25 and drove back to the house. He rolled up in the driveway and stopped. Wilma cried and they both tried to hug him at the same time.

"Oh Tom you are a genius." She cried.

"Shh, the neighbors will hear. You remember that old song, Wait till the sun shines Nellie? Tomorrow I'm going to take you guys for a real ride." They sat there wide-eyed not knowing what to expect. Tom got out and went into the house. When they followed they found Tom sitting on the couch with his feet up watching TV.

"Lupe, do you know what a converter is?"

"It's a thing that changes electricity from AC to DC ain't it?"

Tom poked a finger at his chest. "No I'm a converter. I'm going to convert cars from gas to solar power. I'm going to make a fortune and buy Mom a mansion and build her a solar limo."

The next morning about 10:00 o'clock Tom came out of the bedroom Wilma and Lupe were waiting to see what he would do.

He was carrying some small parts and mounted them on top of the car when they got outside.

"Okay guys lets go for a ride."

They went out and got into the Datsun and Tom backed into the street. He straightened it up and asked,

"You ready?"

They nodded their heads vigorously. Tom yanked the stick back and the little car squealed for about ten feet and zipped up to fifty miles an hour. They were flying down the street with their mouths agape gasping for breath.

"Cool man, so cool!" Lupe was hollering. People watched the car go by silently except for the sound of the tires.

"How did you make it do that man?" Lupe asked.

"Solar intensifiers, my Mexican friend, solar intensifiers.

I can't believe it Tom I can't believe it." Wilma proclaimed.

"Now its time to make this baby look good and I'm going to make it look gorgeous." Lupe said. The next week Lupe worked on the brake system and had the body man in his shop fix the dents and paint it. Tom decided on a copper color. When it sat in the sun it just glowed. They put new rims and tires on it and now it was the most important piece of junk in their life. When Wilma drove it to the store she gloated as she parked it in the lot and looked at the gas guzzlers around her.

Lupe was already working on a model of his own an old American motors version of the rambler. It was a small two door with pea soup colored paint. No one wanted to even look at it, which was fine with the boys they didn't want anyone looking at it anyway, but people couldn't figure out why it was so quiet and there wasn't any exhaust.

Adulthood

When the boys turned twenty-one Lupe became fascinated with the Arizona lottery. Every week he would drive over to the way station on the road to Kingman. It was just a small spot in the road but it had a store and gas station and they sold lottery tickets by the ton. People from Vegas and the surrounding area would flock over there on Friday afternoon and Saturday morning. Lupe was with them every week. He never won much usually he just got his money back, which he invested in more tickets. One Saturday morning he asked Tom to go with him. Tom consented for he liked to use time like this to think about projects he was working on. For the past three years he had something in the workshop he was developing that he couldn't talk to anyone about. His mom didn't question him because she thought he was working on solar systems. He was, but not for cars.

As they glided along in Lupe's Rambler he chatted about the tickets and how he was going to hit it big one day. Tom just grinned and stared off into the distance mulling over more important things in his mind. When they arrived at the store Lupe began trying to get Tom to buy a ticket.

"Come on man, it'll only take one ticket to win two million dollars. I know it's not a lot, but it's a start. It would go along way towards car parts bro." he chided Tom

"Lupe it's a waste of time man. I got better things to do with my money."

Lupe walked around the car flapping his arms like a bird. Squawk! What a chicken."

Finally Tom said, "Alright if it will make you happy, but I'm not going to make this a weekly event." They went inside and stood in line. Tom bought two tickets and it made Lupe

ecstatic.
"You're gonna win, you're gonna win. I just know it". He cried hopping around. Tom grinned and shook his head as he went to the car. On the way home he let his mind drift off into space. He stuck the tickets in his shirt pocket and forgot about them. Lupe chatted about things they were going to accomplish the next week.

Tom nodded silently and stared out the windshield. Tom's true love was lying at home in the shed in pieces.

Meanwhile Lupe hoped he had steered Tom away from the missile project. He knew it meant nothing but trouble. At times he worried about what Tom was thinking for no one knew what went on in his mind. There were some things he didn't talk about even to his closest friend. When they got home Tom threw the lottery tickets on the dresser and forgot them again.

The next Wednesday the numbers came out in the local paper. Wilma was in the kitchen making coffee when Lupe burst in.

I got 'em Mom, I got 'em. He screamed with a wadded section of the newspaper in his fist.

"Shh, what have you got?"

"I got the numbers for the hundred thousand."

"My God Lupe, you're rich." She a said with astonishment. Just then Tom staggered into the kitchen still half asleep.

"What are you hollering about man?" Lupe grabbed the front of Tom's t-shirt.

"I won the hundred thousand man." He screamed.

Tom looked puzzled as if it still hadn't registered. "The Lottery?" he asked.

Yeah, man. Now I'm going to have a real mechanic shop. Did you check yours?"

"What?"

"Your tickets man, go get 'em." Tom thought about the tickets lying on the dresser. He stumbled back to the bedroom as Lupe spread the paper out on the table. Tom came back and threw them on top of the paper. Lupe picked them up and began to mumble. 13, 24, 31, 47, 62, and the extra 6. Lupe fell back in a dead faint. When he hit the floor, Wilma and Tom tried to pick him up, but he was out cold. Wilma ran into the bathroom and got an ammonia ampoule and broke it under Lupe's nose. He came to struggling.

"Take it easy Lupe it's all right." Tom said.

Lupe's eyes opened very big and he spoke in a very forceful tone.

Tom listen to me man, you just won the two million."

"You're crazy."

"Look at the paper and the tickets man." Tom picked up the tickets and laid them on the paper and looked at the numbers. He began to tremble.

"My God Mom, we made it." Wilma began to weep shaking her head; she still couldn't believe it had happened to them.

Lupe shook Tom. "Call the number man, call the number."

Tom picked up the paper and went to the phone. His hand was shaking so bad he couldn't read the number. Lupe grabbed the paper and began to dial. When he finished he handed the phone to Tom. When the woman answered, Tom stammered the information into the phone. When he read the ticket number Lupe put his ear next to Tom's.

He could hear the woman saying, "Congratulations sir you have just won this week's two million dollar lottery." When Tom was finished Lupe took the phone and reported his winning ticket and got instructions where to go to collect his winnings.

Two days later they were in Phoenix on TV holding up two big cardboard checks. One for two million and the other for a hundred thousand dollars. When they got home everyone in the neighborhood was celebrating.

In the next few days Lupe was buying his family all the things they couldn't afford. Tom on the other hand put the money in his mother's account and told her to get whatever she wanted.

"Let's get a new house Mom." He said one morning.

"You know I've thought about this and I would like to stay here Tom. Maybe we could remodel or add on. I kinda like it here, all our friends are in this neighborhood. I know we have money now, but you need to set up this solar business. Tom, you need something to keep you busy. You've got too much time to think and some of your expressions lately make me worry." *Had she figured him out?* Tom wondered. Later he called Lupe on the phone and made a suggestion that they find a place to set up both shops. A shop on each end of a building somewhere would work. Lupe was all for it.

The next week Tom and Wilma found a builder to add on to the house and make the shop out in the back yard bigger and build it of wood frame. Tom and Lupe quietly began to show the solar car and business began to pick up. People were astonished at the possibilities of solar transportation. Tom converted several cars and made a lot of money doing it. Tom worked very hard and his customers couldn't believe a thing like this was possible.

One Friday afternoon a man came into Tom's shop.
"You Tom Mason?"
"Who wants to know?"
"Oh sorry, I'm Ed Parsons."
"From?"
"You're pretty sharp son." The man was older possibly forty-five or fifty with salt and pepper hair, wearing a gray tweed suit. He reached into his shirt pocket and gave Tom a card with his name and a blue oval on it. Tom looked past him and asked,
"Are the rest of them out in the van?"
"Who's that?" he asked.
"General Motors and Chrysler."
"No today it's just me." Tom slowly closed the hood of the car he was working on and started toward the small office. He glanced back and said,
"We can talk in here."
"It's still early, I thought we could go have lunch and talk.

You could give me a ride in your car here."
"That's not my car it belongs to a customer." The man shrugged and started toward the office. Inside, Tom picked up the phone and called Lupe's extension.
"You want to come over we have company from the automotive world.." He hung up the phone and said,
"Have a seat Mr. Parsons my partner will be here in just a moment." Parsons sat down in the padded chair looking at Tom all the while. Lupe came in wide-eyed staring at the visitor. Lupe this is Mr. Ed Parsons from Ford Motor Company. Mr. Parsons this is my partner Lupe Lopez." They shook hands and sat down.
"And now if you will sir, the nature of this visit?" Tom asked.
"Well I'd hoped we wouldn't be quite so formal gentlemen. I just thought maybe our company could help on this project of yours."
"You seem familiar with our business. How did you hear about us sir?"
"Well someone sent an e-mail and the company asked me to come by. The company is looking for alternate sources of transportation and it looks like you fellas have come up with a pretty good idea."
"I've done a little research on a lot of ideas like mine and they all seem to have wound up on the junk pile of history. And the developers have all retired and are living in some neat vacation spot where the weather is balmy."
"That doesn't sound like too bad a deal to me. Now there is no reason to be angry about this, like I said I'm just here to offer help that's all."
"Yeah like the Hydrogen engine we have waited so long for. You guys and Honda still sucking up gas and oil like you always have. You and I both know that project could have come to fruition a long time ago. But we understand it's a matter of weaning. You don't want to let go of the gas hose too quick. And you also know this little project could put you out of

business in short order." Parsons expression wasn't too happy.

"When you leave here you might want to check with the patent office if you haven't already. I don't have many of these cars out there and we have an agreement with the people that own them and your visit tells me that someone has violated that agreement. That's probably why you're here because you can't get your hands on one of them." Tom said.

"Well I guess you've got it nailed down pretty tight. And by your tone I don't suppose you want to talk to anyone about it."

Not from the big three or the foreign folk. I appreciate you stopping by, but if you will excuse us we have work to do."

"Tom I really don't like starting a relationship like this. I want to be your friend. I realize you're a really intelligent person and my company could use your help."

"Well Mr. Parsons I would like to ask you this, where was Ford when I graduated at the top of my class. There were no grants or rewards that came my way and no representative from any of the big three showed up to ask about my progress or any of my needs. And (Tom raised his voice) no one offered a scholarship of any kind. Not a school, not a collage, not a company. I guess their opinion was you've done a fine job kid, but you will have to make it on your own. So that is just exactly what I've been doing. And suddenly when I've made an important discovery everyone needs me. Would you mind telling the rest of them out there not to bother me I'm busy making a fortune. The door is to your right Mr. Parsons. Thank you for stopping by." Parsons stood and walked out not saying anything.

Quietly Lupe said, "Hey man you might have messed up a good deal."

Tom was mad now and he said, "I'm so glad you realized that my friend. I don't suppose you know what happens to people with good ideas in our society. The ideas are in the trash and the people are on skid row thank you very much. Do you know I could put the automotive industry out of business with this technology?" Lupe nodded his head. "Right now every corporation with big money that knows about us is trembling. I'll tell you what I'm going to do bro. I'm going to close down this shop and go home for the night and sleep well and for a change they are going to sit up and worry because they don't know where I'm going to show up next.

Outside Parsons was in his car talking on a cell phone.

"Well you could have some real trouble with this kid. He didn't want to talk to me or anyone else and like I just said he showed me the door. And he's right you know we missed a chance to get him right out of high school. Someone figured we didn't need another electronics expert and didn't bother to check him out. No one did and he's not happy about it. Yeah Bill he realizes the potential of what he's got. I've got to get out of here he and the other boy are coming out. I'll call you when I get back."

Tom and Lupe walked outside and watched Parsons drive away.

"That's not the last we've seen of them Lupe. We are going to have to be careful they are going to be snooping into everything in our lives. You can continue here with business as usual, but I'm going to lay low for a while."

That afternoon Tom bought a white four-wheel drive Chevy truck. The salesman was very happy because Tom didn't haggle about the price. Tom drove home and parked in the driveway. His mom met him at the door.

"Hey, nice truck son."

"Yeah, I needed something to haul parts with. How's the addition coming?"

"They've got the back of the house tore out and the new walls framed in. Your shop is just about finished." Tom had stored all his parts and controls in a storage unit a few miles away.

"A guy from Ford came by the shop today and I sent him packing. The car companies are the last thing I want anything to do with right now."

"You sure that was a wise decision Tom?"

"I wanted to let them know they past us up when I graduated. They are going to feel stupid for a while, but they will find another way to approach me, they'll never give up."

Tom was right, when he went to stand in line at the Motor Vehicle Department to register the truck he was escorted to the front of the line and seated at one of the computer stations where the young lady asked for his driver's license then smiled as she handed him his tags and registration.

"General Motors came by this morning and they took care of this for you; for buying one of their new trucks. Wasn't that nice of them?"

"Yes that was very nice. Uh, who do I thank for this?"

"I guess someone at the dealership where you bought the truck." She smiled and thanked Tom for coming in.

Outside Tom looked around for someone responsible for the gift, but no one was around from the car agency. He took time to put on the plates and tuck the paper work in the glove box and called his mother on his cell.

"Mom if anyone comes by offering you anything don't accept it. I'll be home for lunch. My license and plates were all taken care of when I got here this morning. A gift from the dealer. Yeah right." He went to the insurance agency to take care of the coverage for his truck. Afterwards Tom went to the storage unit and watched for anyone following him. When he was sure he was alone he took out a box with one of his guidance systems in it.

One the way home he stopped at a metal supply company and ordered some high tinsel strength aluminum tubing six inches in diameter and eight feet long. These eight-foot tubes would be the bodies of the next missiles he would make. UPS would deliver them to his shop the next week.

"Well son, what will it be tuna or a roast beef sandwich?"

"Make it roast beef Mom."

As he waited for Wilma to make his sandwich one of the construction workers came to the back door.

"Sir your shop is finished. You can move in any time you

are ready."

"Oh okay, thank you." Tom smiled. His shop a 12x16 building was a bigger place to store items and to work; he could now produce full sized missiles. Now he could work on his true love. He longed to see one of these babies streak through the sky to a predetermined target.

While Tom hadn't been actively working on the missiles he was developing the controls and a special substance in fluid form that he called an attractant. It worked somewhat like the drawing power of two small magnets. When one gets close to the other it draws the opposite one to it. Put on two separate surfaces one was drawn to the other within limits. Tom bought a small twenty-two pistol that held five shots. He wanted something to show Lupe for the first test.

The next day being Saturday, Tom knew Lupe wouldn't be working in the shop so he called early and woke him up.

"Now before you get mad about being disturbed; I want to show you a very amazing test today that is going to make you a good marksman. After we shoot the center out of the bullseye I'll take you out to breakfast. See you in a few minutes." And a few minutes it was. Lupe rushed in his eyes full of wonder.

"Mornin bro." Tom said smiling.

"Yeah mornin to you too." Lupe said in a hoarse voice.

They got into Tom's truck and drove out into the desert quite a ways. Tom took with him a target, the gun, five bullets, and a small vial of the attractant. He hung the target on an old fence post. He then took out the vial and a small brush and dabbed a little of the fluid in the center of the bullseye. Lupe watched with a funny expression on his face. Tom walked away from the target about fifty yards and took the bullets and the vial out of his pocket. He removed the cover and just barely touched the tips of the bullets in the fluid. After he loaded the gun he handed it to Lupe.

"So what's with the goo?" Lupe asked.

"That's what's going to help you shoot a perfect score Bro. Go ahead."

"Kinda far for a pistol ain't it?"

"Yes it is, but you are going to do better than you think." Lupe took aim and fired a shot.

"Go ahead man shoot them all." Lupe fired the rest.

"Okay my friend go check your score." Lupe handed the gun to Tom and walked toward the target. He took the paper down and his eyes opened wide with surprise. He ran back to where Tom stood with his mouth hanging open. All five rounds had almost gone through the same hole. The center of the bullseye was gone.

"Wow! Man you can't miss with that stuff."

"The drawback is it has to be on both surfaces. Projectile and target. Any ideas?"

Lupe stood in thought for a moment then his eyes lit up.

"Yeah man, a paint ball gun could put it on the target."

"Good idea, Lupe We'll have to try that out this weekend."

Lupe went to Big Five, the sporting goods store, and bought the best paint ball set he could find. It was accurate up to thirty yards.

Tom took several of the paint balls and removed some of the paint with a small hypodermic needle and reinserted some of the attractant. On Saturday morning they went out to a favorite spot where there was an abandoned telephone pole that stuck up from the ground about twenty-five feet. Lupe fired one of the special paint balls and hit the middle of the pole about five feet from the top.

"Perfect Lupe, lets go." They drove five miles further out into the hills. Tom had set up a launcher in the back of the truck. It was hydraulically operated. They mounted one of the missiles, which didn't have an explosive warhead that Tom had made from the new tubing he ordered. It was eight feet long. He raised the launcher to maximum height and picked up the joystick.

"Ready man?"

"Go Man." Lupe said with a big grin on his face. Tom pushed the fire button and grabbed the control stick. Tom had wired a small screen to the side of the joystick box so he could see the missiles' progress toward the target. On the top of the screen the target was a white dot and at the bottom the missile was a red dash. The missile traveled about a hundred feet above the ground. When it was ten feet from the post the attractant took over. The point of the nose of the missile split the top of the post in two and what was left landed in the sand fifty feet beyond it. On the screen the white dot disappeared. After they viewed the split in the top of the pole, Tom began to consider an explosive for the warhead.

Disaster

The next week Tom and his mother had been shopping and were turning off a side street on to Lake Mead Boulevard. They were in Tom's electric car. A large older Lincoln came plunging into the intersection and struck the car on Wilma's side driving it through the intersection to the opposite curb. The Datsun was crushed in so badly Wilma's body was pushed against Tom. Fortunately his door popped open and he fell out. Badly shaken Tom's mind wasn't working like it usually did. He finally managed to get up to survey the damage. He saw his mother lying there unconscious. He began to search his pockets for his cell phone. Someone from the gathering crowd stepped up and said,

"I've already called 911."

Tom glanced up and saw the driver of the Lincoln draped over the steering wheel. His forehead was bleeding, his head had hit the steel trim above the windshield and he was unconscious. In moments an ambulance and police units were at the scene because the police station and the hospital were just a mile or so down Lake Mead.

The emergency crew took Wilma out of the driver's side of the car because the passenger side was so badly crushed. Tom found a piece of paper and wrote down the license number and description of the Lincoln. He was also able to get the man's name and insurance information from one of the officers. Tom asked the wrecker driver if he would take the battered car to his driveway and leave it because it was an experimental model. The driver nodded when Tom tucked the hundred dollar bill in his shirt pocket. He then asked another officer if he would take him to the hospital down the street. When Tom reached the emergency room he borrowed a cell phone and called Lupe.

When Lupe answered the phone he listened wide-eyed while Tom described what had happened. All Tom knew was Wilma was unconscious and headed for an operating room somewhere in the depths of the hospital. Tears burst from Lupe's eyes. He dropped the phone and ran from the house.

Not bothering to open the door he slid through the open window of the car and was speeding down the street toward the hospital without even realizing what he was doing. This couldn't be happening to his second mother. He had been close to Wilma all his life. He loved her almost as much as Tom did. This was the woman that had given him advise, made him cakes, given him cards and presents for his birthdays. This couldn't have happened to Mom # 2. He slid sideways in the hospital parking lot and was out running for the emergency room without realizing it. Inside he grabbed Tom crying,

"What happened bro.? What happened?"

"Some guy ran the light and hit us down on the corner of Lake Mead and Walnut. I don't know what he was doing he didn't even slow down and it crushed the side of my electric. Mom never had a chance." Lupe was still blubbering and crying when he called his mother with the news. Maria dropped everything and rushed to the hospital.

An hour later a nurse called Tom to the nurse's station where a young doctor was waiting to talk to Tom.

"Mr. Mason?" Funny no one ever called him that.

"Yeah?"

Your mother suffered some traumatic injuries, we did all we could, but I'm sorry sir, she didn't make it."

Tom's eyes grew wide and his mouth fell open.

First rage took over and Tom screamed at the doctor through gritted teeth, "Where is that scumbag? Is he in here?" Grabbing the doctor's jacket lapels he screamed, "I'll kill him."

One of the security guards rushed from the desk to restrain Tom and Lupe was approaching from behind him. In Tom's fury it was too much for his mind to handle and he collapsed. Lupe caught Tom before he hit the floor. The security guard and the doctor helped Lupe put Tom on a gurney. The doctor called to one of the nurses for an injection to calm him down. They knew when he came to they wouldn't be able to control him.

In another cubicle a doctor was suturing a long cut on the forehead of Miles Burton the man who was driving the Lincoln that killed Wilma. A nurse rushed in and told the doctor he would have to be moved as soon as possible to avoid trouble. The doctor finished hurriedly and had Miles sent to a locked psychiatric room for his safety. What no one but the doctor and the nurse knew was that Miles Burton was drunk. His blood alcohol was twice the legal level.

When Tom came to Lupe took him home and gave him a pill the doctor prescribed for his rest. Soon Tom was in bed breathing deep while Lupe walked the floor and wept. *Who could have done a thing like this?* Lupe wondered.

The days that followed were long and forlorn. Maria came and fixed meals for the boys, but mostly they just picked at their food and drank coffee. Lupe answered the door and the phone and told people Tom could not be disturbed. Four days later at the funeral Tom was looking at the various floral arrangements and came across one from the wife of Miles Burton.

Tom grabbed the flowers and ripped them from the stand screaming, "Get this out of here. Get this trash out of my mother's presence."

The director quickly took the flowers and Lupe and his

sisters tried to calm Tom.

He fell on his knees and cried aloud. The visitors left quickly in embarrassment while Maria and the family hugged Tom. The funeral directors apologized again and again.

Finally Tom told Lupe, "We will get this #@%*! You hear me?"

"Yeah bro, but right now let Mom go in peace, huh?"

Tom's face fell into is hands and he wept sorely. Following the graveside service Tom stood and starred off into space. After a while Maria came and led Tom to a waiting limousine that would take them home. At home Tom took another pill and fell into the bed. Lupe sat in a rocker by the phone and stare at the floor. Maria went home to take care of her household.

Two days after Miles Burton was released from the hospital, and he had to appear before a Judge to give a plea and be charged. His wife brought one of his company lawyers who asked that a manslaughter charge be dropped and felony DUI be considered. The Judge accepted the plea and set another court date. Tom and Lupe were incensed at the Judge's decision and had to be removed from the courtroom, under the threat of contempt.

Not ever having been in a courtroom before Tom had no knowledge of proceedings or the necessity for legal representation. This had been a wakeup call and he realized the need for legal representation. When he got home he looked through the phone book and saw how big the attorneys' section was. When he finally found the listings for criminal law he chose a name and called the number. A female voice confirmed that this was the office of Clemet Stone and asked what Tom's needs were. Tom explained the situation and was asked to come in that afternoon.

Mr. Stone looked almost like a schoolboy. His hair was smothed down and his eyes squinted from behind a pair of granny glasses. His voice was high-pitched, but when he spoke he sounded like he knew law so Tom explained the details of the case and what had happened in court that morning. Mr. Stone said he understood and would notify the court he was representing Tom. When Tom shook hands with him he reassured Tom everything would be done that could be done to prosecute this offender. He was literally getting away with murder.

Outside the law office, Lupe asked, "You sure this guy knows what he's doing bro?"

"Yeah I guess he does. He has a long list of things he covers in the phone book."

At the next appearance Clemet Stone not only looked like a schoolboy, he handled things like one. He forgot, omitted, and lost information pertaining to the case. Miles Burton's lawyer had him for lunch and the judge gave Miles two years probation and the loss of his license. When the judge rapped the gavel Lupe had to drag Tom out of the courtroom all the while hissing in his ear,

"Remember the missile bro, remember the missile. We will get this toad."

After a couple of minutes Tom came to his senses and stopped struggling.

"Okay man that's good. We will do that." After that he was able to contain his anger. Now he had a purpose. Their next destination was the shop where he would prepare a special unit for Mr. Burton.

Since Miles lost his license, his lawyer drove him home. When he dropped Miles in the drive he said, "Whether you know it or not you just came back from the dead. It would be a good idea to get off the bottle and stay off. You are lucky to still have a job. And there will be a civil suit to follow so you can kiss your house goodbye."

Miles glared at the lawyer's Caddie as he pulled away. Then he turned and looked at this huge two-story house. *"Man how stupid. All the years I worked for this and now I'm going to lose it. I need a drink."* When he closed the front door he could already hear his wife's voice.

"Well our favorite alcoholic is home. I'm really surprised they didn't lock you up. Now are you going to quit?"

"If you give me anymore mouth Helen I'm going to knock you out of the park." He doubled up his fist and held it in her face. She turned and walked away quickly because she knew he would do it. He had smacked her before and she didn't want anymore bruises on her face.

Miles went into his office and tried to open the liquor cabinet. It was locked and he couldn't locate the key. He cursed because he couldn't find the key, so he took a letter opener out of a desk drawer, broke the lock and bent the opener. With his hand trembling he grabbed the first glass and filled it with J&B Scotch.

The burning in his throat felt good. It was the relief he needed. He drank the rest and closed his eyes. The buzz would be next and he didn't care.

The next Monday Miles went back to work. After a lecture from the CEO of the company he retreated to his office and sat and sulked from the tongue-lashing and the warnings. But he was lucky to have his job so he would have to be careful. Lana his young secretary came in carrying a cup of his favorite coffee. Lana was a very savvy lady and knew when to say the right words. The company paid her well for it.

"You just have to be more careful boss. Inside you're a good guy and you have done a good job for this company. Right now everybody is down on you, but we all have our bad times and everybody else has his or hers covered. This will dry up in time, but you'll have to be patient." She patted him on the arm.

"Thanks Lana you've always been a source of help and encouragement." She smiled and went back to her desk.

Miles office was on the twelfth floor of the Wells Fargo Tower on Maryland Parkway. There were two offices one each side of an elevator bank, except the floors with conference rooms, which the whole building shared. So there were two offices on each floor on each side. Miles office was on the East side of the center facing the middle window, which was on the South side of the elevator. When he turned his chair around he could see the whole East side of town. First thing in the morning when Lana brought his coffee he would sit and look out the window at the scenery. Somehow it calmed him and started his day off right. Lana would bring in his messages and appointments after he had time to jump-start his mind.

On the North side of North Vegas another person was clearing his mind and getting ready to study a schematic that he found on the internet. It would put his first long range missile together. The body was six inches in diameter and eight feet long with a fourteen inch pointed nose cone with a support rod in the center. Tom had tested one like it and it would go completely through a double metal billboard at about three hundred miles an hour. He had increased the range of his missiles to approximately ten miles. Tom had the body partially assembled. The body and the fins lay on the floor awaiting the internal parts and fuel cell. Tom had honed the guidance system until he could make it work on several hearing aid batteries. And it only had to work once.

A lot of the electronics he purchased from various Radio Shack stores. The rest he got from electronic supply outlets. He was able to put a missile together for thousands less than the government. Of course that's the way it's always been. When the civilian world got their own space shuttle going it would cost everybody a whole lot less.

About 10:00 o'clock Lupe tapped on the door, "Hey bro you in there?"

"Yeah man. Come on in and take a look at this." Lupe's eyes wandered down the length of the tube.

"Too bad we can't put our name on it. A gift from the boys."

"Let's go get some breakfast I want to give you the rest of the plan." They went to Jerry's Nugget Casino and sat in a booth in the back of the restaurant. They talked while they waited for their food to arrive.

"Now partner this is where the paint ball gun comes in. We know this jerk works in the Wells Fargo Tower on Maryland Parkway. The only thing we have to do now is find out which office is his and we can do that this morning if you feel like it." Lupe nodded he was ready for this. At last revenge would be taken for mom's death.

"You think you could learn to fly a hang glider?" Lupe looked up surprised. He couldn't imagine what Tom had in mind.

"Yeah I guess I could."

"Okay we will go to the office building first and locate the drunk's office then we check out hang glider sales. We want the smallest and easiest to hide. We will need a warm morning so you can catch a thermal to give you height. You can glide to your target from there." Lupe looked confused.

"Been studying up on it in my spare time bro."

They found what they were looking for and made a special order for a glider that would fold up and could be easily transported. It would arrive by UPS the following week. Next they went to the tower on Maryland Parkway. Half a block away they stood on the sidewalk and looked up at the building.

"I've come here and watched him go in when he comes to work in the morning. I hired a kid to follow him. He has an office on the twelfth floor in the middle of the hall. I want to go up and see it for myself. I want to get the feeling of the place where havoc will occur."

"Lupe said, "Amen bro."

They walked to the building and took the elevator to the twelfth floor. When they stepped out of the elevator they saw the sign on the door of Miles' company.

"Lupe go in and see which office is his." Lupe opened the door to Lana's outer office. As he stepped in he let his eyes roam the area and spotted Miles' name on the center door.

Lana looked up and said, "May I help you sir?"

Apologetically he answered, "Oh I'm so sorry I've got the

wrong office. I hope I haven't disturbed you."

"That's all right." She smiled, may I help you find someone?"

"I just realized the company I want is on the next floor." He smiled and pointed down. Then he retreated quickly and headed for the elevator. As Lupe approached, Tom had his finger on the elevator button.

"Which one?" Tom asked.

Lupe nodded as he said with a smile, "The middle one."

Down on the sidewalk they stood for a few minutes and looked up at the window Lupe would soon fly past.

In the days that followed the glider was delivered and Lupe learned to launch and glide short distances. When he caught his first thermal he was surprised how quickly he rose into the air and as he circled he shouted with glee, "Look at me bro."

Tom shouted instructions from the ground. Lupe learned quickly and handled the glider very well. Then he practiced swooping in circles and shooting paint balls at various targets. His aim became deadly.

A week later Tom went out into the desert in his four-wheel drive and practiced with one of his missiles. Using the attractant he developed; his accuracy was deadly, if you know what I mean. When he assembled the missile he would use he took great care and made sure everything was just right. He painted the long pointed nose red, and put in a little extra fuel; he didn't care if it went all the way though the building as long as it took Miles Burton with it. This was revenge.

The day they decided to mark Burton's office window they were out before it began to get light in the Eastern sky. In the desert normally there isn't any morning wind, but in July when it's eighty degrees at night sometimes the wind starts early and this was just such a morning. It wasn't blowing hard but it was steady at about fifteen miles an hour. Lupe launched from a place outside North Vegas caught a thermal that took him up very quickly. He was soon above five hundred feet. Tom bought him an altimeter that he wore on his wrist. He watched for planes coming into Mc Carran Airport. At that moment the sky was clear and Lupe banked toward the Wells Fargo Tower. He hoped he could maintain his height all the way to town. Half way to his target he began to lose altitude, but fate was with him and he caught another thermal and was soon up to five hundred feet again gliding through the warm summer air. He watched the streets and traffic below. What an exhilarating feeling cruising along above the rest of the world. The cars and people looked like toys moving along the street. In the distance he now could see the tower looming large in the faint morning light. So far there wasn't anyone standing looking up, pointing at him. As he approached the building he banked to his right and began a long swooping curve so he could pass the window at about fifteen feet away. His paintball gun was clipped to a strap around his neck. He pulled the gun in close as he steered with his other hand. When he passed the window he fired. The shot hit the middle window pane low causing a yellow splatter that looked like a rose to him. He hoped the missile would take Burton's head off as it went in. He smiled as he soared over the palm trees in the courtyard. Lupe leveled off and flew straight away from the building he was much higher than the rest of the buildings around the tower, but he needed another thermal if he was going to make it back to North Vegas. Just then he saw Tom's white truck moving along the street below. His arm was out the window waving slowly. So if he did go down Tom could pick him up. Just then the warm air began to lift him and he began to circle in the thermal and rise quickly. When he was up five hundred feet he glided toward home.

 By the time he reached his house the sun was just clearing the horizon. Lupe came down like an eagle touching lightly on his feet. He quickly unhooked and folded the glider and ran into his garage and let the door down.

 All this and no one noticed. Shortly Tom came by and picked up Lupe and the glider. Lupe was giddy as he told Tom how the shot hit the window at the perfect spot. Tom grinned and nodded. At Tom's they disassembled the glider and disposed of it in several dumpsters around town.

"Now Bro. We will have to get rid of all the electronics for the missiles and the spare parts. I found a cave on the backside of Sunrise Mountain that will be a good place to set up shop temporarily. Its set way back in the rocky part of the hills without an access and even the four-wheel drive has a hard time."

When they reached the cave with the first load Lupe said, "This is perfect man."

"To begin with this cave wasn't very deep but I used small amounts of blasting powder and dug it out to make a room about twenty by twenty. The ceiling is almost eight feet high. I installed a couple of steel posts to support the ceiling. There's a generator for power and I'm going to set up a bench to work on. I've already stored water and some food in case I need to stay a few days."

"That's cool man." Lupe said.

They unloaded everything and headed back to the house for the rest of the equipment. It was almost midnight when they got home from the last trip. They both slept well that night.

When the sunlight shone through Tom's bedroom window it woke him with a start. He got up, showered, dressed and started breakfast. By the time he finished eating Lupe came in the front door.

"Did we get everything out of there last night man?"

"Yeah pretty much. I'll wash down everything tonight and get rid of any traces of chemicals that might have been left. We need to mount that thing in the launcher and cover it with the tarp. We can probably take care of everything tomorrow. You might want to go visit some of your relatives in Mexico after this is over; you know what I mean?"

"Okay man that's what I'll do. How long should I stay?"

"Two maybe three weeks. There will be a big investigation; everybody in the government will be looking into this. I'll be able to handle things up here. I got a pair of those cheap radios to stay in touch until it's over. They're on the counter over there. When we're finished take yours apart and throw it away, I'll do the same with mine. You can sit on Maryland across from the tower and call me. I'll be about five miles East of you over on Harmon. Call me when he goes in and I'll give him time to get to his office."

"He gets there about 9:00 a.m. every morning," Lupe said.

When they were outside Lupe opened the garage door and Tom backed the truck in. Lupe dropped the door and turned on the light. Together they loaded the missile, armed it and covered the truck bed with a bright blue tarp. Lupe put a radio in his car. Now they had to wait, it would be the worst part for them because they probably wouldn't sleep tonight.

Tom and Lupe sat up with a stack of movies watching them on the TV. About 7:00 the next morning Lupe drove slowly toward Maryland Parkway. A few blocks up the street he checked his radio.

"You there bro?"

"Yeah I got my ears on and I'll be ready to leave in a few minutes. Let me know when you're in place."

"Okay man."

By 8:00 o'clock they were both parked and waiting. Lupe couldn't see the yellow dot on the window on the twelfth floor, but he knew right where it was on the pane.

"It's going to be perfect." At fifteen minutes to nine Lupe called.

"Here comes his car man. His wife is driving. They are pulling into the lot. Okay he's getting out and walking toward the doors." A minute later...

"He's probably on the elevator now give him a couple of minutes to get to his office." Lupe raised a small pair of binoculars and peered up at the twelfth floor window.

"Okay man I see movement up there. Anytime you're ready." A smile came across Lupe's face. It wouldn't be long now.

Five miles away Tom pulled the tarp back and looked around to make sure no one was coming. The street was deserted. He held the game pad and looked toward the tower one last time. He pushed a button and the launcher rose to maximum height. With one finger he pressed the fire button and held the joystick with the other hand. The missile fired and streaked off the launcher. Tom watched the screen as he guided the missile toward the building. On the screen the red dash closed on the white dot very quickly. When it hit the window the screen went blank. Now he would have to go somewhere and wait for Lupe to report what happened.

Down on the street below Lupe watched the missile streak across the sky and crash through the window. It hit the area of the yellow spot perfectly.

Up on the twelfth floor Miles came into the office and spoke to Lana and walked into his office. He crossed the room and looked out the window, turned and sat down in his office chair at the desk. Lana came in with his morning coffee, he thanked her and she went back to her desk. He took a sip of his coffee and spun around to look out at the city as he always did. He was smiling thinking life was good. As he started to take another drink he saw a silver glint over the rim of his cup. That was the last thing he saw before the missile crashed through the window on the yellow spot just above the sill. The point of the cone struck him in the middle of his chest at three hundred miles an hour. It went through Miles and through his chair driving him and the chair into the desk and pushing everything across the office to the wall on the other side. Slamming into the wall beside the office door the missile came to rest sticking through the wall about two feet behind Lana's chair. She screamed and turned to see what caused all the noise. Her eyes fell on the bloody tip of the missile, and she fainted. One of the girls in the office next to them came running in to see what had happened. She screamed and ran out for help not thinking to call 911. One of the men from another office came in and saw the carnage and picked up the phone and made the call. He then dared to open the door and saw Miles in the chair thrust through with the missile. The man turned and ran. Thirty minutes later every agency in town was represented on the twelfth floor. The local Police, Detectives, FBI, ATF, Medical Examiner's office and Bomb Squad were all present. All were looking and scratching their heads wondering where this thing came from. There were no Terrorists in Las Vegas. Or were there?

Lupe met Tom on the street and they drove back to North Vegas and went into Tom's house.

Tell my Mom I went to visit my Uncle Rudy. I'll be back sometime."

"Okay bro." Tom hugged Lupe. Lupe picked up two suitcases he brought from home and walked away. Tom didn't know if he would never see him again.

In the investigation of the incident in the Wells Fargo Tower authorities would eventually get to Tom Mason. They would find the records of his mother's death through Miles Burton's driving record and subsequent jail time and probation record. They would find the case proceedings and revenge would come up in someone's mind. That mind was an FBI agent by the name of Vince Gigliani, who was a very sharp man in investigative practices.

In the FBI office the next Monday morning, three days later, two agents were discussing the missile case still baffled by the nature of the crime.

"What do you think considering the info we have so far Vince?" Bill Wyman asked.

"I think we should go ask the kid, who lost his mother, some questions. I understand from checking around he has some very interesting inventions going. I've made a few calls and one of the automotive companies has already approached him and was turned down. This may involve something to the tune of a billion dollars. This kid could be very rich if he wanted so that means maybe he wants to be low profile, but why would he do that unless he had another agenda. Revenge is a very strong motive. I would be very interested in how he covers his tracks on this."

"You got an address on him?" Bill asked.

"Yeah and I think I'll pay him a visit this morning." Vince drove out to North Las Vegas in his plain black agency Ford. When he reached Tom's neighborhood he cruised slowly through the streets looking at the houses and the people. He was trying to get a feel for the people that lived here and it didn't say millionaire to him. Vince would have to remember to get access to Tom's bank account. It would be interesting to know what Mason did with that jackpot money he won a few years ago. He also wanted to talk to this Lopez kid who was Tom's friend. Maybe they were in this together. Vince looked at his note pad for the address of Tom's house, 1164 Stanford that would be another block West. He turned on Stanford and began looking at the addresses. When he came to Tom's house he stopped and studied the wood frame house that was obviously not new. Low profile stayed in the forefront of his mind. Vince looked at the houses around him and they were the same, average or poor. The neighborhood said 2nd class, $15,000 a year type homes. A lot of poor Mexicans that were glad to have a place to live. Working guys. What was Tom Mason doing down here when he could be living in Green Valley or Summerlin, two very affluent communities? Vince also thought about finding Tom's father surely he had one and he would bet the father was a smart cookie too. He picked up the radio mike and spoke into it,

Headquarters, this is unit 22."

"Yeah go ahead 22."

I'm out in North town and I need for someone to check on Tom Mason's father. Where he works and where he lives. If he is local or out of town."

"Right 22. We'll look into it and get back to you." Vince slowly got out of the car watching the front windows for any signs of life. Nothing moved in the windows. He approached the porch casually and rang the doorbell.

Inside Tom let the guy stand there a while before he went to the door. Then he peeked out the hole and looked him over for a few seconds. Finally he turned the knob slowly and opened the door.

He saw a short man with dark hair and a tanned complexion. He wore a black suit, and was a little on the heavy side because of too much pasta maybe. His eyes were dark and serious. Those eyes looked as though they could see right through a person.

"Are you Tom Mason?" he said in a deep voice.

"Who wants to know?" Vince wanted to grab the front of Tom's shirt and scream *I want to know punk!*, but he held himself in check.

In that short moment Vince saw a young boy with blond hair and an innocent face that seemed to say, *I wouldn't hurt anyone.* But Vince knew better than to trust looks, they were deceiving. So Vincent Gigliani retained his 'I'm going to get you boy.' look.

He held out his ID card and said, I'm agent Gigliani from the FBI and I would like to ask you a few questions."

"Sure come on in." Tom said innocently. He backed away from the door as Vince entered. Tom gestured toward a divan in the living room.

"Have a seat."

"Thanks" As Vince sat down Tom took a seat in a recliner across from him.

"So have you lived here long?"

"Sir I think that you, being from the FBI, already know all the pertinent facts about my life. So if we could skip the small talk I think we could get more accomplished if we would be honest with each other." Vince tried not to look surprised.

"We are investigating a crime of a very unusual nature. A man has been killed and that man was involved in the death of your mother several months ago. You know who I'm talking about?"

"Yes, Mr. Miles Burton. I saw the incident on TV last

night. Very unusual death and a shame he couldn't have lived to suffer the mental anguish he deserved for killing someone while in a drunken stupor. I would have hoped he would have gotten time in prison, but I guess that wasn't to be, and I must honor the justice system's decision. Isn't it possible that one of the Air Force missiles could have gone awry and escaped their guidance system? You know that happened in New Mexico once, of course thankfully, no one was killed." That took a little of the air out of Vince's balloon.

"We will be checking that aspect of the incident." He tried to keep his tone casual.

"You know Mr. Mason..."

"We don't have to be formal. You can call me Tom."

"Alright Tom, we have found that you have a very high scholastic ability, bordering on genius if you will and that there are a few inventions to your credit. Some people I've contacted say you have harnessed solar power to drive machines and cars."

"Thanks, but I haven't used that ability to commit murder Mr. Gigliani. If I'm going to be charged I need to speak with my lawyer. If you will get the proper search warrant you may search my property and my business property."

"No one is accusing you Tom, we are just checking out information, we have to see how this could have happened. We've never seen anything of this nature before and with all the terrorist threats we have to look into all aspects of the crime. There was no explosive charge in the head of that missile Tom. Usually terrorists want to blow something up and when they hit they want to get as many people as they can."

"Perhaps they got something they can't handle and it's going wild." Tom said wide-eyed.

"I think some keen minded individual invented that projectile as a murder weapon. You see our lab found a substance on the tip of that missile and on the window glass that is a highly classified material."

"My, my the Islamic world is working overtime, and

someone in our defense system is a little lax I'd say." Tom knew that the material wasn't government property, he made it, but he was sure they knew that.

This kid is real sharp Vince thought. *I'll know how sharp when I talk to his father.* So is your father alive?"

"I don't know, I've never seen him."

"Never?"

"Never!"

"May I ask what happened?"

"He got my Mom pregnant and left her. She never saw him again. He sent the divorce papers in the mail."

"Do you know anything about him?"

"Only what my mother told me."

"Do you know where we could find him? We would like to ask him some questions."

"No, I don't know where he is, I've never tried to make contact with him." Vince could hear the hard edge in Tom's voice.

"I guess there is no love lost between the two of you?" Tom simply shrugged and raised his eyebrows.

"Where were you when this incident took place?"

"Right here. Lupe and I were watching movies. We have a marathon once in a while." He pointed to a stack of tapes on the entertainment center.

"You stay up all night watching movies?"

"Yeah and of course we eat pizza from Domino's up the street. A kid named Greg is the delivery guy. He could probably tell you he dropped off a Hawaiian supreme about 8:00 p.m. and another super supreme about 11:00 p.m.. I slept most of the next day. Mrs. Lopez, that's Lupe's Mom, came late in the afternoon to fix dinner and clean up a little. She could tell you I was here she lives down the street." Tom pointed that way.

"Is Lupe home now?"

"No he's probably at the shop right now."

"What does he do?"

"He's a specialized mechanic. He does engine work and

conversions for me. His shop is over on East Lake Mead, L&L Engines." Vince took a card out of his pocket as he stood and offered it to Tom.

"I will probably want to talk to you again so let me know if you go anywhere out of state."

Tom stood, took the card and nodded.

"What's the number at the Lopez' house?"

"Uh, 1327 Stanford."

"Okay we'll be in touch. Thanks." Vince left and Tom stood at the door watching as he drove away.

Tom smiled because Lupe had already been in Mexico a couple of days. They would have a rough time finding him down there.

That night about 9:00 p.m. Tom jumped over the back fence and trotted down the street to his solar car three blocks away. He drove out to the desert as far as he could and hiked the rest of the way to the cave, which took him two hours to reach the lab. The rest of the night he spent working on special units and setting up targets in the city. The FBI and the rest of them were going to pay a heavy price for this. There was a special explosive unit for each of them. Later Tom would take them out in the desert and bury them with an extended timer to go off in the future. A few days later he planned to go into Vegas and put a mark on each of the places he intended to hit. Just before the sun came up he hiked back to the car and went home and switched to his four-wheeler.

By 8:00 o'clock he was on the Tonopah highway headed toward the test site. When he passed the Lee Canyon exit he pulled off the road onto a dirt trail. He drove far enough so as not to be noticed from the road. Tom stopped and raised the hydraulic unit with a missile on it. When Gigliani's car passed, the missile would follow him up the highway until it hit the rear window. Tom waited and watched the road with a pair of military binoculars. Tom waited a couple of hours before he spotted the agent's car. He picked up the game pad and turned it on. The missile streaked across the desert when he pushed the fire button. Gigliani was about a mile and a half away when the missile struck the back window and exploded. There was very little that was recognizable after the blast. The car behind him skidded to a stop as the fireball rose skyward. The driver was terrified and was afraid there more coming so he drove around the carnage and sped away at high speed. The next driver was a woman who stopped and called 911 on her cell. When they got the fire out there would be very little to recognize and less to examine. Vince Gigliani was a cinder. Tom turned around and drove home. He put the truck in the garage and lowered the door.

About ten minutes after he arrived, he mounted another tube in the bed and covered it with a tarp. A few minutes later he checked the street and drove out headed to the cave behind the mountain. There were a few more things he had to take care of; he knew it wouldn't be long before they caught him. A few blocks down Lake Mead he picked up another FBI car. *Let'em follow, I'll take care of them when I get out in the desert.* He thought. At the end of Lake Meade he picked up Hollywood Road and drove West. The sedan was still behind him. About three miles further he turned left onto a dirt road. He drove fast enough to kick up a dirt cloud behind him and the men in the car behind him couldn't see what he was doing. He pushed the button that raised the launcher and the canvas slid off. He was about a mile ahead of them so it gave him time to stop and push the fire button. The missile streaked off the launcher and a few seconds later there was an explosion. The two men in the Ford were toast.

When Tom arrived at the cave he hurried inside to prepare the last units that would be located out in the desert. He went a few miles out, dug holes and placed the units in the ground and set the timers. Back at the cave he set timers and trip wires for the explosives that would destroy the cave if anyone found it. After he got back to Vegas he knew he couldn't go back to his house so he went to one of the downtown hotels, parked in the garage, rented a room and watched the news.

As usual the police were running around in circles, but eventually they would get him he knew that. He called room service for a good meal, maybe his last.

The FBI was doing a pretty good job of keeping the word missile out of the news stories. If the Associated Press got hold of that the town would be empty in a matter of hours. Tom smiled as the press told of isolated cases and explosives being planted in cars. Tomorrow he would try to put attractant on some of the buildings that were to be targets.

The next morning the places he passed were to heavily guarded to get off a shot so he decided to go back to the cave and wait it out. What he didn't realize was there was a description of his truck out and the streets were loaded with cops. When Tom saw all the patrol cars he used side streets and carefully made his way toward North Las Vegas. When he turned on to Lake Mead Boulevard he picked up a motorcycle cop. At first the cop didn't notice him so Tom stayed cool and watched him in the mirror. Finally he noticed Tom was being careful and that draws a cop quicker than anything. He pulled in behind Tom and turned on his lights. Tom panicked and sped away with the cop in hot pursuit. When Tom left the road to get into the desert the motorcycle was close behind. It was then the cop noticed he was almost out of gas and he wouldn't make it too much further. He called dispatch and reported where he was and said he needed backup. He confirmed that this truck was the one they were looking for and that Tom was dangerous. When the motorcycle sputtered the first time he pulled his gun and took aim, as best he could, on the bumpy road and fired off a shot. The bullet hit the body just below the rear window and went through the seat and into Tom's back behind his heart. Tom slammed forward and into the steering wheel. His vision blurred and only sheer determination kept him going. He left the cop in a cloud of dust for the motorcycle had run out of gas. The pain was unbearable, but he had to make it to the cave. He was bleeding badly and the seat was soaked with blood. When Tom finally pulled up to the cave entrance he had just enough strength to get out and stagger over to a mine shaft a short distance from the cave entrance. It was a black hole with a wood frame around the top that went straight down into the ground. There are a lot of these old mine shafts out there that no one knows about.

As Tom stepped up to the shaft he could hear the roar of engines in the distance. They would be here soon. No use trying to delay. He stepped off the edge and fell down into the darkness. A couple of seconds later there was a splash deep in the ground. Tom Mason was gone. About a half hour later the Police and the FBI found the truck and the cave. They rushed in calling for Tom to surrender and come out. When they discovered the cave was empty several agents went in and finally someone broke a trip wire. When the explosives went off it blew out the front of the cave and killed several agents and some of the cops outside. It also took out the directors SUV.

In the days that followed the FBI searched the area around the site and found several missiles buried in metal boxes with timers on them that would launch on some future date. They were destined for several buildings in Vegas. They were disarmed.

After several days of searching they felt they found all there was and closed the case.

Epilogue

On Thanksgiving day out in the desert to the East of North Las Vegas. The sun was shining brightly the temperature was a warm sixty-eight degrees. About 7:00 o'clock a patch of ground began to shift gradually until a set of metal doors were exposed. The doors slowly opened and there lay a twelve foot missile on a launch rack. The rack slowly rose until it was at a forty-five degree angle. Inside the bottom of the box was a timer with red numerals counting down toward zero. The time left on the timer was **4:38**. Twenty feet away the ground began to shift again and two more doors opened. The timer on the second missile was **4:58**.

Out in Summerlin, one of the affluent communities in Vegas, Thurston Mason was sitting in his dining room waiting for the maid to serve his breakfast. He was reading the Sunday newspaper. Directly above him, on the second floor, a beautiful blond woman is sleeping in Thurston's expensive king-sized bed. Thurston is telling the maid,

"Maria tell the cook not to put any salt on the food."

Three minutes later the first missile streaks away toward its destination. It travels across the Vegas Valley at five hundred miles an hour and crashes into the roof of Thurston's beautiful two story house in Summerlin. It almost takes the second story off the house and the floor collapses on top of Thurston leaving him under a pile of rubble. He is not dead yet and can see through the debris. The top of the house is open and he sees the second missile coming down towards him.

Prodigy

Summerlin is a huge affluent community in the Northeast sector of Las Vegas. It is beautifully laid out with spacious lawns, pools and fountains. The homes are very large and exquisitely decorated. One could only guess at the majestic interiors of some of these homes.

Rashena Moore is one of the many people that live in this community. She is Vice President of a large corporation that produces images of all kinds for everything large and small. This ranges from small cabinet decorations to murals on very large buildings. She has an eye for the pictures she produces and works in the large building sector of the company. Her success in this area has brought her to the position she now holds. There is a reason for her ability however. She has a very sweet personality and a gifted six year old son.

Rashena was married to Brad Moore, after three years they had a boy that turned out to be a very unusual child. When the boy reached the age of five they realized their son had the ability to see into people and knew a stranger's comings and goings before they happened. Of course at the age of six the child didn't know how to handle his gift and sometimes disturbed his parents with his predictions and precognitive abilities. It seemed he knew when things were going to go wrong. Rashena also saw early on that her son could help her to be successful in her job. At times she would ask Robert who he thought she should talk to about helping her get ahead in the company. He would look down and say the person's name even though he had never met them.

Brad on the other hand was horrified by his son's abilities. He was constantly afraid of his son's predictions although at this early age they were mostly innocent. He felt more sinister things would come at an older age perhaps. Brad was so overcome with his son's foresight he could no longer live in the same house with the boy. One day he had a long talk with Rashena and told her his feelings and felt it would be best if he moved out and filed for a divorce. This broke Rashena's heart, but somehow she was able to pick up the pieces, after all she had a son to raise.

Rashena was a beautiful woman with flawless olive skin, very dark brown eyes that seemed to look through people especially when the people were insincere. Her hair was jet black, and very shiny. She was tall at five' ten" and slender, always watching what she ate. When her son was born the couple named him Robert. After the divorce she filed the proper papers and changed his name to Rashid. Amazingly he adapted well to his new name as if it were meant to be. There was very little reaction to the change when his mother told him about it.

"Rashid, nice name Mommy."

Rashid Moore was like his mother in description. He was olive skinned, with dark brown hair, but his eye color was unusual. They were a dark honey color. When people looked at him they were transfixed by their glow. When he smiled it affected everyone around him. It seemed that he did not know how to frown at this age. His expression was either blank or smiling. He didn't cry much except when he fell or was hurt. Rashid didn't show disappointment with life, he seemed to accept whatever came his way. He was overly attached to his mother though and wanted to be around her all the time. She couldn't take Rashid to work with her so she would hire a child specialist to care for him while she was away.

One day Rashena took her son with her to the bank because she had no one to stay with him while she was out and about. The business she had to attend to required she go inside to speak to the manager. She held Rashid's hand as they came out and started toward the parking lot. When they reached the sidewalk she intended to turn toward the parking lot. Rashid pulled away from her grasp and ran over to the curb. His mother thought he was going to run out into the street.

"Rashid! Stop!" He stood at the curb looking out in the street pointing at something.

"Look Mommy it's in there." Rashena's heart was beating fast. Her son had given her a scare. She walked over and squatted down beside him as she usually did to investigate his strange behavior.

"What's in there sweetheart, I don't see anything."

"In there." he repeated, still pointing at the street. She waited until there was no traffic and stepped off the curb and walked out a little way holding him by the hand.

"What do you see Rashid?"

"Down there." he said as he pointed at a manhole cover. "Something down there."

"Honey, this better be important. I don't want to be chasing some kid's lost toy or something." He put his hands together and looked up at his mother and nodded his head.

Rashena took him by the hand and led him back to the curb.

While they were standing there a police car came to a stop and the officer said, "Can I help you folks?"

"Yes officer my son has found something important, I think."

"Just a moment, I'll pull over and park." He pulled over to the curb and got out. He walked back to them with a smile on his face. Rashid was still pointing at the street.

Rashena felt embarrassed. She said to herself, *I know*

he's going to think I'm crazy, but here goes.

"My son is a special child, not impaired but gifted. He tells me there is something important in that manhole." The officer looked down at Rashid and then at the street. Then he looked back at Rashena. He stood in silence for a moment.

"You know this would require a public works truck and two men to investigate this don't you?"

"Uh, yes, maybe we should let this go." She turned to leave and Rashid cried,

"No mommy it's really down there."

The officer squatted down and asked Rashid, "Son can you tell me what's down there?"

He made a few frustrated noises and said, "The thing."

His mother tried to help him, "He doesn't know how describe it. He's only six."

The officer asked, "Is it a bag or a box son?"

"A box." Rashid proclaimed loudly. The officer stood and let out a sigh and walked back to his patrol car. He talked on the radio a moment and came back to them.

"A public works truck will be here in a few minutes."

"Is there anyway I can keep my son out of this?"

"No ma'am, I have to write a report on this now." She rolled her eyes.

"Oh no." A few minutes later a big truck pulled up and the man on the passenger side got out.

"What's up officer?"

Trying to protect the woman and her son he said, "I'd like for you to raise that manhole cover under your truck. There is something in there we need to see."

The man turned to the driver and said, "Pull up a little Carl we need to raise the manhole cover on the street."

The driver pulled the truck up a few feet and turned on his yellow light and set out a vermillion cone in the street behind the truck. Then he pulled a long bar out of the bed. When he put it in the hole the other guy helped him raise the cover. When they had it out of the hole the driver pulled it over to the side and looked down into the hole, shading his eyes with his hand.

"This is an electrical access and there is a box down there that doesn't look like it belongs there." The officer looked down the hole, then he looked at Rashid. Is there any way we can get it out without calling the electrical department?"

"Well maybe, I've got a rod with a hook on the end." He went back to the truck and pulled out a length of rebar with a bend on the end. He lowered it into the hole and slid the hook under the handle. Slowly he raised the box to the top. The officer took it off and walked over to his unit. He put the box on the passenger side of his car. He walked back and told the public works guys the electrician had probably left some of his tools in the hole. He would make sure they got back to him after he wrote up his report.

He asked for the workers names and told them they could leave. As they drove away one said to the other, "You know that ain't no tool box don't you?"

The other man smiled.

"That's a bank security box man. It had First Federal on the side."

The officer took out his report clipboard and started to write. A few moments later he asked for their names and addresses. Rashena gave the officer her license. When he finished he said,

"After we investigate this I'll let you know if there is any reward."

"I just hope we can keep this from the press. My son is too young for the mess this is going to cause."

"I'll be as discreet as I can, but I don't know how it can be explained without telling someone he knew it was down there. Maybe you can come down to the station and talk to the Capitan." the officer advised.

At the station while Rashena waited to speak to the Capitan she thought, *I can just see Brad trying to handle something like this. He would be in a panic.*

When the Capitan called them in of course the first question was, "How did the boy know the box was in the hole."

"My son has psychic abilities and he noticed it when we came out of the bank."

The Capitan smiled and said, "You wouldn't want to hire him out to do a little police work would you?"

"I'm sorry Capitan my son is going to have enough trouble in his young life as it is. He's only six."

"I'm sorry, that was a little crude I guess. If you don't mind waiting someone is counting the money and we will call the bank involved to see if there is a reward."

"I'm really not concerned with a reward. Could you donate it to charity and let us get on with our lives?"

"I'm sorry ma'am we can't do that we have to account for that box and who found it. I appreciate your patience." A few minutes later a female officer came into the office.

"There's fifty thousand in the box and a five thousand dollar reward. The bank president will be here in a few minutes. It's from another bank across town."

Rashena pressed her back against the back of the chair and said under her breath, "Rashid I am not stopping to investigate anymore strange events you hear me."

An hour later the bank president showed up and was all, "Thank you, Thank you, Thank you very much."

He brought a check for five thousand dollars and presented it to her. She gave it back to him and said, "Would you donate this to Opportunity village the children need this more than we do."

The president's eyes widened.

"We will do as you ask. You are very kind." After another half hour of amenities she and Rashid finally got out of there. On the way home she tried to explain the trouble these things could cause.

"Mom I saw the box in the hole."

"Yes Son and next time we leave it there."

Rashena met Salina Rodriguez a young Spanish girl who worked in child care by special appointment at the company she worked for. She was a petite woman, just five foot, but there wasn't a child born she wouldn't tackle. She seemed to move with purpose in everything she did. Salina had met and helped a lot of children in single parent homes. When she saw Rashid she fell in love with him immediately. Seemingly she hadn't seen such innocence in other children.

"Rashena, I want to marry this boy before someone else gets to him. He is gorgeous." His mother laughed at Salina and knew this was the caretaker for her son.

When Rashid was introduced to Salina he shied away from her behind his mother's skirt. Rashena pulled him out from behind her and asked him.

"What do you think about this lady Rashid?"

He looked up at his mother and said, "Nice lady Mommy. She loves me." Then he hid his face in his mother's skirt.

Salina squatted down and said, Maybe we can skip the hug this time, but could I shake your hand?"

He moved behind his mother hugging her leg.

"You are going to be a lady killer I can see it already." Salina said.

The first day they were together Salina didn't try to force herself on him. Rashid did everything she asked of him. When she fixed his lunch he enjoyed everything and later in the afternoon he took a nap. While he was sleeping Salina prepared notes for the lessons she would teach him in the mornings. At four-thirty when his mother came home he was glad to see her and hugged her fiercely when she picked him up.

"Well what do you think of this nice lady Rashid?" his mother asked. Salina stood nearby smiling at him.

Rashid bowed his head and began to weep.

"What's the matter honey?"

He buried his face in his mother's shoulder and wept harder. A look of concern came over Salinas' face.

"Salina I'm so sorry my son is strange at times. I'm sure

this is not your fault. Will you excuse us for a moment we have to have a private talk." Rashena carried Rashid to his bedroom. She set him on the bed and asked again, "Can you tell Mommy what's wrong?"

He shook his head vehemently.

"Rashid if this is something serious Mommy needs to know."

He shook his head again.

She waited for a few seconds while he gathered himself. Then as softly as she could Rashena asked, "Can you tell Mommy anything?"

Rashid sat quietly with a worried look on his face.

"Maybe later when Salina is gone we can talk."

Rashid lay down and put his thumb in his mouth. To Rashena this was strange, her son had never sucked his thumb. It seemed he was trying to put something out of his mind.

In the living room Salina waited anxiously. Rashena came back and said, "Salina I'm so sorry, I don't know what is going on but I need to make you aware of some things so if you can sit down for a moment…" She sat down on the couch.

"My son has an ability to read people. He has precognitive abilities and they have developed too soon in his young life. Sometimes when he sees events he doesn't know how to put them into words. I haven't had him tested yet, but I'm searching for the right person that will understand what he is going through at this tender age. I have no idea what caused him to act like he did, but for sure he has seen something that has made him sad. I don't know if it involves you or someone in your family, or how serious it may be. I've never seen him cry like he did today. I will continue to talk to him and see if I can get anything from him. I will call you as soon as I know. Can you come tomorrow?"

"Sure, that's the reason you hired me Rashena."

"I'm sorry if I seem to make too much of this, but I know things happen the way he sees them."

"It's all right I'm not afraid. When things seem dangerous I carry protection and believe me I know how to use it." Salina said. "Okay I thank you for your patience. I'm sure I will be able to uncover something else when Rashid feels like talking. If he does, I'll tell you in the morning."

"If not, I wouldn't press him about it." Salina said. She left full of concern and wonder.

When Rashena went back to his bedroom Rashid was asleep with his thumb still in his mouth. She went to her office to finish some work she had brought home and later prepared dinner for her and Rashid. She went into his room and he was awake.

"How's Mommy's boy."

He stretched and said, "Okay Mommy."

She gave her a smile and bent down to kiss him.

"Hey tiger how about some supper?"

What we got Mommy?"

Chicken nuggets, vegetables, and cottage cheese. And if you eat good there might be some blackberry pie and ice cream somewhere."

While they were eating Rashena was going on about things they might do on the weekend together. When she looked up she saw a blank stare on Rashid's face.

"What is it, honey?" He came out of the trance and looked down at his pie and ice cream.

"This is sooo good Mommy!" He was bouncing up and down like he might be swinging his leg under the table.

"Everything is all right Son?"

He nodded.

"Okay so we can go see a baseball game or we can go to the movie, or we can have a picnic in the park. What do you want to do?"

"Can we ride the coaster at Circus, Circus?"

"I don't know sweetheart you are still too small for those kind of rides."

"Can we go to the scalaber and ride the one there?" He meant the virtual reality rides at the Excalibur Hotel.

"Well maybe. Those aren't so bad. Do you think you might be able to tell Mommy what you saw this afternoon?"

Rashid was looking down at his bowl.

"Tell her not to let him in."

"Is he a bad man Rashid?" his mother asked softly.

Now he was staring at the wall again with a blank look.

"Very baaad!"

"Can you see what he looks like?"

"Big, mad, dirty man, he gots a rope. He hurts people. Ladies go away when he comes." He began to shake his head vigorously. "No, No, No. Don't open the door. SALINA DON'T OPEN THE DOOR!" he screamed and began to weep again. Rashena ran around the table picked him up and held him.

"It's okay Rashid, he won't get her I promise. Rashena carried him into the living room and dug her cell phone out of her purse and began punching numbers.

Salina. Hi, it's Rashena. Rashid had a vision of a man standing outside of either my house or yours with a rope in his hands. He also saw several dead people somewhere. Salina keep your gun handy. Do you think we should call the police?"

"No Rashena when the time comes we will call the police, besides I have a friend on the force and can call on him for help. I really appreciate your concern. I'll see you in the morning." she pushed the end button. Salina went to a drawer and took out a small Beretta .32 semi-automatic. It was loaded with seven hollow point bullets. She had faced someone in her past who had attacked her. After going through a support program she signed up for self-defense classes. There would be no repeat of anything like that.

She stared into the distance and said to no one in particular, "I shoot until this gun is empty."

Rashena looked at the cell phone with a frown while the dial tone buzzed. Maybe she really didn't know this woman Salina after all. They would have a talk when she got home tomorrow afternoon.

The next morning Salina arrived at Rashena's with the gun in her purse.

Rashena told her not to open the door to anyone.

"I have a camera's that focuses on the front door and the back patio. The monitor is behind a panel in the living room." She turned on the monitor and the cameras. The screen was split to show both areas. The front camera was focused so that it would show the area in front of the windows as well as the door area.

"You are going to be all right Salina."

"Are you going to be all right is what I want to know?" Salina answered.

"If this guy is coming he's going to come when it gets dark. That is usually when they show up under the cover of darkness. If he comes to my place he's in real trouble I've been prepared for this kind of thing for a while now, I was attacked once before and because I didn't roll over and play dead I survived. Then I took self-defense training and found out about all the nice places a woman can hit or punch an unruly creep. I dated a cop a few times and he suggested the Beretta. If I hit him with just one shot he will hurt for a long time, if he lives. If he messes with any of the children I'm watching his days are over."

"I know now that I got the right girl to watch my son. Put my number on your speed dial. If something happens when you get home, call me after you call 911."

Salina smiled and Rashena went to work. When she reached her office someone had left a note for her to contact a company that was considering a large contract job and she would probably be out most of the day.

Salina cleaned up after Rashid had eaten breakfast and they were at the table talking about one of the lessons for the day.

"Today we are going to talk about the letter R which is the first letter in your name." Rashid was staring off into space.

"Did you hearing me Rashid?" she said softly.

"Only taking time until he comes." he said. Salina let out an impatient sigh.

"Rashid let's not have another strange day Okay?"

As if ignoring her he said, "I told Mommy, but I didn't tell you."

"All right, What do you want to tell me? Will this man come to my house or will he come here?"

"Your house. Outside the window. He gots a rope."

"I'm glad you know this Rashid. You have saved my life, because now I can stop him." She glanced out the dining room window as she said this.

"You can't stop him."

"What do you mean?"

"No one can see him." Now Salina was concerned.

"So if I call the police can they stop him?"

"No one can see him." he repeated.

"What if I don't go home?"

"He will wait."

Rashid's eyes rolled up and he fell back against the back of the chair. He had fainted.

"Rashid, Are you all right?" She got out of her chair and picked him up. He was limp as a rag. Salina hurried into the bedroom and lay him on his bed and put a cold rag on his forehead. When he didn't revive she called his mother.

"Hi Rashena, something has happened to Rashid. Maybe you should come home." The next thing Salina heard was the dial tone. Rashena didn't even answer before she hung up.

Salina ran into the living to get her purse. It wasn't a good thing to be separated from the gun. She stepped to the window and looked out. A minute later Rashena's car was already speeding into the driveway. She was just a couple of miles away. She got out and ran for the door. Salina opened the door. Rashena rushed in and ran to her son's bedroom. She moistened the washcloth again and wiped his forehead and blew her breath in his face. Something she did when she came to him when he was asleep. Slowly his eyes opened and he reached for her and hung on tight.

Adversary

He sat in an old dented pickup staring at the field. The truck was black and scratched. The paint was falling off in places, but Jack Larone didn't care he had other things on his mind. What there was left of it. Jack had crossed over into the twilight zone for sure and what was left of his mind didn't operate like anyone else's. He was fresh out of a Northern California maximum mental facility. The way he escaped was truly amazing. When he sunk into the depths of insanity he also received something with it. But first, a little about how Jack got to this point of insanity.

As a boy of about twelve his parents had also reached a point of mindlessness from alcohol consumption to the point that they would rob liquor stores for their habit. Of course they could rob each store only once then they had to move on to another town, but this arrangement worked very well for the Larone's. They were able to rob many stores and get away with it. Their thinking being twisted; they only took the best liquor for a binge and ignored the cash register so the stores didn't pursue the theft too seriously. They figured a few bottles of booze, what the heck. Write if off. All the while Jack sat in the car and watched for the cops. One afternoon he missed an approaching cop car and his parents almost got caught. Thanks to some diligent maneuvering behind the wheel by his mother they got away, but from then on he paid for his mistake. Jack had not been treated to well in the past, but now they both beat him and screamed at him, called him everything they could think of. Finally after a year of this he sunk into the depths of despair and one night he wandered away and was never seen by his drunken parents again. As far as they were concerned, 'Good riddance!' When Jack came to mentally, he was wandering around in the small town of Roseville, California just North of Sacramento. As he wandered the streets a cruising pedophile looking for a new partner spotted Jack and picked him up. Beatings and cursing was mild compared to what Jack would experience as his prisoner.

He went totally insane in a matter of weeks and the abuse went on for months. Finally the Pedophile tired of Jack, would have killed him and left his body in the woods and went in search of a new child, but somehow Jack got out of the bedroom window and escaped while the man was gone in search of drugs. When the guy came back he went wild looking for Jack fearing he would go to the cops. But he didn't have to worry about that Jack didn't have enough mind left to go to anyone.

A day or two later a sweet old grandmother found Jack in a store opening packages for something to eat. She stopped him and said, "Son don't you realize that's stealing."

When she saw the blank expression on Jack's face she took him by the arm, led him to the checkout and paid for what he had eaten and took him home and fixed him a hot meal. He dove in with both hands, forget the fork. Alma tried to get him to talk, but Jack was too far gone for any of that. He didn't even know his name by this time. Finally she gave up and took Jack to child services after he wet his pants a couple of times.

After weeks of tests they determined that Jack was insane, and would have to be cared institutionally for the rest of his life. They transferred him to a mental facility in Sacramento. There they fed him and took him to the bathroom every few hours. No one could get a response from Jack. Doctors or nurses, mental therapists, man or woman it made no difference Jack Larone gave no response. He didn't respond to tickling or pain he was just a living vegetable it seemed. So the child care went on for years until Jack was grown and nearly thirty years old.

One morning Jack was wandering around in the hall and touched his finger to a space heater left unattended by one of the aides. He stopped and looked down at his hand. The finger was red and sore and a blister was soon to follow. The nurse found him standing in the hall looking at his hand.

"What's the matter Jack did you hurt yourself?" She took him by the arm intending to lead him to the nurse's desk to put some ointment on it. A low growl emitted from Jack's lips. When she looked over at him he hit her so hard with his fist he knocked her across the wide hall into the wall. She lay there unconscious.

Jack's face contorted into a fierce animal expression. When he started for the nurse a male aide grabbed Jack and screamed, "Larone has come to get a strait jacket!"

The rest of the aides and nurses at the station looked up in confusion giving Jack time to pull the aide over his shoulder by the front of his uniform and slam him on the hall floor. The quickness of the move was so intense it broke the aides back. A panic button was pushed only too late. Jack had time to beat the male aide to death. In seconds a horde of muscular orderlies with a straight jacket descended on Jack, but he sent two of them to the hospital before they got him subdued.

A nurse slipped a hypodermic into the back of his arm and in a few minutes Jack was out. They put him in a padded cell and good thing they did, because when he woke up he broke the straps that held his arms in the straight jacket and started on the padding on the walls screaming all the way. During the hours Jack was sleeping it off his muscular structure had changed and his muscles began to bulge. Now he was a hundred and eighty pounds of screaming testosterone. Needless to say he destroyed the padded cell, but thank God he couldn't get out.

A couple of doctors watched Jack through the bullet proof glass in the door as he tore up everything he could get his hands on.

"What are they going to do when he gets hungry?" One of the doctors asked.

"This boy is on a fast cause no one is going in there to feed him." The other one answered.

When the doctors walked down to the nurses station one

asked, "How are we going to get control of Larone?"
One of the male aides looked up and said, "You ever heard of a dart gun Doc? You can make it as strong as you want. And I recommend an operation. You know, a lobotomy?"
"I think you're right." the doctor answered as he walked away.
So that is what they decided to do. They waited for Jack to get tired and when he lay down in the rubble they stepped in with a dart gun and gave him a strong sedative. He was put on a gurney and rolled to an operating room to be prepared for surgery. As the anesthesiologist was preparing to give Jack another shot to keep him out for the duration of the operation Jack's knee shot up and cracked the doctor in the side of the head. A loud roar ensued and when Jack discovered a strap across his chest. He raised up against the strap and bent the table he was laying on and it gave him enough slack to slide out from under the strap. A nurse ran at him with a needle and he hit her in the face hard enough to crush her facial structure. She would need many operations to restore her face. When this happened everyone in the OR ran, because anyone else Jack got his hands on was dead.
Jack ignored the doctor and the nurse he had just knocked out. He wanted out of there. From there Jack dashed out of the institution and wandered away. The authorities were notified, but they just couldn't find Jack Larone.
So that brings us to the field where Jack sat in the beat up truck. How he knew how to drive no one knows. Maybe it was in his memory somewhere from the days when his parents robbed liquor stores.
Something else he remembered was where his folks lived. Jack went back to their house. They were home, older now and still drunk. He found them sleeping it off and dragged them both outside, beat them to death, and left their bodies in the back yard. He took some of his Dad's clothes and changed. Down the street he found an old man with a black pickup. He broke his neck and took the truck. Now Jack is sitting next to

this field wondering what to do next.

Suddenly as if he received a mental message he raised his head and started the truck. When he reached Roseville he drove the streets looking for the pedophile. While he drove things were happening in his mind. A strange ability was developing.

In the nineteen forties there was a radio show called, 'The Shadow' in this narrative the main character had an ability to make him self invisible and thereby he could catch criminals without their knowing he was there. This development was happening in Jack's mind. You see Jack's mind was no where near what a normal person's was. One could use the term 'way out there' and be closer to the proper description. Now that he had gotten rid of his parents his rage simmered down to a low boil and he began to gain some control which made him very dangerous. When he drove past the molester's house he recognized it and stopped across the street. Jack sat and watched for a while and finally decided to take a look inside. He got out and crossed the street without looking either way. A soccer mom in a station wagon almost hit him. Fortunately for her she slammed on the brakes and drove around Jack. If she had stopped it would have been her last. Jack continued on to the front door. He tried the knob, it was locked.

As the minutes passed he remembered more of the experience he'd had with the pedophile and his anger was at full rage now. He grabbed the knob a second time and twisted gritting his teeth. Jack twisted the knob completely off the door. He pushed the door hard and broke the jamb. The door swung in. The room was silent. If the man had been there he would not have recognized Jack now. Jack Larone walked in, swung the door closed and sat down on the dirty couch to wait. He just sat there and stared. A couple of hours later the man came back with a little girl about ten. She was an innocent little thing, bone thin from lack of proper nourishment. Her blond hair was dirty and stringy, she might have been pretty otherwise, but that didn't mater to peddie she would be dead in a couple of days anyway.

He stopped at the door, holding the girl by the arm, looked down at the knob laying on the step. Then he saw the lock broken in. His mistake was he pushed the door in. A strong hand on the end of a powerful arm reached out and grabbed him by the shirt. He let go of the girl and grasped the arm that held his shirt. Fortunately the girl ran away and consequently she lived, but not so for peddie. Jack drug him in, took him into the dirty bedroom and did to him what he had done to Jack many times. While that was going on Jack was hitting him in the back of the head about every three seconds. One of the blows was a little low and fractured his brain stem severing the spinal cord at the base of his neck. Peddie died then, which was merciful, because when Jack was through he twisted peddie's head completely off and threw it at the wall. Now Jack's strength was massive he probably could have lifted a car. Rashid's assessment of 'Baad' was pretty close. The song 'Bad to the Bone' comes to mind.

Jack went into the small kitchen and took a knife out of a secret place he remembered. It was a big survival knife and peddie had kept it very sharp. Jack went back into the bedroom and cut peddie into many pieces and left the mess and the knife on the floor.

Driving down the road a few minutes later; for the first time Jack Larone smiled.

Jack drove South and then East toward Nevada. When Jack reached Vegas it was night and he was fascinated by the great glow that lit up the night sky. He pulled over onto the shoulder of I-15 and sat for a long time like a child looking at the blinking lights. Finally seemingly coming to himself, he drove on and took a side exit that led him to the Summerlin area. He came to a fast food restaurant and stopped in the parking lot in front of the big windows. He could smell the greasy fries and he was ravaged. He hadn't eaten in two days. Jack got out and stood by the door of the car. In a minute or two a lady came out with a big bag. Jack charged her and snatched the bag out of her hand. She screamed and he knocked her down. He ripped the bag open and began devouring one of the big hamburgers inside.

The kids at the counter saw what happened and one of them dialed 911. While Jack was consuming his second burger a patrol car sped into the lot. Jack turned to see the officer getting out. He ran around to the back of the restaurant stuffing fries into his mouth. The officer followed with his gun drawn. When he reached the place where he thought Jack should be there was no one there. He turned his head in the direction of the trash area. Something hit him, hard. He went down like a ton of brick.

The patrol car, with lights flashing, sat silent in the parking lot. The kids inside were peeking around equipment trying to see what was going on.

Jack, at the back of the restaurant, was still eating fries. He dropped the empty bag next to the cop and wandered inside. A man at the counter had purchased a burger, large fries and a strawberry milkshake. Jack came in the door eyes wide and rushed the guy at the counter and roared at him. He fled. Jack tore the bag open and consumed the shake. He turned and set the cup on the counter and grunted. A fat Mexican boy edged up to the counter and grabbed the cup and made another shake. He set it down and fled to the back of the restaurant. He didn't know it, but he had just saved several lives. Jack grabbed the cup and began gulping it down. With strawberry shake all over his face he grabbed the bag the patron had left behind and stormed out.

By this time the officer had recovered and was on the radio for back up. Jack smiled and walked over to his truck and drove away with the officer following at a safe distance. Soon other patrol cars followed the first. When there were at least five cars with two officers in each one they tried to surround Jack. Finally they forced him off the road on the 215 freeway. With lights glaring everywhere they raced to overcome Jack. Before they could get to him he was out of the truck climbing the sound barrier wall. The cops were running everywhere, but they couldn't see Jack. He dropped down on the other side of the wall and snuck away quietly. Through the night Jack wandered around the Summerlin area in a trance like state seemingly with no purpose.

The police towed away the truck Jack had been driving. In the process of investigation they discovered he had killed the man who owned the pickup and stolen it. which led to the institution he had been kept in in Sacramento. When they discovered how dangerous Jack was they were shocked. Police were looking for this maniac all over California. They learned his name and how strong he was, but what they didn't know was about this ability he had.

The Swat team was brought in and sent to the Summerlin area, but they didn't know where to look.

In the early morning hour just after six he passed the house where Rashena Moore lived. And when Jack passed the house, walking down the sidewalk Rashid woke with a start. He jumped up and ran to his mother's bedroom.

"Mommy, Mommy" He screamed. He's here! He's here! He's here!"

His mother woke and grabbed him and covered him mouth.

"Shh quiet, he'll hear you." That stopped him long enough for his mother to whisper,

"Is it the bad man Rashid?" His head bobbed up and down under her hand.

"Outside, Outside." he said in a horse whisper and he pointed toward the front door. Rashena set him on the bed and wagged her finger in his face.

"Stay here, don't move." he nodded as she turned and ran to the front door. She pulled the blinds back, but the sidewalk was empty. During the excitement inside Jack had kept walking and was a little way down the street.. If Rashena had opened the door and stepped outside she might have seen him. She went back to the bedroom.

"He came Mommy, He came!"

"All right sweetheart, I believe you. Now stay here while I go make sure the doors are all locked."

She snatched her cell phone off the dresser and went into the kitchen. She dialed Salina's number while checking the patio door. Salina answered on the first ring.

"Yes?"

"It's me. Rashid says the guy passed our house a couple of minutes ago. I don't know how long it will take him to get where you are, but keep your eyes open. Don't come here today. He may come back."

"Okay Rashena, thanks, I'll be watching." she hung up. Then she dialed the cop she had dated. He answered the phone still groggy from sleep.

"Mayhew here."

"Hi Phil, Salina here. I think I need your help there is a guy trying to get to me and I don't know who he is or what he looks like. I got a message from a woman I work for."

"Yeah? I can be over there in a few minutes babe."

"No, no not yet. If something happens I just want you to know what's going on that's all. If I call I'll let you know where I am."

"Okay kid I'll keep my cell with me."

Rashena called the company and told them she wouldn't be in that day. Her childcare person had been threatened and she had to stay with her son. When she hung up she went outside and looked around, but far too late. She went back inside and paced the floor wondering what she could do.

Jack made his way to Rainbow Boulevard and hijacked another fast food joint. It was chicken this time. By now he knew that they would call the cops so he climbed a block wall and listened as they went by, sirens blaring. When things got quiet again he climbed back over and went the other way. Finally he came to a Convenience Store and walked up on a car with the keys in it, and it was running. Some intelligent yuppie was in a hurry and lost his car. Jack just got in and drove away with the kid running and screaming after him. It was a good thing he didn't catch Jack he might have died. Jack looked wild his head had been shaved for the operation and he had a three or four day growth of beard. The clothes he wore were dirty from his travels and from the massacre at the pedophile's house.

Jack followed the 215 around to the Green Valley area and took the exit to Green Valley Parkway. He didn't know he was just two miles from Salina's house. Jack liked the new BMW he had just taken it seemed really nice and fast too. He drove the side streets until the car ran out of gas and left it at the curb only a mile from Salina's house. He got out and wandered the streets until it got dark. Now he was in his element, darkness. He could feel it seeping into his mind and he wanted to do things to people that had misused him since he was a boy. The thing was there was no one left to get even with he had killed everyone that had mistreated him.

Salina looked out the front window to see if anyone was walking the street. She went into her exercise room she had converted from a bedroom. On the Bowflex she went through a few reps of her schedule. Working out made her body hard and released the tension. When she began to perspire a little she stopped and wiped her face with a towel and wandered into the kitchen. The phone rang.

It was Phil. "Salina, how you doin?"

"Hey I'm glad you called. I've got everything caught up for the day and I didn't want to sit in front of the TV. I don't want to sound pushy here, but maybe we could go get a cup of coffee at Starbuck's or something when you get off."

"Hey, I just got off duty and I can be there in fifteen minutes if you want and I know a quiet little place where we can sit and talk."

"Okay that sounds good, I need a little company to settle my nerves."

"Alright I'll give you a few minutes to spruce up and I'll be there." When Salina turned off the phone she thought about Phil. He was really a nice guy and maybe they could get serious.

After all she was nearly thirty and needed to get married and have kids. She didn't know a nicer guy to share life with than Phil. He seemed easy going and considerate of the people around him. He didn't carry the tough cop image. He was a detective and wore good clothes. Well maybe she needed to admit she liked having him around especially now. Since the night air was cool she went and put on a light jacket and made sure the Beretta was in her purse.

Outside up the street Jack stood in the darkness absorbing the night. He could see curtains moving in the houses around him. People were edgy about strangers in their neighborhoods that didn't live there. He stopped and sat down on a low wall that bordered the front of one of the houses. A few minutes later a car passed and stopped down the street; a woman came out and got in and the car drove away. Jack looked at the house she came out of. He knew the house would be empty. Somewhere in the recesses of his mind he remembered the institution where he grew up and he missed the hubbub of the nurses running around and talking to him occasionally. He stood and walked toward the house. When he got there the door was locked, but he didn't feel angry now so he wandered around the side to a locked wrought iron gate and climbed over and went into the back yard. There was grass and a bench under a tree. It was cool and this was the first moment's peace he'd had. He sat down and in a few minutes he was sleepy so, he lay down in the grass and slept.

Salina and Phil talked longer than they thought and it was 10:00 before they got back. In the driveway; Phil kissed Salina goodnight and she hurried into the house. She checked everything before she went to bed. She slid open the patio door and looked out into the yard. She didn't see Jack, he was laying on the other side of the stone bench in the grass. When Salina slid the door shut he heard it and woke up. As he peeked under the bench he could see Salina at the door just before she walked away.

Rashena was walking around her living room worrying about Salina. Rashid was asleep in his room. Finally she could stand no more. She took out her cell phone and dialed Salina's.

"Hi, this is Rashena, I hope you weren't asleep. I was worried, I had to call."

"Oh that's all right you didn't wake me, I just got in. I went out for coffee with a friend. I just got back. Hey, I really appreciate your concern Rashena. I checked everything when I came in and it's all clear for right now." Just then there was a cracking sound in the kitchen.

"I just heard a noise I'll call you back."

Rashena shouted, "Leave your phone on!" But it was too late Salina had shut her phone off. In a panic Rashena ran into Rashid's bedroom and pulled him out of bed and ran for her car. She picked up a blanket on the way and threw it in the back seat and lay Rashid on it and told him to go back to sleep. On the way to Salina's she called again.

Salina heard the phone, but if someone was trying to break in she wanted the line clear to call the police. She took a flashlight out of a drawer and plucked her pistol out of her purse. Slowly she edged down the hall.

Jack had sneaked over to the glass door and grasped the handle. With his massive strength he wrenched the door open and stepped inside. He slid the door closed and stepped over to a pantry and slipped inside. He backed up to the shelves and stood there in the dark.

As Salina stepped into the kitchen she looked at the glass door and thought, I should have put blinds across that door.

The door was closed. She turned toward the pantry in the dark. The door was partly closed. The room was silent. Trembling now she pressed the button on the flashlight and shined it on the door. Her heart was pounding. She slipped the safety off the Beretta. If someone was in that pantry she would fill him so full of lead he couldn't carry it all. Slowly she stepped over to the patio door and checked the door. It was open. Shining the light on the latch she saw it had been forced.

Her blood went cold. He was in the house. She wanted her cell phone, but her hands were full. She laid the light on the counter and ran for the bedroom.

Jack came out of the pantry in his invisible mode and slowly followed her up the hall. In a full panic now she couldn't find the phone. It was in the living room laying on the coffee table. The bedroom door slowly swung open. Salina jumped and pointed the gun in that direction, but there was no one there. Rashid was right she couldn't see him.

Jack stepped in and slapped the gun out of her hand and it went spinning across the carpet toward the hall. And suddenly he was there with his hand on her throat. She tried to scream, but her voice was choked off. She tried to kick him in the groin, but he sidestepped her knee and it hit the outside of his leg. Then he literally lifted her off the carpet. She couldn't get any air and knew she'd pass out soon for lack of oxygen.

Jack grinned and let out a low chuckle. Just then he heard someone beating on the front door. He threw Salina against the wall knocking her unconscious. Then headed for the front door. When he jerked the door open Rashena almost fell in on him. Fortunately she had left Rashid in the back seat of the car. Jack grabbed her hair and hit her knocking her out. He dropped her on the floor and went back to the bedroom for Salina. He had a pull rope in his back pocket he had taken off a lawnmower. When he reached Salina he pulled out the rope and was tying it around her neck intending to hang her somewhere.

Just then he heard a small voice, "Mister."

Jack slowly turned to see a small boy with a gun between both hands less than six feet away. He leaned forward to lunge at him. BOOM!

Shadow Child

Fall weather is still very warm in the desert Southwest were I live. Temperatures reach 100° in the afternoon in the town of Henderson, Nv. Dry and hot. Somehow the thousands of people that come here to live each year seem to ignore the heat. I guess we are all sun worshipers in one form or another. For a lot of them the temperatures where they lived may have been -20°, but the winters are mild here. A little rain at best.

I'm part of the older set and the atmosphere in this area is good for my arthritis. I had reason to be admitted to one of the local hospitals recently. The heat wave had broken and the temperature was in the 90's. So for a time we enjoyed warm days and cool nights. While I was there I was being treated for an infection that required bed rest and medications. In the morning when the nurse comes around for the early vitals check, temp., blood pressure, etc. sometimes they talk about events that have taken place in the medical world. I learned of a strange event that occurred on the floor where I was. It seems that a patient that was in a very serious condition in the last stages of diabetes had been brought in. A couple of his major organs were almost shut down and he was not expected to live. Wide-eyed the nurse spoke of an apparition the man had seen in his room. At first, because of his advanced condition they thought he was having hallucinations.

Like the whirlwinds we see in our open desert that can be as big as a hundred feet in diameter and reach two hundred feet in the air. These circling winds blow fiercely and then dissipate leaving everything in disarray. This story is just such a wind.

I was in a deep sleep when the nurse approached the bed around 3:00 a m.

"Wake up, wake up. Something strange has happened up in 3100. That's the private room in the corner of the hall."

"Uh, I grunted, what's going on?" I was still rubbing my eyes as she related the story, while checking my vitals.

"The old guy that they brought in a couple of days ago with advanced diabetes wasn't expected to live. We called in his family and tried to prepare them as best we could. Everyone loves the old guy. He's a very sweet person, but he's just wore out ya know?" I nodded my understanding.

"Well as I was making my rounds this morning his vitals came up normal. I shake him and try to wake him up wondering what happened. He keeps mumbling something about a little boy in his room last night. He says the kid came out of the bathroom and laid his hand on the old man's arm. Then he retreated back into the dark. He's a little light in the gray matter so we don't pay too much attention to him usually. So I check him again and the numbers are better the second time. Because of the infection in his body his blood sugar usually runs about four to five hundred, which is very high. Blood pressure before he went to sleep last night was off the chart. He was running 102 temp. I give him his meds and tuck him in nothing we can do, but you have to remember he's eighty-two." All the while I'm nodding my head as the excitement builds. She says,

"So when I go in awhile ago everything is way down toward normal. He's mumbling about this little boy. I go check the bath and no sign of the kid. So I check him again and the numbers are still coming down toward normal. Then this is when I see the sores that have been on his feet look like they are drying up, they're not oozing like they usually do. The sores on his hands and arms are already beginning to scab over. It's highly improbable that this could happen in just six hours, but I know what the doc is going to say. It's the antibiotics. Not in that short a time. Not on his best day. I got to get out of here. I'll tell you more later."

"Yeah, keep me posted huh?" I call after her as she goes out the door. This woman is the epitome of efficiency. She has her ducks in a row and works with speed and dexterity. Always moving, doing things without thinking about it as she covers a completely different subject. She has probably been a nurse for many years.

WOW, someone gets healed. I'm excited even though it's not me. I'm glad for the old guy. Maybe he can enjoy his grandkids a little longer. I would like to see what he looks like though. Probably very thin and wrinkled, but it's those old folks smiles I like to see. It changes their whole continence. Grandmas and Grandpas are just sweet people. I'm one myself. I wonder what the boy has to do with all this?

By eight-thirty when my breakfast tray arrives the whole floor is abuzz. Nurses, aides, and even the cleaning people are starting to tell stories of what they heard. Some from the old man and others from other people. I realize I'm going to have to choose who I'm going to listen to, because like the kids game of 'gossip' everything varies and everything changes from ear to ear. So I decide it will be my RN, she sounds credible. While I'm looking under the plate cover to see what I have for breakfast; she rushes in with more of the story.

"Someone told the charge nurse and she called the doctor. You can almost see this guys condition change. Large sores are small now and the little ones are gone. The seeping fluids on his feet have all but dried up. His blood sugar is down to about two fifteen. He's eating breakfast right now and his appetite is better. Man this is so hard to believe, such a sudden change. Nothing normal in this hospital today." Her voice trails away as she rushes out the door.

Nothing is hard to believe when one looks to the source. That source is God. When he decides things will change, they change. Maybe He is using that child as a medium. Maybe someone needs to be convinced of God's presence or even His existence.

Whatever the case I feel people are going to be amazed at what He can do with a little child. The words of the psalmist came to me. "Out of the mouths of babes and sucklings thou hast ordained strength..." No telling what could happen here. No one had a clear description of the boy, but as the stories circulated I could surmise he was under ten years old, blond, and perhaps very shy. I would wait for further news...

By noon everyone was talking and murmuring down on that end of the hall, which was just three rooms away from mine. The hall is six feet wide and there is a large window at the end. Story was the old man was sitting up on the side of the bed. Before my tray came, I decided to sneak down and take a peek. Unfortunately the room was crowded with family members and hospital personal. No chance of seeing him now. I went back to my room before I got caught.

By 3:00 p. m. that afternoon the old man had improved even further. When the nurse came in to pass out meds she said he was really looking good. She said she finally had to put out the snoopers and the family was worn out from the excitement. There is a good chance he may be released by this evening. Most of the family had passed my door on the way home chattering about grandpa's recovery, a couple of teen aged girls, a younger boy, a man and a woman that looked to be in their fifties. All smiling. It even made me feel good. At 5:30 p. m. when the food trays are being brought in a man and woman lead the elderly gent past my door and he is a picture of health. He has on jeans, a western shirt and western boots. He's walking straight and the relatives are holding on to him.

It is a clutch of love not just support. I'm sure they are making plans for when he gets home. Tonight he will be treated like a King. Back from the dead really. Here comes the nurse.

She is all smiles.

"Well what do you think about that? Ready to be released in twelve hours."

"Pretty amazing, and I was just three doors away. I'm glad I was here to see this miracle. It almost makes one envious though. I wonder who will be next in that room?"

"If this continues, these appearances, I would put the worst patients in there."

"Yeah, I nod in agreement, that's what I would do too because they sure aren't going to make a lot of money off them." She wrinkles her nose and snickers.

At 6:00 p m my doctor comes in. She looks like she has had a busy day with all the excitement.

She sits down on the foot of the bed and says, "If this boy makes one trip down the halls he could empty out our hospital."

I nod in agreement and I can't help but smile.

"No matter how many he heals there will be a thousand to take their place Doc."

"Yes you are right. It is a great relief to have one go home whole." A chill goes down my back. His presence is going to affect many lives in this place. I long to see what will happen next.

"So who will be in there next?" I ask.

She gives me a strange look for a few seconds. Then says, "The sickest patient I can find. I hope the boy is still in there somewhere." Then as an after thought she says, "The press is going to get hold of this and then Johnnie bar the door."

"Katie." I correct her, "She was a poor farm girl."

"Okay, let me check your heart." She lifts a cold stethoscope. They must put them in the freezer before they come in. I shiver as she touches me with the icy orb.

During the night I awake to check the door and the doorway to my bathroom in hopes of seeing him standing there watching me sleep. No one. I gradually drift off to slumber's shores once more.

At 3:00 a m my nurse gently wakes me to check blood pressure and temps.

"They brought in another patient late last night." she whispers.

"Man or woman?" I ask.

"Woman; In the last stages of breast cancer. She's fifty and oh so frail from weight loss. Her family has not been told of what happened to the previous patient." She presses her finger to her lips. I nod.

"You want some juice?" she asks as she turns to leave.

"No thanks. I think I'll try to catch another forty winks before the excitement starts. As she goes down the hall I throw the covers back and sneak to the door. Looking after her I see she has already turned the corner down the hall. I sneak down three doors to see the new patient.

The nurse is right, she is a picture of death. Eyes closed, head back and mouth open struggling to breathe. Bone thin. I rush back to my room absorbing the sight, her hair, a shining silver not white like some.

Come young man we await your arrival, this woman needs you,. I think to myself.

At 8:00 o'clock when my breakfast arrives I've had time to wash up and shave. The usual this morning; scrambled eggs, dry toast and a small box of cereal. I uncover the coffee and start there. When I'm finished with breakfast the cleaning lady comes in. She is an older Spanish lady and speaks with somewhat of an accent.

"Good morning sir. How are you today?"

"Doing better today thanks."

"Maybe the boy come and help this lady too?" she asks as she moves the dust mop back and forth across the floor.

"I certainly hope so."

"This is so good, I like to see everybody healed." She says with a broad smile.

"If everybody was healed maybe you would have no job."

"I don't care. I go someplace else to work." I smile. She

feels a lot like I do, we have too many sick in our country. And like the poor we will have them with us always.
I see an older gentleman pass my door walking slow. I figure he's the husband. He has a haggard look on his face weary from hospitals, doctors and treatments. All apparently to no avail. The child seems like her only hope. After the cleaning lady has gone, I step to the door looking both ways. Clear. I wander down toward the window trying to look casual. After a couple of steps I see the door is closed to 3100 so I go back to my bed. I feel a heaviness in my heart. I lower my head and pray the child appears before its too late.

In 3100 the man stands at the edge of the bed holding her hand weeping. He is tall, broad shouldered, balding. His hands are rough and he is a deep tan from years of work outdoors. He has probably exhausted all the insurance and savings trying to save his wife from the inevitable. She lay there skin and bone, mouth open struggling to breathe. Probably on fire inside from the chemo.
Behind them in the shadows, young innocent eyes watch as they both suffer. Her from cancer and him from a broken heart. Haltingly the young child moves closer to the door from the shadows. He is so light he almost looks pale. His eyes are a bright blue, his hair is blond and he is barefoot. The linen garment he wears is white and hangs just above his feet. He raises a small hand and lays it on the door jamb. It is hard to read the expression on his face. Slowly he steps forward until he is at the edge of the bed standing beside the man.
As the man weeps he becomes aware of the presence beside him. He opens his eyes and looks down. His brow wrinkles, he doesn't understand how the child got there. Slowly the boy reaches up and takes hold of the wrist of the hand the man is holding. He holds on for a second or two then lowers his hand to his side still looking at the woman's face. Then he turns as if to return to the bathroom.
"Wait a minute son, where did you come from?" The boy

continues moving toward the door. The man reaches for the child, but his grasp only finds thin air for the boy is gone. A misty shroud covers the space where he just stood. The woman coughs and the mans attention is drawn to her again.

A rough and raspy voice says, "W-a-t-e-r."

He grabs the pitcher and a glass and pours almost spilling it. He lifts her head and says, "Go easy now mom." She sucks at the glass greedily spilling some as she drinks. He smiles, it is so good to see her at least drink some water.

When she stops she gasps and whispers, "Dad, it's going to be all right now." She lays back eyes still closed.

His tears flowed anew, but now they were filled with joy. He still holds her hands with his head lowered. "Thank you, thank you whoever is responsible for this. His head jerks up. He remembers the boy; he's got to tell someone about this.

He goes to the door and out into the hall, "Nurse! Nurse! Come here quick.

The RN comes running, she has a smile on her face, she knows what has happened. She grabs the man's hands and pulls him into the room and closes the door.

"Sit down Mr. Cravats, I have to tell you something before the calamity starts." She relates the story of the man who was in 3100 just before his wife was admitted. He sits, mouth open in wonder, as the nurse tells of the miracle.

"You don't have to tell anyone I told you. They will tell you when your wife starts to improve. No one knows where the child came from, but he need only to touch the sick and their life is changed."

Into our world quietly you've come,
That you might alter the lives of some.
No matter how serious the malady be,
All that is needed is one touch from thee.

Sight returns and cancer flees,
Bones are restructured in old twisted knees.
Come once more sweet child of night,
That you might change man's bitter plight.

Back at the nurses station Margie tells the charge nurse, "Well it has started again. The boy appeared to the man in 3100. He took hold of one of the wife's hands and held on for a few seconds and then retreated toward the bathroom. When the man reached for him he just faded away."

Now the checking starts because Mrs. Cravats is surely on the mend. Her fever is down to 101° from 104.5°. Still she lies with her eyes closed as her husband whispers sweet words of encouragement.

"Mom would you like something to eat? You need your strength, please take a little food. If they don't have it here I'll go and get it whatever it might be." She lies still breathing deeply. He hasn't noticed, but her breathing has improved.

When lunch comes around no one is hungry because of the excitement down the hall. I see more patients moving past my door wanting to see Mrs. Cravats and how she fares. Marge the nurse is constantly shooing them back to their rooms, but she does it with patience and a soft voice. A few minutes later I see the hospital Chaplain pass my door, he is impeccably dressed in a new suit and has a gold chain around his neck. He carries a book and walks slowly. I hear him lightly tap on the door to the room. The man comes out and apologizes asking if the Chaplain might return later, his wife needs rest. The chaplain says certainly and retreats back the other way. As he passes he smiles and waves.

I hear conversation at the nurses desk and I peek out to see what's going on. There is a group of doctors and nurses discussing what to do. My doctor is among them. Mrs. Cravats is one of her patients also. Members of visiting families are wandering over to 3100 to see what they can. Of course the door is closed. The nurse is coming every few minutes to ask visitors to go back to their rooms. A little later a man from security passes and the lookers stop coming. I remember how the crowd pressed Jesus when he was among the people.

Just before lunch my doctor comes in to check me out. After she puts the icy stethoscope away I ask,

"It's happening again isn't it?"

"I dare not talk about it things are heating up and the hospital board is going to get involved. I'm surprised some of them aren't already up here on the floor. She shakes her head and walks toward the door.

She turns and says, "She is improving though."

I can see she feels the weight of the situation. It will not be long before the press arrives and then total chaos. Channel 13 or 8 will get here first sporting cameras and glitzy reporters. Eye Witness News. What a mess they can make sometimes. No wonder the child comes in the night.

My lunch arrives and it looks good, but I will have to make myself eat, the excitement has taken my appetite. After I have eaten what I can, I push my tray away and finish my coffee. The nurse comes in walking fast as usual. She has a pill for me. She lets me know they have asked the staff not to talk about the woman in 3100 to the other patients, but I know she will catch me up when the woman is released and gone. I ask about the board members coming around. She nods and leaves. Well no more info, but I know it will not be long until Mrs. Cravats will be walking out to go home.

1:00 am in the morning

The lights are out in front of the Emergency bay outside. It is quiet and cool. The morning air is refreshing. Traffic on the street is light. Breaking the peace of the atmosphere an ambulance comes speeding into the drive lights flashing, but the siren is silent. The paramedics inside are working feverishly on a man that has had a massive coronary. The doors fly open and for some reason both paramedics rush inside to get the gurney and equipment to hook up the patient. For a few seconds the patient is left alone in the ambulance. Out of the shadows beside the doors the child moves to the back of the ambulance, steps up on the back step and takes hold of the mans big toe. He holds on as long as he dare. Looking toward the doors he sees the paramedics coming with the gurney. He hops down and retreats into the shadows. On the gurney inside the expression of pain changes to one of wonder. The man takes a deep breath and looks at the heart monitor he is hooked up to. The lines have changed to a steady rhythm. The code alarm is no longer beeping. He raises up on one elbow.

"Sir, lie down you are in very serious condition. Don't try to move."

"Hey guys I'm all right. Something happened, my heart is okay."

"Sir, please lie down and let us get you inside and have the doc check you out."

"No, no really I'm okay."

By this time they have him out of the ambulance and are hauling him inside. After everyone has done their job and have the patient hooked up to everything in the ER someone notices his heart rhythm is normal.

One of the paramedics shakes his head and says, "All I know is he was having a massive coronary when we picked him up."

The doctor and the nurse is checking everything. Everything is normal.

"I'm okay folks when that kid took hold of my foot something happened in my chest and the attack stopped." the patient says.

Dead silence. People looking at one another trying to put it together.

The doctor asks, "Do you suppose..."

The nurse drops her head and smiles.

"You might as well send him home Doc." The paramedics stand looking confused. Not able to figure out what has happened. The man on the gurney smiles as he sits up. The nurse helps him to the floor.

The paramedic mumbles, "Never in all my days..."

The patient says, "Call Luxury Cab, I'm going home in style."

The ER nurse hands the man a card and says, "Call me in a couple of days you might want to know what happened."

Outside the main entrance to the hospital the cabbie helps the man into the back seat and closes the door. As the cab pulls away a pair of innocent eyes watch from the darkness. A slight smile crosses his face.

At 6:00 a m, some five hours later, while the nurse is attending to Mrs. Cravats she opens her eyes for the first time and smiles at her husband. He gives her a big broad one back.

The nurse turns to him and says, "Her blood pressure is stronger this morning and her temp is 99.6°. Things are getting better a little at a time, which is not bad for her."

"Mrs. Cravats would you like something to eat? Some graham crackers or some fruit." She gently shakes her head and closes her eyes, headed toward sleep once more.

"Her body is going to need rest she's been through a lot." The nurse tells Mr. Cravats.

After the nurse is gone, in a small voice she says, "Water." He picks up the pitcher and pours a glass and holds up her head. She drinks it all and returns to her sleep. He kisses her on the forehead.

Before she had gotten sick Mrs. Cravats was not long

winded in fact she used a lot of one word answers. Her husband and children had gotten used to this over the years. When she spoke though she meant it and you didn't cross her. Her children, a girl and a boy, both in their late teens now, were bright kids and did well in school. There wasn't the problems a lot of parents had with drinking, smoking, and drugs. She taught them young and they obeyed. She stayed after them everyday and it paid off.

The next morning when the doctor visits I ask how Mrs. Cravats is doing.

"She is improving, but very slowly. Not like the man with diabetes before her. I think this recovery is going to have to be slow because all of the treatment she has had. You know the boy touched a man that was brought to the emergency room last night with a coronary. Before they could get him hooked up to the heart equipment the man was healed and took a cab home."

She smiles.

"You know they didn't like that at all," I say.

The nurse shows up about an hour later and tells me I'm going to be on a new medication. Another antibiotic of some sort. It will start in the morning at 6:00 o'clock.

I try to read a book, but I'm nervous as a long tailed cat in a room full of rockers.

I keep watching the hall to see what's going on. Then I see a new sight, one of the sisters passes the door. Probably from here on, the Church may get involved. I have expected a visit from the Priest across the highway at the big Catholic church. I'm sure word has gotten to him.

If things go the way they want it, room 3100 will probably become a shrine to the boy. And if he doesn't tell them his name they will give him one. Mysteriously someone will gain an audience with the child and he will tell all. I wouldn't bet the farm on it though. In a few minutes the Sister goes back the other way. I rush to the door and peek. She is speaking to the charge nurse. I think about the visitations at Lourdes, France and Fatima, Portugal. This will be considered one of those miracles. I can just imagine the story that will come from this. Now the mystery builds. All is quiet until they bring the lunch trays. I notice a man passing that tells me 'Press.' He is looking in all the rooms as he passes like he is in unfamiliar territory. A minute later Mr. Cravats is telling him to leave, he doesn't want to talk to him his wife needs rest. The man is spouting excuses and questions as fast as he can. Mr. Cravats calls the nurse and tells her to get this guy out of here. He backs up Mr. Cravats is too big to argue with. In a couple of seconds the whole nurses station is on him herding him toward the elevator. The registrar calls security to meet him downstairs. I wish I could see what happens. The parking lot is on the other side of the building.

In 3100 about 3:00 p. m. that afternoon Mrs. Cravats opens her eyes.

"Dad?" Mr. Cravats jumps up he has been nodding in one of the chairs.

"Yes Mom. What is it?"

"Can you get me something to eat?"

"Do you want a tray from the hospital? Can I get you some fried chicken from Kentucky Fried Chicken ?"

"Call for a tray from here I don't want you to leave me. Something has happened in my body Dad. I feel different somehow." He picks up the phone and calls dietary. They say they will be up in a few minutes. He puts down the phone and picks up the water pitcher. After pouring water he raises her head off the bed and holds the glass as she drinks. She lets out a gasp of relief.

"Ah Dad, that cold water is so good."

"More?" She shakes her head.

When the food arrives there is soup and crackers, juice, a fruit cup and pudding. He sits on the edge of the bed and feeds her. With relish she devours it all. Her body is nearly bone thin; it will take a while for her recovery. The nurse comes in to see if they need anything else, more food, pain medication or anything. She tells Mrs. Cravats she is glad to have her back. She smiles and lays back and closes her eyes.

"I have to rest now Dad, stay with me huh?"

"Oh yes you bet I will sweetheart. You sleep I'll be right here." He gently holds her hand. She takes a deep breath and in a minute or two she is asleep once more.

Margie stops in to see how I'm doing. I ask about the woman. She smiles and tells me she is eating. Relief sweeps over me; this is good news. I thank the Lord.

My recovery is also coming along, but the infection is slow leaving my body. I am doing better though, I feel it.

Down in the x-ray hall radiology tech John Pitts pushes a patient along on a gurney. He stops to open the x-ray room door, which is a massive four and a half feet wide. He steps inside then props the door open and the woman tech inside asks which patient is coming in. He walks over to discuss this with her and what type pictures will be taken. John tells her the woman has a broken leg and they need to find the extent of the damage to see if surgery is needed. While he is in the room, across the hall, a door opens and two innocent eyes peer out at the woman grimacing in pain on the gurney. Slowly he steps out and reaches for her hand which is hanging over the edge of the gurney. He takes hold of her index finger. She becomes aware of his presence and looks down and says.

"Are you lost baby?" She turns her head to see if the tech heard her. When she looks back the child is gone. The tech comes out to see what is the matter.

The woman says, "There is a little boy lost down here he went into that room."

The tech stiffens and his eyes get wide. He's heard the stories of 3100. Is it possible the child was that close and he didn't see him? John quickly steps around the gurney and grabs the doorknob. Its locked.

"Gentile, (Gen-ti'-le) do you have the key to this door?" he calls across the hall. She comes to the door and asks what's the matter.

"The boy, the boy he's in this room." Gentile runs for her keys. They open the door to the equipment room and turn on the lights. All is quiet. Nothing there but old gurneys and portable x-ray equipment covered with sheets. They look everywhere. Nothing.

Back in the hall they look at each other eyes wide with anticipation. John says, You call and I'll get the patient ready. He moves the patient into the room while Gentile runs for the phone. She calls security. They come running. She tells the story while John looks on. They go across the hall and check again. When they come back the patient is sitting up on the gurney.

"Folks." She says quietly. "My leg isn't broken anymore." They all stare, chill bumps rising like bumps on a pickle. Almost before their eyes the woman's leg straightened and the bones knitted together. They want a picture anyway to see what happened. When the film is developed they look at it in awe. Then they look at one another and the silence between them is deafening. There is no sign of a break in the bone anywhere. The tibia is whole as it was before the woman fell. Soon there is a crowd in radiology. Gentile is shaking her head and saying she doesn't know what happened, it happened so fast. She is instructed to be alert. Meetings start in every department. The message is, "Keep your eyes open. Expect anything at any time. Disposable cameras will be distributed to every area. Keep them ready."

Margie is talking to the charge nurse at the station on the third floor.

"It happened again Jan. This time he struck down in radiology. The woman had, I repeat, had a broken leg. He stepped in an took hold of her finger while the techs were discussing what was to be done. The woman thought a lost child was wandering the halls looking for his parents. You already know what the film showed. Nothing. Dr. Goetz is not going to be happy about this."

Dr. Goetz has a personality problem, but he is the best bone doctor in the place so they tolerate him. He is a stickler for details and that's what's needed.

In the administrators office one of the board members, a doctor, is talking to the administrator, "I'm not against miracles, Carl, but this hospital has lost over two-hundred and fifty thousand dollars in just a few days. If this keeps on…"

"Look Doc, with all the notoriety this is going to bring us they will be flocking in here in hopes the kid will come to their room. I don't think we have anything to worry about. You have to look at more than the bottom line here."

"I can't help it if these events intensify We stand a chance of losing a lot of revenue."

"Well, don't go stirring up the other board members yet, I don't think we have anything to worry about. We can have a press meeting and the story will bring'em running. This is a Catholic hospital Doc. Let the Priests worry about it. They will make it work.

Just then the Pastor from the church across the highway walks in. A tall white haired man with gold wire frame glasses.

"How're you doing Carl. I'm hearing good things about this place. Doctor, good to see you again." (The doc smiles and shake his hand.)

"Good to see you Father. I think we have a genuine miracle maker here. This boy's appearance has everybody stirred up. Three of the cases have gone home and the fourth is mending, although slower. She was a terminal cancer case, but she's coming along."

"Where did the boy come from? Has his appearances been isolated to 3100?" the priest asks.

"No he's made appearances outside the ER and down in x-ray. These cases were immediate healings. The other two will be healed over a short period of time, giving the body time to put itself back together."

"I'd like to see the room when it's empty to get the feel of things."

"Yeah, you might even mention it in you sermon next Sunday." Carl says. The Priest shakes his head and smiles.

"I wonder if there is any chance of getting close to him."

"Pretty slim Father everyone that tries has come up empty. He touches the patient and fades away." The Priest strokes his chin and nods.

"What's he look like?"

"Blond ,blue eyed, about four feet high. Has a white one piece garment on and goes barefoot. That was the description the lady from radiology gave security after her leg bone fused together."

"Amazing. It's going to be a heyday when the press gets hold of this."

"Yeah, security already escorted one to the front door. They've got a white car parked in the front lot. They're talking to anyone they can. We've asked the employees not to say anything until we can find out how this got started. So far everyone has been pretty tight lipped and it's kept down the confusion. But there is no telling what the three patients will tell when they get home for the money they can make to help with the hospital bills."

Margie the nurse comes in just before lunch and tells me Mrs. Cravats is improving slowly. I will be taking the new antibiotic twice a day. I hope it does what it is supposed to do. The nurse says the doctor will be in after lunch sometime which probably means about 3:00 in the afternoon. No one shows up on time in the hospital. I wish I could get a collaborator to go to one of the hamburger joints. Nothing would taste better than a big double burger with a diet coke. That is verboten here though. One dare not mention fast dietary supplements. Let alone the name of the place.

After lunch the phone rings. It's my daughter apologizing for not calling sooner. She wants to know how I'm doing. I tell her about the antibiotics and tell her I'm stable. Then I take the time to tell her about the boy and the miracles that have taken place. Like everyone else she is amazed and hopes he comes to my room. I tell her there's not much chance of that. The people he has healed have been much worse off and I was glad they were given a new lease on life. I could not be so selfish as to think only of myself. I'm genuinely happy for those people and hope they all live to be a hundred.

My daughter lives in Arizona and says she will come if I want her to. She owns a business and is doing well and I know she works very hard to make a good living. She helps me pay part of my insurance and I'm so glad I've got her to help. My wife passed away a few years ago and Glenda really helped make things easier. She wanted to take me back to Arizona with her, but I like it here in Southern Nevada. So I tell her if things get worse I'll call her. She makes me promise on a stack of Bibles and threatens to call my doctor. She says she will be here to pick me up when I'm released.

Later that night about 9:00 o'clock I'm having trouble sleeping. I flop back and forth like a fish out of water, from one side to the other. I just turn toward the door when I see the boy passing walking right up the middle of the hall. Apparently everyone is occupied, for no one has noticed him. I stare wide eyed and as soon as he is out of sight, I throw back the cover and start to jump to my feet when I catch myself. I think, *If I run after him I may spoil something he is going to do. Maybe he will come back past the door and I can see him again.* I can't contain myself so I get up as quietly as I can and creep to the door. I peek around the jamb and he is standing in front of 3100 like he is waiting for someone to open the door. He doesn't look my way. Then he steps forward entering the room. I wait a second then creep down the hall slowly. At the doorway I carefully peek in and see him standing at the side of the bed. Mr. Cravats has his head down apparently asleep. The boy stands and watches them sleep. Then in a surprise move he touches Mr. Cravats lightly on the temple. So light that is doesn't even wake him. Then he turns to leave and sees me. I run, I don't want to mess things up. Back in bed I watch the hall. In another minute he passes my door. He turns his head toward me and I see a smile on his lips then he is gone. They will never see him at the nurses station. It eats me up to think what Mr. Cravats was delivered from. I guess no one will ever know.

At 11:00 the nurse comes in to take my vitals, everything is normal.

"He was in their room again tonight." I tell her. Her eyes bulge.

"When?"

"About 9:00 o'clock."

"Did you see what happened?" I nod my head.

"Well tell me. Don't sit there like a bump on a log."

"When he went by my door I saw him. After he passed, I crept to the door and watched. He went in and stood by the bed for a moment and then he turned and lightly touched Mr. Cravats on the temple. He was asleep, so he never knew the child was there. And you know what, no one will probably ever know what he was healed of. When he turned around and saw me, I ran back to my bed. I saw him pass and he turned his head and smiled."

"Wow! How lucky you were to see him. Was he dressed like they said?"

"Yeah, he was and the material in that gown must be perfect it seems to flow with him as he walks."

"You know I hope nothing happens to mess this up. When he touches someone I'm so happy for them.." she says.

Somewhere in the great reaches of eternity a tumor the size of a golf ball begins to shrink and finally disappear. Just like the one that was in Mr. Cravats head that he didn't even know was there. When he wakes the headaches will be gone and his vision won't blur anymore, but he won't notice it. His wife's cancer will be his main concern.

At the end of the week, I had been in the hospital for eight days. The doctor came in and told me I would be released the next day. It seemed that the antibiotics were working and the infection was nearly gone. I thanked her and told her I would miss the child and the miracles that were happening. She said she had no idea how long it would go on, but it would be all right with her if he emptied out the hospital. Now I was anxious. I wanted to go see my daughter in Arizona more than ever. Sometimes it takes something like this to make us appreciate our loved ones and the life we have. The nurse comes in a few minutes later and says.

"Okay, the doc says you are going home tomorrow. I'll bet your glad huh?"

"Yeah, I think I'm going to go visit my daughter and take it easy for a while."

"She's writing up a script right now so you'll have a few more pills to take and that should take care of the infection.

By dinner time, I hear that Mrs. Cravats is sitting up eating. Her husband is overjoyed. The kids came in to see their mom. They are so very happy to see her improving.

That night I asked for a sleep aid cause I knew I wouldn't be able to sleep with all the excitement. The nurse brought me the pill and left. It was about 9:30 p. m.. I was just about to lie down again when a big man came into my room. I mean a big man. He must have been seven feet tall with very broad shouldered. He had on a funny sort of shirt and trousers. He had on a pair of sandals. He stopped at my bedrail and looked down at me with a very serious expression. His eyes were piercing and I was frightened.

"Don't be afraid. Come with me." I felt compelled, I couldn't resist. Laying back the covers I sat up and put on my slippers and robe. He turned and walked out the door. I followed like I had no will of my own. When we reached the nurses station it was like there was no one there. Three women were working, but they didn't look up; they talked as if they were alone. We passed them on our way to the elevators and they didn't even see us. When we stepped onto the elevator I noticed his clothes and I felt I had seen that material before. Oh yes, the boy's gown, it was almost the same. He pushed the button for the second floor.

When the door opened we stepped out and walked down a hall. At the end there is a room called the family room. It is where the families of loved ones talk to the Chaplain when their loved ones pass away. When he stopped at the door terror ran up my spine, I almost passed out. I staggered and he took hold of my arm to steady me then he said,

"Do not be afraid. There will be no harm come to you. The boy is inside. He wants to see you." I opened the door and went in. There is a couch on either side of a table and a chair at one end where the doctor or the chaplain sits. A light shined down on the chair from the ceiling. The boy was in it. The big man closed the door. I sat down on the end of the couch. He sat with his arms on the arms of the chair. His poise was like a Prince sitting on a throne. His expression was placid and his eyes stared at me. I was scared and didn't know what to say.

Finally when I couldn't stand the silence anymore, I stammered, "I'm amazed at the things you have done while I've been here. I would like to thank you for having mercy on these people. You have given them a new lease on life. I want to express my appreciation for them since they are not here. I'm sure they would thank you if they had the chance, but I guess you didn't want anyone to see you unless it couldn't be avoided. I hope you will be merciful to many, many more. We have needed someone like you to come and relieve our sufferings. When the Lord sent you it made me want to thank Him a thousand times."

Finally a smile came across his face and he spoke one sentence. "Tell this story to others."

A mist began to rise and in another minute he was gone. He just faded into the mist. I sat there staring, awed by what had happened. A peace came over me and I sat there for awhile and enjoyed the feeling. Then I remembered how long I had been gone from my room. I got up and went out into the hall. The big man was gone too, so I started for the elevator. What an experience! Is anyone going to believe me when I try to tell what happened? But you know I don't have to worry about that the healings will speak for themselves. I can keep this experience in my heart and maybe someday it will become for a testimony to encourage someone to believe in God. The next morning about 9:00 a. m. I was getting ready to leave the hospital. I had been released and everyone wished me well and said goodbye. Inside I had a feeling that my daughter would be downstairs to meet me. As I rode down on the elevator I had another feeling and I was elated. I walked across the lobby to the front door. Sure enough my daughter's car was in front and she was leaning on the fender waiting for me. The other feeling was that I wasn't going to need those antibiotics any longer. The infection was gone.

Protected

A souvenir store in the small town of Soda Springs, Idaho catered to a young Indian woman that brought in her weekly cache of Indian souvenirs. There were cloth dolls, small carved animals, and beaded necklaces that she made herself. She was dark skinned with long dark brown hair. About five foot six. Her eyes were so dark you couldn't see the pupils. Her face wasn't quite round like the other Indian women. There was some oval to it with a little point to her chin. She moved with purpose and at times when she was happy she almost danced as she walked. Everyone called her Kat a nick name her mother gave her when she was a child. That was all anyone ever heard her called since she was a child, but her name was Wynona Johnson, but few people knew it because she never used her last name. Kat was slender, but not skinny. She looked good in a new pair of jeans and western shirt. She always spoke when she met people she knew, but there was no time for gossip. The women of town all respected her for they never saw her at the local saloon and never with any of the local fellas. She wasn't a lone wolf, but the guys didn't interest her seemingly. Kat had just turned thirty and was pretty for her age. She never had time for foolishness. Kat spent most of her time at her small house her parents left her when they passed away. In her craft room (a converted bedroom) was a small loom in one corner, a wood carving table in another and a table in the middle of the floor with cups of beads and thread all over it.

Her father had been a Calvary soldier many years before and spent his retirement years at home mostly. Her mother was a full blooded Piute. She was short almost squat, but not too heavy from married life and children. The tale was Bill had to conquer her before he married her. As the story went she was a wild Indian and drank a lot fire water when she was young. Bill put a stop to the drinking and changed her interests in life. For that the chief at the reservation was thankful. They were an odd looking couple, Bill at over six foot and her at five, but they made a good life together for many years. Beside Kat, they had a boy named Tom who left home when he was eighteen. His Indian name was Sailing Eagle. Kat rarely heard from him. He lived in the South somewhere. Kat's parents passed away close to the same time, both nearing seventy. Afterward she stayed on at the house and set up her souvenir business. It was a simple frame house with three bedrooms. There was about five acres with the place and the strange thing was about fifty yards from the house was a hill that had been man made by her dad for her mom. Her mom would climb the long slope and watch the sun go down and at other times she would go up there to pray for her family. It was probably those times that kept the kids out of trouble when they were in school. Kat went to that hill almost daily now. She didn't pray, she would just stand and stare off into the distance enjoying the peaceful atmosphere...

He father planted a pine tree off to one side. It was now over twenty feet high and a foot thick at the base. At night she would sit at the base of the tree and look up at the sky studying the stars. It was a peaceful existence for her.

As Kat turned to leave the store she noticed a man coming in. He was tall with blond hair sticking out from under his white western hat. His eyes were a deep blue. He had on a colorful western shirt and jeans. He nodded as he passed her and mumbled "Mornin'. She nodded her head and kept going. When she reached the edge of the front porch she glanced back over her shoulder. *Not bad looking, not bad at all.* She thought grinning. He wasn't looking back, but standing at the counter talking to the cashier. She felt something, but she wasn't sure what it was. Fear? Caution?

A strange feeling for sure, then moved on, headed for the grocery.

Inside Mat Carter was looking at the basket of things Kat had just left. He picked up a small carving of a terrier with ears and tail sticking up.

"How much is this?"

"I'm not sure I'll have to check the price with the ones on the shelf," the clerk said.

"These are good carvings."

"The girl that you passed coming in makes them."

"Oh really, good I get to see the artist the day I buy."

"Yeah Kat makes a living at it."

Kat huh, I'll have to keep my eyes open around town in case I meet her again. He thought

"The terriers are four-fifty."

"Let's see, I'll take two of them." he said as he picked up another one. My Mom likes dogs. Dad will only let her have one live one so she collects statues. These are pretty good. When Mom sees these she will want to meet that lady." He gave the girl a ten and took his change as she wrapped the carvings.

When Kat reached her property she was still wondering about the blond guy she had passed. She stopped her old Jeep, left to her by her Dad. It was an old army model M38A1. It was still in good shape and she had no trouble climbing the hills around the open country. When she had a lot of trinkets and small carpets to take to town she hooked up a small trailer to haul them.

She stopped in front of the house and sat thinking for a moment then she turned her head toward the hill. Slowly she slid out and climbed up to the top. There was a slight breeze and Kat faced that way and let it blow into her face.

She closed her eyes and a voice in her mind said, "Keep him out of the bar there will be trouble there."

Concern came across her face and she wondered why this voice was telling her to look out for this guy. She did not question the voice in her head, but made plans to be in town tonight when the action started in the town's largest bar. Which would probably be about seven o'clock. She intended to be at the door by six.

Protected from harm

She had heard the voice before, but not very often. The way this voice started speaking to her was when Kat was at a town hall meeting and took a seat next to an older Indian gent. They talked while they waited for the meeting to get started. The old guy seemed to know quite a bit about her. He said he knew her mom and dad and wished he had gotten to know her brother better before he wandered off. He said he knew she was honest and hard working and wanted to put an Indian blessing on her so the white men wouldn't take advantage of her. This old guy seemed harmless so Kat went along with it when he asked if he could pray an Indian prayer of protection over her after the meeting. She said it probably wouldn't hurt anything. When the meeting started the old guy made a plea for the Indian population and as usual he was ignored. Everybody thought the red skins were getting enough help as it was. It was dark when the meeting let out. Kat looked at the old guy and felt sorry for him and asked if she could give him a few dollars to help out.

He stood and looked at her for a moment and said, "I'm going to give you a special blessing for having compassion on me. I don't need the money I was in the war and I get a check every month so me and my squaw get along pretty good. Step over here a minute."

They moved off to one side of the parking lot and the old man put his hands on her head and began to speak in Piute. When he finished he pulled a small beaded necklace out of his shirt pocket and put it over her head.

"If you wear this until the moon is full you will have protection of the spirits all your days." Kat didn't get any weird feelings or chills she was just going along with the old man because of Indian kinship. He said no more and wandered over to an old pick up and drove away. She tucked the necklace into her shirt and forgot about it. Nothing happened right away because the full moon was two weeks away, but the day after was when the voice started speaking to her. It was a quiet male voice that had authority. Over the few years that followed she learned to trust in the voice that spoke to her mind. Sometimes she did nothing and when an incident took place she felt chastened for not obeying the warning.

This cowboy was young like her and had his whole life ahead of him. That could change if he got into trouble tonight.

At six Kat was just across the street watching the front door of the Golden Crown Saloon. She looked both ways looking for the cowboy. Then she spotted him driving an older Ford Ranchero. There was one parking place in front of the bar, he slid into it. Kat stepped off the curb and crossed the street. He wasn't looking her way as he stepped up on the sidewalk and started in.

Kat gracefully slid in front of him and said, "Hi, Callie at the store said you bought some of my carvings."

"Oh yeah you're the artist. You really do good work. What's your name; my mom likes your work and would like to see more of it when she's in town.

"I'm Kat I have a souvenir business outside of town. What's your name?" He was looking over her head checking out space available at the bar.

He smiled and said, "I'm Mat Carter. Pleased to meet you. Come on in I'll buy you a drink if you like."

"I don't drink. And I don't go into bars. I just stopped by to tell you it's not safe in there and I wouldn't go in there if I were you." His brows knitted together and he looked down into her serious brown eyes.

Just then a big man with a fu man Chu mustache bumped into him and said, "Hey man your blocking the door, and besides that you've got my usual parking place you got fifteen minutes to move it."

Matt looked into his eyes and opened his mouth to say something and Kat pushed him to one side. "Smart move lady, now get him to move his heap of trash." he said as he went inside.

Matt looked down into her eyes and said, "Look lady, I don't need anyone to watch over me I'm a big boy now and I've handled my fair share of broncs."

"Don't go in there, there is danger in this place tonight." she pleaded.

"Hey what's with you? If your not going to have a drink get out of my way and let me have one okay?"

"Angel plane will have to fly you to the nearest city with a hospital and you might not make it." Now she had his attention. He pushed his hat back frustrated. She was spoiling his night of fun.

"I'm not looking for trouble. I just want to go in and have a few drinks and relax."

"You've already got trouble. The guy that just went in will be trouble so why don't you move your car over in front of the café and we'll go in and have a cup of coffee." he gave an exasperated look toward the bar, but finally after thinking it over he turned toward the street.

"This is a funny way to pick up a guy you know it?" he said over his shoulder.

"I'm not trying to pick up anyone. I'm trying to save your life you idiot." he laughed and moved the car over to the other side of the street. As he did another car moved into the space he just left. He got out and Kat was standing on the curb waiting.

"Boy a cold Bud would sure beat a cup of hot coffee right now."

"Let me tell you something there is going to be a fight in there in fifteen minutes. You want to check your watch?" He smiled and held up his wrist.

"Okay, it's ten to seven. Let's go have coffee and I'll see what happens prophetess." She grinned and pushed the restaurant door open.

Fifteen minutes later at exactly five after seven the bar door burst open and the big guy came out carrying the man who took his parking space over his head. He threw the guy and he landed on the roof of his car with a crash. Matt's eyes grew wide as he saw the guy land on the roof of the car. Matt stood up and walked over to the window.

"Wow I just missed all that fun." Kat rolled her eyes and shook her head. Matt looked at his watch.

"Man right on the mark. So you are a seer huh?"

"Okay Matt the rest of the night is yours. I've got to go I've got work to do."

"Well hey; let me show my appreciation somehow you might have saved my life here."

"Yeah, you'll see me around town." Smiling he stepped in front of her.

"Look don't make me be the one to send you to the hospital." she said. He could see the anger in her eyes.

"Will you at least let me take you to dinner? My Mom loves your carvings and she wants to meet you."

"Oh boy! Already wanting to take me home to meet Mom huh?" His face flushed and turned red.

"No I didn't mean anything like that."

"Good might Matt, I'll see you later." She stepped around him and left feeling warm and excited inside.

"I think I'll have another cup of that coffee." he said to the waitress as he watched Kat get into her Jeep and drive away

"Yeah it might be safer." She laughed as she picked up the pot.

"Do you have any idea where she lives?"

"She's got a house a few miles North of town."

A few minutes later a patrol car arrived and took the guy with the mustache down to the police station and an ambulance took the victim to the emergency clinic.

When Kat drove up to the house she went up to the knoll and looked up at the evening sky. This guy had interrupted her evening of peace. Now she wanted to relax and be at peace with the night. When she looked up into the heavens she should have seen stars, but instead there was a little girl running out into the street in front of a truck. Kat squeezed her eyes shut trying to avoid the outcome. The soft voice said,

"Keep her from death."

"When will it be?" she asked.

"You will see." The voice answered. Kat fell back against the tree holding her head. These kind of things had been happening since she was prayed over by that old man. Sometimes she could hardly keep up with the events and sometimes there were long periods of peace and life went on as normal both good and bad. Finally about midnight she went down to the house. Usually these things happened within the normal course of life and gave her time to react. The next morning Kat woke about ten to the sound of the phone. She rolled over and picked it up.

"Yes? Okay I'll pick it up this afternoon. Thanks Paul."

An order of large wood carvings had arrived at the post office. A wooden bear carrying a welcome sign, squirrels sitting up holding a nut and ground hogs with bucked teeth. These items she ordered from another Indian carver in Montana. She would hook up her trailer when she went to town.

Kat put a pot on the fire for herbal tea. She didn't drink much coffee. While she waited for the water to boil she sat down at her bead table and looked through a catalog of beads available. There were glass, plastic and wooden beads. Sometimes she would buy the larger wooden beads and paint lines or designs on them. They sold fairly well. There were plastic beads with florescent colors, but these weren't Indian types so she moved on. The water started to boil and Kat put some herbs in a cup and poured water over them. She sniffed at the steam taking in the rich aroma of the herbal mixture. It was a mixture her mother had taught her to make from plants she raised. Then gently sipping at the tea she continued to look through the catalog. On the back page she saw the face of a woman and a little girl superimposed on the page. A streak of fear ran over her as she jumped up and ran outside to hook up her trailer.

When Kat reached the post office she searched the street for the woman and her little girl. She didn't see them on the sidewalks, maybe they hadn't arrived yet. She went inside.

"Mornin Paul, I wonder if my whole order came in?"

"Well you got a fair sized load; I hope you brought your trailer."

"Yeah, it's outside."

"Wait until I get it this stuff up front and I'll help you load it."

Thanks Paul you've been a lot of help. I hope I can find a way to pay you back some day."

"I wouldn't worry about that. You've been a lot of help to this town that's enough for me." When they were carrying boxes out to the trailer Kat spotted the woman she had seen in the picture. She was carrying her daughter. As Kat watched them the woman met a friend she knew and stopped a minute to talk as townsfolk usually did. The mother put the child down and held her hand. The little girl was holding a ball and dropped it. It bounced off the edge of the curb into the street. When Kat saw the woman put the girl down she started running her long black hair trailing behind her. The postman looked up in surprise and said,

Protecting Others

"Where you goin'?"

The girl pulled away from her mother's grasp and ran toward the street.

The big truck had just shifted into third and was gaining speed. He saw the girl too late to stop and then a woman in jeans ran across the street and snatched the girl up and ran onto the curb. The driver let out a gasp of relief as he rolled by. The mother almost fainted with relief.

"Oh my Lord you saved my daughter. Thank you Kat." The woman took her little girl and tried to hug Kat at the same time.

"It's okay it's just one of those things that happens some times." Kat said as she tried to catch her breath.

Back down at the post office the postman shook his head in wonder.

"That was close Kat. If you hadn't noticed the little girl we would have had a tragedy on our hands." But in his heart he knew that she had been warned, but didn't want to make a big thing of it. That's the way Kat tried to handle these incidents, as low profile as possible. She didn't want some reporter from one of the bigger towns trying to write a story about an Indian wonder woman with a small town rescue service. She would always tell people she helped to keep it quiet. They silently finished loading her boxes. Of course the grapevine would be abuzz about the rescue.

When she had the trailer loaded she walked over to the café to have breakfast. She sat down at the counter and ordered a bowl of oatmeal and a cup of tea.

"Heard you had another close one out there a while ago. What happened?"

"I'm sure you got the story from the girls in the retired section."

"Yeah Kat, but you know how they lie."

Kat smiled as the waitress chuckled. "It was just a case of seeing something and being able to help at just the right time. The little girl was chasing a ball into the street and I just happened to see it and caught her before the truck did. End of

story." She gave the waitress that 'no big deal look.'
"I know you don't say much about it, but you have really been a blessing to this town. I want you to know we appreciate it Kat. I still think you should have shown up for the award they tried to give you last year." Kat was looking down into her oatmeal and slowly shaking her head. She held up her hand to ward off the waitress.
"Please let me finish my breakfast okay?" The waitress smiled and went back to her orders. Under her breath Kat thanked the voice that spoke to her heart. When she finished she went down the street to the local newspaper office. As she walked in she said to the clerk at the counter,
"Let me speak to John Kerry please." The girl smiled and turned to go into Kerry's office, but he was already standing in the doorway.
"Mornin Kat, come on in. I thought you might be stopping by." She skirted the counter and went into the office. The office was messy and in need of a paint job. There were articles covering the editor's desk. He cleared off a chair and motioned for her to sit down. She stood and looked at him.
"Stopped another close one did you?"
"Word gets around quick John."
"Small town what can you expect? He said with a shrug.
"I'd appreciate it if you wouldn't make a big thing out of this."
"That little girl came within a half second of dying out there this morning Kat. You have managed to avoid notoriety on several occasions, but not on this one. I got it from the horse's mouth and I'm printing it. Why do you constantly avoid the townspeople's recognition? They are just trying to show their appreciation. Just take it in stride and don't try to throw it back in their faces."
"I don't try to be superwoman. It just happens that I'm there when these things take place. Like anyone else I won't stand by and let people get hurt or die. Anyone else in my place would do the same thing."

"Ed Garland told me that you were off and running before it happened. We know there is a warning comes before these things take place. I'll make it as low key as I can Kat, but if I don't cover it some hot shot reporter from Boise will show up here one day and he will pry until he blows this wide open. You know how the older women talk in this town. Besides the Boise Herald has their phone number on the front page of their paper. You know these gossipy women can dial faster than you can blink an eye. And with these new cell phones Lord only knows. They're already saying if I won't print it maybe someone else will."

"Nosey old women, they need to mind their own business." Kat muttered.

"When it happens in public it is their business." John said. Kat turned and walked out. As she climbed into her Jeep she realized it could be a lot worse. And if there was anything she didn't want it was a big town newspaper snooping around, because she knew the tabloids would be next. When they arrived the feeding frenzy would be as unbearable as a pool of Piranhas. Of course she knew that some day she would have to answer for her abilities and her gift, but she would hold it at bay as long as she could.

On the road outside of town she saw the old Ranchero making a dust cloud as it approached. Matt hollered as he past going the other way, "Hey Wait I want to talk to you." Kat kept going giving him a wave. When she saw him making a U turn in the middle of the road she slowed and pulled over. She didn't want him to know where she lived. He stopped beside her.

"Mornin, your hard to find."

"Mornin. Not if you know where to look."

"Well where might that be?"

"Sorry cowboy I like my privacy. I'm not giving you my address."

"I heard over at the cafe you saved a little girls life this morning."

"That waitress never could keep her mouth shut." Kat said in a disgusted tone.

"Seems you stay edgy nearly all the time. I'd kinda like to take you to dinner for helpin me out last night."

"Not tonight, I'm runnin behind on my orders. I've got a big day ahead of me. Let's make it later in the week. You'll probably see me around town I'll let you know. See you later." With that she drove off letting him set there in her dust cloud. *Now if he tries to follow me I'll lead him on the merriest chase he's ever known.* She thought as she watched the rear view mirror. A couple miles down the road she turned off on a side road and into some tamarack bushes. Kat watched her mirror to see if he went by. Less than a minute later he rolled by the intersection slow looking to see if she had turned. He guessed she hadn't so he drove on. She backed out on to the side road and continued toward a small lake. At the edge of the water Kat got out and walked along the edge a little way. *It's kind of nice being chased for a change.* She thought smiling.

The state in past years had tried to make a dam at the edge of the downstream side of the lake and the rain was especially heavy that year and the water rose above the dam and stayed there so it left a path wide enough for her Jeep to cross in about two feet of water. She got back in and eased out on to the gravel path and very slowly rolled to the other side, which was about a hundred yards. Kat doubled back and came on to the backside of her property putting the Jeep behind the house where it couldn't be seen from the road. She went in the back door grinning.

The rest of the day she spent working on orders for places out of state and updating her magazine ads. A few calls came in with orders, which she filled and would take to the post office the next day. In between orders she did some loom work on small bath mats and mats for front entries. There didn't seem to be time to do any bead work or carving which took all her concentration that would be for later when it got dark. She would be going to the hill late tonight. Sure enough it was almost ten before she had to give up. She had gotten a lot done and if the crafts kept selling the way they had been she would have a little extra money next week. Kat pushed away from the beads she had been working on and went into the kitchen to make tea. When it was done she took the cup with her to the hill. Climbing the hill she felt a satisfied feeling with what she had accomplished. First thing tomorrow she would go to the post office and send off the orders and pick up anything that had come in. At the top she sat down at the base of the pine and leaned back against the trunk. There was no moon. Kat closed her eyes to relax and that's when she heard a kitten mewing a short distance away. She opened her eyes and stared into the darkness. She could just make out a small form coming up the hill toward her. When it came within ten feet of her it sat down and looked at her.

The Spirits Intervene

"Where did you come from Kitty? Did they desert you on the road? Come here baby, I'll take you down to the house and get you some milk." The cat sat there silent in the dark. Kat waited a moment. Then she noticed there was no night noises, crickets or bugs. Everything was deathly silent. *Oh, Oh, something's coming.* She thought as she got up from the ground. There was a shriek, the definite cry of a mountain lion. *Not down here it's too low.* She thought. Kat looked around in the dark, but it was too dark to make out any forms. The kitten sat silent in the darkness. Kat felt the right side of her belt. The small hunting knife was in the house on the coffee table. *Your mother taught you better than that stupid. Always be ready. That means keep your gun or hunting knife where you can reach it Kat.* She could hear her mother's voice shaming her for forgetting. If the lion was coming up here she wouldn't hear it until it was too late. Turning on her heel she jumped and grabbed one of the lower limbs and hoisted herself on to it. Then climbed three or four courses higher where she could see the road. Nothing approached from where she could see. She checked the trunk of the tree. Still the kitten sat silent in the dark. If a lion was coming he would have scampered. After a half hour Kat didn't want to spend the night up there so she climbed down. When she turned the kitten was gone. *Forget that cat I'm otta here.* She ran down the slope and in the front door closing it behind her. There was a lamp on in the living room and... the kitten was sitting on the coffee table...next to her hunting knife. After she had had time for the situation to sink in the cat batted the knife off the table on the opposite side. Kat made a move toward the coffee table and the kitten jumped down and started toward the kitchen. Kat dove for the side board pulling a drawer open and taking out a thirty-eight revolver. She checked it to make sure it was loaded. She couldn't figure out the reason for the cat...unless it was a diversion. *Don't be distracted by the cat.* She told herself. Her eyes roamed the house as she moved toward the kitchen. The kitten moved into the darkened room. Kat stepped back and picked up her knife and clipped it on her belt. She wondered if these weapons would do her any good. Had an Indian spirit come to her from the past? Slowly she reached around the doorway and flipped on the light. She looked over toward the sink cabinets, no one there. As she turned the other way she saw a man in full Indian dress with a head band and a feather. His face was slightly wrinkled and his hair had strands of gray. He was at least fifty years old. Kat knew he wasn't real for the image wavered from time to time. A messenger, but for what reason?

"I am war lion I have come to tell you that you will go into dangerous places to protect people. Do not fear you have power to overcome the enemy. They are in the forest to the North. Go and stop them from boiling the pot." he said. The image began to fade. In a minute or so it was gone and all was quiet. Kat looked around and the kitten was gone too. *Strange way to get a message. What would they cook?* She wondered.

The next morning she put on a pair of boots instead of the shoes she usually wore so that she would have protection from snakes if she had to walk very far. After breakfast Kat went into town and mailed the packages she had prepared the night before. The gas station was the next stop where she filled the tank and a five gallon can. She wasn't sure how far she would have to drive. Kat took an old road out of town going north. Further out the road became gravel. She listened to the tires crunching on the road. *Too much noise. Someone could hear me approaching.* She thought. A mile or two later she took a dirt trail that circled back to the gravel road further out in the wooded area. She slowed down to about ten miles an hour ambling along in second gear. The Jeep's engine was quiet.

A few minutes later she saw a hat in the distance. She stopped and slid into the under brush and moved toward the hat. As she parted through the brush she came on a guy with a shot gun standing in a clearing. Kat didn't think he was hunting rabbits. She waited and watched.

"What are you doin out here lady?" a voice behind her said.

Oh, Oh busted. She thought. Slowly she turned to she a big rough neck at looked like a logger. "He was holding a shotgun like the other guy and she knew it didn't have bird shot in it. I was looking for herbs that I use in my herbal remedies."

The guy smiled like he really believed her. He nodded and said, "I wouldn't be wandering around out here lady it's not safe. People have been shot by mistake you know what I mean."

She nodded and stepped around him and trotted back to her Jeep. When she reached the gravel road she pulled into a bushy area where she couldn't be seen and shut off the engine. As she sat there she listened to the sounds around her. It was pretty quiet. They had spooked the wildlife. Just then a couple of guys drove by slow in an older Blazer. It was in pretty rough shape, but the engine purred like a kitten.

Just made for this kind of hunting. She thought.

On the passenger side she saw a guy with a gun barrel sticking up. *Man these guy are serious. Probably protecting a Marijuana patch.* When they were gone she quietly got out and took a pair of climbing spikes and a belt out of a bag in the back, the spikes had been altered and were smaller for a woman's use. Kat looked around and found a big pine the trunk was three feet in diameter and probably sixty or seventy feet high. She stood and listened for a few minutes. Then she swung the belt around the tree and caught the other end trying not to make any noise. Clipping the ends to her belt she started to climb. It was about twenty feet to the first limb. She scooted around to the side, but wasn't high enough to see anything. When she finally reached the top she stayed behind the trunk and peeked around the side. Out in the distance she could just make out a small group of men standing around a fire drinking coffee, but there wasn't anything suspicious in the clearing. She decided that she would come back in a day or two after dark in the quiet mode. As she started to descend something caught her eye off to the right. It looked like a small shack. There was a wisp of smoke coming from the stack. It was too far away to tell if there was anyone around. On the ground she took another path back to the gravel road to avoid the blazer.

When she got back to town she stopped by the Sheriff's office. Sheriff Tate was behind his desk with his feet up cleaning his nails. Kat told the girl at the desk she wanted to speak to the Sheriff.

The girl spun around in her chair and said, "You got company Sheriff."

"Oh, hi Kat come on in." she stepped inside the door and said, "May I close the door?"

"Have we got something hush, hush to talk about?" he asked. She nodded and looked over her shoulder. The girl spun around and went back to work.

"I think it might be a good idea until you hear what I've got to say." she said quietly.

"Okay close the door. What's on your mind?"

"Well Sheriff I was out in the woods North of here this morning…"

He held up his hand stopping her.

"Now Kat we all know what's out there and it's not safe for a woman to be out there alone. We have raided those guys before and come up empty handed and until we can get some federal help we are wasting our time."

"There is a shack out there with a stove pipe curling smoke and I've got a feeling they're cooking something besides bacon."

"Yeah I know, but we've raided that shack twice and all we came up with was corn beef and potatoes. Your getting in deep territory here and I'm afraid your going to get hurt. Did anyone see you?"

"Yeah, a guy with a shotgun. I told him I was hunting herbs."

"And I suppose you think he believed you?"

"Well at least I had a viable excuse for being there."

"Did you argue with him?"

"No, I got out of there as quick as I could."

"I know you didn't just drive up on that shack. How did you find that?" She grinned.

"I climbed a tall tree."

The Sheriff shook his head.

"Kat for your own safety please stop this snooping around. You've been a very important help around this town you've been able to avert a lot of trouble. I heard that you kept Matt Carter out of a skirmish the other night. So why don't you just keep your eye on him?" He grinned as he said this.

With an exasperated look she said, "Thanks Sheriff and I guess the good old girls will keep you posted."

She opened the door and left.

The Sheriff got up and closed the door again and picked up his cell phone. He pushed a button on the speed dial.

"We might have to turn the fire off under the pot. We got a local Indian woman looking around. One of the men ran her off this morning."

"Yeah, you better make sure she stays out of the woods.

People come up missing sometimes, you know?" the voice answered. Then there was the dial tone.

As Kat was driving back to her house she said to no one in particular, "For some reason I don't believe you Sheriff." She had detected a tone in his voice that said he might be trying to protect those guys out there. When she arrived at the house she went inside and made some tea and took out her cell phone and dialed the state FBI number from information. The woman she spoke to in Boise said she didn't know of any request for help from that area. Kat thanked her and hung up before she could ask any questions. Then she got the number for the ATF Office. She got the same answer there, but this woman was a little quicker.

"Say, why would someone be calling for help from that area?"

"I don't know for sure I'll have to check it out and get back to you." She hung up before the woman could ask any more questions.

Kat sat thinking for a few moments then she went after her field glasses and tucked her thirty-eight behind her in her belt. The lenses had been dulled to prevent reflection in the day light. She sat down at the kitchen table and thought while she finished her tea.

Seven miles West of where she had been earlier there was a blacktopped road. She might be able to get in if she went further North and doubled back on foot. She thought of a marijuana raid that had been written up in Time magazine in the past. (This one had been in Oregon.) It mentioned the criminals using tree stands for observation points. It might be a good idea to remember that so she wouldn't get caught like she had this morning. *Girl you could have gotten killed out there.* She thought. Then she decided it might be best if she left Sheriff Tate out of this. She didn't trust him. As an afterthought she picked up her cell and dialed the Sheriff's office and asked for him.

"He's not here right now he's gone out on a call. Can I

give him a message?"

"That's okay, I'll call back later." Kat said. *I'll have to remember to follow him sometime when he makes these calls out of town.* She thought.

She called the souvenir shop in town and told the girl if they need anything in the next couple of days make a list and she would take care of it in the next few days. She told the girl she would be out of town for a couple of days and would check when she got back.

Kat made up a camping pack with a light bed roll. Who could she trust? She needed a friend who wouldn't call the newspaper or the Sheriff the moment she hung up. In her mind Kat couldn't come up with a single person. It was supposed to look like a simple camping trip, but if the info got to the paper, or worse, the Sheriff, they would automatically put two and two together. So if she went to Boise first and then came back for a trip to the woods it would give them time to calm down on the Marijuana farm. If there was someone who knew what was going on they might send someone looking for her. She wasn't ready to get caught in that area of the woods again. So she decided it might not be a bad idea if she drove to Boise and talked to someone there in the FBI or ATF offices.

Kat packed a separate overnight case and a change of clothes just to be prepared if she decided to stay overnight. Boise was approximately two hundred and fifty miles away. She could take I-15 to I-80 and make it in six hours if she drove straight through.

Early the next morning Kat left before first light driving West on the freeway. A pair of eyes looking through night vision glasses followed her progress out of town.

On a radio a voice said, "Follow her for a while and see where she goes. Thirty miles later a call went back that said,

"She's headed out of town going Northwest."

"All right come on back. I don't think she going to bother us. Apparently she took the Sheriff's advise, which is lucky for her."

Tribal Help

By noon Kat rolled into Boise and was looking for the FBI office. When she located it she discovered that Alcohol, Tobacco and Firearms was in the same building.

As she walked down the main hall she noticed an Indian woman approaching that looked familiar. When she got closer she recognized the woman almost the same age that had gone to school with her.

"My Lord Tinker is that you?"

"Kat! I can't believe it." She grabbed Kat and hugged her. Tinker was a tall Indian woman with the typical round face, dark skin, and long black hair.

"What are you doing here?" Kat asked.

"I work here lady. I'm a permanent fixture around here. Good Lord girl it's been a long time."

"I wondered what happened to you after school. How did you get here?" Kat asked.

"Well when I graduated I said I wasn't going to be an Indian on the reservation any more and I moved up here and applied. When I passed the test I told them I would mop floors if I could get on here. The next week they put me in an office. I've been here every since. What brings you up here? Tired of beating the boys off with a club?"

No Tinker, we got serious problems down home and I'm looking for someone to help me."

"Well my old friend, you have come to the right person it just so happens I'm in investigations. So why don't we get you a cup of tea and sit down in my office and see what we can do." There was a small snack bar down the hall. They stopped and ordered.

"You know Kat, my problem has always been these stupid donuts. I couldn't be an alcoholic like the rest of my family, so now I'm going to end up a fat old squaw."

The girl behind the counter wiggled her eyebrows and smiled. Tinker said, "And I don't want anything out of you either. You bad mouth me today and I'll lock you up." The girl turned and put her hand over her mouth to keep from laughing out loud.

"Kat I'm like Rodney Dangerfield around here I can't get no respect." Kat laughed.

A few minutes later in Tinker's office Kat was admiring the degrees on the wall and the fine furniture.

"You have made a name for yourself in law enforcement I see."

"I'm working on my masters in one of these fields. And it ain't in rehabilitation either. I like to lock'em up and forget'em. So my friend what can I do to help you?"

"Well you know I've had these premonitions since I got out of school. Now there are more of them and they're getting closer together. I ran on to something the other day and got myself in trouble. So there are people in the woods watching me and I think our Sheriff is involved. The way I got into this was three days ago the image of an Indian on the tribal counsel appeared to me and told me to protect the people and stop someone from cooking in the woods to the North of Soda Springs. I went out and tried to investigate and ran into a guard with a shotgun who forcefully suggested I go home and mind my own business. You know that was the wrong thing to say to Kat Johnson. I drove off to a bushy area, hid my Jeep and climbed a tree. I saw a cabin and I think it's more than just a headquarters for a marijuana operation, which is more like a feeling. I really haven't seen anything illegal yet, but I know it's there."

"Kat honey, I don't have to tell you that this can be very dangerous. If you get caught out there in a hot area you will never be seen again. These people are very cruel and have no conscience. The only thing that means anything to them is the money. I know I'm not going to stop you even though I think that's what you should do. I'm considering the gift you have and the message you received, but let me offer an alternative while the ATF sets up an investigation. Get a good camera with a long telephoto lens; I'm talking about a range of at least a quarter mile or so. Take pictures of anyone you think are involved. This includes the local Sheriff. Don't move in close, our people will do that at the right time. Get the camera here, not at home, it would be a dead give away to buy in a local store or order through the mail, because you don't know who's watching you in Soda Springs. If we have pictures to substantiate our case we will have some idea of who we have to watch. If you happen to get pictures of shipments of material going out in pick ups or larger trucks let me know. Now I know what you are thinking. We need Proof. We have a guy here that can get it if it's there. Everyone calls him sneaky and believe me he is just that. Thank God this man is on the side of the law. I'll introduce you later. I can get you special cell phones that are linked directly to our office. One will be limited to calls to my office and the other will give you contact to any other agent in our department. We will set up an system of initials for prominent characters."

"What if you call when I'm in an awkward position?"

"The red phone will have an extra button that disconnects the call and the caller will know to wait to call back later. And something else you need to know is that when you receive a call these phones operate on vibration, soft vibration only. Now let's go meet Sneaky." They went down the hall to another office Tinker looked in, there was no one there. When they turned to leave a short man with reddish brown hair combed straight back slipped out the door and stopped behind them.

"Good morning ladies." he said in a horse tone. Kat's head snapped around. She hadn't expected anyone to be so close. The guy was short, five feet, with light green eyes and a sharp nose and pointed chin. Tinker smiled as she turned to greet him.

"Good morning sneak. I'd like you to meet a friend of mine. This is Kat. We have been soul sisters since high school."

"Hi Kat. A pleasure."

She grinned a little and said hi.

"I don't mind being called sneaky I'm used to it."

"Kat has brought us an interesting situation from the Southeastern part of the state.

She thinks there is a ring operating in the woods making more than the Marijuana available to our kids in school, but we should have pictures at eleven." Sneaky nodded eyes always wide like he was in eternal surprise.

"Okay talk to you later." He turned and went back into his office silently on tiptoe.

"Strange little man." Kat said softly. "He makes me want to whisper."

Tinker smiled and nodded.

"Should I go to the FBI as well?" Kat asked

"No they will just tell you they have bigger fish to fry. It's a good thing I ran into you it might be the only way you can get any action. Remember though I need pictures incriminating or not. Don't take any chances if this is something big they will wipe you out no questions asked. You're spending the night right?" Kat nodded. "Stop by in the morning before you leave I'll give you the phones. It's been good seeing you again sister." She grabbed Kat by the arms and hugged her and kissed her on the cheek. With that she turned and walked away.

Not like the girl I knew in school. Now she is all business... But in a way I guess that's the way I am too. Kat thought.

Kat rented a room in a Colonial Inn a couple of miles away. The room was bright and spacious. The bath was large and very modern with lots of amenities. The motel also offered a continental breakfast. Kat hoped she could sleep in a little since she was away from home.

The Evil Crystals

A large ton and a half box van rolled off the highway down a worn path several miles outside Soda Springs. Two miles from the highway it drove into a large cluster of trees and underbrush. There was a path just wide enough for the truck. As it progressed a large hole opened up in front of it and it drove down into the ground. The hole closed up after it went in. The hole was actually a hydraulic ramp that led to an underground fortress. Once the truck was below ground it made a U turn and backed up to a door in a white cubicle that was actually a huge laboratory sixty by one hundred feet in size. There were massive beams that held up the roof of the hole. The lab had been built under them. It was an ultra modern structure with all new equipment. Polished stainless tables and new cooking surfaces with special controls that made every batch just the same. It had all the necessary testing equipment necessary to produce the new type of pure Meth that was far more deadly than the stuff that came out of the back rooms and abandoned garages.

A roll up door raised and two men came out and helped the driver get ready to load it's first cargo. The cargo? 3000 pounds of freshly cooked Methamphetamines all prepackaged and ready to sell on the street. The large crew of workers had been working feverishly to meet a deadline that would put the drug on the streets just as school was ending for the summer. This was to be one of the main supply points

Several men came out of the door hurriedly carrying boxes to put into the truck. There was millions of dollars of product here and could leave thousands of teen's lives in danger. It looked like the first load was going to make it to the streets.

Intervention From Beyond

In one corner of the underground hole the area was dimly lit. Most of the lights shined on the building. There was a dark figure watching from the shadows. It waited until the truck was loaded and the driver was getting ready to get in the cab. As he reached for the door handle an arrow came whistling out of the darkness and lodged in his throat just above his collar bone. The driver made a funny noise. "Uhhh!" His body dropped to the ground. A worker heard the noise and turned to see what happened.

When he saw the driver laying on the ground he pulled out a gun and shouted, "Intruder in the hole!"

Everyone stopped and turned. Guns of every description came out of pockets, belts and holsters. They ran out of the lab shining flashlights in every corner. There was no one to be seen. The shadowy figure was gone. A big man came out and stood over the driver's body.

"No one knows about this place. All the people that worked on this project are dead right?" he asked the men around him.

"Yeah Hal, no one knows we made sure of that." a man answered.

"Get the guards to come in closer to the entrance. I can't figure how anyone got in. I also want someone to take care of that Indian woman that got on the property a couple of days ago."

Hal Morris was a real estate broker from the Los Angeles area. He had made a lot of money from the real estate he bought and sold, but the thousands he made every year wasn't enough when he found out how much he could make from these drugs. So he invested all he had in this project and if things had gone without a hitch he would have been a millionaire many times over. Now he was shaking with fury to think, somehow, someone with a bow had killed his driver in his secret lab. The rest of the men were still searching the area. Another man approached Hal.

"Nothing boss. We can't find anyone." he said looking around. Just then another arrow whistled out of the darkness of the other corner. The arrow lodged in the man's eye socket. He fell back dead.

"Quick, inside the lab." Hal screamed.

The men all ran inside firing their weapons as they closed the door. There were no windows so they couldn't see their enemy. The figure approached from the shadows and stood with bow ready as a second figure sneaked up and took the gas cap off the tank and dropped a match in the hole and ran to join the other man. The fumes ignited and there was an explosion and the whole load went up in flames.

The two figures stopped, closed their eyes and turned their faces up and disappeared. A few moments later the door rolled up from the lab and they watched their money go up in flames. After the workers put out the fire and routed the smoke through the filter system which they had to avoid because the fumes were deadly now. Hal Morris went back to his office and fell into a chair and put his hand over his face. A little half breed Indian followed Hal into the office.

"What are we going to do Charlie?"

"I know a medicine man that lives up North of here. He can stop this for a price and it will be a whole lot cheaper than the price we just paid."

"Charlie it will take weeks to replace what we just lost."

"A successful man never gives up is what you told me boss."

"Okay go find this medicine man and get us back on track Charlie. Maybe we can have a smaller shipment by the end of the month." Charlie turned and hurried out.

The next morning Kat woke early and couldn't go back to sleep. She was troubled in her spirit she felt that things might be happening at home and she needed to be there. She got up and took a shower and dressed. When she came back into the room she noticed it was only seven by the clock. If the breakfast bar wasn't ready she could go to a restaurant. Gathering her things she left the room. When she entered the office breakfast was already laid out on a table. There were also cozy places to sit. Kat decided to stay and eat. She picked out cereal, tea, fruit and a small blueberry muffin. At the small table she saw the desk clerk and he bid her good morning.

"You're up early ma'am."

"Yeah got to get on the road got a long way to drive."

"Was everything all right last night?"

"Yes, thank you. It was very comfortable. If I have to come back I'd stay here again."

"Thank you we are glad to be of service."

After she checked out she gassed up her Jeep and checked the oil, water, and gas can. When she finished she sat for a moment. She had an uneasy feeling. Something had gone wrong at home she needed to get out of here. By the time she got to the ATF office it was almost eight o'clock. As she drove into the parking lot she saw Tinker standing outside. She drove up and stopped.

"I'm glad you came early. It's better if no one saw me giving you these phones." They were in a black cloth bag.

"The instructions are inside. Memorize the numbers and burn the paper. Keep me posted." She turned and went inside. Kat drove to I-80 South headed for Soda Springs.

Working for the ATF

That afternoon when she arrived in town she went to the souvenir shop to see if there were any orders. The clerk was glad to see her. Kat held her finger to her lips to keep her from saying she was glad to have her back. There were several costumers in the store.

Kat leaned across the counter and whispered, "I've got some people looking for me that I don't want to see right now."

When she straightened up she said aloud, "So do I have any more orders?"

Yeah, you do, two welcome bears and three squirrels."

Kat wrote them down on her note pad.

"You can bring more small carvings too they seem to be moving pretty good."

"Okay I'll bring in some of the stuff this afternoon and what I don't have I can work on tomorrow. I'll probably see you later" she smiled and turned to leave. She saw the Sheriff standing next to her Jeep. Slowly she ambled outside.

"Afternoon Kat haven't seen you for a couple of days."

"Well I decided to get away for a while and relax from all this souvenir stuff."

"Have you been camping?" She knew what he meant by the question.

"No I stayed at a motel. I'm doing what you told me to do. I'm minding my own business."

"Good girl. Like I said it can be dangerous in the wrong places around here. I'll keep checking on what you told me. Have a good day Kat." He turned and walked back toward his office. Kat watched him leave and now she was sure he was involved. There would probably be someone watching her every move. The hill outside her house came to her mind. She jumped into her Jeep and drove fast toward her property.

When she arrived she found the front door of her house open. She pulled the thirty-eight out of her bag and stalked inside. There was a big man looking through her dresser drawers in the bedroom. His eyes were mean and he had a vicious grin on his face.

"What are you doing in my house?"

"You answer my question and I'll answer yours. What were you doing out there in the woods?" She raised the gun. Someone grabbed her from behind. She raised her leg and racked her boot down his shin and stomped on the arch of his foot. When he danced back in pain she raised the gun again and shot the big guy in the middle of the chest. He hit the floor at her feet and she whipped around and shot the guy behind her in the temple. He jerked sideways and fell against the door jamb and slid down to the floor. After she tucked the gun in her belt she grabbed him by the hair and the collar of his shirt and drug him toward the front door. She drug him outside in the yard and dropped him then went inside for the other one. The big guy wasn't going to be as easy. She pulled his arms from under him and drug him out. With bodies in the yard she pulled out her cell phone.

"Hi Sheriff, I just found a couple of bodies in my front yard and when I'm through talking to you I'm dialing the state police. She punched the end button and started dialing again.

"May I speak to officer Little Cloud please, it's an emergency. Hi Tinker, when I walked in my door a while ago there were two guys taking my house apart. Now they are laying at my feet. You need to get someone down here before I wind up the same way. I'm headed for the forest I'll check in with whoever arrives later." She punched the end button.

Tinker sat staring at the phone. Finally she came to herself and punched a number on the intercom phone.

"Sneak get over to my office right now." She slammed the phone down and leaned back with her arms folded across her chest. Sneaky came running in the door a couple of seconds later eyes wide as usual.

"What happened?"

"I shouldn't have let Kat go back there alone. Now there are two men dead and all hell is going to break loose. Those people will burn her house down and kill her if they find her. I hope Kat is smart enough to stay out of sight until we can get someone down there. Okay sneak take a couple of men and head that way and I'll go to the director and get a team effort started. She lives in a three bedroom frame house out on state road five. The name Johnson is on the mail box. There will probably be a couple of bodies laying somewhere in the shade." Now sneak's eyes were really wide as he gaped at her in surprise.

"Yeah sneak this Indian does not play any games. If a man messes with her he's dead.

Kat was busy gathering the things she would need to survive in the wild. A .22 semi auto rifle, back pack, hunting knife, ammo, traps and wire trips were some of the things she took. A shirt and an extra pair of jeans went with them. And of course her nine millimeter glock, with extra clips.

I've got to hurry and get out of here the Sheriff's probably on his way. I know he's gotten the message by now. She ran outside carrying her rifle and pack. Jumped in the jeep and wound her way through the trees adjacent to her property. About a mile away she came to a deep ditch about a hundred feet long. She cut around to one end and drove down in the ditch about fifty yards from the end. She crawled out and scrambled up the bank and began throwing dead leaves on top and on the hood. This would help keep them from finding it too quickly; it would be difficult to see from the air. Kat ran down the side of the ditch carrying her things into the forest beyond.

While Kat was running through the trees the Sheriff's cruiser was pulling into her front yard. He got out and looked around and saw the two bodies. He shook his head as he approached. Having to deal with the bodies would keep him busy until Kat got away. The Sheriff went back to his car and called the coroner and a couple of deputies. He sat for a moment thinking about what this would cause.

"Kat, you've started a war now and I can't help you anymore." he said.

Sneaky Krebs, ATF agent, was traveling South with two other agents in a new pick up,(Confiscated from a narcotics raid) hoping he could get to Soda Springs in time to prevent any more blood shed. The needle was hovering just above ninety and the other two agents eyes were as big as Sneak's.

"Can you let off of it just a little Sneak." one of the men asked.

"No I can't, one of our best sources of information in this case is probably running from those animals right now. If they catch her we are out of luck. Thank God she is an Indian acquainted with the woods. I hope she's smart enough to stay out of sight." Just then a Highway Patrol unit pulled out on the highway behind them with siren blaring. They pulled over and showed their ID The HP told them to hold it down and let them go.

In the office of the underground lab Hal Morris asked Charlie what happened to the two men he sent out earlier.

"I don't know boss I haven't heard from them since they left."

"Well send someone else out there and see what's going on."

When the messenger from Hal drove past the yard he saw the Sheriff, the coroner and several deputies. He stopped and turned around and sped away. The deputy that did see the car figured it was someone that made a wrong turn. Down the road a ways the driver took out a radio phone and called the lab.

"Charlie this is Ted, both of the men you sent out are out of commission. The Sheriff and the Coroner are on the scene."

"Yeah, that's a 10-4. Come on back in." Charlie answered.

Meanwhile Kat was running at a steady pace hoping it would put her out in the wilderness far enough to be able protect herself from the hoodlums that she felt would be after her. She thought they would probably have access to a helicopter so she would have to be very careful. Kat knew she could take it easy until she made contact with the enemy. She was traveling in a westerly direction away from the dealers hide out.

By the time night fall had come she was several miles away from her house. Fortunately she had hunted deer in this area last fall just before the first snow so she knew her way. As she hurried along she was looking for a hollow tree stump she had seen the year before. The last of the light faded in the distance. It would be possible to spend the night in it without being discovered. The trunk stood about eight feet high and was at least two feet in diameter. Now she went into a quiet mode moving slowly listening for other sounds like men moving in the dark. When she reached the tree trunk she climbed up and peered inside with the help of a small flash light. Someone had used it for a deer blind there were cigarette butts at the bottom. Kat went to a bush and broke off a branch climbed in and pulled it in after her to cover her from the air. She scooted down into a sitting position with her legs folded against her body. She laid the nine millimeter on top of her knees and waited for morning.

Sheriff Tate was at Kat's house searching for evidence of where she had gone. He and a deputy had opened the front door and gone in to search the house. When they looked down the hall they saw a huge brown bear. He growled, they ran, he followed, and they drove away in the patrol car. The Indian spirits had sent help.

Late that same day Sneaky and his fellow agents arrived in Soda Springs and had rented a room as tourists. They tried to contact Kat but she was running and hadn't turned on the phone. They went to the souvenir store and the clerk gave them directions to her house. As they drove toward her house they passed the Sheriff going toward town. Sneaky watched the rear view mirror. Shortly they came to Kat's house. The bear was wandering around in the front yard. They too decided that maybe they would come back later. Back in their motel room they laid out a plan to search the woods and see what they could find. Each one had a small communications radio on a special band so they could keep in contact. Each one carried a Glock .40 semi automatic with two extra clips of ammunition. In Soda springs there was no car rental office so they contacted a town that had an Enterprise Agency. A black Jeep would be delivered later that day. The guy showed with the Jeep and the contract just a couple of hours before dark so they would have to wait until morning. This made Sneaky upset. They were already running behind and couldn't contact Kat. And who knew how fast things were heating up. One of the agents kept calling the red phone. By the time Kat got in the tree she felt the vibration. She answered with a whisper,

"Yeah?"

"This is agent Michaels with the ATF. We are in town at the starlight motel. Where are you?"

"I'm out in the woods a long way from you. I think they have discovered what I'm trying to do. I'll have to lay low for a while until you get a handle on what they are doing."

What direction does the encampment lay from town?" The

agent asked.

"Northeast on the Cumberland road five miles out you can start your search, but watch out for guards with shot guns and AK-47's. You will have to move in and take them out one at a time. There may be some men in the trees on deer stands with automatic weapons. There is a cabin out there that may be their headquarters or storage unit, but I don't know where they are operating from."

"Okay great, we will move into the woods as soon as Sneaky's ready. Are you in a safe place?"

"Yeah, I'll be safe for the night. Check with me in the morning." she pushed the end button and closed her eyes with a smile on her lips. At least she wasn't alone.

Agent Michaels relayed the message to Sneaky.

"Okay then we'll get ready and move into the woods as soon as it gets dark. Let me take point and you guys follow a few yards back. We'll need cuffs and rope to tie them up and haul them to the truck."

The two agents looked at one another strange. One said, "Sneaky, we are in a pick up you gonna put them in the bed?"

I called for another box van while you were gone. It'll be here by dark." They wore special Kevlar vests under hunting jackets with large pockets to carry the cuffs and rope. They had extra clips of ammo. Sneaky had a dart gun used to subdue animals behind the seat of the car. They prepared their equipment at the motel while they waited for the sun to go down.

Sneaky told the other two men, "We can't let the Sheriff know what we are doing until it's almost too late cause we think he is involved and will expose us to the drug boys before we can make any arrests. If this goes all right we'll haul them out of there like hungry bass from a horse trough. When we find them I'll muffle them and you guys move in and tie them up and take them to the truck. Don't try enter any buildings while it's dark you could get trapped. Remember there are only three of us so be careful and be quiet."

They went down to the local restaurant to eat just before dark. Of course all the locals watched them close. While they were eating the Sheriff came in and gave them the once over. They didn't bother to look at him other than an occasional glance. When they left they walked back to the motel so the Sheriff wouldn't see what they were driving. About seven a box van pulled in and parked outside their room and bumped the horn a short toot. After Sneaky gave the driver instructions the three men slipped outside and crawled inside the back and lowered the door. The driver, another agent, backed out and drove Northeast. When they were about five miles from town the driver pulled into the trees and shut it down. Sneaky and the other two agents slipped out of the back and crossed the road. The driver stayed with the truck.

No one quite knew how sneaky could locate a body in the dark, but they will tell you he could when no one else could. He found the first man in a tree on a stand about a half a mile away. When he climbed up to the stand he tapped the guy with the butt of his pistol, tied him to the trunk of the tree and taped his mouth shut. When Michaels asked where the guy was Sneaky pointed skyward. The next one they found behind a rock smoking a cigarette. Peters, (the other agent) knocked him out with a lead sap and they tied him up and carried him back to the truck. Just then a truck came up the road from town and turned into the woods on a narrow path. Sneaky and his men followed. The truck stopped at the base of the tree where the guy was tied to the stand.

The driver got out and called in a husky whisper, "Orin you all right? Come on down and get some coffee. We got some good sandwiches too."

When the guy didn't answer they became curious.

"Orin, you all right?" No answer, no movement. Just as the driver turned to the other man a gun pressed to his throat.

"If you move a whisker you are dead. Sneaky put his pistol to the back of the other guys head at the same time. They tied them up and took them back to the van. They drove the pick up on the rest of the rounds. At every stop there was a man either on the ground or in a tree. At the call for food they came right up and got tied up. When they had them secured, (7men) the driver took them back to town and transferred the prisoners to a paddy wagon and took them to a jail in a neighboring town to be held until reinforcements could transfer them to Boise. Eventually someone was going to miss the guards on the perimeter and things would escalate into a fire fight. Sneaky and the other two agents waited in the woods until the truck came back. They drove back to the motel and waited for the trouble to start. One of the agents watched the Sheriff's office. It wasn't long until there was a lot of traffic in and out.

In the ATF headquarters in Boise Tinker was preparing the paper work to take all the men associated with the drug ring into custody. The Sheriff in the neighboring town related information to Boise. Finally one of the men in exchange for leniency gave Hal Morse's name and his real estate company in California. That was all they needed the investigation went into high gear. But the ATF still didn't have any evidence of drug production they would depend on Kat for that.

When the sky started to lighten Kat crawled out of the tree trunk and looked around. All was quiet. She ate a couple of pieces of jerky while she moved toward the drug compound. She wouldn't be able to do any serious investigating until it was dark again. There were a lot of miles to cover before she got to the drug lab area. Even thought it was daytime she moved quietly and quickly and stayed mostly undercover of bushes and brush. After Kat hade traveled a couple of miles she stopped and called the agents on the red phone.

The agent answered, "Yeah, this Kat?"

"Yeah, I'm on the move Northeast, but have along way to go until I get within striking distance."

"Look Kat I can pick you up and drop you off closer so we can save some time. We have already taken seven men into custody, but we need proof of what's going on. Sneaky says you know where to look and we can get you anywhere in the area much quicker."

"Okay I needed to know about the men taken into custody, now I can go back and get my Jeep and be there before noon. I'll contact you from the cabin in the clearing."

She took off running.

About one o'clock Kat moved close to the cabin and hid her Jeep in the brush making her way on foot. When she could see the cabin she was within thirty yards. Kat waited a few minutes and then made her way to the back of the cabin. There was no window on the back wall so unless someone came around the sides she couldn't be seen. She peeked around one corner and didn't see anyone on the ground or in the trees. Then she heard someone talking in front. She slid up to the corner and peeked around the edge of the building. Both men had their backs to her. In two quick steps she was behind them with her gun out. She hit one on the head and stuck the gun against the others temple. His hands went up.

"Take me to the lab and supply room now." she said through gritted teeth.

"Okay I don't want to die." he whimpered.

She pushed him away far enough so he couldn't grab for her pistol.

"Move!" They walked about an eighth of a mile to a row of trees.

"It's behind those trees; an underground bunker with a hydraulic ramp."

"Do you have the control?"

"No I've never been inside. I just watch for anyone approaching out here."

"Walk over to the ramp." When they were over it Kat could see the out line of the plate.

"Put your hands behind you." With unbelievable swiftness she pulled out a string of rawhide and had the guys hands tied before he could take a deep breath. She stepped back and said, "If you try anything I will kill you no questions asked. Get down on your knees and roll over on your rump. And stay there." He did as she told him. Kat checked the trees for stands and guards on the ground. That was when she saw the camera. There was no one around. She went back and tied the hands and feet of the other guard

"Where's all the guards?'"

"Somebody's kidnapped nearly all of them." She smiled and took out the red cell phone and speed dialed Sneaky.

"Yeah its me I'm about a quarter mile from the cabin in a Northeasterly direction. There is guard sitting on the ground with his hands tied. If you hear a gunshot, he moved." Sneaky hung up and ran in the direction of the cabin he was about a half mile away. As he got close he slowed down and walked carefully over to the man sitting on the ground.

"Don't do nothin man she's going to shoot me," he whimpered. Sneaky looked around and didn't see Kat anywhere. Softly he said, "Kat you there?"

"Yeah." a voice said from above him. He looked up and she had her pistol trained on him. Slowly he dropped his gun and raised his hands. She was between two trees with her feet on one and her back to the other.

"Do I assume you are an ATF agent?"

"Agent Sneaky at your service ma'am."

"You alone?"

There are two more men coming up shortly."

"We've got to find out how to open this underground lab. I think everything we need is down there." Just then a shot rang out. Kat spun around and hugged the tree climbing up on a branch. When she looked down Agent Sneaky was laying face down in the dirt with a blood spot forming on his shirt. Kat's eyes searched the woods, but she couldn't see anyone out there. She grabbed a limb and climbed higher in the pine. A bullet ricocheted off the trunk. She jerked back.

There was a man out there with a .223 survival rifle with a scope. He raised to fire another shot. The last thing he heard was a whistling sound just before an arrow hit him in the temple. It went all the way into his brain. He was dead before he hit the ground. An Indian brave slid behind a tree and disappeared. Kat had peeked around the tree just in time to see the man fall with the arrow in his temple. She smiled for she knew her ancestors were protecting her.

When she was able to get to the ground she realized she was too late to save Sneaky. It looked like the bullet had pierced his heart. Just then a voice called out,

"Drop your weapon, Drop your weapon. Get down on the ground. She did as she was told, but she realized if this man did anything foolish he was dead. Someone was out there with an arrow pointed at his head. The other two agents approached carefully.

"Are you Kat? What happened here?"

"Yes and the guy in the bushes over there with the arrow in his temple shot Sneaky. I couldn't get to him in time to help him. I'm afraid he's dead. There is a camera up in that tree. The second man went over to where the shooters body lay. He picked up the rifle and came back.

"We have got to get into this underground lab" The agent said." Kat looked at him with a grin.

"So what's so funny? He asked.

Do like you always do clean everything up and wait for them to come back and I'll follow them in." The agent just stood there.

"You think that's the way we handle everything?"

"It doesn't matter. Right now it's the best way. Mr. Morris wants to get his stuff out of there in the worst way. I can follow the truck in when he comes back and take pictures and get samples."

"You're pretty sure of yourself aren't you?"

"I'm smart enough not to wind up like Sneaky."

"All right call the guys and tell them to come over here and clean up this site." Kat said,

"I'll be up in one of the trees disconnecting that camera." She walked away into the woods.

When the agents had everything removed they moved out

into the woods and waited. It was nearly four hours before anyone came. A box van pulled up to the approach to the ramp. The guy inside pointed a laser pen at one of the trees and the ramp slid down. By the time the driver started the truck Kat was on the back bumper with the camera. She hung on to one of the handles on the side of the door.

Agent Blackwell was talking to Tinker on the phone when Sheriff Tate drove into the clearing. *Aha, just what we need the Sheriff on the scene. If he goes down there I hope he doesn't see Kat.* He lifted a small camera and took pictures The Sheriff went over to the tree and opened the ramp and drove in.

Charlie was in the office when the Sheriff got out of his car. He punched in the code and the door opened. There were a couple of guys packaging the drugs for shipment. Tate went back to the office and walked in. Charlie jumped up from the desk.

"Sheriff you know you ain't sposed to come out here."

Shut up stupid. The DEA is crawling all over these woods and you're sitting down here like it's a Sunday picnic. Have you checked to see what has happened to your perimeter guards lately?"

"Yeah some of them have gone missing, but Hal doesn't know it yet he's in San Diego at the moment. We knew someone was messing around outside because the camera is off. The second one is blacked out. I've got more guys coming in and whoever is out there is going to be eliminated."

"Has anyone seen the Indian woman?"

"Not yet."

How much have you got ready to go out?"

"Not enough for a truck load. Were cooking as fast as we can, but we have to be careful. One explosion and the whole lab would be history. Right now we are storing the acetone inside."

"Boy that's dangerous. I think the ATF have the outside guards in custody somewhere. I don't think they've had time or proof to take them to Boise. What happened to Bill and Pete?"

"We had something real strange happen last week when we were ready to ship somehow a couple of Indians got in and shot arrows at them. One got Bill in the eye and the other hit Pete in the arm pit. They both died and we had to bury them out in the woods.

The roll up door was open and we ran back inside and locked ourselves in. The Indians set the truck on fire and got out somehow. I think it's an old Indian curse and I've got a medicine man coming in a couple of days to help us out. Maybe he can stop the curse or hold them off until we get the stuff out of here."

"My Lord what a fiasco. Does Hal know about this?"

"Yeah he was here when it happened."

"Okay I'll keep my eyes and ears open. If I find out anything I'll call you on the special phone."

Out of Business

Outside the lab Kat was behind the building waiting for the Sheriff to leave. Every few seconds she would peek around the corner of the building. There was a rear door in the middle of the wall. She slipped over and tried the knob. Though she was unaware of it this door led to the office where Charlie and the Sheriff were talking. When the Sheriff left the office Charlie followed him to the front.

Kat took a credit card out of her wallet to see if she could slip the latch. As she put the card up to the door a big hand grabbed hers. Her head snapped up in terror; eyes wide she saw a big Indian holding her hand shaking his head. She nodded. He turned and walked across the space and melted into the wall. Kat went to the corner again and waited for the Sheriff to leave. When she heard Charlie close the door she rounded the corner and tip toed to the front. A pick up was parked in front of the building just a few feet away. She slipped around to the back and opened the window to the camper cover. As quietly as she could she put on a pair of gloves and opened the window and crawled over the tail gate. She turned on a small pen light and swept the interior. She found two rows of boxes across the front of the bed. She examined them. They were about twelve by eighteen and the were sealed with tape. She slid one off the stack and laid it by the tail gate and crawled out. She snapped a couple of pictures of the inside and the license plate. Then reached back and picked up the box. She walked over to where the ramp met the floor and stepped on a bar imbedded in the floor. The ramp started to descend. Before it was all the way down Kat climbed on it and ran out. By the time Charlie noticed the ramp light Kat was already giving the box to one of the agents who ran as fast as he could to where the vehicles were parked. He jumped in a truck and drove away.

Kat and Michael moved out into the woods to a hiding place where the agents were setting up.

"Michael I'm sorry about what happened to Sneaky. I wouldn't have wanted that for anything in the world. I'm sure he was a good agent."

"Yeah, we are sure going to miss him. If there is meth in that box I'm going to clean this place out and put Hal Morris in jail for a long time."

As the agent in the truck drove North he called Tinker for a helicopter to meet him in a small town away from Soda Springs. She had a bell bubble copter on the way in minutes.

Tinker gave the agent authorization to open the box while they were on the phone. He cut the lid open and inside were hundreds of zip lock packets with measured amounts of the drug ready for sale. This was the new stuff stronger, more powerful. It could have been the ruination of many young lives.

Hal Morris was at a San Diego airport getting ready to fly back to Idaho when his cell phone rang. He took it out and pushed the on button.

"Yeah."

"Hal this is Charlie. Are you at the office?"

"No I'm in my plane getting ready to leave. What's going on?"

"Don't come up yet the ATF has arrested several of our agents, but they haven't found the lab, though it may not be long before they do. Should we clean up this place and get out?"

"Not yet, if you can hold out a while longer until I can get our lawyer up there and protect the property. Just hide everything in the secret place and get ready to setup our alternate operation. When the ATF comes with a search warrant they won't be able to find a thing. I'll stay here keep me posted." He punched the end button and cursed under his breath. It was time to move to another state. He had another crew he could activate to build another lab in neighboring Wyoming or further North in Montana. Last year he had bought fifty acres in Wyoming so it might be quicker to start there. Setting up the lab wouldn't be too much work, but the hole and the roof support would take some time. He decided to use all new people that knew nothing about this operation in Idaho. He could have the equipment from here loaded into a van and left at predestined place then have a driver from the new team take it East to Wyarno just North of Sheridan.

Now he would have one of his salesmen, Kevin Marshal, start combing the back streets of San Diego for an new operator that liked money. Kevin would know the kind of person that would be a good operator for the lab. Cookers were a dime a dozen, but a shrewd operator that knew how to move the stuff wasn't easy to find.

That same day Tinker was on the phone to the ATF office in San Diego giving them the info about Hal Morris.

"If Morris runs he will need someone to handle things wherever he moves. See if you have someone on the street. If not we can send an undercover agent down. His name is Mat Carter. Just maybe we might get lucky. Morris might be dumb enough to hire one of our guys." Standing behind Tinkers chair was a ghost of an Indian that she couldn't see, but he was feeding her mind.

The big guns from the DEA and the ATF would be moving in now so Kat thought it was time to go home. They wouldn't need her any longer now that they had the evidence they needed to prosecute and the town would be getting a new Sheriff once they searched Tate's bank account.

In the floor of the lab Morris had dug another hole down about thirty feet and had the entrance covered over with concrete so that it could be broken up easily to give anyone access. The room at the bottom was about fifteen feet square all covered with concrete walls and ceiling. There was a small metal ladder that went down to the room. Charlie was breaking up the cover and the others in the lab were packing electric hot plates and mixing equipment to put in the storage hole. When all of the stuff was in the hole it would be cemented over again. Below the concrete would be a special locking plate a half inch thick making it very hard to get in.

An hour later the men had the equipment in the room below and Charlie was getting ready to seal the hole. The men had loaded other equipment into the truck to be driven out. They were outside waiting for Charlie to finish. An Indian crept out of the office and eased up behind Charlie and pulled out his knife. He grasped the blade and hit Charlie on the back of the head with the handle. Charlie rolled forward and fell into the shaft. When he hit the bottom his neck was broken. The Indian put the locking plate in place and went back through the office wall.

One of the men came back to see how Charlie was doing as they were anxious to get out of there. He didn't see Charlie anywhere so he began to mix the concrete. It was time to get this done. When he had it mixed he poured it in and troweled it over and covered it with a plastic mat. No one would see Charlie again for a long time. The pick up drove out of the hole and left the site.

When agent Michael Long came back to the hole with his

agents everyone was gone. The activator button on the tree next to it wasn't working. Long suspected that the power source, wherever it was located, had been shut down. Now perhaps they would have to dig out a space and use a torch or blow a concrete wall with explosives. In a few seconds he was on the phone talking to his equipment man in the van in town. The guy said he had a small amount of explosive, if the wall was block or concrete, and it might be enough. If it was metal he had a small oxygen cutting torch that would do the trick… Long sent one of his men back to town to buy a couple of shovels. Later when they started to dig one of the agents hit the side of a control box. They uncovered it and pried off the lid. Inside there was a valve; long turned the handle and the ramp slowly dropped to the floor. He called the explosives man and cancelled the exercise.

Inside one could tell that all had been abandoned. They pried open the rollup door with a tire tool and went in with big flood lights. No one was there and all the equipment had been removed and all that was left was long stainless tables and refrigerators. The team searched the lab area and the office. The computers were gone and they had even ripped out the data plug. They would have to leave the rest to the fingerprint team. No one noticed the mat on the floor.

When Kat arrived in town she saw several unmarked cars at the Sheriff's office. She parked across the street and watched. About thirty minutes later they came out with the Sheriff and his secretary in handcuffs. They put them in a car and drove away.

Kat called Tinker on the cell phone she had given her.

"Hi Tinker. I guess they have pretty well cleaned them out here. The sample box was good? All right. What next? Did you hear about sneaky? Yeah they shot him and he was gone before I could get help. I'm so sorry. The pick up with the Meth is on the road somewhere. I've got pictures. We need to stop that truck. The license number is… Okay I'll talk to you later."

Under Cover

Hal Morris was waiting for his private jet to take him to his property in Wyoming. Kevin His contact on the street met with his people and the name of Mat Carter was dropped. He found Carter in a booth in a back street dive with a woman drinking beer. She had on a tight red dress. When he walked in and asked the bartender he pointed toward the darkness in the back. Kevin knew where to go. He stopped at the table.

Mat looked up and asked, "Can I help you?"

"Maybe. Can you get rid of the lady for awhile I would like to talk to you."

"Sammy go powder your nose, but come back in a few minutes. Okay?"

"Yeah shug, but don't you sneak out on me." She squeezed out of the booth and walked away. Kevin slipped in across from Matt.

Word on the street is that you know how to handle and sell."

"Yeah I've handled a few ventures in my time. What can I do for you?"

"Ever heard of Hal Morris?"

"No can't say I have."

Hal has an operation in the woods and needs man to move things in the city. You open for some work running things?"

"Yeah I might be at that. Things have been slow lately and I need some action. What's it worth?"

"Twenty five percent of the street price."

"Boy you need someone bad. No one pays twenty-five percent."

"Yeah, I know. You also get a truck and whatever hardware you need."

"All the latest toys huh? This guy must be in big time."

"It'll be a few days he's setting up things in Wyoming. Where can I find you?"

Matt took a card out of his wallet and handed it to Kevin.

Matt Carter
Retirement Investments

It gave a cell phone number and an office address.

"Give me a call when you are ready. And maybe sometime I could meet Mr. Morris." Kevin slid out and walked away.

When Sammy came back she sat down and said, "So, what happened?"

"I've got to call Tinker I think I'm in."

When Matt talked to Tinker she told him she was going to have to leave him out there on his own for a while.

"We're going to leave you there alone until we know for sure where you stand with these guys. We think Morris is desperate right now and he might be setting up a new HQ. You might have to let the first shipment go to the street, but I don't think it will be too big and we'll can see if we can get the pressure turned up on the street which will slow things down a little. We've got a license number on the truck. If we make a few arrests on the rich kids we can get a few parents stirred up. Keep me posted." Matt went to his apartment to wait for a call. If Morris was as desperate as he thought it wouldn't be long until he called.

He had just dozed off when his cell phone started chirping. He reached over to the night stand and picked it up pressing the on button at the same time.

"Yeah."

"The shipment will be in tomorrow. Kevin will give you the delivery schedule. Meet him at the mall at the Star Buck's coffee shop." Dial tone. Mat lay there staring into the darkness. He pushed the light button on his Timex. Four seventeen. Almost six hours until the mall opened. He thought of Kat. Mat wished she was here now. The other agents had told him how sharp she was and he could use her help, anybodies help actually.

He needed someone to watch his back. It was a dangerous situation walking into a new territory where no one knew you. Being around fidgety people got you killed. Mat knew what was coming though he had been in this situation before and he became nervous thinking about it. He got up and went into the bath room and splashed cold water on his face. He put on his shirt and pants and headed for the first place he could find that served coffee. This would be a delivery day dropping off packages all day.

At ten when Starbuck's opened Mat was already in the parking lot. He got out of the car and looked at it thinking about how nice it was. It wasn't the normal agency hack. A nice new Crown Victoria all black and done up slick. It would pass for a delivery car, but Tinker had warned him, "Mat if you mess this one up you'll be riding a bicycle" He grinned as he pictured her in his mind. She was all business, but she was a good person to work for. If an agent was careful she kept her eye on him. She took good care of her people. He hoped she had someone out there watching him. As he walked toward the coffee shop his eyes combed the parking lot. He didn't see anyone watching him that might be a delivery boy. Once inside he had time to get a cup of coffee and sit down. He had just taken his first sip when he saw Kevin come in. He walked up to the table and dropped a piece of folded paper turned and walked out. Mat waited until he got in the car and drove away. He opened the note and a hundred fell out. On the paper at the top was **GAS MONEY**. Below it was an address and eleven o'clock. Mat put the hundred in his pocket and started tearing up the paper until it was in tiny pieces. When he left he dropped it in the trash.

At five minutes before eleven he found the house and parked across the street. It had a small porch with three steps up to the front door. When he raised his hand to knock the door swung open. Inside was a big man. He looked like he could be Hawaiian or Philipino. Mat tried to keep a neutral expression on his face as the big guy glared at him.

"YOU LOST?"
"NO I'M NOT!"
"How'd you get this address?"
"Louise gave it to me." The big guy smiled and stepped back.
"Come on in." He patted Mat down for weapons. Finding none he said,
"Follow me." as he started toward the back of the house. Mat followed him to a back room that had probably once been a bedroom. It had been converted to an office and had boxes sitting on the floor behind the desk. The hulk sitting behind the desk had the same glare that the Hawaiian had.
"You know the San Diego area?"
"Yeah. I grew up here." It was a lie, but he hoped the slug bought it.
With a sick smile he said to the Hawaiian, "Hey Polo we got a home boy."
The big guy's expression never changed.
"Okay homie the box with the tags in it is yours. Get the route down quick cause the tags are going to disappear. You don't need to know no names. And we will be watching you. You got to be sharp cause these jerks will short you. If that happens we take it out of your money. Got it?"
"Yeah."
"You only got seventeen deliveries cause we never got the big load, but it's supposed to be coming." Count the money and a guy named Benny will pick it up over on Market and Harbor."
"Wait a minute, I didn't get this stuff from Benny and I'm not delivering it to Benny, so you better be some where around when I get through cause I'm gonna be looking for you." The fat guy grinned.
"Okay so you're pretty sharp. I'll be here when you get through. Pull your car around to the alley and Polo will put it in your trunk." Mat drove around behind the house and popped the trunk lid and got out. Polo came out and set the box in. Mat stepped over and counted the bags inside there were eighteen.

He pulled out the extra and tossed it and it landed on polo's chest.

"The man said seventeen." Polo held it out.

"Just a little bonus, you know."

"Not today. I don't get paid for somthin I ain't done yet." Polo smiled and went back inside. Mat closed the trunk and drove off.

The drop offs were all over the city. As Mat made each drop he checked the money and drove off. At the fifth stop the guy was jittery and wanted to stuff the money in Mat's hand and run. He grabbed the bag and shoved the folded bills toward Mat. Mat grabbed his coat and pulled him close.

"Just cause I'm new that don't mean I'm stupid. Count the money out loud."

"Look man the narcs..."

"Count it." The guy came up short ten bucks.

"You got two seconds to come up with the rest or you don't get no bag this week."

The guy shuffled through his pockets and found the errant ten.

"You ever try to stiff me again and you wind up standing in front of the man. Got it?"

"Yeah, yeah. I got it." Mat got in the car and drove off.

The pick up man took out a cell and dialed, "Okay boss he's pretty sharp. I think he'll be good for business."

When Mat was through with the deliveries he went to the back door of the house and knocked. The fat man opened it. Mat handed the money to him and said, "Call me."

Mat went back to his apartment and called Tinker on a special phone. As he dialed he stepped out into the hall.

When she answered he said, "Gotta be quick I'm out in the hall. They've had time to bug this place they are watching me pretty close but I think I'm in for deliveries.

The man tried to give me some extra stuff and I think it may be cause they're short of cash because of the lost load.

"I turned it down so they can't accuse me of using it for

evidence if I get caught. He's got stoolies on the street checking me out too so no one comes around for a while. Get me an address for Morris I want to check him out. Don't call me I'll call you." He pushed the end button and stepped back into his apartment and started looking around. He felt under the edges of tables, cabinets and counters. When he was just about through he checked the edges of the drapery linings. Maybe they hadn't bugged him yet, but he would check again after the next delivery he would have to be gone at least a half a day. Mat thought Cameras? He walked the floors of each room checking for spot cameras in the pop-corn ceiling texture. He knew they would look like a small dark spot the size of a pencil lead. As he was going into the second bedroom he noticed it. It was on the back edge of the door at the top. A shallow hole had been drilled and a small disk the size of a small hearing aid battery was inserted into the hole. Mat took out his pocket knife and dug it out. Sure enough it was a pick up. When he checked the other doors he found one in every one throughout the apartment. He replaced the one he found in the bedroom door. Back in the living room he turned on some music. The only thing he could do now was wait until Morris called him in.

The next morning he went to the house to make the usual deliveries.

The fat man was there waiting for him. Mat went in looking for his delivery packs.

"Hey Mat, how you doin?"

"Okay, what we got for today?"

"Look man the boss wants to see you. He's at this real estate company. Go by there first." he handed Mat a business card.

"Okay I'll check it out." he already knew Morris' office was downtown. When he pulled out into traffic he could see the Hawaiian following him.

At the real estate office he parked and went in. The secretary was on the phone, he waited.

"Hi I'm Mat Carter. Mr. Morris wanted to see me."

"Just a moment I'll see if he's busy." In a few moments the phone buzzed. The secretary picked it up. 'You can go in now Mr. Morris will see you." Mat went into an office of all warm woods and velvet furniture. The book cases were dark Mahogany.

"Hi Mat have a seat." Mat shook Morris' hand and sat down in the closest chair.

Mat I'm going to get right down to brass tacks here I need someone who can run things in my field offices. I've had you checked out and I think in can trust you. The feds got to me in in Idaho and shut me down so I'm going to have to move to Wyoming. I've got a plot of land there and I need someone who can over see things and you seem like you could qualify. In a few days I can have a kitchen going that will produce the best Meth in the country and get top prices for it, but I can' be in two places at once. So that's where you come in. If you will go up there and run things for me and make sure shipments get out on time I will give you a healthy percentage."

"What happened in Idaho?" Mat asked.

"I'm not really sure. Some Indians got into the lab and put arrows in all my main people. I'll never understand how it all happened. Something to do with an Indian girl that could call up spirits." he put his head in his hands. Oh I don't know Mat there is too much I don't understand so I think it would be better to start over. Anyway they are digging the hole for the new lab as we speak. Everything will be underground. There will be a hydraulic ramp that drops for the vehicles to drive in. We can load underground and drive away with everything hidden."

"Yeah, that sounds pretty good. Pretty expensive huh?"

"Over three quarters of a million dollars, but I can make that back in a couple of weeks if I can get this stuff on the market."

"Okay Mr. Morris..."

"Call me Hal."

"Okay Hal I'm your man I will get this thing off the ground

as quick as I can. I can be up there as soon as you are ready."
"Well I have to get the lab ready and make sure no one knows where it is. I have to make sure the workers are blindfolded in and out. They will have to be housed up there on the property until the lab is through."

Mat's blood ran cold he knew what had happened to the first work crew in Oregon. No one came out alive. Morris was a cold blooded killer and would stop at nothing to get his way. Mat would have to use the utmost caution if he wanted to save these men's lives. He had to find out where this property was. The Indian girl was his best bet. He wondered who she was.

That night before he went into his into his apartment he called Tinker.

"Hi Tinker, he offered me the head spot setting up the lab in Wyoming. He's going to do the same thing to the workers up there as he did in Oregon. If I can find out where the property is located I may be able to save those men's lives. By the way who is the Indian girl this guy keeps referring to?"

"Well Mat as I understand it you two have already met. She kept you from getting your butt whipped one night."

"Oh no! You mean Kat?"

"That's right Kat Johnson. If anyone can keep you out of trouble she can. But let me tell you if she's going to help you you'll have to convince her because no one pushes Kat. She does what she wants to. And remember Wyoming is not her tribe's territory. She will have to convince the spirits to go with her. She protected at home, but will that work somewhere else? I don't know."

Help Comes Again

"Okay I've got a lot of work to do. Can you give me a number where I can reach her?"

"Yeah she's on one of our red cells. Here's the number..."

Later Mat sat on the bed and stared at the wall thinking... If there was anyone he wanted to get next to it would be Kat.

He would have to be careful though he made the wrong impression to begin with. Of course she didn't know he was an ATF agent.

Kat was up on the knoll setting at the base of the pine meditating when the phone chirped. She answered it thinking it was Tinker.

"Tinker what are you doing calling me so late?"

"Kat it's not Tinker, it's Mat, Mat Carter."

"Where did you get this number? I can't talk to you on this phone."

"Wait Kat don't hang up. I need to explain some things. You still there?" his heart was pumping double time.

Her pulse had also quickened.

"Yeah I'm here."

"Hold on a few seconds I need to go outside so no one will hear."

Once outside he said, "Look I'm with the ATF. I work for Tinker up in Boise."

"WHAT! You pullin my chain?"

"No Kat I really do and I need your help."

"Oh no. You got a lot of explaining to do before you get any help from me."

"Look Kat I'm undercover down here in Southern California. I'm in with Morris and he wants me to set up a new Lab in Wyoming. I know what he did to the crew in Idaho. A lot of men could die if I don't find a way to protect them. He wants this place secret and the best way to keep it that way is kill all the workers afterward. Believe me he won't hesitate to do just that."

"Okay let me speak to the spirits and see what they will do. What is your number so I can call you back?" Mat gave her his number. And pressed the end button.

Kat sat in the darkness a moment thinking. She knew that they would protect her in the interest of the tribe, but would they move in a different territory? All she could do was call on them and see if they would answer.

Kat knelt in the dirt and put her forehead on the ground. She said, "OH great warrior, War lion come and speak to my heart I need your help." she waited. Then she repeated the plea.

There was a crackle in the air. Kat knew he was coming through. A male voice said, "Rise and listen." she stood up. He was there glowing softly in the dark.

"Why do you call me? The evil has been stopped in this place. They make no more powder here."

"They have moved to Wyoming and are setting up a lab there to do the same thing again."

"The tribes there will plead to the great spirit to stop the evil white man."

"The white agent is going there to help and he wants me to help him. The white crystal will take many lives."

"Do you love this man?" A lump formed in Kat's throat.

"It is not a case of love Oh great War Lion. I want to save the Indian children in Wyoming."

"I will ask once more and do not speak to War lion with forked tongue."

Kat was crushed inside torn between two things love and Indian honor. She considered her answer. War Lion crossed his arms and waited.

"I could love him yes, but I don't know if he will be good to me."

"You are avoiding the truth. Do you love him?"

Tears ran off her nose. "Yes I do love him."

"When help is finished you will become his squaw. This is the only way. Your father was a white man and so shall your husband be."

She knelt and touched her forehead to the ground.

"Yes great warrior. As you speak so it shall be." Kat remained in that position for several minutes. When she looked up War Lion was gone.

Mat called his mother to let her know everything was all right. She worried about him constantly. Since he became an undercover agent she didn't see him much.

Her Mat was the adventurous kind always wanting to look into things. Now he might be in over his head.

After Kat got up she sat on the hill smiling in the dark. She liked Mat, but his work might present a danger she could not handle. His being undercover was a shock to her. He was so cool she never suspected he was an ATF agent. She liked that. Kat got up and started down the hill.

"Well I got to go pack my duds again. I'm off on another adventure." Inside the house she pulled out as large canvass bag. When she had it packed there was her clothes personal items and the guns and extra ammo. She would put the hard top on her jeep and be ready to travel by eight in the morning. After she laid down she went to sleep quickly and dreamed of Mat.

Six o'clock the next morning Kat was under the carport letting the top down onto her jeep. It was hung on four hooks that went to pulleys and could be operated by one rope. She snapped it into place and put her bag inside. She wondered where she would meet Mat. He would be traveling today too only he had further to go. By eight o'clock she was ready to leave. The red phone in her pocket chirped.

"Yeah this is Kat."

"Kat we got information last night on the new property in Wyoming. It's in the Southeast part of the state in the Washakie Wilderness a couple of miles from Horse Creek. By the time you get there the equipment should be there to start the hole. And materials will be coming in all the time. Any way you can slow down production will keep the workers alive that much longer. When its time to install the equipment we will make sure the crates get mixed up or lost in transit. When zero hour comes we will replace the workers and leave a team of agents to take over. I'll get information and descriptions to you who the men are that work for Morris beside Mat. Be careful over there girl. Watch your back."

"Okay Tinker thanks. Talk to you later."

By eight-thirty in San Diego Hal Morris was entering his office. When he put the key in the door lock he stopped. He noticed something that told him someone had been in his office illegally. He had put a hair across the bottom of the door as a seal. It was gone. Inside he went straight to the file cabinets and all the safeguards had been breeched. Now he knew they were on to him. A phone call to a hired fingerprint man would tell him who had been in his office.

"Yeah this is Morris I need you to come over and dust my office someone has been here and I want to know who." Twenty minutes later the print guy showed up and dusted the office and checked his lap top for a match in a few minutes he had the agent's name. Gil Trent out of Illinois. He called a local hit man and made a deal. They had messed with Hal Morris for the last time. Now he knew he could set up in Montana where he intended to go all the time.

When the ATF showed up in the place in Wyoming they would waste a lot of time waiting for someone to show up.

"Carl this is Morris. Go ahead with the plan. No one knows but us. The workers won't have any idea where they are until it's too late. The ground team called, the hole is ready and they can install the steel and cover it up. We can assemble the lab when it's finished. If anything goes wrong we can be across the Canadian border in a matter of minutes. A transport plane with twenty construction workers is on the runway preparing to take off. I'll be out of here in a couple of hours. I can pick up the helicopter in Butte."

"This is the pilot, are we cleared for take off?"

"You are clear. Out."

The pilot pushed the throttle forward and the plane began to move. This was a one way trip for the workers only they didn't know it...

In Soda Springs Kat was driving out of town when the engine died and she rolled to a stop along side the road. An Indian walked out of the trees approaching the Jeep. Kat looked eyes wide.

"Go to Montana. Near the Canadian border in the flathead forest. I will guide you when you get there. The white man must stay with you to be protected. If you get separated he will die." He turned and walked back into the trees. Kat was in shock she didn't know what to think. She assumed the lab would be set up in Wyoming. Morris had created a double cross to protect himself and what men he had left. She pulled out the red cell and dialed Mat's number. No answer. She dialed Tinker. After a few rings, which seemed like an eternity, she finally answered.

"Tinker, Kat. There has been a change in the plan. Morris is going to Montana. It's a switch to buy him time and leave us out in the cold. There is probably a team of people somewhere getting ready to leave now. The lab will be up near the Canadian border in the Flathead forest. We have to get word to Mat before he heads the wrong way."

"Wait a minute. Slow down Indian sister you're not making any sense here. How did you find out about this and how are we going to get there if we don't know where it is?"

"Come on Tinker think. You are the ATF. Satellite surveillance and GPS tracking. Remember?"

"Where did you get this Kat?"

"I'm the one who's protected. I told you that. An Indian brave just walked out of the woods and spoke to me. Your wasting time here. You need to get this to Mat so he can change his plan. When I tried his phone it was off. I'm leaving right now."

"Okay Kat listen I'll have a helicopter pick you up in Idaho Falls and fly you the rest of the way. Kat pushed the end button.

She put the Jeep in gear. When she turned the key it started.

Tinker pushed the intercom button and told a secretary, "Get hold of Mat Carter if he doesn't answer keep trying until you get him. Transfer the call to my line."

She called in a team of twenty-five agents that she would replace the workers with in Montana. They could be in helicopters in an hour.

Mat was driving North toward Nevada. He was trying to get on I-10 and transfer to I-15. Once out of California he could move through the desert at a faster pace. He had turned off his phone to make sure they didn't make him as an ATF agent, but something kept nagging at him to try Tinker again. Just before he reached the San Bernardino mountains he tired again. The message center answered and asked for his code. He tapped it in and a message came back. "Montana. Meet at the forestry station South of the Flathead forest outside the park."

"What's going on?" he said to himself. While he puzzled over the plan he realized it was a switch in plans to keep the ATF out of the loop. The Wyoming site was a ruse. He could have wound up standing at the site in Wyoming with nothing happening there. On his GPS Locator he mapped out a route to the flathead forestry station and got an estimated time of arrival. Tomorrow evening. He could loose a day because it was a hard area to get into. The only approach was secondary roads. Then he realized how close it was to the Canadian border.

If we tip our hand they could be gone inside of an hour. He thought. He was three states away from his objective no way he could get there in time. His phone chirped.

"Mat where are you?" it was Tinker.

"I'm still in California moving North."

"When you reach the Nevada go to Las Vegas. We'll have a plane waiting for you. Kat got a message from the protector and told her about the change of plans. Morris has a place up there and is probably putting it together as we speak. Those workers are in serious trouble if we can't get some men up there."

"Okay Tinker you're a life saver. Don't worry we'll get them out alive." He let the hammer down he had a plane to meet.

Morris left the office and headed for the airport to catch his private jet. He would land in Helena and go the rest of the way by helicopter.

By the time Mat got to Las Vegas Kat was already in the air. He had all his equipment on a Chinook in thirty minutes and was waiting for agents that were to go with him. When they were airborne Mat explained the situation to them. Everything they carried was semi automatic. AK-47's and machine pistols with thirty round clips.

Kat reached Idaho Falls that after noon and was flying out in fifteen minutes. She told the pilot she hoped they could get there before Mat's helicopter arrived. So they could go in together.

"Okay Ma'am we will put the pedal to the metal and I guarantee you we will get there first.

Zoom!

Mat wasn't aware that he had to be with Kat to be protected.

In the mountains in Montana the heavy equipment had arrived and the hole to house the lab was already dug. They would start putting steel in as soon as the semi arrived. The workers were working on cement forms and deep blocks to support the posts for the ceiling. The posts would be on the first truck and the steel beams on the second. The hole was fifteen feet deep and one hundred by one hundred and fifty feet. They had wet down the sides to keep them from caving in. Ten of the twenty construction workers had already arrived and was helping lay the foundation.

Up on the mountain side above the construction site was a DEA spotter with a high powered spotting scope and a radio watching the progress in the hole. He was on the same channel as the radio in Mat's helicopter.

"They're coming along too good Mat. If they can get concrete in here the steel can go in early tomorrow morning and I'm talking about six a.m. They'll be using quick dry and twelve hours will be plenty. Those support posts are what bother me. The floor can be finished after they are in."

"Hang in there Kenny we are moving as fast as we can. Thanks for keeping us up to snuff."

Kenny, an agent for the DEA, was parachuted in the day before with orders to observe and report. He was located on a cliff almost directly above the hole. If he had to move he would do it at night. So far no one was looking up. Off a short distance away the crew's quarters could be seen at the base of another cliff. It was a long narrow building with a door at each end. The mess hall was a small square building in the middle of the open area. The only other building was a small office for Hal that would be moved inside once the lab was finished. These buildings would be disassembled after the hole was finished. Kenny was bundled up in artic gear because it was still cold at night and he had to sleep at his hidden position. The wind gave no mercy and seemingly blew like a gale all night. He would have to exist on jerky and hard biscuits for a couple of days, but he would get paid well for it. He was invaluable. He called in an update to Tinker every two hours.

The Indian medicine man that was hired by Morris was brought in a few days before to work spells to protect the site. Inside the mess hall he was mixing powders to sprinkle around the work area. When he was finished he went outside to begin. He sang an Indian chant while he worked. His steps were positive and sure footed as he moved around the encampment. When he reached the far end of the site beyond the office. Two braves stepped out of the trees and grabbed him and pulled him into the brush.

"Timikowa your protective spell will work while the building goes on, but you will not live to see it." Both braves had sharp hunting knives in their hands. One pulled his head back as the other cut his throat. While the blood ran down the front of his clothes the brave cut him down the middle as if doing a standing autopsy. His insides fell out on the ground. They laid him down and walked away. When the men found the medicine man's body panic would ensue. Mat would need that to convince the workers to leave and let the ATF and DEA take their place. A rendezvous would be set up down the road where a helicopter could pick it up and fly them to safety.

The helicopter with Mat and Kat in them landed several miles South of the encampment. The other agents began setting up a base of operations to take the workers out and replace them with agents. They were picked up by agents driving combat Hummers and driven in as close as they could get without being seen.

When they stopped and were getting their gear ready Mat said, "Look Kat I'm sorry I couldn't let you know and besides I didn't have a chance before it got serious."

"Okay, Okay, things got worked out. Now I need to tell you something. You listen to me because your life is on the line. What ever happens up here you need to stay with me. I don't know if you understand that I'm protected by the spirits and I've made an agreement with them to keep you safe, but the deal is you and I stay together. If we get separated and you get killed it's not my fault."

"All right sweet thing how close can I get?" he smiled. She pushed her hand in his face.

"This is not the time for sweet nothings stupid. We got peoples lives to protect here. Now What's the plan?" Mat smiled and said, "We exchange the workers for agents and wait until Morris shows up and take everybody into custody. Hopefully we can shut this place down before it gets started."

They moved into the trees about a hundred yards from the encampment and watched with binoculars. Just before they were scheduled to eat supper Mat moved in with the workers in a bold move. Some of the workers gave him strange looks, but said nothing.

Inside the mess hall he took a tray and sat down with the rest of the guys. He told the guy next to him he was a new worker just sent in to help get set up. They struck up a conversation and finally Mat asked him who the foreman was. They guy pointed him out. He was a big guy with light brown hair and a broad moustache. He looked to weigh about two fifty which was all muscle. Mat slipped over and sat down next to him.

"Hi My name's Mat. I just came in." They shook hands the guy was big, but seemed like the gentle type. "I need to talk to you in private. I have an important message to give you. Things are going to get dicey here pretty soon and I need to let you know what's going on so none of your men get hurt."

The furrow between the big guy's eyes deepened. "We'll finish eating and go outside so Morris' men won't suspect anything.

Mat handed him his ATF ID.

The guy nodded and handed it back to Mat.

"I'll meet you outside when you're through." Mat got up and put his tray on the wash rack and went outside. He could see Morris' men standing around he knew they had guns under their coats in case anything went wrong. When the foreman came out he walked toward the sleeping quarters Mat caught up with him.

"What's going on here?" The foreman asked in a quiet tone.

"The guy that hired you fellows wants complete secrecy here. So when you guys are through instead of a bonus he plans to kill all of you so no one will know where this place is. We have a whole team of agents out there in the woods waiting to take your men's places, but we have to make the switch gradually so these men won't know what's going on. They don't recognize your men by sight yet so we will replace them one at a time since they know you are the foreman, I'm sorry, but you will have to be last. We will have you covered don't worry. When the workers get in the sleeping quarters let everybody know and don't act surprised when my men start coming in."

"Okay partner thanks a lot. You've saved our lives. I'll let'em know."

Mat looked around. When no one was watching he slipped back out into the trees. He sided up to Kat.

"Okay they know what's coming down. Now we have to

watch our step as we replace these guys. If Morris' men suspect anything they will start shooting."

"So you need to know that things are going to start happening tonight when everybody goes to bed. Don't get jumpy. The Indians are going to have a little party. Tell your men not to interfere."

What about the workers?"

"Don't worry about it they won't be able to get out of the building in time to do anything about it. Just let it come down and stay out of it."

"Okay So when do we get close?"

"Listen mister you and I are going to have an understanding before anything happens between us. Right now we have work to do."

"You said we have to stay together so do we share the same sleeping bag?"

"No you jerk we don't. Sometimes you seem pretty smart and other times you are pretty stupid." She walked away. Mat's face flushed. He was embarrassed.

The DEA team leader was giving instructions for the switch and what to look for when they were in place. They would take Morris' men into custody cuff them and put them in a special vehicle then move them off site once the workers were safe.

About ten thirty after everyone was in bed. The walls of the hole gradually began to slide in. The two long sides slid down and completely covered the concrete forms where the posts would be placed. Now they would have to be dug out again. Which would take several hours.

The next morning when workers went to the outside toilets five men were replaced by ATF agents. No one noticed. One of the workers discovered the Indian medicine man's body he turned and went back to the other workers. When he arrived there was quite a stir. The sides of the hole had collapsed and there was a great amount of dirt and rock in the hole covering the foundation area. One end had been graded off so that it created a natural ramp to get equipment in and out. All of Morris' men were in the hole trying to figure out what had happened. They had brought in a big front loader to remove the dirt and rock as quickly as possible. Suddenly all of Morris' men became irritable and demanding.

An ATF agent walked up to the group of workers and gently nudged one of the men in the back when he turned the agent gave him the nod. The worker walked away out into the trees. The agent stood there watching. For the rest of the morning when a man went to the out house he was replaced by an agent. By noon when they took a break for lunch all of the workers had been replaced with DEA agents with guns in their coat pockets. More agents waited out in the trees for a signal to move in.

"What are you guys waiting for? Get in there and move some of the dirt." the agents were instructed to take orders up to a point. They began picking up shovels and going around to the end of the hole. One of Morris' men stepped over to one of the others.

"Something doesn't look right here. There is something different about these guys."

"Look man you don't make decisions here just make sure they get the job done. Okay?" The man moved away. Cautious. While the front loader was removing the fallen dirt the far end of the hole fell in. There was a pine next to the edge of the hole. The loose dirt fell away from the roots and the tree tumbled into the hole. The watcher, cussed and ranted now more nervous than ever. If Morris arrived and saw this mess he would be mad and might start killing people. He had to make a call. Morris didn't like surprises. He started moving toward the office. When he went in there was an agent there waiting for him. He had a Glock forty pointed at his chest.

"Get your hands away from your pockets." he turned him around and searched him and took his pistol and cell phone and cuffed him. Then the agent put him in an office chair and taped his mouth. Then he taped his legs to the legs of the chair. He stood waiting to see if anyone else came in. Now there were only four more men out there with guns. They couldn't take them all if Morris showed up and no one was there he would know something was wrong.

Mat couldn't be caught with the agents posing as workers if someone showed up that knew him from San Diego his cover would be blown. He looked up at Kat in the tree he was standing behind. She was up about thirty-five or forty feet on a limb with her survival rifle watching through the scope. He smiled. She was all business. He really liked her.

Morris' Hummer turned off the paved road five miles from the site.

"Funny Callus hasn't called. I hope everything is going smooth up there. I can't get him on the cell."

"It'll be okay boss no one could possibly know about this place." The driver said.

The other man pulled out his pistol and put a round in the chamber. Morris said,

"Yeah, Cane, I feel the same way. Then he followed suite. The gravel road was rough from the rainwater that ran down from the mountain rain. There were lots of ruts and they needed the all terrain vehicle to make any time.

As the agents with shovels labored with the dirt they worked slowly keeping their eyes on the men with guns. The front loader had one side cleared and had started on the other when the diesel engine stalled. Then the operator couldn't get it started again. Morris' men were in a panic. The only civilian workers left was the foreman and the heavy equipment operator. Their eyes were as big as silver dollars. Scared.

The DEA leader was on the radio with one of his men who had an ear plug in his ear.

"Williams, get those two guys out of there things could go South any minute. The front loader operator climbed down. One of the agents with a shovel turned to him and whispered,

"Head for the potty." he took off. When the foreman saw him leave he followed. When they were out of range they were put in vehicles and moved out. Now all of the workers were out of harms way. The DEA agents began to spread out.

Three miles.

"There is something wrong we can't get them on the phone."

"It might be the reception up here boss. We could be in a pocket where the signal don't go through," the driver said.

"Okay, so we stop a half mile from the site and walk in. I don't want no surprises. I got a funny feeling in my gut."

Morris' men came up out of the hole looking for Morris' Hummer. They knew he would be there any time. One of them ran for the office. The agent inside saw him coming. The other man he had taken into custody was outside the back door taped to the chair. The agent was behind the door. When the guy came in he stuck the gun to his temple and said,

"Come on in and keep your hands up. The agent took his pistol and phone and closed the door. He cuffed him and taped his mouth. He laid the man down behind the desk so if anyone else came in they wouldn't see him. An ATF agent that saw the second man enter the office came to the back door to assist.

"It's me, everything's fine. There's only two more out there." Still they waited.

A mile and a half.

At the edge of the hole the two remaining watchers were nervous. They looked around and discovered they were alone and the workers were watching them now. The feeling of being out numbered sank in quick. One asked the other where everybody went. He shook his head. The both started toward trees. The knew something was wrong it was too quiet. The team leader in the hole said to the others,

"Let'em go the men in the trees will get'em."

The agents stopped shoveling and waited. When the two men were out in the woods the agents stopped them and took them into custody. Now Morris and his two men were the only ones left. From the agents in the woods several men started

down the gravel road to meet whoever was coming.
A mile. Morris was edgy now. Knowing something was wrong. The agents moved fast through the trees staying well back from the road. Finally he could stand no more.
"Stop!" He shouted then crawled out looking around for movement in the woods. There was none. He started up the road moving fast. The other two men followed.
When the agents saw the Hummer parked they knew Morris was on foot. They radioed to make the pick up. Now the other agents were moving toward them fast hoping they could avoid a shoot out.
Morris and the other two men heard someone shout, Hey!" When they turned they saw nine men moving to surround them.
"Don't reach for any weapons or your dead." They were taken into custody.
Morris and his men were brought to the site and Mat identified Morris as the head of the operation. They brought in vehicles to carry the drug men to jail. The operation went off without a hitch and the workers were all safe. Mat was standing watching the criminals being taken away. Kat ran up to him and threw her arms around him and kissed him.
"Maybe we could go somewhere warm tonight and have a nice dinner by candle light."
"I didn't think Indians liked candle light." Mat said.
"Mat you are so dumb some times. I've got a lot of work to do on you."

Groeler

The state of Iowa is mostly vast farmlands that raises a major portion of the country's corn and soy beans. They also raise a lot of the pork we eat today. In the Southeastern part of the state, there lies the small town of Burlington where this story begins. Burlington lies near the Mississippi. In addition, Burlington had suffered much damage from the torrential rains in 1993. However, the people involved in this story lived outside the town far enough that they did not loose everything in the floods.

 This family owns about forty acres and raises corn and hogs like everyone else in the area. They are the Tillman family, Ed, Martha, their son and daughter, John and Emily. Ed works part time in town and Martha and the kids keep the farm since the kids are now old enough to help. In the heart of his boy there is a secret desire. He wants to join the circus. His parents had taken the children to the yearly circus ever since he could remember. John, now twelve, lived for the yearly event and always minded his P's and Q's when late spring drew near. He would begin to retrace the previous year's events to warm up on the subject of this year's circus. Emily, eleven, liked the circus for something to do in the spring but after it was gone, she went back to her dolls and chores. John on the other hand talked for weeks after about the things they have seen. He made a large pine tree a place to practice tight rope and aerial tricks until his dad made him come down before he hurt himself. "John, he would explain, we need you to help out and if you are laid up with a broken bone you can't do that." So John would go back to his chores and at times he would sit under the pine and remember the great events he had seen. The circus was always in his thoughts.

This year in late April, knowing the circus was coming, John performed his work with precision. Ed and Martha would look at each other and smile, while Emily would shake her head in disgust knowing it was all a sham. That next week when the mail came (There was a row of community mail boxes on a beam a quarter mile down the road.)

John and Emily were riding their bikes down to the mail box and as they rode up they saw a big poster on the fence advertising a circus similar to the one that had been there last year. They both let out a yelp and jumped up and down. John jumped on his bike and rode off toward the house.

Emily watched him go, shook her head, opened the mailbox and took out the mail. She said to no one in particular, "John boy you ain't going to be good for nothin until that circus leaves town."

He rode up into the yard and dropped his bike and ran inside shouting, "Mom, Dad the circus will be here in two days! It will be in town for three days. Kin we go the first day?"

In the kitchen Martha was standing at the stove fixing breakfast. Looking down at the bacon she said, "Lord, give us patience, until that circus is gone he's not going to be worth a dime."

From the table Ed said, "He just twelve Martha, he'll git over it in a year or two."

John broke into the kitchen beaming with joy. His dad smiled at him waiting for the onslaught of expectation. "Hey Dad! The poster had a big elephant on it standing on his hind legs and a lady riding on his head with a big feathery bonnet on. They're from Barnum and Bailey this year and it's gonna have three rings. Kin we go the first day Dad? I saved some of my money for my ticket and I'll buy Emily's too."

"Well by the looks of it Son you forgot the mail."

"Oh, the mail. I'll have to go back and git it."

Just then Emily came into the kitchen carrying some letters and ads. "Don't fret yourself John boy I got it. At least I membered what I went after."

"Now don't be rude sugar, John just offered to buy your ticket this year." Martha said.

Emily looked away and shrugged her shoulders. "You know Mom, when you seen one you seen'em all."

"You're growing up too quick Darlin. When I have to ask you to be patient with the yearly circus you're growin' up too quick."

"Well some of the aerial acts aren't that bad, but all that horsin around on the ground don't amount to much." she said as she laid the mail down next to her dad's plate. John looked at his sister in awe he couldn't believe this was coming out of her mouth. The circus was the greatest event ever. Girls, he would never understand them.

"Well Dad kin we go the first day?"

"Yeah I guess so. Git this thing out of the way so I can go back to farming."

When the circus set up at the fair grounds kids went to the office to hire on to pass out leaflets to the surrounding area. John's dad wouldn't let John go he might not remember to come home.

The first day the Big Top was crammed full of farmers and their families. John wanted to sit right down front, but dad thought they could see better half way up the bleachers. John knew better than to put up a fuss his dad might haul him to the car and that meant no circus. All the acts were better this year and it seemed everyone had a great time. They laughed as the clowns threw confetti on the people in the front row and the aerial acts took their breath away. John was ecstatic through the whole thing, but he liked the animal acts the best. The tricks the lions and tigers performed put him on the edge of his seat. Dad bought them cotton candy and coke. Nothing was better than this.

After it was all over Emily thanked her brother for buying her ticket. "It was really good this year bubby thanks a bunch."

John's heart swelled with pride that he was able to buy his sister's ticket. Ed and Martha were even bubbly that day and Martha giggled at Ed as he cavorted going to the parking lot. In their hearts though they said thank God it was over. Now they could go back to being normal, except for John who usually took a few days to get over the excitement.

The forth morning after, before dawn, John was sitting on the edge of his bed putting on his socks daydreaming, a voice in his head said, "John you're a big boy now why don't you go join the circus this year?"

John's vision came back into focus looking at the light outside his doorway. Now he could see himself carrying a pack walking toward the circus manager's trailer. Yes! That was what he would do. What an adventure. He thought of sending money home in the future to help Mom and Dad with the expenses and he could send Emily a gift occasionally. But right now he had to get there and get on the team that made the circus run. That day when he had time he would put things he needed in a small gunny sack that he kept under the bed. He could buy a nice suitcase later.

That night after everyone else had gone to sleep John was still up packing clothes into the sack. Tomorrow would be the fifth day, the day for the circus to leave. He crept out into the living room to see what time it was. The big clock on the wall showed ten-thirty. He could hear everyone else in the house snoring deeply.

He went into the kitchen and took some left over biscuits and a little meat

No sense dragging this out I could be gone six hours before Dad wakes up. he thought.

Back in the bed room he dressed, picked up his bag and

crawled out his window. The moon was in the second quarter and gave him enough light to see his way to the road. It was only four miles to town. As he walked along in the dark he listened to the crickets and the frogs in the ponds on the other farms.
Wow! It's really going to happen. He thought.

Circus life

When he approached the edge of town he headed toward the fair grounds. In a few minutes he could see the campers and trailers where circus people lived. The huge tent was gone and the vehicles were lined up The big tractors in front and the campers and RV's behind. Personal cars were last. The animals were bedded down for the night and all was quiet. This was the real circus. Now John would see a different side of circus life. He would get to meet the people that made it happen.

John crossed the fair grounds and began to tip-toe as he approached the convoy. He found a large storage compartment on the side of one of the semi trailers and crawled in. After he closed the door he lay down on his sack and went to sleep. He didn't want anyone to know he was there until they made their next stop. He slept until about five when he heard noise outside. Two people were talking and John heard them say something about going North to Davenport and then East to Chicago. *Wow! The big city.* John thought. Just then someone started to open the door. John scooted back into the depths of the storage compartment.

When the door opened someone said, "Yeah we got room to put it in here."

They slid in a big box and closed the door. Well he was in for the duration of the trip now. He began to feel around the compartment and above his head it felt like a trap door. He found the handle and turned it and opened it slightly. Right above his head a camel grunted. Whew! What a smell. He closed the trap door and turned the handle tight. The first reality of circus life landed in his mind.

The big trailer had large air shocks and made the trip smooth and pleasant considering his surroundings. He lay back on his sack and napped a while. About five hours later they pulled into Davenport and stopped in a big open area just outside of town. John woke with a start and anticipation began to build. How was he going to reveal himself and convince someone to let him stay? To start with he would have to wait and let this play out. After what seemed like forever some men began to unload the animals above him. He could hear hooves thundering over his head and the camel bawling. The odor came back to him something he would never forget.

A while later a man opened the door and pulled out the box and another guy helped him carry it away. The door swung shut but no one locked it. At least he could get out.

He heard a voice in the distance, but he didn't understand what they were saying or he would have got out and run for it.

"Tate, the voice said, we got a stowaway in twelve storage."

"Oh, okay I'll take care of it. Tate was the animal caretaker. He didn't train, he just fed and cared for the animals. Tate had the type of personality that just understood animals so the circus was glad to have him. He was a big man about fifty and was graying fast. His hands were big and rough, but his heart was tender, especially toward kids, now he had another one on his hands. He had helped several of these type youths and knew how to handle them and get them back home safe and sound. He usually let them learn a lesson or two before he sent them home on the bus. He hoped this one would be no different.

These kids were always boys with a love for circus adventure and Tate saw to it they got it before they decided to go back home. He remembered the wide eyed fascination on their faces and the awe as they learned a little about how the circus worked from the other side. He was supposed to go to the wild animal cages next, but he had to get the kid before he got away and got hurt. So when he tied the camels down and gave them feed he headed toward the storage compartment in #12.

John wasn't expecting the door to come open again, but when it did a rough voice said, "All right, come out of there. I see ya."

John now petrified scooted toward the door. When he crawled out he saw the big man and he didn't have a smile on his face.

He grabbed John by the arm and leaned down into his face and asked, "What are you doing in there? This is not a Gray hound bus it's a storage hole. Where did you come from boy?" he said in his gruff voice.

"I-I-I come from Burlington. I wanted to travel with the circus. I'll work for you and earn my keep. Please let me stay." he said in a fearful voice. Tate turned and walked away with John in tow. When he reached one of the other trailers he stepped up into it and hoisted John in after him. It was nearly dark inside. As smooth as clock work he pulled the boy over to a cabinet with a drawer in it. He jerked the drawer open and pulled out a pair of handcuffs and snapped them on John's wrists. A short chain had been welded to the link in the middle. This he wired above John's head to a vertical bar. Then he left John in the semi dark to go finish his work. When John looked up he was face to face with the biggest lion he had ever seen. His mouth dropped open and he wanted to scream but he was afraid he would spook the huge cat. This animal did not look pleasant. He just stood and stared at John.

"Oh God I hope they fed him." John whispered.

The lion looked like he could come right through those bars. John tried to back up but arms length was the best he could do. If he stuck his big paw through those bars John was a goner. A low rumble came from the throat of the beast. John was terrified and wet his trousers. When the scent hit the lion's nose he let out a roar and John passed out. In a few minutes Tate came back into the trailer and took John down and carried him to his RV trailer and laid him on a cot and wired him to a big nail in the wall over his head. When John came to his eyes were as big a silver dollars, but at least the lion didn't eat him.

A few minutes later Tate came in carrying John's sack. He dropped it on the cot beside John and said, "Well I see you had enough sense to bring some meat and biscuits. We don't have to feed runaways you know. "

John just nodded his head.

Tate took John's hands down, but left the cuffs on. He went into the other end and came back with a pair of pants. "Put these on. Better eat what you got it'll be a while before you get anything again." He went to a cabinet and took out a glass and poured milk from a small fridge. Sit up!"

He handed John the glass and pulled up a chair. The boy dug into his sack and pulled out the meat and biscuits. He stuffed his mouth full and drank between bites while Tate sat and stared at him with a scowl. When he was finished he held out the glass and Tate snatched it out of John's hand and filled it again. The kid was probably dry from those biscuits. John drank half the second glass before he came up for air.

"So what makes you think you can be any help to the circus?" Tate said in a milder tone.

"I'm strong and I do what I'm told."

"I don't know so much about the strong part, but doing what you're told will help you stay alive around here. What's your name?"

"John Tillman, sir."

And I'll bet you come from a farm." John nodded his head.

"Does your momma know your gone?"

John shook his head.

Tate wiped his hand over his face and let out a sigh. *How many times had he seen this sort of thing?* he wondered.

"You got any brothers or sisters?"

"A sister."

Tate's eyes bore into him as he asked, "And?"

"Emily, she's eleven."

"How old are you?"

"Twelve sir."

"And that almost makes you a man, huh?"

John knew better than to answer that one. He just stared down at his fingers.

Well I been thinking John Tillman I could use some help around here, but if I let you stay we are going to have an understanding. And that is you never go any where by yourself and you do exactly as I tell you. I take care of the animals around here and as far as I know there isn't one of them that likes a man, except to eat. The only reason they put up with us is because we feed'em and give them a place to sleep. The rest we force them to do.

Now my name is Tate and I take care of all the animals and get them ready for the show. There is a lot of work to be done and you don't stand in the wings and watch. While the show goes on there's a lot to be done to get ready for the next act. You will be working for me and no one else. If anyone asks you to do anything you tell them you will have to ask Mr. Tate first. You got that?"

"Yes sir."

"Okay now I have to get some work done. I'm going to take off the cuffs, but you stay in this trailer until I come back then I'll show you around. Just in case you're thinkin about it don't try to run off. If you do I'll find you and it won't be pleasant."

John nodded his head. "I won't go nowhere."

Tate removed the cuffs and put them back in a drawer.

"There's more milk and some Jell-O in the fridge. I'll have to go to town later and get some grub for supper. With that Tate left and slammed the door.

"Whew! John let out a breath and looked around The trailer looked just about new. John got up and wandered toward the other end. Past a petition there was what could be considered to be a living room and beyond that a big bedroom at the end. There were two beds. A queen sized and a twin. *Maybe this is where the other boys slept.* John thought. Back in the front room he looked out the window and saw people passing both ways getting ready to unload and set up. He hoped he would get a chance to see them set up the big top.

It was just about noon when Tate came in. He was sweating from some heavy labor he had been doing. John was sitting on the cot where Tate left him.

"John we have a sort of group lunch the day we set up and everyone gets together and eats in the community tent. Might be a good time for you to meet the folks that work in the circus. John nodded and stood up.

"They'll know I ran away huh?" he said quietly.

"That's not the thing to worry about now John. These people like kids and they'll help you in every way they can if you'll let'em. And you can learn something from everyone of them. Don't say nothin but hi and smile and they will understand. Remember you're not the first boy they've seen join the circus. Tate thought of the year he sneaked away to join the circus. He never left.

Tate led the way over to the tent where they would have lunch. Tate pulled back the flap and John stepped in. Before him was a very long table and some of the women were putting big bowls of food on it. Gradually everyone began to look his way and smile. Tate put his hand on John's shoulder and led him to the end of the table. Then he put his arm around him and said out loud,

"Everybody, we have a new helper with us today." Everyone stopped what they were doing and looked his way. They were still smiling.

"This is John and he wants to work with us. He'll be working with me cause he says he likes animals. He would appreciate it if you all would help him get broke in."

Then simultaneously they all began to applaud.

Johns' face turn crimson as he looked down.

Tate led him down to the middle of the table and set him in chair. He sat down beside him and said in a low tone, "When they pass the bowl if you want some take it and pass the bowl on."

A man with dark skin and big muscles stepped up to the end of the table.

"Gimme your attention a minute. John we are glad to have you with us. Now let's be thankful for what we have. Lord we give thanks today for a safe trip and no one was hurt. We ask that you will be with us while we get this show set up. Now we thank you for all this food and fellowship. Keep us in peace. Amen." There was a clatter of table ware and bowls being moved around the table. It seemed like everyone was talking at the same time. John was glad cause it would take their attention away from him. He had never seen so much food in one place at one time and it all smelled good too.

When everyone was through eating The dark skinned man stepped up to the end of the table again. "Alright folks let's get this show set up. Report to me with anything torn or broken. We'll get it fixed. Be careful and work safe everyone." With that he walked away.

"That's Indian Joe. He's the circus manager. He's not a bad guy, but for the time being you might want to stay out of his way. He's not too patient with kids. Let's go take care of the animals."

When they reached the trailers and cages where the animals were Tate walked him by the cages and explained about each one and what they ate. When they reached the end Tate took him by the shoulder and looked in his eyes, "John, you see this red tape and the white tape behind it?"

"Yes sir."

"No one but me and the trainers go beyond those. Your line is the white line. (Which was about five feet back.) You stay behind it all the time. Never go any closer.

John nodded. They were standing outside a panther cage and the cat was pacing back and forth letting out a low growl occasionally.

Tate pointed at the cat and said, "He knows he can't bite you, but if he can get a claw on you he can rip you in half and pull what's hooked in his claw into the cage and eat. Don't go past the white line. Don't do anything with the horses, camels or llamas unless I'm with you. The same with the elephants if they step on your foot it will crush your foot. Now I guess that's the first place we are going." As Tate walked away John hurried after him. Tate opened the doors to a big heavy trailer and pulled out a heavy ramp on wheels and pushed it up to the back of the trailer.

"Okay Susie come on out girl, it's time to come out and eat. The elephant gave a loud roar and tugged at the chain holding her to the side of the trailer wall.

"John over there on that small trailer is some hay. Go get an arm load and put it right here." Then he hurried up the ramp and patted Susie on the rump.

He went in front of the elephant and released the chain. Meanwhile she was parting through his hair with her trunk.

"Okay, okay Huh, Huh. He raised his leg. Then Susie raised hers and turned her head, And Tate held on to her trunk and stepped up on her leg and climbed on and sat behind her head.

"Okay Girl let's go." The big elephant turned around and walked out to the ramp. Tate goaded her behind her ears and she walked down the ramp and stopped at the pile of hay.

"Alright John, now we can get her baby out. You can go in with me." Inside, the elephant in the front of the trailer was smaller but it was still higher than John's head.

"John when he puts his leg up step up on it and slide on behind his head. I'll lead him out. When the baby raised it's foot John was clumsy, but he finally got on the elephant's back. The baby turned and started for the exit and John almost fell off.

"Whoa!"

"Hold on John." Tate said.

The baby hurried down the ramp to join it's mother.

Tate and John brought two more arm loads of hay and moved on to the next cage. When they were finished feeding the animals Tate took John to his office. It was a shed that the circus hauled around on a trailer. They set it on the ground with a forklift when they were performing.

"You sit down and rest a bit while I fill out my paper work." John hardly heard Tate he was so mesmerized by all the animals he had seen and touched. He sat on a chair and stared off into space with a grin. He had also met some of the trainers and acrobats. Most of them spoke with an accent, but they were all nice to John. Tate looked at John with a smile. He remembered other boys that had been elated by the sights they had seen and tales they heard. John's mind came back to earth when he heard a noise coming from a large box setting in the far corner of the trailer. The box was covered with a canvas cover made to fit. John listened as the noise continued like something rustling around in there. He looked at Tate, but Tate didn't pay any attention to the noise he was busy with his papers.

When Tate was finished he stood and said, "Well John, it's just about time for supper, you hungry?"

"Yes sir, I guess I could eat bite."

"Okay let's go back to the RV and I'll see what I can rustle up."

As they left the office the noise continued, but Tate never said a word and John thought he better not say anything either. John wondered what was in that box.

When they got in the trailer Tate took a can of vegetables out of a cabinet and some roast beef out of the fridge. When he put it in the microwave it gave off a delicious odor. John's mouth began to water.

When they sat down to eat Tate said, "Well John you seem like you will be a good hand. Just remember in this line of work you've got to be careful."

John smiled and nodded.

"Tate I shore appreciate you giving me a chance to stay with the circus. It would be hard to tell my folks all the things I saw today there was so much."

You're a very observant boy John and that's good. You'll learn that if anything is out of place you'll have give folks a warning. Like if one of the cats gets out, or if an elephant gets loose. Don't try to stop them because someone or something has probably spooked them. They get scared just like we do sometimes. That's why we don't allow any dogs or cats around cause they can spook the bigger animals."

John nodded his head in understanding.

Someone knocked on the door and John jumped.

"Come in." Tate said grinning. Lasa a dark haired woman came in with a book in her hand. She was part of one of the aerial acts. She was short, but very light on her feet.

"Hi John How do you like the circus?"

"It's great ma'am."

She glanced at Tate. "A boy with manners." she said softly.

"Yeah, he's gonna be a good hand too. He learns quick."

"I brought your book back it's very good."

Tate nodded.

"Care for some supper?" Tate asked.

She smiled and said, "You need to come down to my trailer and have a good meal."

"Thanks, I may do that."

"John, you come too. I make delicious short cake with huge strawberries on it with mounds of whipped cream."

John's eyes got big. He hadn't had too much short cake at home. Lasa lay the book on a shelf and stopped at the door. She smiled at Tate and blew him a kiss then left a wink for John and slipped out.

"She's a pretty good cook huh?" John asked.

"Don't let the strawberries throw you boy, she's got marriage on her mind. And you might remember this when you meet a woman. You know what a snare is don't you?"

"Yeah?"

"Well her short cake is one of several she's got. When a man gets married he gets fat and lazy most of the time. I ain't quite ready for that yet. So this fox don't stick his foot in that snare."

John nodded and went back to his supper.

Rendezvous

After dinner Tate turned on the television and they watched the news. Afterward He put a movie in the VCR for John to watch. The never ending story, a tale of a boy that goes to a very strange land and finds a beautiful stallion and a very strange dog. John really enjoyed that. Tate found some phone calls to make and some paperwork he had to do.

After the movie he told John, "I'm going to turn in. We have to get an early start, You can stay up a while if you like. Let me show you where your bed is."

They went into the bedroom and as John had expected he would have the twin bed. He thanked Tate for everything and went back to the living room for a while. The way Tate treated him he almost felt like a man. About nine he went to bed. Lying there before he went to sleep he thought of his Mom, he missed her a little and his sister too. He was afraid his Dad was going to be very mad. But he thought running away to circus life was worth it.

Finally he dozed off and what seemed like a few minutes he heard Tate saying, "Come on boy get up we got a full day ahead of us." He jumped up trying to get his mind working. Tate was standing there grinning at him. The clock on Tate's headboard said five o'clock. Wow! The night went quick.

"The bath is in there." John picked up his burlap sack and went in to take a shower. He put on the other set of clothes he had and some clean socks. When he came out Tate was frying bacon and eggs. Boy it sure smelled good.

"Where did you learn to cook so good Tate?" Tate grinned.

"Well, my momma taught me some and the circus women taught me the rest." John stared off thinking.

"I guess I should learn to cook huh?"

"It might not be a bad idea, but for now I'll do the cooking. You didn't bring much with you. I might have some jeans and a couple of shirts that would fit you. When we get some time today I'm going to show you how to wash your clothes. That's one thing you need to learn early in life if you are going to be a bachelor."

"Yes sir. I will."

After breakfast they were out feeding the circus animals theirs. Tate fed them and John pulled the cart and watched his every move. Maybe some day he would be doing this and he wanted to do it right. When the other circus people passed they greeted him cheerfully and made John feel like he was part of the gang. The only one he was afraid of was the circus manager because he always had a scowl on his face.

"Don't you let this kid get in any trouble." he told Tate.

Tate assured him he wouldn't.

"Is he gonna run me off Tate?" John asked.

"Don't worry I'll take care of him. You just learn what you can. It'll turn out all right John you'll see. Just before we go have lunch I'll take you over to the side show. You'll see some really strange things over there." By eleven thirty they were finished with the animals and went to get grain and hay. On the way back Tate stopped at a tent that was separated from the rest.

"Come on John let's go meet the funny folk. John was wide eyed not knowing what to expect. He hadn't seen any funny folk in the other circuses he had been to.

When they went into the tent the whole place was abuzz with all kinds of people. John gaped in amazement. It seemed like everybody was doing something. He couldn't believe his eyes. There were midgets smaller than him, a lady with half a beard down the middle of her face, A huge lady with a satin dress that sat in an equally big chair.

"She weighs eight hundred pounds John, course the circus claims it's a thousand."

There was man swallowing swords, and another guy with scaly skin they called the human lizard. There was a huge guy they called a weight lifter he was lifting heavy bars with weights on them and a lady dancing with a filmy dress that sang in a strange language. John never realized that there were people in the world like this. He had blown a fuse his twelve year old mind couldn't handle it. One of the midget women approached and greeted them.

"Hi Tate. Hello there young fella. What's your name?" She said in her tiny voice.

John had trouble finding his.

"Uh, uh John ma'am."

She looked up at Tate and said, "I guess this is his first time huh?"

Tate nodded. "Yeah Nelly I thought I would bring him by and let him see the rest of the world."

"Well I got to get back to work we got a new gag and I got to get it straight see you at the show this afternoon."

"Show?" John asked.

"Yeah, we got a matinee at two-thirty this afternoon. We better go eat lunch and get ready."

In Tate's RV he showed John how to operate the washer while he fixed sandwiches. By the time they finished it was almost time for the afternoon show. John could see all the towns people gathering at the gate. The band was warming up in the big tent. John could see in his mind the three big rings they set up in the middle. He was excited. Now he would see the show from this side.

"Now John when things start they happen pretty fast at first so it might be best if you went into my office for a few minutes. In the opening parade everyone gets involved and there is a lot happening fast and I don't want you to get in the way Okay?"

John nodded.

"You can watch out the window."

John saw that someone had moved the shed over to the back of the main tent. He went into the office and pulled back the curtain. He could hear the music and he was excited inside. Trainers were lining up the animals outside and people were gathering to march around the rings inside. John remembered this from the circuses he had seen in the past. It was all so great he swelled up inside to think he was a part of all this. As he watched all the excitement he heard a noise in the corner. John had forgotten about the box with the canvas over it. It was about three foot high and four foot wide and deep. He saw the front flap moving a little and something whining inside. It was a funny noise he couldn't quite place it. It seemed like he had heard a sound like it but he didn't know what it came from. He stood looking at the box wondering why it wasn't with the other animals. The noise it uttered made John feel sorry for it being covered up all the time. He couldn't understand why anyone would treat an animal that way. Maybe it was sick.

He thought of farmers that had to cover horses eyes to keep the flies away and causing infection.

Maybe that was it, but he still felt sorry for it because of the sound it made. So pitiful. He stood staring at the canvas flap. Curiosity had John in it's grip. Tate hadn't mentioned the box or what was inside. He wondered if Tate would be mad if he peeked. He took a step toward the box and looked at the door.

If Tate came in…

Another step. He watched the door. What? Two more steps.

If Tate comes…

Two more steps.

When he was standing in front of the box it seemed like the noise inside became excited like it would be glad to see John. Like a new puppy that whined when it first saw him. He looked down at the flap. There was snap on each side of the bottom. John reached out and touched the canvas then turned his head toward the door.

If Tate…

He squatted down and touched the snap at the bottom. Then looked at the door again. He pulled the snap and it came loose. The noise inside stopped. He lifted the corner a little but he couldn't see anything it was dark in there. He raised it a little higher still couldn't see anything. A little higher, a bare foot and a pants leg? He looked back at the door. He reached over and pulled the other snap loose. Did he have a small boy in there? He couldn't stand the mystery so he stood up and raised the flap all the way. Before him was the strangest sight he had ever seen.

John stepped to one side and laid the flap on top of the box, no cage was what it was. There were thick bars on the front and close together too. The cage was heavy metal like the lion cages he had seen. What was this? The thing inside looked like a little boy…almost. It also had a questioning look on it's face. Like who are you? John couldn't quite figure it out. If one didn't look close it looked like a child, but then when you noticed it's features weren't quite childlike. It's head was a little bigger than it should be. It's ears were larger too and it's eyes were a light blue. But it's nose was almost flat and it's upper lip was longer than it should be. There was a small patch of hair in the middle of its cheek. It's neck was short, almost none. For a boy it's arms were a little longer than they should be. The boy had on a small pair of bib overalls and a small blue shirt. Then another shock hit John, a chain led from behind the boy to the wall of the cage. How could a small thing like this be dangerous? Yet it was caged and chained he better be careful. It was so hard to pull his eyes away from those gripping blue eyes in the cage. They almost held him. He stood up and pulled the flap down and snapped the buttons. The frail whining started again. John backed away to the window and looked out. Now the circus parade didn't mean as much as it had a little while ago. He felt sorry for the little boy. Boy? No, not quite. What was that thing? He wondered if he should mention it to Tate. Fear began to rise up John's back and the hair on the back of his neck began to prickle. Caged and chained? What was that thing?

When Tate finally came in he was going to ask John if he enjoyed the parade, but he could see that John was troubled.

He sat down in his office chair and pulled John over by his arms and said, "I guess you saw what was in the cage huh?"

All John could do was nod his head.

"Listen John I should have told you last night , but I got busy with the paperwork and forgot. I'll tell you what that is, it's a Groeler. And I know, it looks like a little kid, but son, it's not. I got it from a gypsy in another circus he was old and about to die and the Groeler was his pet and he didn't want it killed so he asked me to take care of it. I should have been careful not to let it loose he warned me but I didn't pay close enough attention.

He told me to keep it in a heavy cage, but the first one I got wasn't heavy enough and he got out. I didn't know how dangerous he was and someone went missing and we never found him.. The only way I got the Groeler back was a special language the gypsy wrote down on a paper. It seems he has gotten used to me and he doesn't try to hurt me. I keep him fed and covered up so no one sees him. I wouldn't get around him if I were you his eyes seem to pull a person in and if he grabs you I don't know what he will do."

Now John was trembling.

"It's okay John he can't hurt you as long as he is in the cage."

John had a blank stare on his face. Then he said, "Can I go back to your RV?"

"Sure John you might want to lay down and rest a while."

When he got back to the RV he lay down on his bed and tears ran down his nose. John Tillman had never been so frightened in his life. He trembled all over and couldn't control himself. Those blue eyes loomed large before him. He couldn't get them out of his mind. It looked so innocent, but had it actually killed someone? He never wanted to go into that office again. Now he missed his family more than ever.

Confrontation

When the show closed John helped get the animals loaded. When they were ready to leave he sat in the front seat of Tate's big truck. They would be going to Chicago next, the big city. Beside John's fear of the Groeler there was a little excitement. He was anxious to see a big town. He had been gone from home over a week now and if it wasn't for that thing in the cage he might have wanted to stay gone, but he thought of home more and more now. How safe things were with Mom and Dad.

When they set up in Chicago one of the aerial men taught John to climb a rope and Lasa showed him how to scamper up a rope ladder. He actually climbed up to the platform where the high wire people performed. It was one of the greatest thrills he had ever had. When all the excitement was over though he still thought of the thing in the cage.

After the third day the show moved to another part of Chicago and set up for another three days. By now John realized it was always the same thing set up and move, set up and move. And that thing in the cage.

The last night when everyone was gone the big tent was empty but they hadn't turned out the lights. John wanted to take a walk so he went over to the big tent and went inside. In the area outside the arena was a place where the performers got ready to go on. John had to pass through there to get to the arena. It was in that area he noticed that someone had moved the Groeler's cage out of the shed and left it in there. Then the worst shock he had ever had hit him. The cage door was open and the cage was empty. He froze in his tracks. Where was that thing? He mustered up all the courage he had and turned his head. Then he looked the other way. Nothing. No one here to help him either. He began to tremble. He shook all over. *That thing is loose.* his mind screamed. *I got to get otta here.* Finally he dredged up enough nerve to turn around and look the area over. No one there. He took a couple of steps toward the big tent. *If I go outside its dark out there and he'll get me for sure.* The tent was the only choice he had. He ran through the flaps and into the arena looking around, but no one was there. What could he do?

Under the seats a pair of blue eyes watched the boy as he ran around. *He would be easy to catch* it thought. *He's scared. Fear loses every time.* Slowly the Groeler began to move. It moved under the benches until it was close to the boy then it stepped out into one of the aisles and started toward him. Excitement grew in the Groeler now and he began to drool a little. He didn't have to run the boy was slow.

John turned and saw the Groeler coming. He quickly looked around his blood throbbing in his temples. Where could he go? Then he spotted a rope hanging down from the trapeze area. He bolted for the rope and started to climb. When he was about half way up the Groeler approached the rope and took hold. He raised one foot and grasped the rope between his toes. Something else John hadn't noticed the Groeler's feet were a little different also. He moved up slowly hand over hand and foot over foot like walking up the rope. John reached the platform and looked down the Groeler was still coming. He quickly looked around and he spotted a swinging ladder that led to the high wire. He released the strap that held it and swung over to the other platform, but he forgot to hook it to the pole beside him and the ladder swung the other way. The pole next to John was one of the main supports for the tent. There were three. As he looked up he saw the opening at the top, which was an air vent also. There were ropes tying the canvas to the pole. If he could climb up there and get through he might get away.

The Groeler leaped off the platform and caught the bottom rung of the ladder as it swung back. Now he was headed to the platform John had just left. He landed with ease and looked up at John struggling to climb the pole. *There's no hurry he's getting tired.*

John finally reached the top and was struggling to get

through the hole in the canvas. He pulled himself through, but he made the mistake of looking back. He was looking into the face of the Groeler. Slowly it began to open it's mouth. John Tillman was face to face with the biggest set of fangs he had ever seen. The teeth around them weren't much better. John let go of the rope and started to slide down the canvas top.

Just then a voice rang out across the empty arena, "TINKMON JU JU MOD LA COT. EN BEBE AWS MAL" The Groeler stopped and closed his jaws. He turned his head to see his keeper below. He turned and climbed down the pole. Tate snapped a chain on the back of his belt and led him back to the cage. He closed the door and put the big lock on the hasp. Someone had not put the chain back and locked the door when they fed and exercised the Groeler.

Outside John had hit the edge of the canvas and climbed down. He was running toward the RV and he wasn't looking back. Once inside he locked the door and held on to the knob tight. He was out of breath, but that thing wasn't going to get him. A couple of minutes later he heard a tapping on the outside.

"John, the voice said, it's all right he's back in the cage and he can't get out.

"Ezat you Tate." he called.

"Yeah John, it's me and everything is okay you can open the door."

John turned the lock and slowly opened the barrier and peeked through the crack.

Tate stood back and smiled not wanting to frighten John any further. John leaped through the door way and landed in Tate's arms sobbing on his shoulder.

"It's okay buddy he's locked up again. You'll be okay."

The next morning after Tate made his rounds he went back to the RV. He didn't bother to wake John. When he went in John was fixing a bowl of cereal. He sat down and took hold of John's arm.

"You okay partner?"

John smiled and nodded with a shy grin.

"Well John the time of truth has come. What do you think?"

"You know Tate I been thinkin' my folks are probably missing me as much as I miss them. It might be best if I went back home. I was wonderin' if maybe you could lend me enough to get a bus ticket I could send it back when I get home." John was looking down playing with his fingers.

Well son that's not a bad idea and I just happened to have a little extra so I can help you out."

Outside the window the circus manager was listening. He walked away chuckling to himself.

When John got off the bus in Burlington he grabbed his sack and headed toward home. He crossed a little rise as he got close to the house and the prettiest sight he ever saw was his Daddy' farm